LOVE, I
HEAVEN
&
HELL

SHAMAN
with
Roche Bentley

Terms and Conditions

The spirit Shaman is declared as the official author of this book. His able assistant and scribe (that's me) was able to convey Shaman's thoughts to the page and whilst the scribe is entitled to some small measure of credit (or blame!) he is also entitled to the profits that are to be made from the book in the form of sales, royalties and of course the eventual film rights and the opportunity to sit chatting to beautiful film stars on set.

It should also be pointed out that the reader of this book agrees beforehand that he will not hold the scribe (that's me again…) responsible for any damages however caused nor will the scribe be blamed for any actions of religious nutters who may wish to cause havoc as a result of reading it.

As this book is based on a true story (apparently) and as the author is dead, then any action that anyone may wish to bring must be done in the spirit world. In any event, as you will read, all actions, good or bad, are resolved in the spirit world. If you think that this is tough, hard luck!

It is a condition of acceptance that you agree to these terms before you read this book and that if you do not agree to these terms then you will not read it.

Understood?
Good.
Now start reading – I hope you enjoy it…

Roche Bentley, 2019

Any references to persons alive or dead is purely accidental and descriptions of methods used are completely fabricated and are fiction.

This book is dedicated to every person who ever helps another without any thought of reward, thanks or gain.

This book is therefore dedicated to you.

Reviews

"Verily better than any tragic comedy that I ever penned."
– W. Shakespeare

"Hey dis boy, he gets it right!"
– Pope John 23rd

"I am deeply ashamed of what I did and all of the suffering I caused. Now that I know I have to answer for my sins I am bloody scared."
– Bin Laden

"Ditto."
– G. W. Bush

"I now wish that I asked for more than Ten Commandments, some of those listed 21-39 are quite fun."
– Moses

"This book is nothing like 'The Bible' or that 'A Short History of Time' by Stephen Hawkins which sell quite well. Don't just buy it and put it on your shelf to impress your friends, read it too."
– The Manager, your local book shop

"If this book was a car it would be a Ferrari with a V24 engine and no brakes, I never wanted it to stop."
– Jeremy Clarkson's spirit

"Writing this book under the direction of Shaman was a pleasure, I can't wait for the sequel."
– Roche Bentley

"Looking forward to meeting you all soon…"
– Steve Rogers, Michael Shepherd, Rosie, Helen, lots of other lovely spirits and of course Boo!

CONTENTS

INTRODUCTION

A note from the author

This book about Love, Life, Heaven and Hell is based on a true story which I can personally vouch for because I was there to witness the life of Steve Rogers, his Life Appraisal and his subsequent vocation. I am still here on Earth and will always be there in Heaven and Hell just as you will be quite soon for you own Life Appraisal. All the characters that you will read about, existed and still exist either as humans or as spirits. One day you will meet them or others just like them.

Some of the things you will learn about, happened in your past and my past, others will happen in your future which incidentally also happens to be my past and future too.

I am indebted to my scribe, Roche Bentley, who spent many long hours writing down what I told him to write and he did this dutifully even though on some occasions he didn't like or understand where the story was going. Please don't give him a hard time over any of the revelations that are described to you. He's just the messenger and I take full responsibility for everything that I say and do – just as you will too!

Live your life and be considerate to all others and treat everyone, including animals, fish, insects and birds as you would like to be treated if the roles were reversed. If you do this, you will find joy. But if you don't and you cause pain, then you will experience what they went through – only worse. Don't worry, it's okay to carry on eating as before, you don't have to become a vegan.

When you have finished this book you will know where Heaven and Hell are and why you have had a chance to experience life and love as a human being. You are very privileged; I hope that you enjoy all that is to come. Shaman.

(A note from the scribe while the author isn't looking –

Shaman is the author of the book (Shaman is apparently a Mongolian name which means "he who knows everything" and he is a medium between us and spirits). Thankfully this spooky lunatic has, at last, finished dictating his book to me and I hope now that he'll leave me in peace and able to collect the royalties which he told me I could keep. To be fair, some parts are quite funny even though other parts are scary and if you think about it, the whole thing about Life, Love, Heaven and Hell is really quite simple and deep down inside us we know that we will… Oh no! He is now saying, "Wait for the sequel!" Good luck, I'm off!

– Roche Bentley, somewhere near Cambridge, Autumn 2007)

PREFACE

He couldn't find the trapdoor. As the frightened young man in the crumpled grey suit stumbled forward along the corridor in the dark, his right hand brushed the wall and the coarse stone grazed the skin on his knuckles for the second time as he winced in pain. The faint glimmer of the red light twenty yards behind him disappeared and Steve Rogers found that it was difficult to keep his balance in total darkness. His left arm stretched ahead with his fingers probing for any more painful obstacles in his path and Steve sensed the floor tilting slightly. Then he felt it, he was almost on it and he swore as his toe stubbed the iron hinge.

He had been told to find the trapdoor and stand on it as it was the only way out. His left foot moved gingerly over the hinge and Steve steadied himself again with his right palm pressing on the wall. He could now feel cold dirty water flowing down the concrete and onto the floor, it had started as a trickle but now there was a definite increase in volume. He knew that if he couldn't find the trapdoor and get it to open, the water level would rise and he would drown. He could hear the water as well as feel it and he sighed as he felt it seep into his shoes, the corridor was filling fast. He knew that he had very little time and he planted his right foot firmly next to his left but the trapdoor still didn't open. He stamped firmly. The door remained shut and he remembered his instructions, he mustn't have any part of his body touching anything else. He knew that he had to take his right hand from the wall and stand unaided, he breathed hard and carefully moved his palm away, his fingers hesitated for a second. He put both arms down and pressed the palms of his hands firmly against his legs but still the trapdoor wouldn't open. Steve clenched his fists and was about to stamp hard with his left foot when he realised that his feet might not be completely on the door but one shoe could be covering an edge, he knew that he must be on the door completely to get it to open.

He slowly shuffled his left foot forward an inch and hesitated, again nothing happened. He pressed the toes of his right foot forward and the heel of his right shoe moved clear of the crack and the trapdoor fell back noisily as the hinges swung open at last. Steve instantly felt very light as the wood gave way and his body dropped, he gasped as the putrid air hit him and he looked down to see where he would land, but there was nothing to see apart from a grey mist far below. The speed of his fall surprised him and he screamed and tried to look down as his body reached its maximum velocity as the shaft swallowed its victim. Then he hit the icy cold underground lake and gasped as the freezing water wrapped itself around him clutching him to its heart. Steve grasped madly at the water, his arms flailing as he felt himself slowing down, the fall was over. Steve was well below the surface of the underground lake and he knew that he would drown if he didn't kick out with his legs. The water broke as his head emerged into the cavern and shafts of light welcomed him as they flickered over the surface. Steve sucked the stale air into his lungs and he saw the shadow of the wooden pier in front of him. He swam towards it, the weight of his clothes made it harder but he struggled and spat out the ice cold water as he grabbed the base of the pier.

"You were too long in finding the trapdoor," his tormentor snarled as Steve tried to pull himself up onto the split planks. Steve knew from experience that he wouldn't be helped so he didn't bother asking. He tugged at the frame and tried to pull himself up but was surprised to feel a strong arm grasp his shoulder and he mumbled his thanks as he was pulled clear of the water, no one had ever helped him before. This was the hardest course he had been on and all the instructors had been cruel, he expected no sympathy and he received none.

"Dry yourself and then clear off!" A dirty, damp towel hit him in the face. The instructor turned away, he felt no remorse in treating his pupils badly, that was his job, but his time with Steve had come to an end and his student would now move on to another stage and experience more of the delights of his course.

Steve sat down heavily on the metal chair, the water dripped from his clothes and made puddles on the floor and he knew that he had no option but to endure whatever challenges were presented to him. His clothes were wet through and Steve shivered as he closed his eyes and thought back to the day when everything changed and he began his real journey. He was starting to find out why he was here as he remembered where he was and what he was doing on the day that he arrived in Hell. He thought of Sharon, he wanted to cry. He would have given anything to go back.

BOOK ONE

CHAPTER 1

We have to know suffering in order to know joy.

There is no possible shortcut.

(Shaman)

Sharon smiled at Steve as she opened the door of her Golf and climbed in, she let her split skirt show her legs as she eased herself behind the wheel and she knew he was watching her. Steve winked as he acknowledged the message, he was looking forward to the night ahead and there would be no way that Sharon's husband or his wife Jane would find out. Sharon was a sensible girl, a very sexy one and Steve looked forward to her undressing him as he lay on the hotel bed, he wondered, did she deliberately wear a bra that seemed too small for her? Steve felt for the keys of his Porsche and he noticed that his hand was shaking slightly as he fumbled for the lock. He preferred the classic line of the 911 to the later models and he loved driving it and the power of the Porsche engine was simply breathtaking. Most of the other salesmen had company estate cars or hatchbacks, some even had the firm's name written on the side, he hated that and although it was frowned upon, Steve used his own car instead of a company car and he claimed extra expenses, it's amazing what a top salesman can get away with. Steve wasn't arrogant, he knew that his success was based on hard work and a stubborn refusal to give up and he was under no illusions about his skills either. He left school with average qualifications and whilst he didn't know what he wanted to do for a career, he knew what he didn't want. He didn't want to work in an office or in a factory, he didn't want to work as a labourer on a building site and he didn't have the patience or the aptitude to be an electrician or a plumber. But he knew that he wanted to make money to enjoy a nice lifestyle and he decided that selling would give him freedom and that if he was good at his job, his earnings were limitless.

At thirty-four he had topped the national sales charts for five years and he earned more than the company's managing director. Being paid only on commission was far better than receiving a salary and he knew that if his terms and conditions were changed, he'd simply go to another company. His bosses knew that too and they appreciated that Steve's success and earning potential spurred others to work hard too. Steve relaxed a little as the Porsche engine fired and settled down to a satisfying rumble. He would lead the way to the hotel, Sharon would follow and they would park at the back so no one could see their cars from the road.

The silver sports car pulled out into the main road leaving the bright lights of the offices behind him, it had been raining and the wet road glistened under the glare of the streetlights and shadows flickered as the Porsche picked up speed. In his mirror Steve could see Sharon's Golf pulling out behind his car and he enjoyed driving alone with his thoughts. Sharon was a stunning woman, she could drive fast, was good at her job and she was the only woman on an all-male sales team and he grinned at the thought that their affair was a secret. Sharon was discreet and she was great fun, she would never let Steve undress himself, she loved doing that, he was much too polite and delighted to argue. His grin broadened into a smile as he thought about what they would be doing over the next few hours.

The road headed out of town, the countryside on either side was cloaked in darkness but the visibility ahead was good. The soft moonlight touched the road and glinted off the bonnet as the clouds drifted eastwards. Steve pushed the clutch to the floor as his left hand flicked the gear lever from fourth to third ready to overtake a Volvo and Steve felt the car surge as he sped passed and tucked in well before the oncoming traffic passed him. But he sighed when the

8

driver of the approaching white van felt the need to flash him full beam. He glanced in his mirror at the driver dawdling along behind him and he muttered.

"Why do old people insist on wearing their hats, scarves and overcoats when bumbling along getting in everybody's way and couldn't that van driver see that I had plenty of room? This is a Porsche after all." Steve often talked to himself when driving, the car handled beautifully, he loved it and he glanced in his mirror again and was pleased to see that Sharon had overtaken the slow Volvo too and was at a safe distance behind. Steve disliked drivers who couldn't follow and were too hesitant about overtaking, he thought that it was a shame that most drivers couldn't drive as well as he could.

Just ahead there was a fast left-hand bend. Steve knew the road well and as he eased the gear lever into top the exhaust burbled nicely.

"Who needs music when the sounds of an engine are so satisfying?" In front he could see the lights of another slower car and a lorry but they were well ahead and just over the brow the road widened into two lanes. He had to be careful because there was a speed camera ahead and the limit was sixty.

Steve didn't give a thought to the T-junction ahead, it was only a minor road and he'd never seen anyone using it and as he approached the junction his speed nudged a steady sixty-five, just fast enough for the conditions and not too fast to trigger the camera. A beam of headlights appeared and Steve saw a lorry approach the junction from the right, there was nothing coming from ahead but Steve wasn't worried, the driver would obviously stop at the double white line on the minor road and wait until the Porsche and the Golf had passed before pulling out. At first Steve was more surprised than alarmed and he merely lifted his foot slightly off the pedal.

'This chap's not stopping, surely he'll see me, wait and then go after we've passed.' Then Steve's heart missed a beat, this was serious. He braked hard and the driver kept coming, he could see the giant front wheel getting too close and he realised that he was going to hit the near side of the lorry. His horn continued to blare as he felt an ice-cold tremor run through his body. Steve pressed harder on the horn as if the extra pressure would make the lorry disappear, it didn't. Steve's jaw fell open in shock and his right foot pressed the brake pedal so hard, he thought it might go through the floor. He felt the wheels lock up and the car started to slide, the 911's front wheels hissed on the wet road and the lorry was too close to miss. Steve aimed at the verge, he could sense safety on the grass bank and as he eased the wheel to the left his nearside front wheel hit the kerb. The car bounced into the air and cleared the concrete edge, Steve was concentrating hard and decided to aim along the grass bank and try and get back onto the road ahead of the lorry, the gap was big enough, the verge was clear of obstacles and in dry conditions Steve might have got away with it but the grass was soaking wet and it was long. The Porsche slewed around, skidded sideways and when the nearside wheel hit a rut Steve lost control completely. The back of the car flipped up, Steve swung the steering wheel in vain and in his mind Steve noticed that everything had slowed down almost to a standstill. An unseen hand seemed to guide the car, not a sound could be heard and the effect was surreal. The car glided through the air as if it was born to fly but as it rolled over any onlooker could see that the landing would not be a smooth one, the roof hit first and the window shattered, then the car flipped noisily onto its side, up onto its nose and thudded to a stop back on all four wheels. Steve sat there astonished, he could see that the front of the car was badly dented, the glistening bodywork reflected the light and shadows at an angle he'd not seen before. The roof on the passenger side was almost level with the door handle but the driver's door had come open, torn off by the impact during one of the rolls and Steve found that he was able to ease himself out onto the grass. His shoe slipped on some mud but Steve steadied himself and walked back to the road. The lorry had stopped halfway across and the driver was getting out. He was at least sixty and his faded yellow reflective jacket was grubby with years of grime from brushing out the back of the lorry after deliveries. Gordon Brownlow was shocked, this was his first accident since he had skidded on black ice twenty-two years ago and slightly damaged a parked car, he had the best driving record in the firm. He hoped that the Porsche driver wouldn't be badly hurt but the accident did look serious. Gordon felt a knot start to tighten in his stomach, he was a big man and his friends liked his kindly nature, his wife loved him too, she said that he was the most gentle person she'd ever known. She told everyone that's why she married him. But Gordon didn't feel gentle, he felt a strong desire to be sick.

Steve looked at the lorry driver and his hands closed into tight fists, he had a few words to say to this chap and none would be polite. But the idiot lorry driver would keep, he needed to talk to Sharon first. He looked back along the road, Sharon's Golf had stopped barely three feet from the lorry and had skidded to one side.

"Sharon stopped in time, thank God!" Steve muttered under his breath. Sharon sat in her car, her face was white with fright and Steve ran to her to reassure her that he was okay, the meal and the night of passion would have to be postponed. Thank goodness he hadn't been drinking, he'd call Jane on his mobile phone and she'd come and take him home. Sharon suddenly moved, she tugged at her seat belt and opened her car door. Steve asked if she was okay but she ignored him, she ran towards the Porsche, her high heels clicked on the road and she shouted at Gordon Brownlow who had left his lorry in the middle of the road and was now walking towards the wrecked car.

"You bloody maniac! You pulled right out. Are you mad?" Gordon Brownlow didn't reply, he was peering into the car and jerked back when Sharon pulled sharply at his arm.

"Quick, get him out of there I can smell petrol."

Steve stood next to her. "It's okay, I'm okay, get on home and I'll sort this out, get on home." Sharon ignored him and ran past him back to her car, the lorry driver stood and stared, obviously in shock. Steve turned to Sharon and noticed that she was feeling in her bag, she pulled out her mobile phone and punched the numbers.

"Police please and an ambulance, get an ambulance now please, hurry." The operator seemed painfully slow as she put Sharon through to the police and quoted the mobile's phone number slowly and carefully. Sharon was beside herself with impatience.

"Hurry, hurry." Steve went to her.

"It's okay love I'm okay. The car is smashed but I'm okay. It's all right." Sharon was asked for the road number and where the accident happened. She was flustered and the driver of the Volvo stopped. He parked his car in the middle of the road with its hazard lights flashing and he looked at the crashed car and thought about taking off his jacket to put over the driver. Barry Johnson used to have a Ford Escort but bought the Volvo after he had been involved in a motorway pile-up on a foggy November morning and others around him had died or been badly hurt. He had been lucky as he managed to open his door and get out just as his car was shunted hard from behind. He had never forgotten the images he saw that morning and he could see that the Porsche driver was badly injured or maybe even dead. Barry heard Sharon speaking into her mobile phone, he saw her pause and look around and guessed what she needed to know, he nodded at Sharon and spoke.

"We are on the A429, eight miles east of Newton approaching the village of Little Welling." Sharon relayed this to the operator, she ignored Steve as if she hadn't seen him.

"Quick!" she called to the Volvo driver, "see if you can help." Steve was shocked as they ducked to look inside the 911. What on earth was she so upset about, it was as if it was her car that had been wrecked? He couldn't see what they were looking at and he nearly slipped again on the wet grass as he looked into the interior from the other side. It had started to rain hard but Steve didn't notice, there in the driving seat crumpled up against the wheel lay a man. He couldn't tell who it was, the head had fallen forwards and the hair was matted with blood. Sharon obviously knew this guy, she was talking to him, reassuring him, trying to make him comfortable without actually moving him.

In the distance Steve could hear a siren and he turned back to Sharon, this time she noticed him, at least he thought that she did.

"Sharon, who is that guy in my car, I didn't see any pedestrians?" Sharon was crying, she could hardly see him through her tears but she saw the police car pull up and ran to the driver.

"It's my boyfriend," Steve was amazed at her outburst, what she was saying, people weren't supposed to know. She continued, "Help him, help him." Steve was astonished, who was this guy in his car, how did she know him, did she have another boyfriend? The rain was falling harder now but Steve didn't notice, the policeman pulled back from the car and was speaking into his radio, his colleague was urging Sharon back to the police car as the ambulance arrived, the flashing blue lights and the rain on the moonlit road had an eerie effect. Steve was determined to find out what was going on, it was bad enough crashing his car and writing the damn thing off but to find that he's somehow collided with someone who was badly hurt or even dead and who Sharon actually knew and called her boyfriend, well that was too much. He moved towards the police car and fumbled for his wallet, he'd need to show his licence. A hand held him back, he turned and a man stood there in a dark blue raincoat. He had fair hair, looked about forty and had deep blue eyes, no lines showed on

12

his face but Steve didn't notice that, he didn't pay that much attention.

"Are you okay?" the stranger asked. Steve was relieved.

"Yes I'm perfectly fine, that idiot lorry driver pulled out and I've smashed up my car but yes, I'm fine, thank you." Steve paused. "I don't suppose you saw it did you, can you be a witness?"

The stranger smiled. "Yes I did see it, it wasn't your fault, it was an accident." He took Steve by the arm.

"My name is Michael Shepherd, I can see that you are shaken up. Come with me and we can sort this out, the police are busy at the moment." Steve saw that he was right. The ambulance team and the police had freed the man from the car and had put him on a stretcher. Sharon was watching and crying. Gordon Brownlow stood to one side, he hadn't spoken to anyone except to nod when the police asked if he was the driver of the lorry, Steve watched as the blanket was pulled up to the man's chin.

"Well he's not dead," Steve whispered, "otherwise they would have covered his face." The men lifted the stretcher and carried it back to the ambulance. As they passed, Steve recognised the victim, he gasped, he started to move towards him but Michael Shepherd firmly held his arm just below his elbow.

"Don't move," he said, "it will be okay."

The stretcher was put into the ambulance, Sharon was still crying and talking to the policeman, he was asking her if there was a friend she could phone, or could they give her a lift somewhere? A recovery truck had been called, there was no point in hanging about here. Steve wanted to approach her but the man at his side said,

"You can't help her now, you have to go through." Steve was puzzled and repeated the words.

"Go through?" The man beckoned him to his car. A powerful black classic model that Steve didn't recognise. He opened the front passenger door and Steve got in, at once he smelled the musty aroma of the black leather seats and polished wooden dashboard. The man went around to the driver's side and sat behind the wheel, he buckled his seat belt, Steve took the hint and did the same. He sat there in silence thinking about what was happening but there were no answers only questions. Michael started the engine and the car moved off, there was no other traffic, the road ahead was clear, the rain had stopped and the road surface was perfectly dry. Steve knew the A429 well but this part was completely new to him. Michael Shepherd was very caring and talked quietly.

"It will be all sorted out when you go through. Have a sleep now, I'll wake you when we arrive." Steve was just about to say that he wasn't tired and had no desire to sleep but as he started to speak he felt himself getting very drowsy, he closed his eyes and within moments, he was sound asleep.

The black car purred through the night leaving the scene of the accident far behind. Sharon had the Volvo driver's coat around her shoulders and she gave her details to the police, Gordon Brownlow had been asked to move his lorry, in fact, it was more of a command than a request and Gordon realised that he was in serious trouble. The police cautioned him and he was told to wait with his vehicle, once the police were satisfied as to his identity, he would be allowed to leave. He watched the girl being sick on the grass verge and he started to think about his story.

"The road was clear, it was safe to turn right and the Porsche driver was going much too fast and was already out of control before I pulled out. No that wouldn't be any good, if I had seen the Porsche out of control, why would I try and make a right turn in front of it? Better to say that I was turning right and the Porsche must have been doing over a hundred."

Yes, that would do, if that chap were dead, Gordon might be believed. Of course there would be an inquest. Gordon wondered what relationship the girl was to the car driver. Gordon had a lot of thoughts that night when he finally climbed into bed next to his sleeping wife, if he was convicted of causing death by dangerous driving he could go to prison. Gordon wished that he'd paid more attention before turning right that evening.

CHAPTER 2

"Wake up Steve, you won't want to miss this." Michael Shepherd gently shook Steve's shoulder and he opened his eyes. The road was clear ahead and there was no other traffic, the moonlight sparkled through the tall trees at the side of the road and the strobe effect mesmerised him. As the silver light danced along the bonnet of the car and around him, Steve sat comfortably in his seat, he loved the natural beauty and the sensation of night time driving.

The bends in the road allowed for a satisfying steady speed and Steve glanced at the dimly lit instrument panel, a faint green light glowed around the edges of the glass set in walnut and Steve could see the luminous needle flickering around the seventy mark. The driver looked relaxed, he was enjoying the drive and he loved the car. Not many people were lucky enough to own a Bristol and few recognised the make. The radio reminded Steve of the old radios from the nineteen-sixties, five black push buttons selected the stations and the tiny red glow of the radio's light illuminated the glass strip. The driver leaned across and turned the black knob. Steve liked the song, 'Take it Easy' by the Eagles. A bright light appeared ahead, he could see it getting bigger and it got even brighter as they approached and he saw that it was in the middle of the road.

"Hey that's bright," said Steve, "he's on full beam, it must be enormous." What looked like a huge lorry appeared to sit right in their path and Steve suddenly became alarmed.

"He's on our side of the road!" The driver didn't slow.

"Take it easy, you'll enjoy this, I always do." Steve looked hard at the driver, he was going to collide head on with this lorry and Steve was about to protest, he even thought about grabbing the wheel.

"I said take it easy Steve, listen to the words of the song." Steve suddenly realised something, "How do you know my na…?" He didn't finish the question. The car burst into the light and Steve put his hands over his eyes, a huge crash was inevitable but nothing happened. The engine continued to purr but Steve needed to be reassured, he peeped through his fingers. The long, black bonnet stretched ahead and he saw that the car was in a tunnel just like the one he drove through last year between France and Italy. It was very long, well-lit and perfectly straight but this tunnel was different, there was no other traffic. The car sped on as the yellow lights from the tunnel roof beat steadily around them reflecting off the windows. After a moment, Steve could see the end of the tunnel approaching and another burst of light awaited them. Steve didn't speak, he looked at the driver who looked back at him and smiled.

"Not much longer. We are nearly there and of course I know your name, I've been with you for all of your life." Steve was amazed but somehow he felt that this man was telling the truth. He did feel that he knew him and he felt that he could trust him completely.

"Watch this." The car accelerated hard towards the brilliant light, Steve could see that the speedometer needle was hovering at just over a hundred miles an hour. The light got closer, it got even brighter, it didn't seem possible, Steve had never seen a light so bright. The Eagles song was just about to end. He could feel the hairs on the back of his neck prickle. Steve swallowed hard, he could sense that this was a momentous occasion. Suddenly they were through as the final chord played. The light flashed for a split second, then it was gone. Steve looked around. The car had stopped although Steve felt no signs of braking and he didn't even recall slowing down. One moment they had been speeding towards a very bright light, then they were in it for a split second and immediately they were perfectly parked in a large car park outside a very impressive set of offices. The driver left the car, walked around to Steve's door and opened it. Steve got out. The man wasn't wearing his coat anymore. Steve saw that he had a smart blue suit and a yellow tie with small dark blue crosses.

"Let's go to Reception, you can register and then we'll have a coffee and I'll explain everything to you." Steve wasn't often short for words but he said nothing and followed the man through the revolving doors. Steve almost stepped on the back of his heel but checked himself and waited for the next section to come around. The reception area was bright and airy and the wood panelling was beautiful, the ceiling might have been painted by Michelangelo. If Steve had looked up, he would have seen hundreds of cherubs smiling down at him, but Steve didn't notice them at all, the receptionist had his full attention, she was quite stunning and without doubt this was the woman that Steve had wanted all his life but had never met. Her name was Julie, so helpful these badges. She smiled at him.

"Welcome Mr. Rogers, allow me please." She tore a card from a book with Steve's name printed on it, she placed it inside a plastic clip and she smiled at him as she pinned the nametag to his lapel. Her white soft silk blouse had the top button undone and her pinstriped black suit jacket fitted perfectly. Steve noticed that her lips were full, she had a perfect complexion and hardly a hint of make-up. Steve didn't like too much make-up on a woman, most didn't need a lot and when he met women who seemed to plaster it on with a scraper he always thought that it was a shame. Steve liked women but once in a while he met one that stood out as special. This woman was beautiful, she was very special indeed.

"If there's anything you need ..." she left the sentence unfinished and Steve gazed at her. Normally even he would have been flustered at meeting his perfect match but he found his voice to be calm and the words came out smoothly.

"Thank you Julie, you are very kind." She smiled again at him and spoke to his companion.

"Welcome back Michael, it's lovely to see you again." Michael nodded pleasantly.

A door slid open and Steve followed Michael into a spacious lounge. He stopped as he watched him walk past the long brown leather sofas and turn before he reached the glass-topped table. He stood perfectly still for a moment and looked out of the window into a grassed area newly planted with young trees, he then turned and faced Steve.

"May I introduce myself to you properly? My name is Michael Shepherd and I am one of your guides. You can ask me anything you want, I'll show you everything I can and you must remember at all times that you are with friends, everyone here is looking out for you and will do all they can to help you." He invited Steve to sit down and he walked over to an automatic coffee machine stood against the wall. Steve sat on the brown leather sofa as Michael poured out the coffee.

"It's cappuccino, you like cappuccino." Michael pushed the coffee in front of Steve who took it, sipped at the froth and got some on his nose, he wiped it with the back of his hand and leaned forward.

"I feel that I am dreaming, in fact I know I must be but I feel very much awake and this place, and you, it all reminds me of somewhere," he paused, "I know I've never been here before, what's happened, what is happening?"

Michael stood up, turned his back on Steve and looked out of the window again. He always did this when breaking the news, he would turn and face Steve as the impact hit him. He spoke carefully.

"Steve," he paused. "You were killed in that accident. That's it! You are quite dead; you are no longer a member of the human race." He turned and faced Steve and he wasn't disappointed, the look on Steve's face was hysterical. At first Steve smiled, then he frowned, his mouth opened to speak, then he changed his mind and tightened his lips. A look of realisation came over him and he stood and faced Michael.

"Yeah right, yes very funny. Look Michael. I don't know who you are, how you did it but you are brilliant. I have seen these hypnosis stunts on stage and they are very good. I've been hypnotised, yes? You really are very good. Who put you up to this?" Steve paused. "I bet it was Malcolm, he loves jokes like this. And I suppose you are an angel. What's the matter got no wings? Why not? They sell them in that joke shop he goes to in Cambridge. Yes brilliant. Very funny! Trouble is Michael, I had other plans for tonight and this game of yours has spoiled them." Michael said nothing, he just smiled, Steve would have to work this out by himself.

"But hang on, I remember the crash and I remember Sharon crying, I remember rolling my car, we weren't at a hypnosis show." He paused, looked at Michael and said, "I'm pretty screwed up, this is too much for me." He paused again, unsure of what was happening to him. He felt a real need to sit down.

"How about I listen and you talk or whatever?" Steve sat back on the sofa, the leather creaked slightly under his weight. Michael sat down next to him and looked into Steve's eyes.

"It's not hypnosis; it's not a practical joke. You were in that accident, would you like to see it, you were driving far too fast for the conditions?" Michael picked up a remote control handset from the table and pressed a button. The lights dimmed as a screen rolled down from the ceiling onto a wall. Steve watched as he saw himself get into the Porsche as Sharon closed the door on the Golf, he watched as they drove out of the town and was amazed as the various camera angles captured the images.

"Who was filming this?" He was motioned to be quiet. The camera showed the speedometer needle flicker around the sixty mark and then rise to seventy.

"It was raining," said Michael with emphasis on the raining. Another camera had shot a view of the lorry coming down the side road, the driver looked right, saw nothing coming, looked left and saw the Porsche way off in the distance and he looked right again. He pulled out onto the main road. Steve watched as the wheels of the Porsche locked up, he stared as the silver 911 hit the kerb stone and rose into the air and he winced as the car rolled over, hit the ground and the rear engine cover and the driver's door opened and tore off under the impact. Steve's eyes were wide open as he saw his beloved Porsche crunch down onto four wheels and stop. The camera shot changed to Steve getting out of the wrecked car and then it showed a close up of the crumpled body, the matted blood and a shot of Steve staring into the car under the crushed roof. The video stopped, the light went on and Michael looked at Steve.

"Nice car that Porsche, well it was. I would have loved to have had one but I never earned as much as you did, besides Porsches weren't around then." Steve sat there stunned.

"Bloody hell!" he said.

Michael shot back. "Less of the bad language if you don't mind Steve, we don't mind the bloodies, we don't mind even the occasional ... you know what, but we don't use the word H. E. L. L. here unless we need to." He spelt out the letters in a whisper.

Steve looked at him. He wasn't used to situations where he was not in control but now he felt that he might have to get used to it. He shrugged.

"Okay I'm listening, what happens now?"

Michael motioned to the door. "I'll use an analogy to help you understand what will happen to you. First, I have to start you on an induction course, just like the one you had when you trained to sell office equipment at Dawson and Peacocks. I'll show you around the HQ, I'll talk you through the whole company, you'll see the products, meet the staff and ..." he paused, "you'll then have your career appraisal," he wagged a finger at Steve. "But it won't really be a career appraisal; it will be your life appraisal. Then you'll make a personal decision on what you want to do, where you want to be and that will all be taken into consideration when the directors make their decision." Michael laughed as he saw the serious expression on Steve's face. "But most of all Steve, I want you to enjoy yourself. And lighten up! It's not every day you get to look around Heaven and H. E. L. L."

"You are going to show me around Heaven and Hell?" Steve was shocked. He didn't believe in anything like life after death when he was alive, he was proud to be a definite non-believer. Religion for him was a way of controlling ignorant people. As far as he was concerned, when someone died, that was it, in the box or down to the crematorium and then the ashes spread over the garden or kept in an urn on the mantelpiece. Disgusting! Most of the other salesmen he knew felt the same. But he thought about it. Perhaps if they knew that something did happen after they died they would be amazed, he wondered if he would have a chance to tell them. Malcolm wouldn't believe it, neither would Mike, Harry Warner would just puff away on his pipe and tut.

Steve followed Michael through the door, he straightened his tie and smoothed his hair. If he was going to be shown around Heaven and Hell, he wanted to be smart for the occasion. He found himself thinking, 'I wonder what Heaven is really like?' he was excited. 'I hope it's fantastic! But what about Hell? I'm not sure I'm looking forward to that very much.'

He frowned as he followed Michael. 'I hope it's not too hot and horrible.'

Michael smiled to himself. He liked showing new arrivals around Heaven and Hell. He had first become a spirit in the middle of Earth's fifteenth century, in his human life he had been a merchant and owned a beautiful and very fast ship. The captain he employed was popular with his crew and sailing the ship between Europe and the Far East was a challenging and wonderful experience. Michael Shepherd would buy the cloths, seeds and spices that were craved by the aristocracy and the Chinese would buy the guns and ammunition he bought from Britain's finest craftsmen. Michael was looking forward to settling down, he had made his fortune and a friend offered to buy his ship after Michael's last voyage but just three weeks from home, pirates had attacked his vessel and their guns had wrecked his rigging. His crew had fought bravely and Michael killed two of the pirates before he too was felled with a cutlass. As he fell to the wooden deck he knew that he had been badly injured but he felt no pain and as his life ebbed away, Michael imagined that a misty veil covered his eyes as he felt a compelling urge to sleep. A sailor who had sailed with Vikings for Northern Europe arranged his arrival in the next world and as he was introduced to Heaven and Hell they spent many happy hours swapping stories of their adventures at sea. Michael appreciated the skill and care of the spirit who arranged his introduction to eternity and he hoped that Steve would enjoy the transition too.

CHAPTER 3

Michael led Steve along a narrow corridor, it was just like any other corridor in any typical company's modern office block but there were no names on the doors and the blinds were drawn in every window. There were no prints on the walls either but apart from that, it was typical of the hundreds of corridors that Steve had seen. Steve stopped, opened a door and peeked inside but there was absolutely nothing in the room, it appeared vast with the floors, doors and ceiling painted a brilliant white. There were no pictures, no furniture; the room had literally nothing in it. Steve paused and Michael stepped back to where Steve stood, he leaned forward, grasped the door handle and pulled it shut.

"What did you expect to see Steve?" Michael politely enquired.

"Er … nothing," said Steve.

"Then you weren't disappointed were you?" Steve looked puzzled but Michael laughed. Michael was about to go on down the corridor but instead he stopped, looked at Steve and decided to ask him a question.

"Okay Steve, if you were back on Earth and you had the whole day to do just as you wanted, what would you like to do? What for you would be a perfect day?"

Steve paused. "I'm not sure, I like doing so many things." He started to smile then realised that the smile was possibly turning into a leer and then he checked himself as Michael began to frown.

"I love golf," he said suddenly, "I'm not much good at it but I do enjoy a good game, not too serious, just a good day, a good game and good company." Michael leaned forward again to hold the door handle.

"Right, you will have a new set of the best clubs ever made and a putter that's magic. You can play in a foursome with Tiger Woods and you will be playing against Colin Montgomerie and Jimmy Tarbuck. It's not a championship game, just a friendly, would you enjoy that?"

Michael opened the door and instead of the pure white walls and ceiling Steve now saw the most magnificent golf course with beautifully tendered fairways and immaculate greens, the sun was shining and the temperature was perfect. Colin Montgomerie was about to select a club from his bag for the 1st tee but stopped as he saw Steve hesitate at the doorway and he smiled and waved at him to come in. Michael stepped in front of Steve and held up his hand.

"Good morning gentlemen. Steve's not quite ready to play now." He looked at Steve who had stepped into the room and was suddenly dressed for golf in the most amazing but tasteful outfit.

"Oh! Perhaps he is but sorry Steve, you have to come back and play later." He smiled at the three golfers and motioned to Steve to leave. As he shut the door he quipped, "We've got things to see and people to do." He chuckled at his joke and gently pulled Steve out of the room and back into the corridor. "Sorry but I have to show you other things first before we relax and enjoy ourselves too much." Steve was disappointed and said so.

"Come along, there's so much on the agenda." Michael smiled as he moved down the corridor but Steve was still very curious and opened the door once more. This time the room was totally white again so he pulled it shut and walked on. He followed Michael past the next door and before Michael could stop him, Steve opened that door and again was presented with a pure white expanse. Michael sighed.

"Okay you want to know about these rooms." Steve nodded. "It's simple really. When you have the right accreditation and you've been admitted to Heaven you can come here when you want to relax and enjoy whatever you love doing. You stand outside one of these doors, picture in your mind just what you'd really like to do and when you have thought of it and got it clear in your mind, you open the door and there it is." Michael smiled. "Alright, go on. You can pretend that you've won your golf match and it's now the evening, where would you like to be?" Steve wanted to think about what he was thinking of before when his leer gave him away but Michael smiled. "It's alright, I know what you are thinking, go ahead, you'll get over it." Steve frowned on hearing the 'you'll get over it' but he concentrated carefully then opened the door again. The scene was the most amazing nightclub. Lights flashed and speakers thumped out a steady beat. He could see his friends from work around a stage and on the stage dancing topless and very erotically was the lovely and very sexy Julie from Reception. She turned towards him, smiled and waved and it was the most erotic moment that Steve had ever experienced. He sighed. He ignored the other beautiful sexily dressed women standing around the bar and talking to his friends, he only had eyes for Julie but Michael pulled him back and firmly closed the door.

"Bloody he …" Steve checked his language. "I mean, Bloody Nora, wow what a place, what else can I do here?" Michael laughed.

"You like skiing don't you?"

"I love it."

"Open the door again Steve." Steve pushed the handle down and gasped. The scene opened up onto the start of the men's downhill course at Sestriere, a slim blonde was skiing beautifully to the side of the piste and she stopped, turned and waved at Steve to follow. Steve turned to Michael.

"I don't suppose …". Steve really wanted to ski. Surely they could try just one taste of Heaven? Michael looked up and down the full length of the corridor, there was no one there.

"Come on then, be quick, I love skiing too." They stepped into the room and found themselves at the top of the mountain outside the exit to a cable car. Lots of people were milling around, all of them smiling, very happy and enjoying the fantastic scenery and superb conditions. Michael handed Steve the latest top of the range racing skis. Steve looked at Michael's trim ski suit and at his own one piece racing outfit, it was bright yellow with large black diamonds.

"I look ridiculous," he laughed.

"Designed for speed." Michael grinned. "Ready to race?" But Steve was off down the slope and although he could ski moderately well on Earth, he could now ski brilliantly. He twisted and turned, keeping his shoulders steady and his skis flashed over the perfectly groomed piste, the sun shone in a clear blue sky and the temperature must have been around plus two, there was hardly any wind, just enough breeze to cool Steve's face. The blonde had already gone ahead and Steve decided to chase after her. Once he thought he was catching her up, then she increased the distance between them. He saw her making some tight turns to slow down for a bend and he decided to go flat out without braking. Steve didn't even slow down a little bit, he put his head down to minimise the drag from the wind, held his pole tips behind him and he crouched down as far as he could. He flashed past all the other skiers on the piste and edged his left ski hard into the snow as he leaned over to take the sharp right bend. He leaned further, the snow held, the skis slid harmlessly over some ice and Steve straightened, he needed to turn left, enormous black and white arrows warned him of the sheer drop ahead. Pressing even harder down on his right ski and bending his knees Steve lined up perfectly for the next bend. The blonde was just ahead and he was catching her. Suddenly she stopped, she looked over the side of the piste and jumped down over what Steve thought was a sheer drop. Steve nearly fell in astonishment but he did the most amazing emergency stop and showered the piste ahead with snow. He stopped exactly where the girl had jumped and he carefully peered over the edge. Her tracks had disappeared for a few metres but here was the most amazing sight, fresh powder snow stretched before him, a few trees and down below, a bowl where he could see other skiers arriving at the bottom of a chair lift. There was only one set of ski tracks, those made by the girl and Steve hesitated. Steve had never liked deep powder skiing, he wasn't confident but he heard Michael speak as he arrived behind him.

"Go for it, bounce through the snow, you can do it." Steve launched himself off the cliff edge and instead of falling headfirst into a pile of deep snow and losing his skis, Steve found that he had the position and the style just right. Bounce, bounce, poles in front, bounce again. Steve laughed out loud with pleasure. He came through the deep snow, rejoined the piste and arrived at the chair lift just as the blonde was getting on the chair ahead. Michael arrived at his side.

"Perhaps you will get to meet her later." He laughed. They passed through the gate and waited for the next chair to arrive, they both sat down together and Steve grinned as pulled the safety bar down.

"This is wonderful, what a place, this is like ..." he paused and then became serious, then he laughed again, "it's like Heaven."

"No Steve, it's not like Heaven, it IS Heaven."

Steve looked around him, he was happy. Michael spoke. "Just don't come here when the children are on half term," he smiled and whispered. "Then it can be Hell!" They both grinned at each other. Steve liked Michael a lot and he liked Heaven even more.

"The only thing is," Michael turned to warn Steve gently as the chair climbed to the end of its run, "it's not all fun and doing what you want, that's nice enough but you'll find the real Heaven quite unexpectedly. Doing nice things and having material things is fine for limited periods but do you know where the real Heaven is for most spirits?" Steve shook his head.

"It's found in relationships. Really good ones, where spirits love and trust each other, the kind of relationships that are without conditions. The kind of relationship that God has with you and maybe you will have with God."

The skiers left the chair together at the top of the hill, the girl had gone and Michael drew Steve to a door next to the cable car station.

"Come on, there's lots more for us to see."

As they went through the door, Steve found himself back in the corridor and in his ordinary clothes.

"Fancy some lunch?" asked Michael.

"You bet! That wonderful ski we just had has left me starving." Michael frowned.

"Talking of starving. Later I have to show you some rather less pleasant scenes, it's all a necessary part of your induction and education I fear."

CHAPTER 4

Lunch was taken in a large canteen, there were no menus and no queues for food and the diners enjoyed the relaxed atmosphere and food from many different countries. Some people were dressed in ordinary everyday clothes and Steve spotted a Bishop in full regalia slurping down a forkful of spaghetti, another character was eating heartily from what looked like the leg of a lamb or a goat. He was dressed as a Roman Centurion and he drew his short, heavy sword and hacked another chunk of meat which he munched happily. Steve felt like he was on a lunch break on the set of a film and around him were actors and support staff. A group of lepers came through the door, they looked like some of the cast from *Ben Hur*.

Steve whispered to Michael, "Why are some people in costume, is there a play on or something?"

"Can you see all these people?" Michael was surprised. "Normally new intakes can't see any other spirits for quite a while after they arrive. You are obviously starting to adapt to your new surroundings."

Steve was puzzled but he didn't say anything, he looked down at his place setting. Whereas before they had sat at an empty table, now there was a steaming hot bowl of soup in front of him. Michael had a chocolate éclair. Steve picked up a spoon.

"I didn't see this arrive, I didn't order it either, did you bring it?" Steve immediately felt stupid for asking the question, he knew that Michael hadn't moved from the table.

"The food comes automatically; the chefs know what you want before you come in. They know, for example, that your favourite soup is tomato with a touch of Tabasco to make it just that little bit spicier. That's what you've got, eat and enjoy."

Steve was impressed and he looked at Michael's chocolate éclair.

"That looks nice." Michael smiled.

"We don't actually need food in heaven but I love these. You'll quickly arrive at your perfect figure," he paused, "but of course you won't have a perfect figure because here we exist in spirit form only. You only sense and feel your body and you see our bodies because to take you straight into the spirit form will confuse you even more than you have been already. Now eat your soup, we have to go to deepest Hell after lunch and I never look forward to showing new arrivals around there." Steve couldn't pass up asking the question that wouldn't stop nagging him.

"I never imagined that spirits would need to eat after they died, surely food is just for humans?"

"Of course it's just for humans and other living creatures on Earth, but many humans enjoyed their food just as good chefs enjoyed preparing it and they want to carry on enjoying it in Heaven. You and I and all these spirits don't actually need food to exist, we eat what we want, when we want and only if we want to. There are lots of things that humans enjoyed doing when they were alive that they don't need to do here. You might not have wanted to sleep late on a lazy weekend but lots of humans love to, you can sleep all day here if that's what you want. But what you will find is that people who loved sleeping late when they were human now regret the time they wasted. Still, the choice is there whether you wish to eat or sleep or whatever, enjoy it whilst you can."

"But that Centurion is eating meat, I would have thought that spirits might be vegetarians or even vegans."

Michael smiled. "Some of them are, it's all a matter of personal taste, no one pressures anyone else here to do what they want them to do. If you enjoy meat, eat it, if you prefer a non-meat diet that's fine too."

"But isn't killing animals for food wrong? I was seriously considering becoming a vegetarian when I was alive."

"It's not wrong, it's not right, it's all decided in your own mind. If you feel that meat is good for you, then it is but don't worry about killing animals, every animal, even the human animal is part of someone's or something's food chain. You'll see that in close up later on, I hope you are not too squeamish."

The soup was delicious, Michael finished his éclair and stood up as Steve put down his spoon. When Steve stood, he saw that his bowl and spoon had vanished.

"Saves on the washing up," Michael grinned. They left the dining area and Michael nodded at a few people who said "hello" to him.

As they entered a lift in the corridor Michael explained. "They haven't been here that long, they are adapting to eternity and some are taking their time about it. That Centurion, he's been here two thousand Earth years, and those lepers you saw, they arrived four years ago in your time but they are acting in a play. We often have *Ben Hur* on after lunch on Christmas Day, or sometimes Steve McQueen in *The Great Escape* and we celebrate all the world's religious holidays here."

Steve interrupted. "I bet you also show *The Sound of Music?*"

Michael was surprised. "Yes how did you know?" Steve grinned but stopped as Michael raised his finger to his lips and told him to be very quiet.

The lift door opened and Michael whispered to Steve, "You will be upset by some of the things you see here. I ask you to speak to no one, to smile at no one, just look and listen, I'll do all the talking, if you have any questions, save them until afterwards." He didn't need to whisper and Steve thought that it was odd that he did but he did feel a little bit scared and if Michael wanted him to be quiet then he would be.

They stepped out onto a metal grille, the walls around them were made of cold, grey steel and were damp, the lighting was poor and there were shadows everywhere. A groaning sound filled the air and even Michael shivered in the cold atmosphere. Steve was soaked through and could feel the damp coming through his shoes and socks. Michael put his mouth close to Steve's ear.

"People think that Hell is hot but sometimes it isn't. If it were always hot, spirits would get used to the heat. What they do here is to change the conditions so that they are always unpleasant. Sometimes it's too windy to stand, sometimes it gets flooded and everyone is up to their shoulders in filthy water. At other times it's so hot you feel that you will suffocate. You've experienced unpleasant weather conditions in your human life on Earth, that was just a tiny taste of the real Hell to come."

Michael led the way and Steve stayed close behind him.

"Don't get the idea to open any doors down here, there are some very powerful devils at work and even I have trouble with them. With all my experience and I've been here," he paused, "ten trillion mos."

Steve wanted to ask but didn't dare, "ten trillion mos?" he'd have to ask later what a mo was, then he realised that he'd often said he'd be along in half a mo, he could work out what a full mo was and then he'd know roughly how long Michael had been here.

The iron grille continued along a narrow corridor and was raised high above a flat expanse of cold, wet metal flooring; the grille glistened with dirty water droplets. Steve tried to see through the holes, he wondered what was below but the holes seemed partly obscured by filthy cobwebs. Steve looked around and below, he could see the shadows of people loading sacks, others were stooping over tiny bits of coal and were picking them up one by one. As they turned a corner Steve saw a figure that he was sure that he recognised, it was dressed in a brown uniform with a group of others in the same clothes. The man pulled himself straight and glared at him.

"My God it's Adolf Hitler! There's Goering!" Steve almost collided with Michael as he stopped, turned and looked at Steve hard.

"Keep quiet please!" Michael hissed. Steve saw that he was annoyed and he was sorry but he didn't dare say so.

As they progressed along what seemed like a very large dark and damp basement, they came to the end of the grille walkway and Steve grabbed a rail as they descended the iron steps. The rail seemed sticky, he looked and saw old blood stains. Michael put his hand close to his mouth and whispered,

"We are in the bowels of Hell. The very worst devils live here and they love to play tricks on new arrivals. Some of them were in the Nazi SS, you'll have read about them and seen films of their atrocities but they were no different than other murderers that went before them or after them. Some of the Crusaders who decided to spread the word of Christianity were not too polite to those who refused to be converted and many extremists from various religions who killed others in the name of their God have earned their right to spend eternity in Hell. Some even prefer it and rejected the idea of Heaven outright because they thought it was too lax and too tolerant of others, I bet you've got a thousand questions but please save them for later."

Steve nodded. They were just about to leave the basement area when a woman stumbled in the dark ahead of them, she was carrying a heavy bucket and she crashed to the floor. Michael moved out of her way but Steve stopped to help her up and he saw that her clothes were rags and her feet were bare except for dirty strips of cloth around her ankles, her knotted hair straggled across her face. She had never washed and her neck was black with dirt, her lips parted and Steve saw her brown and rotted teeth but the look in her eyes rooted him to the spot, he saw a flash of recognition and a memory from the past flooded into his brain. As she rose, she smiled and he saw more of those disgusting teeth. She looked into Steve's face and smiled and his heart stopped, her searching eyes gazed into his and Steve stood transfixed to the spot. Michael paused and looked back and he immediately saw the confusion on Steve's face. He shook Steve roughly by the arm and pulled him away.

"But, but, but!!!" Steve stuttered.

"Save it! Don't speak again." Michael was annoyed and hurried Steve along. They came to a door, it was locked but Michael moved his hand across the doorknob. The door opened and they entered a small room. Michael closed the door and sat down heavily on a wooden chair. He was upset and Steve stood and waited for him to speak. Michael motioned Steve to sit in the other chair. He did. This time there were no smiles, no cappuccino.

"I should have guessed, those devils have been too quiet lately. What must I have been thinking of? Tell me Steve what do you think you saw back there?" Steve had almost recovered his composure but he was still breathing hard.

"I didn't think I saw ..." he paused, "I did saw, I mean I did see my mother, she was the woman who fell carrying that bucket."

Michael sighed. "You weren't supposed to see anyone you knew for quite a while into your induction course, those devils sent her to fall in front of you on purpose, that's their idea of a joke." Michael hadn't been prepared for this and he sat forward in his chair, there was no point in trying to be evasive, better to come out with it.

"The thing is Steve, that was, or rather is, your mother." Michael glanced at Steve who was staring at Michael hard. "Your mother passed through three years ago in your time, right?" Steve nodded. Michael continued. "When she and your father were together they were good parents but your mum wasn't always the mum you knew, she had a life before you were born." Steve waited. "The thing is, your mum wasn't", he paused again, "how shall I put this ...?" Michael considered his words carefully, "She wasn't always a nice person. But ..." and he paused again, "you will have an opportunity to hear her story and understand what she did, in the meantime, you've seen the depths of misery down here for people who deserve Hell, but there are other places too where Hell exists for people who don't deserve it and I'm going to take you there now."

Steve spoke firmly, "And where is this Hell for people who don't deserve it? Michael answered softly. "On Earth Steve. We are going back to Earth."

CHAPTER 5

Michael pressed the button on the lift, he leant back against the wall and the lift started to move.

"Was Hell as you imagined?"

Steve didn't know what to say, he thought that it would be fires, volcanoes and molten lava covering burning and tortured people but the cold, damp metal, the groaning and the expression on the faces of those there seemed worse. Being burned alive in the fires of an imagined Hell might be awful but at least it would be finite, unless they had to do it again and again of course. Having to exist in such a horrible place with constantly changing conditions seemed worse somehow.

"At least they work, what were they doing, collecting coal for the furnaces?"

"Yes the ones you saw were collecting bits of coal but coal isn't needed, what they were doing was and always will be a completely useless job. Not being occupied for eternity is pretty awful but to be occupied doing something that is of no benefit to anyone, well that's ..." he paused.

"Hell?" suggested Steve.

"Precisely." He decided to change the subject and spread his hands.

"This isn't really a lift, it might look and work like a lift but really it's an illusion. We use offices, corridors, rooms and lifts because that's what you are used to, anyone who works or is associated with offices sees their surroundings here as offices. If you were a doctor, this would be a hospital, a lecturer would be in a college, an actor would be in a theatre and a book publisher or an author's agent would be in a pub. He laughed and Steve got the joke. Steve had written a book called *Cheeky Chat Lines For Cheeky Chaps*. His friends contributed with their best opening gambits and some of them were very funny and others were rude. His personal favourite was 'I don't normally rush things but will you marry me?' but his pal Mike Steadman swore that the most successful line he used was as the disco closed and he'd say to a girl, 'Would you like to come back and see my wallpaper?' Apparently that worked on most women that chewed gum openly whilst waiting for a taxi or a bus. Everyone said that it was a great book but although he sent manuscripts to twenty-nine publishers and authors' agents carefully including the cartoon that included a drawing of a cat speaking on the telephone and saying 'Bonjour! C'est un chat line' all he received was a collection of rejection letters, most of them pre-printed.

Michael explained. "It's all arranged for your benefit and comfort and so that you can adapt more easily. One new spirit I showed around was an Eskimo and we spent a lot of our time in an igloo and we travelled around on sledges pulled by dogs. It was great fun."

"An Eskimo? Are you teasing me?"

"Of course not, Eskimos die too you know, Heaven is full of Eskimos."

"So besides Eskimos in igloos, a soldier would be in a typical army HQ, a sailor would be on board ship and a policeman in a police station or in a court," Steve understood. "It's all adapted to suit the person who's just died?" Steve thought it was a great idea.

"But not everything is an illusion created for your benefit, what we are going to see now is certainly not a mirage. I regret that I have to show you Hell on Earth." The lift doors opened and Michael politely invited Steve to step out first, he followed and they moved through a set of glass swing doors and onto the street. Steve thought that he recognised the city but he wasn't sure. Michael led the way and Steve walked beside him along the pavement.

"We are going to meet some people who experience Hell on Earth but before we do, I need to explain something." Michael entered a park gate and they walked along the path, it led to a pond and Steve noticed children and their parents throwing bread to the ducks. The sun shone, it was a warm day, Michael stopped at a bench and sat down. Steve sat at the far end of the bench, crossed his legs and folded his arms, he was ready to listen.

"To be in Hell, there have to be certain factors present." Michael gazed ahead as he spoke. "The Mother of Hell is Fear. Not the kind of fear that you feel when you are nervous of diving off a high board into a swimming pool or the trepidation you sense when you are about to do something you consider scary, that's not the fear I mean. The kind of fear that is Hell is the type that knots your stomach, that freezes you ice cold, that makes your hands shake uncontrollably. The kind of fear that you have when you are really very very frightened and you know that you are totally helpless, yet there might be a way to get away if only you can find it, but of course you can't find it. When you taste that fear, then you taste Hell."

As Steve listened he watched a young mother pushing a baby in a buggy and holding on to the buggy with one hand was a two-year-old boy. Jessica Clarke wore a coat that her mother had given her and her shoes were from the charity shop and were scuffed but comfortable. She saved her new shoes for special occasions. Unfortunately she was so busy with the children she was too tired to go out with her husband and there were no special occasions for her at the moment, unless of course you count taking the children to the park as a special occasion and if you did, the shoes from the charity shop were just fine for that. The toddler pointed to the ducks and wanted to run to them but his mother grabbed at his hand and tried to stop him but he evaded her grasp and ran quickly past two older women who were walking ahead. The mother left the buggy, shouted after the child and pushed past the women mumbling an apology, she clutched the boy as he ran at the ducks and scattered them. They were annoyed and fluttered into the air only to land again a few yards away. She bent down, scolded him and turned towards the buggy just as it increased speed on the sloping path and toppled into the pond. For a second she froze, then she screamed. The women looked at her in amazement and a man with a black Labrador turned and stared at her. The handles of the buggy disappeared under the surface and the mother left the child and ran to the water's edge. She screamed for her baby and dropped to the ground, her hand flailing uselessly in the water trying to reach the buggy. The two women ran to her side and looked into the deep water, the man with the dog stood there rooted to the spot, he hadn't seen the buggy rolling off the path but he then realised what had happened.

"She's in the water, Sarah's in the water." The mother thought that she would faint. "Please somebody help!"

A young lad on a skateboard stopped, flicked his board up and caught it neatly. He immediately understood what had happened and placing his board on the ground, he sat on the edge of the pond where the tarmac of the path met the pond edge and he lowered himself into the water feeling for the bottom with his feet. He then pushed himself away from the edge and dived down, a few moments later he spluttered to the surface, looked at the mother as if to say, don't worry I'm still trying, and he dived down again. When he appeared he seemed to be in difficulty treading water, he tried to get to the edge and he put out his hand. The man with the dog tied the lead to the bench and leaned over trying to take the swimmer's hand, he grabbed it and pulled the lad onto the path. The boy twisted and sat on the tarmac, he had something heavy in his left hand and as he pulled the buggy handle emerged from the water. The mother was on her knees and trying to reach it but the man had a longer arm and he grabbed it first and pulled it hard. The buggy streamed out of the water and was plonked down on its wheels, water poured from it and Steve and Michael watched as the mother realised that the baby was no longer in it. The lad stood up and dived straight in. The man dropped his coat, stepped out of his shoes and followed him, the water swallowed them both and for a few moments it was quiet, no one spoke, all that Steve could hear was the mother whimpering and crying.

The man appeared first, he shook his head to free the water from his hair and his legs splashed as he bent over and dived again for the bottom of the pond. Then the lad came up for air, he had been unable to find the baby either and yet again he dived. As Steve watched the appalling tragedy he said that he would help but Michael's hand held him back.

"There's nothing you can do even if you wanted to."

The man and the boy pulled themselves onto the path and coughed up the dirty water that they had swallowed and they were really upset because they hadn't found the baby. Jessica Clarke wanted to jump in but one of the women stood between her and the water's edge and spoke firmly.

"My friend has called the police on her mobile phone; they will be here in a minute. Stay calm."

Steve and Michael watched as the police appeared. Roger Bennett had finished his probation three years ago and he complained yesterday that he was fed up with moving beggars out of doorways, they only returned a few minutes later and if he arrested them, the custody sergeant told him to take them back to where he found them. Roger longed to catch a proper villain but the best he'd done was to arrest two schoolgirls caught shoplifting. His shift today was with Jenny Bryant, he enjoyed her company and he thought that she would be a good WPC, she seemed very capable. He and Jenny had been patrolling in the park and were chatting about car chases when he got the call to say that a baby had fallen in the water in South Park in the pond behind the bandstand. They ran as fast as they could and he spotted the buggy on the path and pointed. Jenny tried to comfort the mother but Roger interrupted and asked how long the baby had been in the water. When he learned that two or three minutes had passed, he immediately unbuttoned his jacket but instead of diving in where the others had, he plunged in by the reeds and came towards the path under the water. He seemed to be down a long time but suddenly his head burst from the water and he gasped for air. In his right hand he held the baby clear of the surface and as water streamed from its wrap he stretched for the pond edge and thrust the baby into the hands of the policewoman. Jenny Bryant was two months into her probation but she knew what she had to do. She laid the baby on the grass and pulled weed and bits of algae from its mouth, she then made sure that the baby's throat was clear and as she could see that the baby wasn't moving, she placed her mouth over the baby's mouth and started to breathe air into its tiny lungs. The mother stood there in horror, she felt totally helpless but she knew that she could do no more. Jenny's left hand went to the baby's stomach and chest, she realised that she couldn't exert too much force so she tried to massage the baby's lungs with her fingers. Nothing happened at first but then the baby moved, its head twitched and dirty water gulped from its mouth onto the grass. Jenny picked the baby up and put it over her shoulder trying to burp it. She slapped it firmly and to her delight another gulp flowed onto her back. She patted the baby's back a few more times and then looked at its face, she was ready to breathe for the child but she hesitated, the baby was breathing, she could see colour returning to its cheeks and the child moved its mouth and began to cry.

Jenny held the baby in her arms as if she was the mother, tears streamed down her face. Jessica Clarke reached out her hands, she was crying too. Roger Bennett was grinning, a small crowd gathered and people congratulated him, he picked up his jacket and took his radio out of its leather holder.

"This is Sierra Two at South Park by the grandstand. Send an ambulance please, we have a baby that needs a check-up, oh and can someone bring my spare uniform from my locker please?"

Michael turned to Steve and asked him a question. "Can you imagine, if only for a moment, how that mother felt when she saw the child fall into the pond? How she felt when someone was trying to save it and then what her feelings were when she realised that she had lost it?"

Steve said nothing but he could feel the most awful pain in his stomach. It felt as if someone had reached into his tummy and was trying to pull his insides out. He suddenly felt extremely cold, he wanted to vomit, but he couldn't. His body started to shake and he felt as if a very large and very black cloud had covered his head. He couldn't think straight, he couldn't make sense of anything except the most awful feeling of emptiness and despair. He suddenly realised that this was his fault. If he hadn't left the buggy to run after Jonathan, if he had bothered to tie on his reins, if he had chased after Jonathan with the buggy... His thoughts were confused and he blamed himself totally. He felt a coat being put over his shoulders and through his tears he could see that someone else had arrived. A policewoman was comforting him and her colleague was taking off his jacket and his belt. Steve snapped out of his dream.

"How would you describe that mother's experience this morning?" Michael asked as he walked beside Steve as they left the pond.

"It was awful, poor woman. Thank goodness it ended all right. If that policeman hadn't guessed that the baby was trapped under the ledge, then it would have died."

Michael suggested what might have happened if the baby had drowned.

"She wouldn't ever forgive herself for her baby's death. That would have just been the start of it for her, her worst ever day. She would be taken to hospital, her husband would be called. He won't believe it at first, then he'll question her, he'll almost interrogate her.

He'll blame her, then he'll blame himself, then he will have to call her parents, then his parents. Next week they will have a very sad funeral service. Time will heal the pain to a degree but the mother will never ever forget and despite all the counselling she will receive, she will always blame herself for her daughter's death."

"But it was an accident."

"Yes it was but she'll still blame herself even though it wasn't her fault."

Michael paused. "Every second of every day, someone somewhere goes through the pain that the baby's mother experienced. Her pain was short-lived, her baby was saved, but every few seconds someone dies like that, children are lost, killed, they disappear. The people who are left behind are the ones who experience Hell on Earth. No one is exempt from this Hell, everyone at some time in their lives knows and feels the terrible bitter pain of fear and loss, unfortunately we have to know suffering in order to know joy. When that mother held her baby safe in her arms, then she felt pure joy. How did you think that mother felt when she realised that her baby was safe after all?"

Steve was about to answer when he felt his heart nearly burst, he felt as if he was ten feet tall and he felt truly wonderful. He looked down at the baby in his arms and a sensation of pure love came over him as the inside of his body became very warm. He felt that he could achieve anything and that his baby would be safe forever and he would never, ever be parted from her. Michael looked at Steve's face and saw his joy. He didn't need to ask again.

Michael turned off the path and walked up a grassy mound. He spoke quietly to Steve. "I'm going to introduce you now to two men who will tell you about the Hell they experienced on Earth through fear. The big chap is Tommy MacNeil, the other man is Dave O'Reilly. Tommy is a Protestant and hated Catholics. Dave's a Catholic and he was in the IRA. Listen to their story."

CHAPTER 6

Few things sharpen a man's mind more than when he discovers that his own side
has said that he is 'bad for business'.
(based on experiences in Northern Ireland)

"Lord God give me patience, but give it to me now!" Dave O'Reilly smacked his forehead with his palm and lay back on the grass in the sunshine, Tommy grinned at him.

"You're a bigot and that's sure enough." Tommy and Dave were relaxing in South Park not far from where Jessica Clarke nearly lost her baby but they didn't see or hear anything of the drama that had unfolded less than a hundred yards away. They were too busy arguing over a subject that they had often argued about before, but they were great friends and enjoyed their banter enormously.

"If I'm a bigot, then you're a bigger bigot." Dave realised what he had said and burst out laughing. The two men chuckled at the joke. Tommy saw Michael and Steve approaching.

"Watch it now, it's the bloody Garda." Dave deliberately spoke in a mock whisper that was loud enough to be heard by Michael and Steve.

"Sure it's the man himself." Then he looked at Steve. "Is he the man or are you the man?" Steve was puzzled but Michael spoke.

"He means am I the boss or are you the boss?" He called to Dave and Tommy. "Morning to you both, have you got time for a chat?"

"Well that depends, it's been a long time since we had a drop, if you have brought some with you, we could have a wee chat."

Michael was carrying a small bag over his shoulder, Steve hadn't noticed it before but Michael must have had it all along. Michael sat down on the grass and opened the flap, he took out two cans of Guinness and handed one to Dave and the other to Tommy, he then reached into his bag again and took out a can of bitter and a can of lager. He gave the bitter to Steve who accepted it gratefully and he flicked open his can of lager and took a drink.

"We don't get the opportunity to drink very often these days, on account of our situation." Tommy winked at Steve as he put the can to his lips.

"You wouldn't have a cigarette by any chance?" Steve was about to shake his head but Michael leant across and handed Tommy a cigarette. He offered one to Dave who looked at it before putting it to his lips.

Steve looked at Tommy and smiled to show friendship as he didn't want to cause offence by staring. Tommy had a haunted look, the lines in his face belied his forty-nine years, he looked well over sixty. The grey hair was receding and Steve thought that a trim was long overdue. The suit was cheap and the trousers were shiny. Steve looked at Tommy's shoes, they were scuffed and had probably never been polished since they were new, Tommy clearly didn't take any pride in his appearance. The man held out his hand to Steve and as he shook it, Steve noticed the faded yellow nicotine stain on his fingers, the nails were grubby and bitten. Steve looked into the man's eyes and he saw eyes that had lived with fear. The man sat back down on the grass and fumbled in his pocket.

"I don't suppose you have any matches?"

Steve apologised and looked at Michael. He handed him a box.

"Tommy doesn't smoke much anymore."

Tommy snapped back. "Not by bloody choice!"

"Tell your story Tommy, I may find you a whole packet later." Tommy smiled and Steve could see he had told it before, probably many times.

"As you can tell from my accent, I'm from Belfast. I am a Protestant and I was a loyal member of the UVF." He spat on the grass. "I believed in what I was doing. The IRA murdered my father and my brother and I wanted revenge and I wanted the Catholics crushed, as far as I was concerned, the only good Catholic was a dead one. I hated them, I hated the IRA and I hated the British soldiers who had to poke their noses into our business. I was a soldier, a soldier at war and my orders were to kill Catholics. I despised them sure enough but I hated those Brits more, they arrested me three times and beat me up. Then they sent me to the H block, they called me scum and they were supposed to be on our side," he turned to Dave, "they were worse than your bloody lot." He didn't smile, he wasn't joking.

"I wasn't very high up in the hierarchy but I was expert in explosives and automatic weaponry. I killed Catholics and traitors. That was my job and I was good at it, but the traitors got me, I was sold out."

Tommy put his can of beer to his lips and took a long draught. He paused for a moment, enjoying the taste of the beer and thinking how he could best explain what happened to him.

"Have you ever heard the phrase 'Bad for Business'?" Tommy glanced at Steve but Steve shook his head. "Bad for Business is when your own side decides that they don't want you anymore. When you have been so great at doing what they themselves trained you to do, they decide that you have gone too far and that it's time for you to stop. But I didn't want to stop. My duty was to kill Catholics and traitors. Until we were rid of them, they had to be killed or forced out. If we lost the war, we would be finished, they told me to stop but I wouldn't, I couldn't. I didn't realise it then but some people at the top on both sides were making a fortune in cash from extortion, protection, robbery, smuggling, stealing donations from the public, at home and abroad and taking money from other countries. Irish Americans poured huge amounts into IRA funds, they might have thought that they were soothing their consciences and helping out the old country but what they gave was shared out on both sides. There were big frauds too against the aid agencies and when the British Government attracted investment from foreign firms those firms had to pay insurance money to prevent their executives being kidnapped and held to ransom. Those who paid were left alone, those that refused got more trouble than they needed. Millions of pounds were being creamed off and when a factory or shop got blown up, the British Government would pay compensation and where do you think that went?"

Steve shook his head, he had no idea.

"It went to the bosses of our lot and their lot." He looked at Dave and Dave nodded. "It was shared out and some people got very rich. But I didn't get rich, neither did thousands of others who dedicated themselves to what they believed in. We thought that what we were doing was right, but we were conned." Tommy took a long draw on his cigarette and flicked the ash on his shoe. "I didn't realise it at first and I didn't know why but my commanding officer really did want me to stop killing Catholics for a while. He had orders from above and I think now that someone had done a deal. But if he knew, he wasn't telling, he hinted that I should relax a bit and take a holiday but I didn't understand what he was saying. At the time I was just about to hit a house just off the Falls Road and execute a man who had been involved in hiding an IRA bomb team after they blew up a car in Belfast and killed four people. I got a message saying that I was to delay the killing until I received further instructions but I discovered that my target would be going to Dublin in a day or so and that if I wanted to get him I had to take him now. I went with another man to his house. We knocked on the door; he opened it, saw my gun and he ran back into the house. He tried to hide behind a chair but I saw him and shot him once in the stomach, he was slobbering and begging me not to shoot him again. His children were in the room and saw the whole thing. His wife came at me screaming and as I shot him in the heart she tried to hit me with a saucepan but I brushed her aside and went out."

"When I told my commanding officer what I had done he went crazy and shouted and yelled at me, you'd think I'd shot his mother or something. Anyway he told me to get out and that as far as he was concerned I was to lay low if I knew what was good for me. He said that he'd try and sort it out and maybe hint that I hadn't received his message but he told me that I was an eejit and that I had embarrassed him. I didn't go home for a while, I guessed that someone might come after me. I had known of others who had upset him and I knew for certain that one particular man had disobeyed an order that he didn't agree with and he was kneecapped. I hid out for a while and stayed in pubs on the coast but when I ran out of money I had to go home. Walking up the hill to my street was the worst part. Not being able to sleep at night can be cured with a few whiskies but going home was scary. I felt that everyone was looking at me and that they all knew that I was in trouble. My wife didn't look at me when I pushed the door open, she was ironing and she didn't ask where I had been and I didn't tell her. I think she knew. I asked if any of my friends had been round. Normally a few of the lads would come over and we'd go to the pub, or we'd go and play snooker but she said that no one had been at all.

"I asked her for money and told her that I had to get out of the area for a while. She went upstairs for her purse, came down and gave me thirty pounds and told me to go to Hell. She told me that I had been nothing but trouble to her and that as far as she was concerned I was dead already. I was shocked and demanded to know what she meant but she wouldn't say. In the end she threatened to hit me with the iron. I decided to go to the pub on the corner. I knew people there, I'd known some of them for forty years, if I was in trouble they would help me, I was sure of that. But when I pushed open the door of that pub, I sensed a strange atmosphere. No one spoke to me, indeed I thought I must have leprosy or something. I tried to talk to my mates but they made excuses. Then when I went to the toilet one of them followed me. He told me that he had heard that I was to be set up because I was bad for business. I grabbed him and he thought I was going to strangle him right there in the jacks. He told me that he had heard that my name had been passed to an IRA hit team by my own side. I was expendable, bad for business. I had been sentenced to death and the IRA would execute me."

"I dropped the man where he stood and left the pub. First I went home, my wife had gone out and she'd taken her purse so I went upstairs and threw some clothes into a bag. My wife then came in, she'd been next door and saw me come home. I told her that I was going and that if anyone came calling I was in England. But I was laying a false trail. I wouldn't go to England, I would go to Spain, I knew someone there who had a bar. There was a bus into town in ten minutes but I never made it. As I walked away from my house for the last time, a car pulled up, I didn't know the men. One of them asked if I was Tommy MacNeil. I said no. They moved on and then their car stopped at the top of the road. Two of them got out and walked towards me. I looked over my shoulder in case I had to run but there was another man behind me. He called to me. 'Hello Tommy, remember Sean O'Shea? He was my brother, Tommy.' By this time I was really scared and looked for somewhere to hide. I knew if I could get someone to open their door I could duck inside. Just two doors along lived John McColl. He was in the UVF and I'd known him since we were snotty kids, he'd hide me. I took two long paces and hit his door hard. I shouted for him to let me in. He had a gun did John, we could fight. But John didn't open the door, I saw him at the window and yelled at him, I thought he would help, but he didn't. He moved out of sight. I thumped hard on his door again but it held firm. O'Shea's brother stood behind me and he pointed a gun at my head. The car reversed up and stopped. I was given a choice to get in or die like a dog in the street. I got in. Immediately someone hit me in the mouth with the barrel of a pistol. I was frightened and my mouth started to fill with blood. The driver moved off. We passed a car parked at the top. We slowed right down and stopped level with the door. I looked at the man in the driving seat, it was my commanding officer. He looked at me hard, then he nodded at the man in the front seat of my car and no one spoke. I realised that I had pissed my trousers. The men laughed. I was tortured for three days but I didn't give any information away because I wasn't asked to, they knew what they wanted to know. By day I was beaten, frozen, cut and by night I was tied up so tightly I couldn't sleep. If I tried to doze, I was kicked and punched. On the last day I was taken into the yard of a farm, tied up and shot in the head. My body was dumped and there was just one mention of my murder on the news. It said. 'A 49 year old man was found bound and shot in a lane. The police believe that it was a sectarian murder.' But do you know what really got to me? The fact that my own side had arranged it with these murdering bastards. When I realised that I had nowhere to run, when I realised that my side was also my enemies and that I had been given up to be executed, I was scared beyond belief. Do you know what it's like to be scared, to be really frightened? When you know that someone is going to kill you and you don't know where or when. You can't go to your own people because they set you up. You can't go to the police, you can't go to the army. All you can do is wait. Believe me, it's not something I recommend unless you're an effing eejit like this fella." He pointed at Dave and finished his beer in one gulp.

CHAPTER 7

Dave grinned and smacked Tommy playfully on the head. "I may have been an effing eejit but at least I wasn't the only one to be set up by my own side."

Michael rummaged around in his bag and found two more beers, Dave accepted his with a grunt and took a swig. Steve looked at him. Unlike Tommy, Dave was podgy and being bald suited him. He had a cheery face, round cheeks and at some time when he was young he may have had a twinkle in his eye, the girls would have liked him especially before he lost most of his hair. He noticed Steve looking at him and he patted his shiny head.

"I'm just a little tall for my height, if I was smaller you'd see my hair, but as I'm too tall, you can't," he grinned at his joke. "The girls love me, you see this," he patted his head again, "I am a solar powered sex machine."

Tommy leaned back and laughed so much he nearly spilt his beer. Michael pretended to enjoy the fooling about but wanted Dave to tell Steve his story, he said that they needed to be going soon, could Dave be sensible for a moment? Steve was quite surprised at Tommy's change of mood, one minute he was recounting the story of his fear and his terrifying death, the next minute, he was laughing and fooling about, maybe being in the spirit world helped him see things in their proper perspective?

Dave looked seriously at Steve as if he understood what Steve was thinking, he winked and smiled but he didn't make another joke, suddenly he became as serious as Tommy had been when he told his story.

"Let me tell you Steve, war is hell, all war. Soldiers do their duty but they are trained not to think, just to obey orders and try to be lucky and stay alive. Some people want to be soldiers, some people don't. I didn't want to be a soldier but I became one. An English soldier once told me that a soldier's duty is to die but I didn't want to die. I saw men getting caught, I saw two get killed, a man in a car shot them in the street when they were walking to church. If we had uniforms at least we'd know who was on our side, who was on the other side, but in our kind of war, the enemy looks like a friend and the next knock on the door could be some kid coming round to play with your kids or someone who doesn't know me but who has been told to kill me and ask no questions. Rumours are the worst, our orders are passed to us and we do as we are told but when we hear that someone has been caught by the army or by the UVF and that we might be next," he paused, "well I'll tell you, sleep doesn't come easy to a committed man who doesn't know if he'll survive the next day. And there's nowhere to run of course, if you hide, the word is out that you are a possible informer. Once you're in, you are in, the only way out is death. I believed passionately in The Cause and sometimes I used to rattle a tin outside our church. Catholics were treated like shit and we'd had enough. I didn't intend to be a killer, I got involved when I was twenty because someone asked me to come with them to do a bit of poaching, I had nothing better to do and I was promised a share so I went. But we didn't go poaching rabbits, we went poaching to catch someone we were told was an informer.

"I was in the car, sitting in the back when our driver stopped outside a house. I was given a handgun and told to wait in an alley and to shoot anyone who challenged us or who interfered. The lad in the front, he was only about eighteen, he got out and went to the door of a house, he knocked and waited. The curtain moved and a face looked out. The door opened. I remember that the fella inside welcomed the lad, he knew him. The lad went into the house but he didn't stay long enough to close the door behind him. I heard three shots, then the lad came out, walked calmly to the car and got in. Someone called me and I got into the back again. We drove off. We went to a pub and I met a man I didn't know. He bought us a drink and said that we had done well. I was given fifty pounds. I tried to refuse it but I was told that to refuse a drink would be an insult. I didn't want the money but I was scared and I took it. Later I was driven home. Again I was thanked. They'd see me around. I didn't sleep for two nights, I kept thinking about that man who got shot and the expression on the lad's face as he came back to the car. He was grinning, he'd enjoyed it. The following Saturday night I was playing darts and someone I didn't know spoke to me by name and told me to be ready Wednesday evening at eight in the evening. I wasn't given a chance to ask why or refuse. He walked away.

"On Wednesday I was crapping myself, I kept looking out of my window and my wife was asking me what the matter was but I couldn't tell her. Then the car arrived and someone knocked on the door, it was the man from the pub. He told me that I would be needed to help carry a milk churn. A milk churn for God's sake! He opened the car door for me and I got in, there were three others in the car and no one spoke. Then the driver said that he'd drop us off at Benny's in the High Street. We stopped outside Benny's and the driver got out and opened the car boot. I stood with the others and saw a milk churn wrapped in a blanket. I had to help lift it out, it was heavy. I did what I was told and we rolled and dragged the milk churn into the shop doorway. An old man saw us but he immediately crossed the road. One of the lads stood over the churn and unscrewed the lid. He fiddled inside and then screwed the lid back on. He got back in the car and told us to do the same. We drove off. I heard later that someone called out the army to handle a suspected bomb outside the department store. The army arrived and blocked off the street but our churn was in the doorway of Benny's. It was detonated by remote control just as the soldiers were setting up their equipment to defuse a suspect suitcase in a dustbin outside the store. The army truck took the full blast of our bomb and the building that was Benny's collapsed into the street, a mass of fire, rubble, dust and smoke. Three soldiers were killed immediately, four more were cut to pieces by glass and nails and one of them died later that night. Again I was given money but this time I refused it. My refusal was accepted and the man who offered it said that I was a true patriot and a credit to The Cause. He thought that I refused to accept money because I was dedicated.

"Three days later I was arrested. The whole bloody British Army turned up to arrest me at dawn at my house. They broke the door down, my family was terrified, my wife tried to hide the twins but the soldiers smashed up the house and threw her and the boys into the street. They then broke every bit of furniture, tore down the curtains and wrecked everything they could see. I was dragged to an armoured van and thrown inside. I was kicked and punched and then someone must have clubbed me because I passed out. I woke naked on the floor of a cell and I was chained hand and foot. When my guard saw that I was awake he kicked me and made me stand up, he undid the rusty chain holding my ankles together and he unlocked the handcuffs, put my hands behind my back and cuffed me again. He then leaned me against the wall with my feet spread-eagled behind me and my forehead pressed against the wall. He told me if that I moved, he'd personally cut my balls off. It was agony, try standing like that sometime. The muscle pain is immense."

"Over the next few days I was questioned, beaten, questioned and beaten. I was not fed and if I tried to sit down without permission I was kicked and punched. I told them everything I knew, it didn't take long for them to break me and besides I didn't know anything but what I'd done. They told me that they had arrested the others and that they had given my name. Then for some reason the torture stopped and I was handed back my clothes, I was given some food and even a beer. An officer I hadn't seen before introduced himself, he was going to be my minder. I told him I didn't need a minder. He said that I did because now I was working for the British. In return for my life and my family's safety I would be released back home and the word would be put out that I was of no use to them because I didn't know anything. That in itself was true, but he added that I would be contacted again and next time I was asked to go poaching or moving milk churns or whatever, I was to make a signal by opening one of the upstairs curtains and closing the other and leaving the window like that. I refused point blank and said that I wouldn't be helping on any more jobs for anyone. I was then told that if I refused to work for my minder, I would be released anyway but that the word would go out that I had informed on others and was now working for the British. The bastard asked me if I liked having two kneecaps.

"When I was released they arranged for a taxi to take me home. A taxi! People in our street didn't take taxis, they got the bus or walked. My wife was there when I got home and the house had new furniture. Apparently two days after my arrest, a van arrived with a new bed for us, new beds for the twins and everything that had been broken was replaced. Sheila, my wife, was given a hundred pounds in cash. I asked her who had done this, she said that a nice man had called with a priest and told me that I would be properly looked after. The man said that good friends look after each other. I didn't know what to do or think. I wanted to move. I told my wife what I had done and at first she didn't say anything. Then she stood up and slapped me as hard as she could in the face. Of course I didn't tell her that I was supposed to be working for the British and about the bedroom curtains. She said that I was an effing eejit.

"Had the IRA brought the furniture, had they given us the money or was it my Army Officer minder? I had no idea. I tell you it was hell for me. Every time someone came near the house I wanted to hide. Sheila suggested that we go to her cousin who lived near Cork but I didn't dare. If I left the area, my minder would spread the word that I was an informer. I was trapped and there was no way out, there was no one I could call and no one I could speak to. Yes I had friends but no one that I knew would hide me and risk their own lives or kneecaps. I just hoped that I wouldn't be required to do any more little jobs. Nothing happened for three months, I had just begun to think that we would be all right then one night in the pub, I was playing darts and someone I didn't know asked me if I would play an away game for a good cause. I wanted the ground to swallow me up but the man smiled and placed a fresh pint next to my glass. He told me to keep Friday free and that the dart team's captain would collect me at eight in the evening. It was exactly the same time as before. What could I do? Should I move the curtains, should I leave them alone? I couldn't sleep for worrying and I didn't dare tell Sheila. But I had an idea. I told Sheila that I'd won some money on the horses and that I planned to take her and the twins on Friday to Cork to see her cousin. But as I was playing darts on Friday I wouldn't be able to go until Saturday. She was pleased but said that she'd wait until Saturday and that we'd all go to Cork together. I persuaded her that she should go with her sister and I gave her some money and promised I'd join her on Saturday afternoon or early evening.

"I decided not to move the curtains. After all, nothing had happened for three months, I was only going to play darts and even if this was something that I didn't want to be involved in, I could always say that I didn't know it was a job. Justifying my decision not to move the curtains got easier and I decided to cross my fingers and hope for the best. I lay awake that night. In the distance I heard a shot; it was about two in the morning, then I heard a siren, some poor bastard had taken a bullet. I lay there and wondered what it would be like to be shot. Would I just keel over and be immediately dead like the baddies in the cowboy films or would the bullet really hurt as it tore into my flesh, cut through muscle and splinter my bones? I felt my right hand touching the back of my knee, I knew a man that had been kneecapped, the doctors at the hospital tried to repair the wound as best they could but he would never be able to walk properly and would be in pain for the rest of his life. How did I get into this mess? I had a horrible feeling that I knew how it might end. Just as it got light I fell asleep but I dreamed that my wife was shooting me with a gun and the twins were laughing at me and shouting, 'Daddy is dead, Daddy is dead.'"

CHAPTER 8

"On Friday evening I waited alone in the house, I was tempted to go out but the look I got from the man who told me to wait implied that I should not disobey. The clock on the mantelpiece chimed eight times and I wanted to go to the toilet again. I'd been four times since the early evening news and I looked again at the bottle of Jameson's in the cupboard. Sod it! I unscrewed the cap and put the bottle to my lips. Someone banged hard on the door, I jumped and nearly dropped the bottle. I took a tiny bit and felt my heart burn as the spirit warmed me. I didn't want to open the door but I did and a man stood there in a coat, his hat pulled down over his eyes. He asked me if I was okay and when I nodded he asked if I had my darts! I said no and he said well you better get them then. I found them in the sideboard drawer and tried to control my nausea, maybe we were really going to play darts after all, what an eejit I am. There was a car against the kerb. The man opened the door for me as if I was important, I got in. It was an old green Ford estate with a long rip in the seat, it stank of stale cigarettes, the ashtray was overflowing with dog ends and the floor was littered with bits of old newspaper. There were even old chips from a takeaway, it was disgusting. There was another chap in the front seat. But he didn't look at me, he just stared straight ahead and smoked. I'd never seen him before either. The driver seemed cheerful and friendly but there was something about his manner that chilled me, he didn't have to be too polite and I felt he was making a special effort to make me feel welcome but he overdid it and that worried me. Then he said that he heard that I was a great team player. That worried me even more. I fingered my darts box, what a bloody mess I was in.

"We drove out of Belfast and past a few pubs, I recognised some of the names. One pub had recently been bombed with a solution made with weed killer and sugar. The sugar was designed to melt in the explosion and stick to the people that got caught in the blast, it made the injuries more severe because it melted exposed skin. I looked at the others in the car, no one spoke. Eventually we arrived at a pub used by weekend fishermen, it was packed for a Friday night and the cigarette smoke hit me as we pushed through the door and into the bar. We didn't stop for a drink. I followed the car driver, the other man was behind me and we went through the restaurant area and into a room at the back. A brown door opened, I remember that there were scratches on it as if a dog or large cat had tried to get out. We went upstairs. A man stood in front of another door, he recognised the man leading us and opened it. There was a long black table, seven or eight men in their sixties and seventies were seated and each had a whiskey glass in front of him. I remember that each wore a tie, not any special tie but a tie worn because the meeting would be important. I couldn't see any windows, old red velvet drapes ran from the ceiling to the floor along two walls. One light on an old brown cord with an upside down green tin shade hung from the ceiling and spread a pool of light on the middle of the table. Maybe this was a private room for playing cards. There were three bottles of Irish whiskey on the table and several ashtrays, the room was smoky but not as bad as downstairs. I didn't know any of the men but they appeared to know me and I was invited to sit down. The leader of the group spoke. The ash hung long from his cigarette and I thought that it must fall off but it didn't. He told me that I was a great soldier, an asset to the Irish Republican Army and that my loyalty and courage were an example to them all. I blushed and decided that I might need to go to the toilet again. A glass was put in front of me and it was filled to the top. Everyone stood and so did I. They toasted Ireland, the IRA and every man downed his whiskey in one go and almost slammed their glasses hard on the table. I gulped mine down and nearly coughed it all up again but thankfully I didn't. The men sat down again and so did I, they appeared to be friendly but I knew that they weren't, I felt as if I was on trial. I was then told that they were aware of my conversation with the British officer who wanted to be my minder. I wasn't to worry, everyone who was picked up by the army was given a tough time and invited to become a spy for the British. One man slapped me on the back, he seemed friendly;

he said that he hoped that I'd agreed. They looked at me and waited for an answer. What could I say? If I told them the truth they would believe that I was a spy for the British, if I lied they wouldn't believe me especially if others had been made the same offer. I decided to tell the truth. I told them exactly what happened and what I had been told to do and what I didn't do. The leader looked at me and thought for a while. He asked why I hadn't set the curtains that evening as instructed. I said that I had no reason to as far as I was concerned, I was off to play darts. I'd been told to bring them and I had. I showed them my darts. The man opposite me leant over and asked if he could see them. I handed him the box. He took them out and put the flights onto the brass points. He toyed with them. Then he pointed a dart at me and asked if I was a stupid man. I said that I wasn't. He asked if I thought that they were stupid. I didn't like the way this conversation was going. No I didn't think they were stupid.

"Another man with a very soft voice spoke. He said that I was going to be given a chance if the others agreed. What did I think? Would I accept their offer of a chance? I didn't want anything to do with anything and I didn't want to accept any chance. I asked as politely as I could what my options were. The man with the dart interrupted, he said that I could accept a chance or refuse it. If I accepted the chance, then I would have a chance. I could understand that bit. But if I didn't accept the chance then I would be shot. I was told not to worry because if I elected to be shot my wife and children would be given money and helped to make a new home in Cork near to my wife's cousin. My blood ran cold. They knew where my wife had gone. I didn't hesitate. I told them that I was dedicated to The Cause and they had no reason not to give me any chance to prove myself. I was frightened for myself but the thought that these people knew where my wife and children were terrified me. I wanted to go to the toilet even more but didn't dare ask.

"The leader asked if everyone agreed that I should be given a chance. The second bottle of whiskey was opened and each glass was topped up. The leader asked again. 'Shall we give this man a chance?' To a man they lifted their glasses and downed the whiskey in one go. Seven of the men put their glasses down normally; one put his glass down upside down, this appeared to indicate a vote against. The leader held on to his glass and said that it looked like I would be given a chance. I breathed a sigh of relief but the man who voted against me said that he hoped that I would prove him wrong but that he didn't think I would. I tried to smile at him, I must have looked stupid. The meeting ended and the driver and the other chap were called in, they had been in the bar downstairs. I was told that the meeting was over and that I would be briefed later.

The car turned into our street, the driver turned to me and told me that I would be picked up for a little job with a milk churn on Monday at eight sharp. I was to set the curtains tomorrow at first light to tip off my British Army minder. That was it. Goodnight!

"On Saturday morning I telephoned my wife and told her that I had a hangover from the Friday night darts session, I suggested that she stay in Cork for a few days and that I'd get down to see her next week. Thankfully she agreed. I checked my wallet, I needed some food for the weekend and I walked down to the corner shop. I was just about to go in when a man bumped into me and dropped his newspaper. I bent down to pick it up for him and he said that he had seen the curtains, I had to tell him the date and time. I whispered and he nodded. He took the paper, thanked me and walked away. Monday took forever to come and the days dragged by and someone at my work noticed that I looked awful and suggested a good night's sleep. As the clock struck seven on Monday evening I sat in the front room and put the newspaper down for the third time. Someone knocked softly at the door, I nearly wet myself! I thought that my army minder had arrived early. I opened the door, a boy of about fifteen stood there. He asked if I would come to Mr O'Leary's house as Mr O'Leary needed me to help move a wardrobe. I said that I couldn't as I had an appointment. The boy said not to worry, I would be back before eight! I hadn't told him when my appointment was, obviously this was either an early call from the IRA or a quick chat with my minder, I had no idea which. I grabbed my jacket and cap. The boy led the way and as we turned the corner a car pulled up and the driver waved to me. I hadn't seen him before and I wondered who he worked for. I was told to get in, I did and the car moved off. The car left Belfast and as I checked my watch for the tenth time, we passed a farm entrance just as the minute hand reached twelve. The car stopped and reversed into the farm entrance. Someone opened the boot and a milk churn was put in the back, I could see the movement through the rear window.

"The boot slammed shut and the car moved off. There was

nothing on the road and as we drove away, the man in the passenger seat turned to me and smiled. He asked if I knew why I'd been arrested. I didn't. Apparently somebody had said to Danny, the shop owner that he had heard about his shop being blown up. Danny hushed him up and told him that the bombing was tomorrow! The others laughed and the man grinned at me. We drove back through Belfast and didn't stop. The car eventually pulled up in the street next to ours and I got out. The man in the passenger seat said that the job had been called off, he wished me goodnight. The following day I watched the news. A car had been driving out of Belfast yesterday evening. It had stopped at a junction. A pillion passenger on a motorcycle had taken a light machine gun from under his coat and when the rider stopped alongside the stationary car, the gunman sprayed the car with bullets killing the occupants. The police were asking for any witnesses to the shooting to come forward. Later I discovered that my army minder had arranged for two plain-clothes soldiers to watch my house, they had arrived three hours before the appointed time and had been surprised to see me leave the house an hour early. They had seen me get into the car and guessed that my appointment had been brought forward. They didn't have time to make any changes to their plans to have me watched and decided to follow me. They may have thought that it might be a trap but couldn't risk losing me especially if I was on another bombing mission. I know this is true because my army minder briefed me when I agreed to become a double agent."

CHAPTER 9

Steve was very interested in Dave's story. He'd been to Northern Ireland on business with his previous job, he sold paper-cutting machines and they were made in Dundonald. It was during the troubles and he had been nervous but he found the people to be lovely and the people he met came from both the Catholic and Protestant communities yet they got on well. It was only late at night in the hotel bar or the room of a colleague's house when the conversation would turn to the problems of the region. On the surface the people were positive and friendly, underneath he noticed an underlying worry. Everyone he spoke to was deeply concerned for their families and their future, just like anywhere else in the world stuck with a war that very few people actually wanted. Steve decided to ask Dave a question.

"I appreciate that you were frightened and didn't want to get involved in the mess that you found yourself but why didn't you just refuse to get involved, would they really have shot you or anyone else who refused to do what they wanted?"

"Are you talking about the IRA or the British Army?" Dave looked at Steve.

"Well, er, both I suppose."

"Listen Steve, if I had refused to do what the IRA men wanted, they would have shot me and no mistake. If I had refused to spy for the army they wouldn't have shot me themselves I suppose, but the word would be out that I was informer, either way I'd be dead."

"And that is hell," said Steve.

"Too right! Every minute of every day was spent worrying myself sick. It's no way for a man to live. In fact it wasn't a life, it was a real hell."

"So what happened?"

"Just after the soldiers were shot there was a clampdown by the army and anyone even remotely suspect was pulled in. I got taken in too of course but I wasn't taken to the police station as others were, I was blindfolded and taken to a safe house. The officer was there, he was extremely upset and he asked me if I had set the whole thing up. He asked me where I had been and what had I done. As he spoke, he took out a pistol and he put the barrel in my ear, I remember it was very cold. He told me to tell the truth and that if I told just one little lie he wouldn't hesitate to blow my brains out right there.

"Of course I told him everything, I was sure he would kill me when I explained about the curtain and the job. When I finished, he sat down and put the gun away. He thought for a very long time. I didn't speak. Then he asked me if I would still send him a signal if I was asked to go on any more jobs. I said that I would. Then he got up from his chair and pulled up a stool and sat extremely close to me. His mouth was an inch or less away from my ear and he said that he would ask me just one question. He paused and I knew that this question would have to be answered correctly. A shiver went up my spine and I knew that I had to be very careful, I suddenly felt that only this man could protect me and I felt almost a love for him. It was really strange, I felt I was making a pact with the devil himself. He spoke very carefully and very slowly.

'When you meet the IRA leaders again, would you tell them that you were still working for the British Army?' I hesitated. I knew that I would. If I told him that, he wouldn't trust me. I tell you Steve I was so scared. I knew that I would be a dead man soon. I was just about to try and answer but I couldn't decide what answer he wanted. He then did an amazing thing, he stood up, patted me on the head and told me that I was free to go. I couldn't believe it. I was blindfolded again and taken to a car. The blindfold was taken off and I was dropped outside my house. That same evening a man came for me, he said that I was playing darts with him, I had to go. I didn't have my darts, that man at the meeting had kept them. I told him that but he said not to worry. We travelled out of Belfast and we stopped once to pick up another man. He seemed very nice and we chatted about everything and anything. Then the car stopped and he asked me if the police had picked me up in the latest round up of suspects. I told him that the army had arrested me. He asked what happened and I told him everything and when he heard that the army officer had let me go with no strings attached he didn't believe me. I told him that it was true, he said I was lying. He then told me to get out of the car, I was very scared. I got out and the car drove off. Two men appeared, they had been hiding behind a hedge. They called me over, they knew my name, I didn't even see the gun. One minute I'm alive in a country lane, the next, I'm going through a very long tunnel to a bright light and then I'm being told that I'm dead and that I am going to learn about Heaven and Hell and be judged. I didn't need to know any more about hell. I'd been there."

Michael and Tommy had also listened carefully to Dave's story and Steve swallowed hard. He could imagine that the experience had been horrible. Dave asked Michael for more cigarettes. He rummaged in his bag and pulled out two packets which he gave to Dave and Tommy.

"Come on Steve." He turned to the two men. "Thanks for that, I'll see you."

Michael and Steve left the park and Michael spoke.

"Real fear, the sort that twists your stomach is a hell in itself. When the cause of that fear affects you, it's awful but when you are frightened for someone you love, then the pain is multiplied many times. That's what hell is like on earth."

Steve didn't speak. He thought about the two men and then asked, "Tommy and Dave are friends, they get along fine now?"

"Oh yes, they came from opposite sides of a bitter war yet when they met here they found that they liked each other. Having passed through the experiences that you are having now they have completed some of their learning stages and they are involved in helping spirits who arrive from war zones all over the world, you'll see more of this as we progress. But you know, it's very sad but nearly everyone who lives a more or less full life on Earth experiences hell at least once, very few people escape it. When it happens, they think that they can't cope but in fact they can and do cope. The spirit is tough and from the pain of fear, depravation and loss often comes peace and sometimes joy. In fact, it's necessary to know sorrow before anyone can fully experience pure joy. I've told you that before. Now I want to show you something else before we put hell's experiences behind us for a moment and cover topics that are a little more enjoyable."

Michael and Steve crossed the road, a shop window caught Steve's eye. It was full of televisions, they were showing various channels and it was time for the midday news. Michael stopped and they watched the news unfold. Severe floods and a mudslide in a South American country had washed away a village, rescuers were struggling to dig out bodies whilst survivors looked on in horror. Another channel showed the remains of an aircraft that had crashed and burned out, there were no survivors and the camera switched to the airport terminal where people were weeping uncontrollably. An African country at war was the next news item and children as young as ten were armed with machine guns. The look on their faces belied their age. They looked much older.

Steve realised that the television news had been like this ever since he could remember. He understood that every day, somewhere in the world, people were experiencing fear, loss and deprivation. It was truly a living hell. He wanted to ask Michael something.

"Why does all this have to happen, why doesn't God prevent all this suffering?" Michael smiled at him. "Patience Steve, that's exactly what you are going to find out for yourself."

CHAPTER 10

Steve thought that he had never felt more sadness. When he watched the news of world events and personal tragedies before, he always thought that it was something that happened to someone else. He always felt remote, as long as he had his health, his money, a job, car and everything he wanted he felt immune to the problems of others.

Someone screamed in the street behind them and Steve turned around to see two teenagers dressed in black and grey hoodies, one grabbed a girl's bag and the other pushed her against the wall as they ran. A typical handbag snatch. Steve immediately wanted to chase them and moved forward, Michael stopped him and said, "I don't often get a chance to do this but watch."

Michael clasped his hands in front of him but he didn't pray, he pointed the tips of his fingers at the taller boy running ahead of his friend. The lad tried to run around a street corner but he slipped and crashed heavily to the ground. The second lad tried to stop and nearly made it but collided with the first boy and as they scrambled to get up in the gutter, the bag slid out of the boy's hand into the road. Steve saw the car and heard the tyres squeal, he realised that it was a police car and as the driver skidded to a halt, his colleague was out of the car, saw the handbag and took both lads firmly in his grasp. One tried to wriggle free but the other policeman jumped from the car, grabbed him and spread-eagled him onto the bonnet. A click of the cuffs and the thieves were arrested and pushed into the back of the patrol car. The girl smiled at the policeman who handed her the bag, he asked her name, she blushed. The policeman also blushed and Steve noticed that the policeman obviously fancied the girl and she was gazing back at him. Michael looked down at his hands, still clasped as if in prayer and pointing at the couple. He shook them apart.

"Whoops! I didn't mean that to happen but hey, so what, she's single and just out of a bad relationship and he's a lovely guy who hasn't got a girlfriend."

"Did you make that happen?" Steve was very interested. "Does clasping your hands make things happen like that?"

"Well yes, but in fact that's something we are not supposed to do often. You may be taught to do that and you will be able to help people occasionally but you won't be able to ..." He paused and looked at the couple who were now swapping telephone numbers. "You won't be able to help people fall in love until you are qualified to do so." He added, "So many spirits try and get it wrong, indeed some spirits are always trying to make perfect matches and never, ever seem to get it right. The lawyers love them."

"But what if we weren't around just then? Those robbers would have escaped."

"Yes probably but we were around and as they have done over thirty muggings so far, it was about time that their luck ran out."

"Can every spirit affect people's lives like that?"

"Well they can but as I said, they are not supposed to until their training is complete. Then their powers are fantastic and they can alter events and help save people."

Steve thought for a moment. "But terrible things keep happening. What ...?

His question was cut short.

"Of course we can't help in every case, and as you'll discover that there are well trained, very capable spirits able to affect people's lives positively, but then there are the spirits from hell, you'll know them as devils. As we work to help and to spread love, they work even harder to ruin people's lives by spreading hate. You'll come across some very powerful evil spirits and you'll see some of the problems that we face."

Steve was very interested. "Will I be trained to do good things?"

Michael paused. "Yes you will but you will also have the opportunity to choose to do the opposite. It depends on how you progress with me and your other guides, decisions will be made as to where you go and what you do."

Steve stopped him. "And who decides?" he paused, "God?"

"Yes but you are very much a part of the decision process too. It's got a lot to do with you and what you yourself want."

"Well I'm for good, not evil, I know about all that and the good guys always win."

"You'd think so." Michael shrugged. "It's a long battle and we are not always winning. Sometimes," Michael continued after a pause, "sometimes spirits get very powerful and get carried away doing good deeds. We expect the powerful bad ones to do something terrible but occasionally good spirits go crazy too." He turned to Steve and faced him.

"You remember Superman?"

Steve smiled, of course he did.

"Superman the comic book hero was based on a spirit we had who took doing good deeds far too far. He'd appear sometimes too and as you'll learn, that is not normally allowed."

"But Superman didn't exist, everyone knows he was a fantasy comic book hero."

"Actually he did exist, we knew him as Marvel. He was seen by thousands of people, he got mistaken for a UFO, he even got caught a few times on camera in the 1950s. We had to hush the whole thing up and because so many people saw him we couldn't completely deny his existence so we added to the myth and influenced some artists and writers to write a comic book. We called the firm Marvel in honour of him."

Steve asked, "What happened to him?" Michael smiled.

"You remember that green stuff Kryptonite? It was supposed to rob him of his powers. That was made up of course but in fact he was moved to another planet and he works well there and the people are used to seeing him. He's passed into folklore on Earth and most people knew him as a comic hero though there are those who remember actually seeing him. He eventually did marry Lois Lane and Batman and Robin were their sons." He could no longer suppress his giggles. Michael grinned at Steve and laughed.

"You are winding me up," Steve grinned. "Nice one!"

"Yes you'll find that we like our little jokes, I shouldn't tell you this but God is a great practical joker and his influence and sense of humour rubs off on most of us, though there are a few spirits around that would rather he didn't. Later, when we have finished this session, and when you will be feeling rather miserable after seeing more of what you have to see, I'll show you some of the jokes of the present and future, we can look forward to that, eh?" Michael stepped out into the road and flagged down a taxi. It wasn't a typical London cab but one of those mid-fifties American classics used as private taxis in Cuba. Steve had seen these on television and always wanted to go in one. The rusty chrome bumper was held on with wire and the windscreen had a long crack in it, a plastic Virgin Mary holding the baby Jesus was stuck to the dashboard. The driver looked Cuban, his deeply tanned face and long hair didn't disguise his poverty but his genuine smile showed that he was a happy man. His name was Tony Santez and he liked picking up tourists because he knew he'd be paid in dollars. He smiled showing his gold teeth.

"Hey Senor, you lika my car? I take you everywhere you wanna go for ten dollars."

Michael grinned as he and Steve climbed in the back.

"Thanks Tony but we'll just be going back and forth in time a bit. How are Maria and the boys?" Tony shrugged. He recognised Michael and knew that he'd be paid five dollars as usual and that would keep him and his family in food for three days. Michael sat back in his seat and took something out of his pocket, he flicked a few switches and punched in a date. The car filled full of smoke and then the smoke cleared. Steve thought that the old Chevy had caught fire and was relieved to breathe fresh air again.

Michael got out; Steve opened the door and faced him over the large green roof of the car, the paint was faded and peeling. He looked around at all the activity. Exhausted people in clothes that seemed too big for them were being herded out of cattle trucks. The old black locomotive steamed and hissed, it had been the smoke from the engine that had filled the car. German soldiers were pushing people along and roughly treating them. Steve immediately realised where they were. As they walked with the crowds towards the brick built buildings, enormous towers belched smoke, children were crying and the faces of the people were of fear and acceptance of a terrible fate. Some tried to slow their pace, others just looked down at the ground and walked.

"You know where we are, you know what happened." Michael

took Steve to one side and explained. "You've seen films of this, you have seen photographs, you have seen this suffering. What amazes me is that history is so well documented and yet the ethnic race still practices what is now called genocide or human cleansing and it has learned absolutely nothing."

Steve didn't say anything, he leaned over to pick up a rag doll that a little girl had dropped, he handed it to her and she smiled at him. Clearly she had seen him, Steve had tears in his eyes and looked at Michael.

"Yes she can see you. She doesn't know it but she's very near to death and her own spirit is aware of this and is preparing her for the passing and her new life after death. She and her family have been starved and bullied for months, her death will be a welcome release and it will be for the rest of her family too."

Her Jewish family walked on through the great wooden doors, Michael and Steve went to the rear of the building and watched. Standing around were scores of spirits in shimmering form, they looked like a crowd of eager parents awaiting the arrival of the school bus after a children's school outing. As they watched, shimmering spirits came from the building's rear and were greeted by the waiting spirits. Steve saw what looked like mums and dads, aunts and uncles, even some children. They greeted the spirits who appeared to know them. They then moved away and as they walked arm in arm, pleased and joyful to see each other, their vision melted and they were gone.

"Those spirits waiting?" he paused, "are they dead relatives of those who have just died?" Michael beamed at him.

"Yes they are," Michael continued. "from the beginning of life everyone is born to his or her generation. A baby is born, it becomes a child, then an adult, then an old person, possibly needing help and care again, as it did when it was a baby, and then when the cycle is complete, the whole thing starts again. Of course some babies don't make it to childhood and some children don't make it to becoming an adult and so on. But in the main, the cycle of life is through generations. As one generation dies, the previous generation greets it in spirit. I'm sure you know all that anyway."

They continued to watch as the new spirits emerged into the sunlight and Steve saw that whilst the weather was miserable, cold and blowing with rain at the entrance, the weather at the exit was lovely and the spirits emerged into sunlight to be greeted by those waiting for them.

Michael continued, "As the life cycle ends, the spirit passes from the body and is where you are now."

"And where exactly am I now?" Steve asked.

"You are at the beginning of a great adventure and one which will either see you enriched with all the joys that you ever imagined or one where you will have to spend what will feel like an eternity doing nothing of any value to you or anyone else."

"But I will end up okay won't I?"

Michael frowned.

"You have so much to learn, come with me. I'm going to introduce you to a German soldier. His name is Hans Schmidt and he recently passed into spirit form. He's here now with his guide, he's at a similar stage to you and you will get a chance to speak to him."

Hans Schmidt was beaten, his tired eyes looked at Steve and he glanced down at the floor, he seemed ashamed. He moved back a couple of feet and sat on a crumbling stone wall, his guide stood to one side, a slim, whitehaired man in a German officer's uniform. He nodded to Michael and touched Hans on the shoulder. Hans cleared his throat.

"I thought I would be shot but I had to risk it. I refused to work anymore at the camp. The suffering was so awful, I couldn't sleep or eat. I went to my senior officer and asked him for a transfer. He asked why and I told him that I couldn't stand the killing. He said that we must obey orders or be shot. I told him that I would rather fight and be a soldier than a shepherd of death and when he dismissed me I refused to leave and stood my ground. I was very frightened. One of the other soldiers had been caught giving food to a Jewish child and he was executed by firing squad. We were told that unless we did our duty, we too would be killed. But I couldn't carry on, my own children back home in Munich were just three and five years old, the same age as many of the Jewish children being gassed. I said that I would rather die as a soldier than be a murderer of children. I thought that he would explode, he shouted and screamed at me and accused me of being stupid. He said that I was safe in the camp as long as I did what I was ordered, he asked if I would prefer fighting against partisans. He thought that I would say that I would not, but I didn't. I said that I would much rather fight partisans and that if he transferred me I would die as a soldier for Germany and be proud. Thankfully he agreed and I was posted to Evosges, a mountain village in South East France. For three months we chased partisans, it was dangerous work because they knew the land and we didn't. Then one day we laid a trap and six men and boys walked straight into it. We surrounded them like rats in a barn. They fought but it was no use. I thought that they would be killed there and then but the officers demanded that they surrender. They refused as they wanted to die fighting. But the officer seized one of the village girls and told the partisans that if they didn't surrender, the girl would be shot. They still refused. The officer then knocked the girl to the floor, pulled out his pistol and aimed it at her head. She was crying. She was probably only about fourteen, I knew that he would shoot her. One of the partisans shouted. The officer demanded to know if he should shoot the girl or would they surrender? They were told that they had fought bravely, that France would be proud of them and that they would be treated well as prisoners. Two of them wanted to surrender and they stood up and the straw fell from their clothes. The officer demanded that they all surrendered but the oldest one refused. The officer clicked back the hammer of the gun and aimed again at the girl's head. The oldest partisan realised that there was nothing he could do, he called out that he was coming out from his hiding place. One after the other, they surrendered. But the officer had lied, he wanted to show the villagers what would happen to partisans who terrorised the German Army. He made the whole village watch as a firing squad was formed. I was in that squad and when the order was given, we shot them, some were only young boys. One was called Brun, another was Cavell and they are remembered on a plaque. The young lad Goldberg was only eighteen so again I was killing children. Long after the war I went back to that village, I didn't expect anyone to recognise me and they didn't. I saw the place where I stood holding my rifle. There was a plaque on the wall and there were photographs on the headstones in the village cemetery. I sat down on a bench and I wrote down my thoughts in a poem. Here, I'll read it to you."

Hans took out a piece of crumpled paper and read.

A Plaque By the Well

A plaque by the well shows where you fell,
Nineteen Forty-Four, during the war.
When I half close one eye I can see the surprise
On your face as you die, your mother she cries.
The order is called and the shots they ring out,
Your mother she sways, I hear her shout,
Her grief and her pain, she feels it again,
Tomorrow your father is caught in the lane.

In the hotel that night we Germans get tight,
We laugh and we cry, there's no question of why
You had to die…
For us it was clear as we drank down our beer
That you were a soldier and should have no fear
Of dying for France, let's have the next dance,
The girl is your sister; I'm in with a chance.

Your father he heard, someone gave him the word
Of what happened today, his friends heard him say
That he'd come to the bar and kill all the guards
But they say that he mustn't, there'd be repercussions
And we Germans would loot, we'd burn and we'd shoot,
We'll kill everyone including your son,
He's only two and that wouldn't do
He'll be needed to fight and die in the night
The next time we came…"

Steve noticed that Hans was crying when he finished his poem.
His German officer guide took him gently by the arm. He nodded to
Michael who smiled at him. Michael turned to Steve and opened the
door of their American taxi. As they got in, Tony nodded at them, he
turned the key and the starter struggled with its weak battery. The

engine coughed into life and then rumbled noisily.

Michael did his trick with his remote control and they arrived outside a hospital in a small town somewhere in America. Michael and Steve left Tony in his cab and they followed a worried looking father rushing to greet his wife crying by the bed of their fourteen-year-old son. Michael whispered to Steve that the boy had been in a road accident and wasn't expected to survive. The shimmering spirit of an old man took a more stable form and stood waiting by the bed. He nodded at Michael and Steve, they nodded back and turned to the parents. The mother was sobbing, the heart monitor on the wall, flickered and then became a flat line. The father, tears running down his face, gripped his son's hand as he died and the boy's spirit rose from his body, moved to stand behind his parents and embraced them. He stood there for a few moments and then he left his crying mother and father and moved through the wall holding the hand of the spirit of the old man. Michael told Steve that it was the boy's grandfather. The spirit of the boy looked sad as he gazed at his parents but he smiled at Michael and Steve and kissed his grandfather. He obviously knew and loved him. Michael and Steve left the room and walked outside to Tony's car. Michael took out his remote device again and punched in another number, immediately the scene changed and the American car was parked in the countryside by a river. Michael and Steve looked out of the window at the setting.

The sun shone and the riverbank was a mass of long grass and butterflies. The boy's parents sat beside a blanket and their two children chatted as they munched on sandwiches and drank from plastic cups. The mother, her hair free in the gentle breeze was laughing as her youngest son was pretending to eat worms and his sister was squealing with mock horror. The happy, family scene vanished as Michael set more numbers on his handheld device and another new scene emerged.

They were in a pleasant family home and sitting comfortably in the lounge, the furniture and décor were typical of thousands of middleclass American homes. The parents of the dead boy were sitting together on the sofa, a girl in her early twenties sat opposite. A cameraman positioned himself to start filming. The reporter was talking about road accidents and she said to camera that the Fowlers had lost their son Tom as a result of a speeding driver five years ago.

She asked the parents how they were coping with the loss of their child.

The father spoke gently, "Some people, indeed most people will be shocked to hear what we have discovered, but," and he paused for a moment, "when Tom died, we thought that we would never again, ever, be happy." He stressed the word ever. "But then we realised that Tom's death was the best thing that could have happened. Marion and I realised that we really hadn't ever known each other and our family properly. It sounds an awful thing to say, but whilst Tom gave us so much pleasure when he was alive, he gave us so very much more after he died."

The reporter looked stunned but she leaned forward with the microphone sensing that something very important was being said.

"When Tom was alive, I was working at ACG. I rarely got home before nine. The children were usually asleep and all I wanted to do was have my meal and go to bed. At weekends I would work and maybe on Sunday, if I wasn't away, we might have a meal as a family but after that, everyone would do his or her own thing. We worked hard, we struggled, we had to have a newer car, a more expensive holiday, everything that other people had, we had to have. We bought things, we got into debt and we had to work even harder. Marion got a job at the store and we had no time for the children and they had no time for us. We gave them everything, yet we gave them nothing. Then Tom got hit cycling home from his friend's house, he died and after the funeral we locked ourselves away. Marion and I even talked about a divorce. But then we realised that we felt the spirit of Tom around us and I started to work less. I made more time for Marion and Georgie and Katie and instead of working at weekends we made a special effort to get out together as a family. If it was raining, we'd go to a museum or a show. If it was sunny, we'd go outside. We found that we loved picnics and Georgie developed a real talent for painting watercolours. I know that no one will understand this but Tom dying was the best thing that happened to this family. His gift to us was life and love."

Marion chipped in. "We also found that when we didn't buy the things we didn't need, we didn't have to work so hard and John realised that working all hours didn't earn him any extra money or promotion. I still work at the store and I enjoy it but the family comes first for us now and it will always come first."

Michael and Steve left the room as the interview continued, Steve turned at the door and noticed the handsome teenager standing in the corner listening to his parents. He smiled at Steve and gave him the thumbs up.

"Do spirits still live with people they have left behind?" Steve was interested. "Obviously I know about ghosts and poltergeists and all that but do dead people come back?" Tony's taxi was waiting outside for them. They got in and the car moved off down the leafy suburban road and through the town. The scenery changed as the car moved along the country road. Tony then indicated and slowed. He turned into a large office car park. Steve recognised the building; this is where he had come to first, just after his death. Michael got out and thanked the driver. He and Steve walked over to Michael's black saloon.

Michael opened the car door and got in. He switched on the ignition and the radio came on softly. Steve settled into his seat. He liked this car almost as much as he liked the American classic taxi, it was very comfortable.

"You'll come to realise that the perception of live people and dead people is just a perception, it's understandable if you get confused at this stage of course and you'll have to accept that it's a perception and only that. Spirits and humans live together. Spirits see everything, most humans only see other humans."

"There are a few more things to show you, relax and listen to the music."

Steve sat back in the black leather seat, Michael started the engine and drove out of the car park and onto the main road. He switched on the radio. Neil Diamond's 'Love on the Rocks' played quietly in the background.

"I prefer to drive now and we have lots of places to visit."

The song ended and a preacher launched into an enthusiastic sermon prompting his audience to send donations if they wanted to be saved and live in heaven. Michael tuned to another station and a Carpenter's record came on, he fiddled with the knob again and quickly found another station playing Beatles songs. He seemed happier with that.

CHAPTER 11

You might think that Mother Nature is wonderful but have you any idea what

she'll do to you if you get old?

(Shaman)

"Don't you like The Carpenters?" Steve smiled at Michael who was twiddling the radio knob, he stopped when he found that John Lennon's 'Imagine' was playing.

"Yes, er, it's not actually the song, it's the station, I don't, correction, we don't," he glared at Steve, "we don't normally listen to that station or any station where people are persuaded to send money to ministers in order to be saved, there's too much to explain now, you'll understand later."

Steve sat back and sighed. "Everything's going to be explained later."

Michael gave in. "We have free radio in Heaven and that's where you are now. Okay, you are not in central Heaven at the moment; we are touring the outskirts and looking at different areas. Much of your assessment is based on how much you learn from your lessons and if you are accepted, indeed, if you yourself decide to move on through the training programme, then what you have learned so far and what you are learning now counts towards your training. Is that clear?"

Steve shrugged. "So although we are in Heaven, we are not in Heaven and though we are not in Hell, we are in parts of Hell." Steve was pretending to take a rise out of Michael but his mischievous grin vanished when Michael responded.

"Precisely!"

"Heaven is everywhere, Hell is everywhere, you go from one to the other throughout your human life and what determines how much Heaven you have and how much Hell you have is based on a whole casebook of variables."

"A casebook of variables?" Steve tried to take this in as he looked out of the window. The car drove along an ordinary high road in the suburbs of a typical British small town with the usual shops and people going about their daily business, the traffic was light and the black car moved swiftly towards the traffic lights. They turned green as the car approached, just like all the other traffic lights on their stretch of road.

"Don't worry about understanding a casebook of variables," Michael laughed, "that just describes the varieties of life that we go through as a human and as a spirit. Whether you live in Hell or Heaven depends mainly on your outlook, your acceptance of what you cannot change, a tiny bit of good or bad luck and how you handle the challenges set to test your resolve. You know that there are rich people who have material wealth yet they are miserable and there are poor people who have little, yet they live happy and contented lives. "I'm now going to introduce you to Mother Nature, she's someone you don't know and she's a casebook of variables in herself."

"Of course I've heard of Mother Nature, everyone's heard of Mother Nature."

"Ah yes you might have heard of her," the word might was long and drawn-out, "but do you know her?" He looked at Steve, "I thought not. "Come on, we'll take her as we find her and we'll hope that she's in a good mood. Last time I went to visit her I was trapped for three days in a snow drift."

Michael indicated and turned left at the traffic lights, he stopped the car outside an incredible building and Steve gasped when he saw it. He was used to the solid glass monuments to business that he'd seen in London and in other cities but this was truly astonishing. It was shaped like a dome but had a centre that twisted to the sky in several directions, the base of the structure was clear ice and waterfalls ran freely, some even flowed upwards. Parts of the walls were terraced and layers of grasses and flowers merged with snow and fields of corn and it seemed as if the building consisted of a patched quilt of every aspect of nature. At the sides, puffs of smoke drifted outwards, in other places, ribbons of fire tickled at solid wooden posts that seemed to hold up nothing. Yet, on the top of these posts were large discs of what looked like thin ice where birds sat watching rabbits and ducks enjoying themselves in the balmy weather of a perfect evening in late summer. A minor earthquake could be felt, it came from the bowels of the building and as the floor beneath them trembled so very slightly, a loud and rasping fart shook the walls and the whole building vibrated gently. A cat sat at the entrance to the building, ignored the movement and sniffed Michael's leg as he waited politely for the cat to inspect him. The cat then rubbed itself against Michael's other leg and the door opened. The cat moved to one side, took absolutely no interest in Steve and then it jumped onto a ledge and continued to watch the world pass by. Steve hadn't noticed any cars in the car park but he did see two coaches and from one of them came around thirty Japanese tourists armed with cameras. A few people were in the foyer of the building and were picking up leaflets. 'All you wanted to know about Nature', Steve could read the title, he wanted to pick one up but Michael urged him to come through before the tourists arrived.

Steve was transfixed by the splendour of the interior of the building. A million lights sparkled above and straight lines of colour from the rainbow shone from the sides through ceilings and bounced off walls and windows. No part of the building was in shade and no part was too well lit and though it felt that the building was moving and swaying, the sounds were of gentle winds blowing through tall trees in Spring. The fart noise came again. Now they could feel the floor and walls moving from side to side and Steve steadied himself as Michael took hold of a looped strap that Steve remembered from the underground trains. He looked up and saw one over his head, he gripped it and turned to Michael and was about to speak but something was happening.

Steve's hand went to his mouth, he gasped, as he looked into the centrepiece of the building where a giant waterfall that was gushing down in many directions started to flow to two sides. In the middle, an expanse of what looked like sand appeared and two rock pools emerged as the sand above them moved upwards and away. The rock pools appeared brilliant blue, then they turned green, brown and turquoise. Below, the sand moved as a rock started to appear, it was brown, pink and perfectly formed. Steve could see the image become a face as the chin started to wobble and two very bright red lips became clear. The giant face smiled, or rather, it leered. The mouth formed a smile but the eyes weren't shining, they seemed angry. Steve wasn't sure at first, then he saw it again, the lady definitely winked at him.

"Oh My God!" Steve gasped as Michael punched him to be quiet. Steve couldn't contain himself and started to laugh. He trembled, he shook, he put his hand in his mouth but the laughter forced itself out of the sides. Michael glared at him to be quiet and this time he was very cross. Steve tried to mumble an apology but nearly laughed again. Michael could see that Steve was almost unable to control himself, he pulled Steve sharply and almost dragged him to a corner where the face might not see them.

"What IS the matter with you?" Michael hissed at Steve. Steve lifted Michael's hand from his arm.

"Sorry, look I'm sorry, It's just that," he looked again at the face. "I think she fancies me."

"What?"

Steve calmed down and Michael led him forward to a rope fence that surrounded the water feature that had become the face of Mother Nature.

The lady had finished evolving from the centrepiece and her face and expressions were clear. She smiled at Michael and then scowled at him, she smiled at Steve and then scowled at him too. Now he wasn't so sure, was he fancied or not? He felt a stinging burst of ice cold rain straight in his eyes, he jumped back and covered his face with his arm.

"You might laugh," she boomed, "but I am able to make your life a misery young man and I don't like men at the best of times." She laughed and Steve wanted the ground to swallow him up. She spoke again, her voice was deep but not threatening.

"So you wish the ground would swallow you up, I can arrange that!" she ended the sentence abruptly and a fissure appeared at Steve's feet, Michael caught him just in time and pulled him to safety.

"No Ma'am," Michael pleaded. "This man has been chosen, he has potential and I'm training him, please don't ..." He stopped. Steve was looking at him oddly. Steve had just learned something very important. Michael hadn't wanted to reveal that information just then, he wasn't pleased.

"I didn't expect you to choose another man after the last fiasco." The lady was stern.

"There are plenty of women able to do your work. One woman is brighter and better than ten men and yet you do insist on bringing me men!" She was now quite annoyed and Michael put his hands between his legs as if his testicles were frozen. Indeed they were already very cold and getting colder by the second. The cat appeared at Michael's side and hissed, Michael knew they had to go.

Michael didn't switch the radio on, he drove in silence and with one hand on the steering wheel and the other cupping his testicles. Steve looked at him.

"Mother Nature is something else," Steve wanted Michael to speak. He pressed.

"Imagine an angel with ice cold balls and feeling very unhappy about everything."

Michael said nothing, he was very uncomfortable.

"Do you have a hot water bottle?" Steve thought that it was a sensible question but Michael seemed to ignore him. He then braked and stopped the car in a layby, he leaned forward to pull a lever and the bonnet clicked open. He got out of the driver's door and went to the front of the car and lifted the bonnet to its full extent. Michael fiddled for a few moments and a great hiss of steam shot out from the radiator, he stood there for a moment, then put the radiator cap back on and closed the bonnet firmly. Michael got back in and Steve saw that his trousers were soaked, steam came from them.

"Thanks for that. Good idea, that feels better." Michael was much happier. He told Steve what happened last time.

"I was rude to Mother Nature. She didn't like it and as my trainee and I left her palace we were covered in a giant snowfall. Our heads weren't covered but we were stuck firmly and she left us there for three days. I was cold all over and today she reminded me of it by giving me that icy blast. She was quite lenient with you, one smack of sleet at gale force wind was quite kind under the circumstances. Mother Nature doesn't like people laughing at her."

"Well she's not very pretty and if she starts winking seductively at men, she shouldn't be too surprised if they laugh at her." Steve tried to make a joke but Michael didn't laugh.

"Mother Nature can be the most beautiful woman you have ever seen. She can be lovely, she will smile and capture your heart and hold it forever, then like a flash of lightning, her mood can change and she can become dark and moody and if she's upset, well," he paused, "you don't want to be around if she's upset. She can be wonderful, she can be cruel, she can give life, she can take it away. In Heaven we have absolutely no say in what she does or how she behaves. The devils in Hell try to influence her and just when they think that they have her doing what they want, she changes her mood completely and is sweetness and light and boy does that make them mad."

Steve smiled but said nothing.

Michael continued. "When the Earth was formed and the universe came into being, Mother Nature was given the task of arranging things, creating the land and seas and generally acting like an interior designer with a free hand and an unlimited budget but unlike an interior designer, this lady knew that she would only be given and only ever have one job. She therefore secured a contract whereby she would be in charge of nature and no one, not anyone, would interfere. God, in his wisdom agreed and the rest is history, or should I say, nature."

Steve thought. "So when earthquakes happen and kill people, when floods drown thousands, when hurricanes create havoc, that's Mother Nature having a laugh?"

"Goodness no, she's not laughing, she's doing what she is supposed to do, she's trying to create a balance and she has to continue with that balance. She arranges the weather, the seasons, the temperature changes, all of the adjustments are made by her striving for that balanced world that you lived in. Humans think that they are powerful, they build rockets, they build bombs, they create cities and countries but they are only really like ants scratching around in the dust. They never had any major positive impact on Mother Nature and when they tried to change things by spraying clouds to create rain in the desert and other daft ideas, she just laughed." He paused. "Just as she laughs at us when we ask her not to crush a village with a landslide or make thousands die of thirst and hunger. Mind you, when the devils ask her to blow up a city with a volcano or collapse it with an earthquake because it suits their needs, she will ignore them too. To be fair to her, although she can be cruel and terrible, she rarely acts without warning and humans do apply some intelligence to try and read those warnings. Trying to cut down on pollution goes down well with her but if your attempts are inadequate then she can warm or freeze the planet to ensure its survival. If there is a huge nuclear war, sure it will make a big mess but Mother Nature will find a way to regenerate life over a matter of time. That's her job and she's good at balancing things."

"But if she's trying to keep a balance, why are there so many changes and differences?"

"Keeping a balance doesn't mean keeping everything calm. It's not that kind of balance, what this lady does is to maintain ups and downs, ins and outs, hots and colds …"

"Hots and colds?" Steve teased Michael.

"You know what I mean. It's a balance where everything evens itself out in confusion."

"Well I'm confused, so it's working." Steve thought for a moment. "I'd like to see her when she's beautiful." Steve tried to imagine that face turning into a vision of loveliness.

"You will, she's at her best in the Spring but she can be beautiful and let's say," he paused, "less beautiful at any time. It just depends on her mood."

Steve wanted to interrupt but Michael carried on.

"And don't go thinking you can change her. You can shout and wave at a blizzard, you can scream and shout, you might as well try picking up leaves and putting them back on trees in an Autumn gale. We can try and influence her but she will always have the upper hand. The secret of getting on with her is to understand that and love her for it. The planet is blessed with Mother Nature and would be poorer and bleaker without her."

"But you have lovely weather here," Steve claimed. "I accept it's been nice so far and not even rained, doesn't she give this place a hard time sometimes?"

Michael sighed. "Steve, this place doesn't exist as you sense it. The reason you see a blue sky and fluffy clouds is perhaps because you expect to see it or you'd prefer to see it rather than have it rain and blow an icy wind. There's no bad weather here, just a surrounding of love and of purpose and hope. You and I sit in a car, we drive and we see roads. But that car, those roads aren't here, they are in our minds and in the minds of those who will one day read about you or see you in films. You saw me in an office block because your background is office blocks and business. You and I travel by car because you know cars get people from place to place. But if you had been a horseman fighting with Genghis Khan, you wouldn't be seeing office blocks and cars, you'd be on the Russian Steppes and we'd meet in village huts and travel around on horses. All this is an illusion to suit you, I told you all this before, do you remember our conversation about Eskimos?"

"And Mother Nature, is she an illusion too? Is Heaven an illusion and Hell? Is everything on Earth an illusion, are we the victims of some great practical joke?" Steve had been indulging himself in the luxury of the thought that he was adapting to his new surroundings, the fact that everything was an illusion upset him.

"No, everything is not an illusion. You will see what is real and what is not and then you'll understand. I promise you, it's just easier for me to explain how things are if you are comfortable with your surroundings." They left the car park and walked to a grass field.

Michael pointed, Steve followed his gaze. Michael sat down on the warm grass and patted the ground beside him. Steve took the hint and sat down too and he looked to see where Michael was pointing. He saw that they were on a cliff edge overlooking the most magnificent Scottish loch. Steve could see what Michael was pointing at, away in the distance, an eagle soared in the sunlight.

"This grass that we are sitting on, this loch that we see, that eagle. If it's all an illusion then it's a very good one. Mother Nature is a part of it all, just as you, the Earth, your family and your world are also part of it all. I am part of it all, though not a very important part and indeed you will become more of a part as you learn, understand and develop. That's why I am here. Your grandfather didn't meet you when you passed through. Yes he wanted to greet you and lead you through and he was disappointed to be told that he couldn't. But when it was explained what you would be doing, he was delighted for you. He watches over you and he hopes that he will be able to help with your training, indeed we'll meet him later. You were three years old when he passed through, look there he is, he's on time."

Steve turned and smiled. The old motorcycle and sidecar came up the trail and stopped as the rider leaned forward to switch off the ignition. He climbed off, removed a giant waterproof cape and pulled off his helmet and goggles. Steve's grandfather was small with white hair and a full white fluffy beard. He stood next to Steve as Steve got up from the ground, his feet shuffled and his eyes, bright and shining, darted from Steve to Michael and back to Steve. His jacket sleeves were too long for his arms and he continually fiddled with his cuffs. He removed an old leather glove and put his arm around Steve and hugged him tight. Steve hugged him back and then realised something.

"I'm sure I've seen you many times before." Steve gazed at his grandfather. "I definitely saw you on TV, you've been in films, in adverts, you were Father Christmas once in my local store."

The old man smiled. "Yes I do get around, and yes, I do a lot of character work, I love it."

"You mean that dead people are on television and in films?"

He was offended. "I'm not dead Steven. I'm as alive as you are, as Michael is. And yes we do work with people on Earth, we give them ideas, we make suggestions, we help create stories and situations. Unlike most spirits I'm allowed to work in human form, I've done lots of work on TV all over the world." He put his cape on the ground and sat down next to where Steve had been sitting and motioned to Steve to sit down by his side. He continued. "When someone writes a wonderful song or tells an incredible story, they don't just have their own life experiences to help them, they are assisted, even directed by anything up to a dozen helpers. When Elton John and Bernie Taupin wrote 'Candle in the Wind', do you think they wrote that all by themselves? Of course they didn't. Their names might have been on the credits but I know for a fact that Norma herself worked for ages on those words and that tune. She wanted to be seen as something more than sexual, more than just our Marilyn Monroe. She was with them when they wrote it and she helped them to create a song that will be remembered forever. Not like some of the stuff that you hear these days. Yuck!" he grimaced.

"And the musicals." He was getting excited now, his eyes flashed back and forth and he waggled his hands. "Tim Rice and Andrew Lloyd Webber might have earned all that money from their hits but who do you think helped them in their subconscious? Why, Gilbert and Sullivan, Noel Coward and Rogers and Hammerstein. And not forgetting Freda Appleyard of course!"

"Freda Appleyard?" I never heard of her." Steve started at his grandfather then looked at Michael. "This isn't another Superman joke is it?"

CHAPTER 12

"No, it's not." Michael said before his grandfather could speak. "Freda Appleyard is a brilliant composer, she writes wonderful music. She's quite shy though and never wants her name used; unlike her cousin Eleanor Rigby. Remember her?"

Steve nodded. "But she wasn't famous, didn't she die in a church and get buried along with her name? A great song, a classic, but sad words."

"That's right," smiled Grandad. "John Lennon and Paul McCartney were loved and admired for their writing everywhere and not just on Earth. I believe that they were influenced by spirits just as other great composers were and always will be. John Lennon's 'Imagine' has been in Heaven's top ten forever."

Grandad started to sing 'Imagine' in a cockney voice, Michael and Steve joined in the yoo hoo hoo and it sounded awful. They laughed.

Michael stood. "I have to be somewhere else, you and Aloysius go and have a nice time, I'll see you later."

Steve suppressed a giggle, "Aloysius?"

"You call me Grandad, if you don't mind." He looked thoughtful, "And I'll tell you something odd. John Lennon loved his wife Yoko very deeply and whilst he may have sensed the presence of Freda and Eleanor when he was writing and singing, he also got tremendous help from Yoko and her spirit as well and he later arranged for a rather odd credit to appear."

"What did he do?" Steve was very interested.

"Well, if you use a personal computer's spellcheck and type in 'Yoo Hoo Hoo', one of the alternative spellings for Yoo comes up as Yoko."

"Wow," said Steve, "that's weird."

Steve and his grandad walked to the bike. Grandad handed Steve an antique crash helmet and a pair of old goggles.

"What a lovely old bike!"

Grandad swung at the kick-start and the engine rumbled happily. They climbed on and the old man steered the bike off the trail, onto the grass and back the way he had come. Steve hung on and grinned.

At the end of the trail, the tarmac road rose over a crest and swept around a bend and an old MG burbled past. The roof off, the windscreen flat and a young couple dressed in flying jackets, the woman wore a scarf. The man waved at them as he accelerated away. The motorbike chugged onto the road and followed the MG as an old Jaguar saloon came from the other direction and flashed a greeting. A mile further on, the bike slowed and they turned into a pub car park. The pub was called 'From Life to Eternity,' and a blackboard sign had the word karaoke in red chalk.

Steve climbed off the bike and handed Grandad the helmet and goggles which he tossed into the sidecar. The old man said. "Normally I can't stand karaoke but this place is great. They only have people who can sing. Any drunken idiots trying to ruin 'Bohemian Rhapsody' or 'We are The Champions' are discouraged. Sometimes I sing too."

"Thanks for the warning." Steve pushed the old oak door open. The landlord looked up at Steve and smiled, he saw Grandad and the smile froze for an instant.

"Well young sir what will you have?" He looked at Steve who noticed that the glass was already under the spout and being filled with what looked like Guinness but the pump handle had a badge stating that the beer was called 'Heaven's Cream.' The landlord moved the top of the glass deftly and Steve saw that he had made a little cross in the foamy, cream top. The glass was placed in front of Grandad, the landlord said, "Nice to see you Al, you won't sing too soon I hope?"

Grandad took his beer and grunted, he was offended.

Steve looked at the pump names. Besides 'Heaven's Cream', the beers included 'Old Frothy', 'Legless Lizzie', 'Scrimpy' and an ale called 'Less'. He pointed at the pump handle and the glass was placed under the spout, the landlord pulled and a clear, light brown liquid frothed into the mug. He beamed again at Steve and his cheery face typified the perfect landlord, happy and willing to discuss any subject with any customer – except politics and religion of course – and well able to produce a delicious bar meal in one moment or to diplomatically handle a drunk in another.

"So you bin to see Doc Rafferty, then?" Steve looked puzzled at the landlord's question. "Only you are drinking Less, see."

"Sorry, I'm not with you." Steve looked quizzically at the landlord.

Grandad interrupted. "Bill likes his joke. His trade started to drop and he discovered that the good doctor was telling everyone to drink less so he came up with the idea to call his beer 'Less'. Good idea really, keeps everyone happy except for the doctor of course. But he'll be in later, he drinks Scrimpy and he'll never buy you a drink even if you buy him one. Aptly named, a Scrimpy beer for a scrimpy old ..."

"Now, now!" The landlord waggled his finger and Grandad stopped speaking. The girl who had been singing a lovely Celine Dion number had left the microphone to polite applause and now four men, pint glasses in their hands got up and were obviously tipsy as they fought over the mics and started to sing Frank Sinatra's 'My Way'. They started to yell the words, the sound was awful and the landlord bent down and pulled a lever. Immediately the floor gave way and the singers shouted as they fell into the cellar. The trap door closed and their muffled cries and shouts of anger could be heard, the other customers clapped and cheered. The pub door opened and the lads came back in, they were still holding their glasses, not a drop had been spilt. They mumbled an apology and sat down at their seats.

A small man with a round face stood and spoke in a high voice.

"My turn I think." The audience seemed pleased and the little man took the mic. A wonderful Joe Cocker sound erupted and the man had Joe Cocker's 'Unchain My Heart' off to perfection. He finished, Steve clapped and everyone else hooted and roared, they loved it. The little man beamed at the applause, put the mike back in its stand holder and joined Steve at the bar.

The landlord poured him a scotch and he knocked it back in one go, turned to Steve and said in his high voice, "Will you sing? They got everything here." Steve blushed.

"No I don't sing, I am hopeless."

The man waggled his finger. "If you come in here to enjoy the singing then you must sing if you are asked to. Then if we realise that you can't sing you never have to sing again, but if you can, we are all happy."

Steve started to apologise and make excuses but another man stood in front of him, a big gruff chap. He looked like a bear and wore a navy service jumper. His black beard hid his mouth but an old wooden pipe revealed the source of his grunt.

"Sing, it's your turn."

Steve knew that he shouldn't refuse and joked, "Well I did warn you." He moved through the drinkers sitting around the tables.

Steve took the mic and went to the small stage. A row of faces looked at him, some were smiling, he noticed a very pretty girl sitting next to a young man in a college scarf. The girl's eyes met Steve's, he looked at her, what a beauty. From the speakers came the sound of the start of Elvis Presley's, 'The Wonder of You'. As Steve looked at the words on the screen, he heard the words come from his mouth. No longer was he a tone deaf, flat, absolutely awful singer, he was now Elvis! The words came out perfectly, the notes were spot on and Steve realised that he sounded just like Elvis. When he got to the chorus, everyone joined in and the song was superb. He finished to a rousing applause and he bowed delighted to the others in the pub. He then spotted a man in the corner wearing a white suit with gold trimming; it glistened with diamonds and rubies, his face turned towards him and smiled. Steve gasped, the hair was unmistakable. The King himself was congratulating him.

CHAPTER 13

Steve stood at the bar, everyone listened as The King sang the lovely ballad, 'Fools Rush In.' Steve was happy and said, "This place is great."

Grandad smiled at him. "You are due in court tomorrow," he paused, the smile on Steve's face faded. "Don't look so worried, you'll be taken through your life, asked to explain a few, er, well let's say, misdemeanours and you'll be given the chance to justify where you go."

"Where I go?" Steve wasn't happy with the way this conversation was leading.

"Michael explained it to you, your life is presented to you like in a film. You may be asked to account for some of your actions and explain your reasons for doing what you did, how you treated your family, your friends, your young wife." He paused. "You married that lovely girl but continued to have girlfriends, didn't you think that she would be hurt and upset if she found out?"

Steve was quiet for a moment, "You know I feel terrible about Jane. I do love her, but ..." his voice trailed away. Then he added, "She would have been really upset to hear about my death."

His grandad lifted his hand. "She doesn't know yet, you may have sensed the passing of time since you've been here but less than a millionth of a second has passed in Earth time. When she is told, you will be there, she won't be able to see or hear you of course but you'll be able to meet her spirit and you and he will communicate."

Steve interrupted. "He! Jane's spirit is a He?"

"Most certainly, many men have women spirit guides, many have men and it's the same with women. Some men have dogs as spirit guides." Steve looked at him astonished.

"That might explain a few things!" The interruption came from the pretty redhead Steve had noticed when he sung. "Some men act like dogs, I had one and I called it Martini, he'd be off doing it, anytime, any place, anywhere."

Steve looked at the girl. He wasn't sure if the girl was saying that she had a man called Martini or a dog called Martini. He decided not to ask. She was about five feet four inches, slim figure, short red hair but not too short, her dark red jumper with a brown stripe showed an interesting figure. 'She really is lovely' he thought.

"Thank you," she said and smiled. She looked into his eyes and saw them widen as Steve realised that she had read his thoughts.

"Can you read my mind?"

"Oh yes, it's not very difficult to read your mind, you are a man after all. I've been studying it and as it's my job to represent you in court, I need to know what you are thinking as well as saying. Certainly the other side will be reading your mind too."

"The other side?" Steve asked.

"The other side," she teased. "Your life will be examined, you will explain yourself and I'll try to help you put yourself in a good light. The counsel for the other side will pick up on your mistakes, highlight your bad points and try to prove that you don't deserve Heaven. You and I have to show that you can become a better spirit and become qualified for the job expected of you in eternity, but more of that later."

Steve asked, "Okay, so you are representing me, who will be against me?" He looked at his grandad. "No one I know I hope." If Steve was hoping for a friendly opposition then he was unlucky.

The girl answered, "Funny you should say that. The other side is the spirit of your wife's mother. Mrs Crompton specifically asked for the case."

"Mrs Crompton! Helen Crompton!" Steve was horrified. "She'll hate me when she realises that I was cheating on her daughter with …" his voice tailed off as he counted several names in his head.

"No she won't, it will make no difference."

"Really?" Steve wasn't so sure.

"No difference at all Steve, she didn't like you much before she found out what kind of husband you were."

Steve groaned. He then realised that the girl had taken his hands in hers and was stroking his fingers. He gazed at her and was about to ask her name.

"What is your—"

She interrupted him. "Rosie," she whispered. "it's Helen's job to put you through Hell and my job to make you look better, through rose-tinted glasses if you like? I'll see you at the court at ten." She turned to Grandad. "Make sure he's ready, I suggest a good night's sleep."

Grandad nodded. He took Steve by his arm, they left the bar area, walked through a doorway and upstairs to a large double room. Grandad pointed at the bed.

"When you have been here a while you won't need sleep because your mind will clear itself quickly but your mind and spirit are not yet ready for total unity yet and you'll need to rest. Sleep well." Steve wasn't in the least bit tired. He was about to complain that he didn't need sleep but his grandad had vanished. Steve looked around the room; he couldn't believe that the old man had just disappeared. Steve looked in the wardrobe, he leaned under the bed. Grandad had gone.

Steve kicked off his shoes, he didn't undress, he lay on the bed and looked at the ceiling. The sound of the music came from downstairs as someone sang 'Unchained Melody' beautifully. Within seconds he was fast asleep.

The court building was huge. They climbed up a hundred rows of wide steps that gleamed a brilliant white. Gold marble towers stretched as high as Steve could see and he was reminded of those impressive court buildings in America which are enormous and very intimidating. Other people were walking up and down, some looking worried, others carrying books, folders and papers. Grandad was at his side and taking the steps with ease as Steve struggled to keep up. They passed through the giant entrance where huge statues of angels looked down at them.

Grandad arrived at the reception desk and smiled at the clerk. The clerk beamed brightly at Steve. He lisped,

"Good luck in there Stephen," his eyes lowered as he said the name. Steve was too shocked to reply. He and Grandad walked past reception and the admiring clerk.

"He's a nice boy." But it wasn't a compliment and Grandad understood his tone.

"Actually he IS a very nice boy and like everyone else here he is being polite and wants you to do well." He frowned at Steve and Steve regretted his comment.

A woman in a black gown approached them and without asking them she ticked off their names on her pad. She didn't ask if they were ready either, she leaned forward and opened the door and Steve stood back to let his grandad go first. Grandad stopped and motioned for Steve to pass through before him.

"Don't try and be clever, don't make jokes, be yourself and whatever you do, don't try to pretend, your thoughts and feelings are open for all to hear."

The usher motioned Steve to the box placed to one side. Steve looked around for a bible but there wasn't one. He looked up at the bench but there was no one there. But there was something there and Steve studied it. It was a black cube supporting what looked like a large oval Easter egg. One moment it was a clear colour, then it turned blue, it changed to red, pink, brown and as it changed colour each time it vibrated as well and Steve could feel the vibration and he could almost perceive the movement visually. The egg turned clear again and finished vibrating.

He looked to his right, he saw Rosie sitting at her bench. She wore the black gown typical of a barrister and a small white wig. She felt his gaze on her and turned and smiled. Steve's heart seemed to jump.

"She is gorgeous!" he thought and the words were heard around the large room. Rosie put her finger to her lips, she mouthed, "Shh!"

Steve heard a door open and he stared. His mother-in-law entered, also dressed in a long black gown and white wig but Steve didn't find her as attractive as Rosie. She looked straight at him as she settled at her desk and she smiled, but Steve could see that this wasn't a friendly smile, the woman's lips bared, she gritted her teeth and her eyes revealed the contempt she had for him. He shuddered and thought 'what a bitch.' Too late he realised that she and everyone else would hear his comment and her face jerked back at him. This time the false smile had gone to be replaced by a look of hate.

'I must be careful, but...' he struggled with his thoughts that he knew were being broadcast throughout the court. 'I must disguise my thoughts but I can't do that so I must think nice things; I know; he looked at Helen Crompton's black gown. She looks smart in that.' His thoughts again echoed around the room. Mrs Crompton glared at him and he decided to think of more nice thoughts. He couldn't, it's hard to think nice thoughts when you want to think, 'oh get me out of here.'

Rosie stood and waved her arm. Someone pressed a button and a wall moved to reveal a large screen, the film started and Steve was fascinated. The scene was of a young child aged around ten months old. The child's mother came into view. Steve was stunned. It was his mum and the baby looked familiar. She was trying to feed the boy but the child resisted all attempts as he kept his mouth tight shut. He moved his head and every attempt by the mother to feed the child was thwarted. Steve watched in amazement, this was him as a baby.

Then Dad offered to have a go and Steve smiled as he saw his dad younger than he remembered him. Mum wearily handed over the jar of baby food and the spoon.

Dad spoke, "Come on sweetie bumpkins, try some nicey wicey, tasty, basty, yummy gummy," he looked at the jar, "peasy weasy and carrot," he stalled, looking for a word to rhyme with carrot. The baby looked at his dad and everyone in the court could hear the baby's thoughts.

'Nicey wicey, tasty basty, oh you silly daddy.' And with that, the child grinned and opened its mouth. Daddy was triumphant.

"Look he eats for me, it's just the way I handle him."

The food continued from jar to spoon and from spoon to mouth but silly Daddy didn't realise that Steve wasn't swallowing. His mouth filled, his cheeks swelled and as Dad leaned forward for the final time with the last little bit, he noticed the child's expression but was marginally too late to get out of the way. Steve puffed himself up, now he let Dad have it. Almost a complete jar of pea and carrot puree hit Dad in the face from a distance of eight inches. He was covered in it. The baby's dinner was in his hair, his eyes and on his chin.

Dad fell back. Mum was angry.

"Look what you have done," she blasted at her husband. "That's all I had until I go to the shops tomorrow. Some help you are. Men!"

Rosie now addressed the court, the chuckles had died down and

Steve realised that there was no judge, just the black cube box and the oval egg. The colour remained clear.

Rosie said, "Whilst you were naughty, you could be forgiven. Silly Daddy deserved the practical joke but Mummy didn't deserve to experience your tantrums."

The scene moved forwards. Steve was now nearly three. His mother tried to restrain him in his pushchair whilst she spoke with other mothers in the street but Steve wanted attention, he was bored and he didn't see why Mum should get what she wanted. He screamed, he kicked, he tried to cry but Mum could see that there were no tears. She pulled a baby's rattle out of her bag, waggled it in Steve's face and put it in his hand. Steve fell silent for a moment and then when Mum wasn't watching, he threw it away with all his might. The rattle sailed through the air and caught the face of a cyclist, the man wobbled, almost regained his balance and fell heavily in the road. He shook himself clear of his machine and stood up, blood poured from a cut to his forehead.

Mum and her friends were horrified, the other babies slept through it all but Steve was smiling, he had done this. Mum left the pushchair and tried to help the cyclist but he waved her away, he was pretty upset but he didn't want to make a fuss. He struggled to get back on his bike, almost fell off and wobbled away as he regained control.

The scene faded as Helen Crompton barked at Steve, "You did that on purpose, didn't you?"

Rosie addressed the bench where Steve expected the judge to be sat. He looked at the solitary egg that had now turned light brown. She spoke clearly.

"If we can rewind the tape back to where baby Steve spat his food at his dad," she paused as the scene was repeated. "Now stop." The frame froze and Steve noticed a silvery shadow of another baby behind and to the side of his pushchair. Rosie continued. "You'll notice baby Steve's spirit guide, he's given the idea to Steve and Steve loved it. Now, fast forward to the part where toddler Steve threw the rattle at the cyclist." The film froze at the point where Steve drew his arm back ready to make the throw. "If you look, you'll see Steve's spirit guide place his hands over his eyes and if you look to the left…"

Steve could see it, so could everyone else. On toddler Steve's left shoulder was a grey coloured spirit. His expression was obvious; he was urging the toddler to throw the rattle.

Steve felt the vibration from the egg. It had turned a clear colour. Rosie sat down.

Helen Crompton addressed the court. "I accept that the toddler Steve was influenced on this occasion but as we will see, later in life Steve's behaviour is unacceptable with no bad influences to tempt him."

Rosie turned to Steve. "You may leave your place now. You are to be offered the opportunity to discover answers to some of the questions that you may wish to ask and to solve any of life's mysteries that have been troubling you. You will return here afterwards and explain why you acted as you did in certain situations. Is that clear?"

Although Rosie had spoken kindly, her last question revealed that whilst she might be fond of Steve, she had to act professionally. Steve nodded.

A black man appeared at Steve's side. He was firm but gentle as he took Steve's arm.

"I will brief you on some questions that you might want to ask but haven't yet thought of. It would be a pity to waste this opportunity as your place in eternity depends on your understanding of the answers."

Steve found himself sitting in a wide corridor with doors leading to several rooms. There were no signs, no bells or buttons and no handles. The black man introduced himself as Peter.

"Have you a question?" Peter asked as he smiled at Steve. "You can ask anything you like, indeed I urge you to ask whatever comes into your head."

"Er," Steve hesitated and looked at Peter who nodded his head and encouraged him to ask something.

"Okay," Steve started and then stopped. He paused for a few more seconds and then asked, "Why is so much trouble in the world caused by religion? Wars are fought, thousands of people suffer and most of it seems to have God behind it all." Steve couldn't believe that he had been so bold but then so what, he had been told to ask a question.

Peter had been asked this question before and said so, he added,

"The trouble is that many people confuse God with religion." He stopped and Steve looked at him oddly.

"But religion is supposed to be about worshipping God," Steve stopped. Peter was nodding his head.

"Supposed to be is a good term, of course many people use a religion to pray to God for what they want but sadly over the centuries people in power used religion to control others, to get power, to keep power, to make money, to control whole countries. Basically religions are very similar until they are corrupted. All religions have their share of leaders that are corrupted at some time or another, but most of the time their leaders are good and bring spiritual pleasure and contentment but when they aren't good, they spread terror and evil. You know some history; you have seen it happen in your own life."

"So why does God let it happen? If corrupt religious leaders use his name, why does he seem to protect evil people and let them harm others?"

"You could extend that question to ask why does God let bad things happen?"

Steve accepted the prompt.

"Just imagine if God didn't let bad things happen, suppose that when a terrible catastrophe was about to occur, instead of it happening, God suddenly took control and prevented it? Suppose for example that an earthquake or landslide was about to crush a building and kill people, what would be the situation if this was not allowed to happen?"

"Everyone would be saved of course." Steve smiled at his cleverness.

"Yes everyone would be saved. And if a plane were about to crash or a bus about to slide off a mountain road, if those things were stopped, what would happen?"

"Everyone would be saved." Steve repeated his point but he frowned, he started to appreciate that there might be a reason after all.

"Of course if the control, the stopping of tragedies were implemented, everyone would always be safe, no one would ever come to any harm and everything would be perfect." Steve had made what he thought was a logical answer but he could see where this line of thought was taking him. Peter spoke again.

"If a world existed where nothing bad ever happened, where people were always happy and safe, where no one ever died or got injured, would that really be a perfect place to live bearing in mind that the freedom of choice given to us at birth would no longer be necessary?"

"But we don't have a freedom of choice over natural disasters?"

"No you don't, but Mother Nature, you remember her? Her task is to balance the planet and in bringing beauty she also brings joy and in bringing life she also brings death. She brings sadness too and she can create fear and terror. Her four natural balances, Fire, Earth, Air and Water can and do offer life in all its beauty and the death that it can offer can be sudden, horrific and very ugly."

He looked at Steve as he was explaining this. Steve listened, trying to understand.

"But God lets people kill each other and innocent children in his name."

If Peter was annoyed, he tried not to show it.

"People have a choice; do you want to know what happens on Earth in the future, in the years after your own death?"

Steve nodded.

Peter stood and walked towards a door and Steve followed him. The door opened and Peter motioned for Steve to enter. A large hall was before him, the floor was marble with stars, lines, some straight, some wiggly, a mass of colours. In the centre of the floor was a form that for a moment was a circle, then it became a pentacle, then a square, then a diamond. As Steve defined a shape, it changed again.

In the middle of the hall stood a dozen or so men and women in a variety of costumes. Steve recognised a Bishop, next to him a Rabbi, a Muslim Cleric, a Buddhist Monk, a Sikh. Some he knew, others he didn't. They turned to him and said together,

"We are of one voice, we are of one voice." They all smiled at him and their expression was of welcome. Steve moved towards them and stopped, one spoke.

"Ask your questions, we are of one voice."

Steve looked down at his feet and thought. He then spoke clearly. "You represent probably every religion I know of." He looked at a very tall man in a long black cloak who smiled at him. "And a few that I don't know. It's nice to see you all happy together," he wanted to add, "and not killing each other," but he didn't dare. "What happened to change you?"

The Bishop stepped forward.

"We used to argue over our differences. Some of us used weapons to make others conform or die." Steve saw a Roman Soldier waving a sword, he too was smiling. "Things then got out of hand and religions were set against each other. The planet was set on destruction and we overcame our prejudices to hold a meeting of world religious leaders. Everyone was given a chance to speak and at the end, when everyone had spoken we realised that we all had so much in common. We all wanted the same things and we all wanted what we thought was best for our families and our followers. We then wrote out two manuscripts. One showed everything that we agreed on, the other showed everything that we disagreed on. When we looked at those manuscripts we realised that we agreed on so much and disagreed on so little. We then showed them to the world and we could all see that if we concentrated on where we agreed rather than where we disagreed, we could all live in peace."

The man in the black cloak added, "We realised that we all basically wanted what was best for our families. We wanted to bring up our children in peace, with food to eat, on soil that we could grow things, in a land where we could have pride and not be fighting to take something from someone else or have to be defending our land from someone else. Where we could go about our daily lives without the fear of arrest or being killed and where our children wouldn't be influenced to sacrifice themselves to kill others. We all agreed that's what we all wanted. Where we disagreed was on how we could achieve that goal. We realised that the laws we passed and the rules we made were there not to protect everyone but to protect ourselves. We then went back to the Commandments, they became the strength." Here he paused and laughed. "But we didn't realise that the Commandments we had weren't complete. But when they were, agreeing on world peace with God's help was assured."

The Rabbi took up the story. "When Moses met God and was offered the Commandments for the Jews he didn't know that God had already offered them to others. The first religious leader to be offered them said that he couldn't accept them without consultation with his fellow leaders and he warned that not all might agree.

Another group said that they would have to look at them carefully and decide which to accept and which to reject. God wasn't too impressed with their indecision." As he spoke, the Rabbi blushed. "Moses wasn't sure either and he asked God how much they cost? God said, 'They cost nothing Moses.' Moses said, 'In that case I'll take ten.'"

The others laughed at the story.

The Rabbi continued. "What Moses didn't realise was that there were many more than ten but God didn't tell him, he let him take his bargain. We found out later that the first fifteen or so were negative, thou shall not do this, thou shall not do that, thou shall not commit etc. It turned out that Commandment number eleven was 'Thou shalt not committee.' If we had known that it would have saved a lot of time arguing. And number twenty-four was, 'Thou shall go dancing and having fun at least one night a week.' And number sixteen was 'Thou shall not get upset when another person's views differ from your own.' But the most important one we missed was the last one, 'Thou shalt not ever take the life of another person or unlawfully imprison him or act in any unsociable way towards him.' It was a great pity that we found that one so late."

Steve asked, "How did you find them?"

"Mother Theresa made a visit back to her hospital in India and appeared in a vision before hundreds of witnesses. She thanked everyone for making her a saint and handed over the rest of the Commandments."

An Anglican Vicar spoke in a beautifully cultured English accent. "Mother Theresa gave us a message and she said that we would find it helpful. She told us that we should look after every other person as if he or she was our best friend. In turn, they would watch out for us as we would watch out for them. With children, we needed to be especially careful. Every child was to be helped as if it were our own child. If it were hungry or in danger we would care for it as we would our own. We were told that if we did this, love would spread around the planet faster than the wind could blow. We were asked to grant personal favours, if someone needed assistance we would offer it without any demand for payment, in turn, when we asked for assistance, it would be given to us freely. It didn't stop us arranging our daily business but it did mean that life was easier. When a person became successful in a career, they were encouraged to help others do well too. Anyone who jealously guarded what they had achieved or who did their best to push others back was discouraged and often they lost it all or never found real happiness. Those who helped others found the joy that they were seeking."

Another religious leader interrupted. "What is given out, comes back. When someone offers help to others freely, that help is given without cost and without conditions. It took a while for this to get through to some people but as soon as most people grasped the concept, the mood of everyone changed for the better."

Steve decided to risk a question. "When I was five I asked my dad, 'why are we here?'"

The priest said, "And what did he say?"

CHAPTER 14

"He said he didn't know, but what he did know was that life wasn't fair."

A Priest interrupted. "A lot of people complain that life isn't fair but when we meet them here we ask them when they were told that life would be fair?"

The Rabbi butted in. "I mean..." he spread his hands, "when you were born, did your mum say, 'Welcome to the world, life is fair?' Of course not! Did your priests, your teachers, your bosses, your customers ever say, 'hey you, don't worry, life is fair?' I think not."

The little Priest spoke again. "When you were born, you were supplied with a sense of humour. You might hide it well or you might use it, it's your choice. You were also selected for birth because it was felt that you could take a joke. If you can't take a joke, you shouldn't have joined. Hee Hee!" The little Priest laughed, Steve didn't think it was funny. "We Catholic priests had to be able to take a joke. For hundreds of years we were told that we couldn't marry or have children. Then one day, one of the Cardinals in Rome was found crying in the library. Do you know what he discovered? He was reading some old parchments and found that someone had been confused. The word 'celibate' wasn't in the original text, the word written there in faded ink was 'celebrate!'"

Peter spoke to Steve who had covered his mouth with his hand to suppress his giggles. "Mentioning the 'you can't take a joke' reminds me. If you have finished asking them questions for the moment, let's move on, you'll have plenty of time in eternity to come back and ask as many questions as you want."

Steve asked, "Can I ask two last questions for now?"

Peter nodded and Steve referred back to the time when he asked his father why they were here. Steve's dad didn't know but Peter did.

He said, "Without making too much of a point of it we are here because of love. Love and life go hand in hand for all creatures and humans. We give love, we receive love, sometimes we go through periods where we get very little or none at all and at other times we give a lot and receive a lot. No spirit goes through life on Earth or here without experiencing the giving or receiving of love at one time or another. Indeed I could go on to say that no one is ever denied that experience nor the opportunity. Love and life are linked together always, that's what motivates all creatures and humans to exist." He put his arm around Steve's shoulder and smiled at him. "You had another question?" Steve nodded and pointed politely to the Rabbi and the Arab standing together.

"It's good to see you together as friends ..." he paused. "Are you friends?" The men nodded. "Okay then, can you just tell me how does the Arab/Israeli conflict end? When I came here it looked as if there would never ever be peace in the region."

The Rabbi smiled at the question. "It was referred to as the A solution. If you put an A in front of the word Rabbi, it makes it Arabbi. It was an Arab religious leader and a Rabbi who came up with the idea together. Basically Palestinians wouldn't rest until they had their own homeland, they wanted Jews to leave occupied territories and whilst many Jews weren't completely opposed to Palestinians having their own homeland, they didn't want to leave the homes that they had built. If you recall, each side kept on killing, there was no let up and as each atrocity was met with revenge, it seemed as if the war would go on forever. Everyone was suffering, no one was winning and in the end the Arab and the Rabbi struck a deal and each went back to his people to present it. Not everyone was in favour of course but as no one could think of a better idea, it was approved. Like most good ideas, it was very simple. The Palestinians and Israelis agreed on territorial boundaries and formed the land now known as Holy Palestine. The Israelis called their country by the new name of Holy Israel and both agreed to respect the two new Holy Lands for ever. Leaders of both peoples signed a guarantee of peace by taking a trillion year lease on their land agreeing to support a fund to the Palestinians of billions of US dollars. The Americans and most countries in Europe contributed towards this massive fund to provide Palestinians with infrastructure, schools, hospitals, even complete towns. Of course there were those on both sides who hated the idea and there were those who wanted to deny one side or the other any peace but when they saw the possibility of the end of suicide bombings and the end of action from Israeli soldiers they realised that the Arabbi plan might work. Four generations passed however before the Palestinians and Israelis held their historical football match. And before you ask, yes it was a great game, it passed without trouble and the score was 3 – 3."

Peter added, "Someone finally realised that there were only two ways for anyone to overcome a hated enemy. One sure way was to successfully attack, bomb, kill and maim their way to victory and although that method might be effective in the short term, it would always cost the winning side dearly in respect of lives, retribution and expense. The second sure way to come to terms with an enemy was to talk with them and that would always happen sooner or later. In talking they would search for common aims and try to find ways to overcome objections from the zealots. Yes it would be true that often it would be impossible for the people who were in the war at the beginning to agree to talks but as these people grew older and wiser or when they died and were replaced by others it always became evident to those in charge that talking was infinitely better than fighting. A wag even invented a slogan, 'Jaw Jaw is better than War War!'"

Steve thanked the group who clapped and nodded at Peter's joke; he waved them all farewell and followed Peter out of the large room.

"Come on, you'll enjoy this." Peter pointed to another door.

They went through the door out into the corridor where there were still many people moving around. The receptionist who had lisped at Steve looked up and he wasn't sure how Steve would react but Steve gave him a genuine smile and asked if he was okay. The man nodded and smiled.

Peter led Steve across a marble floor and stopped outside a door. He looked up and a green light was on, he pushed the door and Steve followed him in.

There were rows of seats with only four or five occupied. The wall lights were on and in front of the curtain covering the screen there was a small stage with a stand and a microphone. Peter sat in the second row from the back and motioned Steve to sit next to him. They settled down into their seats as a man came on the stage, he had white, wavy hair, his bright red jacket was borrowed from the old music hall days and he sported a magnificent twirly moustache. He spoke very clearly and waved his hands about.

"Ladies and gentlemen, it is my proud and overwhelming pleasure to show you an extravaganza of humour, straight from the rumbling tummies of our spirits. I implore you, I beseech you, I beg you, take everything you hear with a huge pinch of salt but remember," he paused and waggled his finger, "everything you see and hear is absolutely and perfectly unintentionally, and intentionally true!" He emphasised his nonsense as he banged his gavel on the lectern. He then read aloud the caption on the screen.

CHAPTER 15

A sign was positioned on an easel, it read…

"GOLF IS A GAME PLAYED BY SPIRITS WHO
TEASE HUMANS TO SEE HOW FAR THEY
CAN PUSH THEM.
THE WINNER IS THE SPIRIT WHO
ANTICIPATES THE BEHAVIOUR OF HIS
HUMAN PLAYER CORRECTLY."

The curtain opened and the scene was of four middle-aged men preparing to play golf, they were business colleagues rather than close friends and they liked each other and enjoyed their game. Two of the players would turn out to be quite skilled, one would reveal himself to be truly hopeless by making all the classic golfing errors and the last was the kind of player that would play good shots and bad shots and had no consistency in his game.

Peter whispered, "We chose a golf example for you because you tried to play it."

"Tried to …" Steve objected.

Peter put his finger to his lips and then pointed at the screen. "Shh."

The camera moved to one side of the tee where the golfers prepared to start. Steve saw four shimmering figures, they were giggling to themselves and were picking players and obviously they were making a bet and selecting their players whilst deciding on the odds of each player winning. But as Steve listened and read the subtitles they weren't betting on who would win the golf game but on how each player would react under the different circumstances of each shot whether it be a good one or not.

The speaker spoke over the film. "There are many games of golf played by spirits, this one is regarded as one of the classics as it combines the best and worst of this wonderful game and of the real challenge. Not the challenge of the player against his opponents or the challenge of the player against the course but of the player against himself. That's where the fun begins." He smiled and turned to watch the screen.

The first player in the red jumper addressed the ball. He wiggled and jiggled and measured his stroke and as he performed a perfect shot, the ball flew straight and long and landed well down the fairway. "Good shot!"

The second player in the tartan hat moved to the tee and did exactly the same. His wiggling and jiggling were spot on, his slow back swing was perfect. He did exactly the same shot as the first chap but as he did so, Steve noticed that one of the spirits to the side gently moved his arm to point to the right, away from him. The ball left the tee and sliced high into the air, turned gently to the right and splashed into the lake.

He grimaced and strode off the tee. The spirits looked at the player, he brandished his club but controlled himself and he grinned weakly at the others. The third player took up his stance, his pullover was yellow and brand-new. His shoes, trousers and cap were all new, indeed his clubs were only on their second outing, they were expensive and each club had its own place in the latest state of the art golf bag. Money could buy expensive gear but it couldn't buy talent.

The man took up his stance, wiggled, jiggled and did a few practice shots in slow and perfect time. He then moved up to the ball, wiggled and jiggled again but this time he performed a very fast back swing, an even faster through swing and the club came down towards the ball. At the same moment, one of the spirits opened the palm of his hand and lifted it slightly. The club head missed the ball altogether. It was obviously an air-shot and one that counted. Instead of admitting the error, he jiggled again, muttered, "this is it" and swung again. The bottom of the club hit the top of the ball; it shot forward three feet and stopped. The man sighed.

Red-faced and furious he stood back to let the last player tee off. Only five-foot tall and with a wide girth, the player didn't look as if he could see the ball when he addressed it. He wobbled backwards and forwards, didn't jiggle or wiggle and didn't do a practice shot. He performed the most ungainly stroke, the club connected and the man toppled backwards, his balance upset. The ball rose three or four feet off the ground and whizzed long and low. It bounced once off a path, hit a tree and spun crazily towards the green where it stopped a yard from the pin. The man whooped with delight and the others were disgusted but said, "Good shot."

The spirits grinned at each other and marked their cards. Mr Red Jumper took a grip on his trolley and was keen to move on. Mr Tartan Hat said that he wanted another tee shot but the others reminded him that he could take a penalty shot by the lake. Mr Everything New took out his iron, addressed the ball by the Ladies Tee and let rip. The ball sailed into the air, a glorious strike. It hit the green just by the pin and bounced once more as it cleared the back of the green and landed deep in the bushes. His face was a picture but he said nothing as the fat man said,

"Oh hard luck, super shot, what was that, a five iron?" He didn't hear the reply made under the other man's breath.

As the game continued, Mr Red Jumper played consistently well and looked set to win the match. The short fat man thought that he had lost lots of balls but found most of them and he recovered well from bad shots and was in second place. He bounced off boulders and off trees and on one occasion he would have gone straight through the green but his ball hit a rake on the edge of the bunker and the ball stopped short of the pin by six inches. Mr Tartan Hat found his first ball on the edge of the lake and decided to try and hit it out saving the lost shot. As his right foot squelched into the mud, his shoe filled with water and it came off. He nearly fell but caught his balance by putting his club to the bottom. His intention was to save himself from falling as he bent to pick up his shoe. But the mud didn't support the club and it slowly but firmly sank halfway up its shaft. The spirits watched and one put his arms into the air. At the same moment, the golfer lost his balance and toppled after his club and fell onto his side into the muddy water. The others looked in horror but the fat man called out,

"Sorry, no swimming allowed," and shrieked with laughter.

Under the circumstances the golfer handled it quite well. He dragged his trolley and club to the drier ground and then proceeded to search in his bag. He pulled out his waterproof trousers and waterproof jacket. He kicked off his other shoe, pulled off his soaking wet trousers and started to remove his jumper. He pulled it hard over his head but he'd forgotten about his tartan hat, which was now caught in the wet jumper. He struggled to pull the jumper back on, retrieved his hat and threw it down by his bag. His jumper came off, he put on his waterproof trousers, pulled on his jacket and struggled with the zip. He then bent over and put on first his dry shoe, then, and very gingerly, his wet shoe. The others watched as he took another ball from his bag and when he half threw, half dropped his ball it landed on a dry area of grass about ten feet from the edge of the pond. He took a club and was about to strike when Mr Red Jumper offered a suggestion.

"You have to drop the ball two lengths from the place of entry, that would be over there." He pointed and Mr Tartan Hat looked back. The area was part rough, part swamp. Some of it was dry, most of it was bog.

"The ball sliced right, it went in over here and it's far too boggy, this will do!" He spoke firmly but Mr Red Jumper was a good golfer and a stickler for the rules.

"Sorry Giles but if you take your shot from there, you will forfeit the hole."

"Right then!" Giles was furious and picked up the ball. "Simon is by the pin for one, that's minus one with his handicap. I'll pick up." And with that he thrust the ball into his pocket, picked up his club, threw it into his bag and stormed off in the direction of the green, his bag bouncing on its trolley behind him.

Giles had enjoyed better days, he lost nine balls. He'd played a ball from another foursome and experienced the wrath of a stout Ladies Captain and as they started the seventeenth he was more than upset. The others had done fairly well. His Red Jumpered colleague had parred nearly every hole and was saying that he hoped to play as well in the forthcoming club match. The small fat man had the most unorthodox style yet he was finishing in second place and his friend from the office with the new clubs, new gear and new balls had lost four balls, scored no points on most of his holes but he'd enjoyed two birdies and a par. He was excited and thought that he had done well.

Giles had no more balls left as he took the last one. The others had teed off, it was his turn. The three balls sat in the middle of the fairway and all Giles had to do was take it easy and gently make a swing, the club head would do the rest. But one of the spirits was tapping himself on the head and pointing left. Giles decided that he would hit a perfect shot, over the top of the other three balls and that his ball would bounce between the bunkers and with luck, hit the edge of the green and roll on. As the club came down Giles knew that it would be a great shot and as the club connected the ball clicked and soared into the air. It went high and it went straight but the wind seemed to catch it just a little bit and as the ball gained height it started to veer. Giles watched. It might be all right, the ball would land just to the left of the green. It did, it bounced once, then twice and then as it started to roll to the left, it picked up speed and Giles watched in dismay as the ball trickled over the edge of the bank into the water hazard.

Giles was furious, his wife had been complaining that he was spending too much time and money on golf and she felt that golf for him was a waste of time. He had argued, he'd said that the fresh air and exercise did him good, but now he made a decision. He walked defiantly and rudely past the balls waiting on the fairway and he ignored the calls of "Hard luck Giles" as he did what he knew he had to do. The spirits moved to one side as he marched through them and he stopped at the edge of the water and peered in. He could see his ball not more than two feet from the edge but at least a foot under the surface. He took his bag and his trolley in his hands and as the others gasped he raised the whole thing above his head. The clubs started to slide out as if they were protesting at their fate but before the clubs could fall, Giles threw the complete set right into the middle of the pond, they hit the water and sank but the depth wasn't sufficient to submerge them and the driver poked its head out of the water. Even the clubs seemed to mock him.

"That's it. I'm finished. I am totally fed up with this bloody game. I'm off." The others stood there, their mouths gaping. Giles had passed the seventeenth green and was on the path to the car park adjacent to the eighteenth when he suddenly stopped. He stood still for nearly ten seconds with his hands clenched. The spirits who had been laughing and congratulating each other had seen Giles stop and they watched in silence as he walked back to the pond and stood there looking at his clubs. Then he bent down, removed his shoes and socks and then his trousers. He left his pants and jacket on. He slipped off the bank and took a step forward, the bottom was firm. He reached his clubs in five steps and stood up to his waist in cold water. A moorhen scuttled away. With his left hand he lifted his bag clear of the weeds. His right hand fumbled in the side pocket and located something. He removed his hand and the others could see that Giles had retrieved his car keys. The bag fell back into the water as Giles moved back to the bank. He climbed out, put his clothes back on and said,

"I'll see you tomorrow Simon, goodbye Barry, talk to you later Bill." He seemed to be a happier person as he left his friends, his golf bag and the game of golf behind forever. The spirits stood there stunned.

One said, "You went too far, he's given it up. That's not supposed to happen, you've lost the bet."

"Just watch, trust me, he won't give it up, mind you when he came back for his keys I thought he'd changed his mind then. I'll double your winnings if he doesn't come back again within two hours, pick up his clubs and play again at the weekend."

The other spirits didn't hesitate, "You are on!"

Giles had reached his car and was about to get in. He felt a bit bad walking off without saying a proper goodbye to the others. He could see them on the eighteenth tee, it was a difficult par three, the green was small and it was easy to catch one of the many deep bunkers that protected it. Barry teed off first, his ball fell just short of the largest bunker and sat there nicely for a chip on. Bill took up his stance, it was a nice shot but too short. The sand flew up as the ball landed in the middle of the trap. Then Simon took his turn. Giles could see his funny swing, it was amazing that he could even hit the ball. The club connected and the ball soared into the sky, it was too long, it would land behind. Giles watched as the ball seemed to stop in mid-air. It dropped almost vertically, hit the green, bounced once and then rolled. The ball hit the pin as it stopped moving and dropped into the hole. He heard the shriek, Simon was jumping up and down and it was comical. Bill and Barry were slapping him on the back and Giles felt awful, he had made an enormous decision to give up golf, he had thrown his clubs and trolley away and now Simon had got a hole in one.

Simon handed over four twenty-pound notes. The bar was packed, everyone was delighted and Simon handed the whiskey to Giles.

"Have you ever had a hole in one Giles?"

"Yes I did once, it was on a par three in Spain. It was a club society day, it cost me a fortune in drinks for everyone, so yes I did have a hole in one." Simon was being congratulated by the very happy bar steward and no one noticed Giles slip out the side door and walk back to the pond. For the third time that day he shuddered at the temperature of the cold water but he knew he was doing the right thing. He placed the clubs carefully in the boot of his car. he would be back on Saturday.

The spirits watched this, one was happy and grinning, the other three had lost their bet, but they didn't seem too sad or upset.

"A great day's golf," one said.

"Did you see when my chap bounced off two trees and onto the green for a birdie?"

"And when your man threw those clubs into the pond, what a sight, you were amazing getting him so wound up, it was brilliant. And you were right, he came back for his clubs just as you said he would."

They walked away happily.

CHAPTER 16

"Golf is one of the greatest practical jokes we ever played on mankind. It's a game played by spirits who use players on Earth. The players think that they are ones doing the playing but in truth, it's us who play with them. Unfortunately some players have started to realise that and no longer treat their game so seriously. But many still do and we have great fun teasing them."

Steve looked at Peter. He was a powerful man with strong shoulders and his black suit and black open-necked shirt gave him a gangster look. For a black man to dress completely in black showed poise and confidence and his body was firm and showed no signs of fat. Steve sensed that Peter was a hard man and not one to upset. He certainly would not want to have to fight him as he could probably break an opponent's neck or arm with ease. Steve had always been fairly fit but didn't work out at a gym and he didn't jog either, he sensed that golf might not be Peter's favourite game and asked him if he played.

"No I don't play golf," Peter smiled. "I like to box, maybe you'd like to go a couple of rounds in the gym sometime?"

"Er thanks but no thanks. I'm not much of a physical fighter." Steve thought it wise to change the subject. "What other things do you do?"

"I'm on the reception team with Michael and others and my job is to introduce you to spirits who can answer questions and unravel mysteries for you. You'll never understand what you have to learn until you have a better appreciation of important matters. Take religion for example, would you say that you were a religious person on Earth and would you feel any different now that you are here?"

"Wow, that's a heavy question. No I wasn't religious on earth though I did believe that there was something more than just living, dying and being buried but I just didn't know what. Frankly I found religion very boring and I'd rather stay in bed on a Sunday than go to church."

Peter explained, "Most people think that life, death, God and religion need to be taken very seriously with no pleasure or humour. Most Jews have a wonderful sense of humour, sometimes they need it! And gospel singers are a great example to everyone. They love religion, they enjoy their music, and worshipping God brings them pleasure and genuinely uplifts them. Other forms of worship seem to warrant such seriousness that pleasure and laughter are frowned upon. Often you find that the most serious followers of religion have no time for other people, for their lives, for their suffering or joy and no time at all for humour. We don't actually encourage those people at all and when they arrive here they need to adjust. What is funny is when we tell them to 'Get a Life', they even miss the irony of that and the really bigoted ones never get the joke, they really are hard work."

"So which religion gets it right?" Steve was really interested.

"Prior to the World Meeting of Religious Leaders they all got some of it right and they all got some of it wrong. The ones who were tolerant, friendly and forgiving were nearest, those that tried to impose controls, collect money in return for salvation, or violently force their beliefs on others; they really did have a lot to learn. But to answer your question, no one religion was ever spot on a hundred per cent although some were much closer than others. After the World Meeting of Religious Leaders people realised that it's the individual spirit that's important to God not solely the religion or the method of teaching." Peter opened another door to reveal a laboratory filled with scientific projects, designs and new ideas. Steve recognised some of them as being used in science and medicine, others were completely new to him.

He said, "This looks interesting, are these inventions?"

"Absolutely right." Peter grinned. "They have all been developed here and spirits have introduced them to humans as they have been needed. The saying 'Necessity is the Mother of Invention' was a good one. As you needed these things for your development, and sometimes to be able to live with nature and her ups and downs, so these aids were designed and introduced."

"What's this?" Steve picked up a circular disc about the size of a penny and as he examined it, a madcap inventor crashed through a door in the corner and shouted at them.

"Ah there you are! I expected you to be invisible but clearly you are not!" He seemed pleased to see them but also very agitated. Steve was reminded of a cross between the white-haired crazed inventor who built the special De Lorean in *Back to the Future* and the white rabbit from *Alice in Wonderland*. His silver hair was long and it flowed over his shoulders. Steve noticed that his trousers were too short and he had odd shoes on, one was brown with a lace, the other was black with elastic sides. He either didn't care what he looked like or else he simply couldn't dress himself. His crumpled jacket seemed to have over fifty pockets, some large and bulging, others were tiny with a small piece of paper poking out.

He looked closely at the disc through his bottle-lensed glasses then stepped back, took the glasses off, said, "That's better," and studied what Steve was holding. "Ah yes, this is due on Earth in about fifteen of your years. We may use it to replace golf for our games, certainly it's got great potential." He laughed. "Yes we can make a lot of mischief with this one."

He giggled again and Steve asked, "What does it do?"

"Do? What does it do? It doesn't do anything. What a strange question." He looked at Steve oddly. "It's an Embryonic Translator. It's been invented already of course but the spirit responsible won't pass it to his Earth contact until we have modified it for fun. Golf still has a long way to go but this will be a great game for all of us. It's almost as good as the Quadrantal Transporter. Great fun! Great fun!" Steve held it in his fingers and looked at it closely.

Peter added, "Anyone wanting to meet someone from a different country can have this disc planted in their body. Most people will have a plastic sleeve sewn in just under the armpit." He lifted his left arm to point with his right hand. "When you speak to a foreigner you have to try and speak in his language or he has to speak in yours. But with this, you simply select the disc for the language you want and insert that into the sleeve." He pointed to his armpit. "When you speak in your language, the person you speak to hears what you say in their language and when they speak to you, they use their language and you hear what they are saying in yours."

"That's brilliant." Steve moved back as Peter motioned him to one side. A screen opened up on the wall and a film showed a tourist who was obviously American and most certainly from Texas as he approached a Japanese lady on the streets of Tokyo.

"Excuse me," the American drawled as he raised his hat. "I'm looking for the Hasawoto Hotel."

"Sim wah, hurro naya bora." She pointed and smiled.

"Thanks lady, that's great, you have a nice day now ya hear." The lady gave a slight nod and the American removed his hat and bowed. The three musketeers couldn't have shown more gallantry. The Texan walked off towards his hotel and the Japanese lady continued on her way.

"Now watch this next scene. This gives you an idea of the fun we can have when the Embryonic Translator apparently malfunctions."

A smooth young man, beautifully dressed, approached a blonde girl in a nightclub. The man looked Italian and ultra-cool and he acted as if he were a gift to women. He smoothed back his hair and smiled at a lovely girl and his manners were exquisite; the girl blushed as he took her hand and kissed it. He spoke in Italian and the subtitles appeared on the screen for Steve's benefit.

"Oh you are so beautiful. It is lovely to meet you."

The girl frowned and became annoyed. She spoke to him in Swedish and again the subtitles showed what she had said.

"I beg your pardon?"

The Italian smiled and said, "You are indeed a treasure, I would be honoured if you would join me at my table."

He was astonished at her response. Her face looked like thunder and she drew back her arm and slapped him hard in the face. He tumbled backward over a table, scattering bottles and glasses and landing in a heap at the feet of another girl. Her boyfriend looked very annoyed.

The blonde retreated to the bar where her friend asked in Swedish, "What did he say to you?" The subtitles again showed the words.

"First he said, 'you are not so beautiful but I would love to eat you' and when I asked him to repeat it he said, 'I don't know from which stone you crawled out from but I will have you now right over this table!"'

The Italian had got to his feet and was apologising to the people whose drinks he had spilled but his words were being translated as 'You might at least say sorry for your behaviour and if your ugly woman could get off my scarf, I would like it back please.'

The Italian then backed off saying "Scuzi, Scuzi", this was being translated as "pigs, pigs."

The scene ended with two burly bouncers picking him up bodily from the floor and the subtitles showing the words, "I'll beat you both up outside, you …"

Peter and the mad inventor thought that this was very funny. Steve wasn't so sure, he'd been slapped by a Swedish girl once when he asked if her breasts were real.

CHAPTER 17

Steve wandered over to a tall blue police box standing against a wall. Its door had one large silver knob and a pad with lots of numbers. He was interested in the advice printed on a notice. 'Ensure you are wearing the correct clothes before transporting.'

"This looks good, what is it Mr... er?"

The inventor apologised. "So sorry, I forgot to introduce myself. I am Professor Knob. I invented the Knob many moons ago and I've been famous for it ever since. Every invention apart from a very few has to have a Knob somewhere and without my Knobs, Earth and Heaven would be a sadder place."

Steve gazed at him in astonishment and decided not to ask him why.

Professor Knob continued. "Handles are one thing but Knobs are far more useful." He pulled at the Knob on the police box but nothing happened. He tried it again and then remembered that he had to enter a code first. He explained, "News of this marvellous device was leaked prematurely to a British inventor in the 1960s. Fortunately it wasn't properly understood and all that was produced was a TV programme called *Doctor Who'*. The box and the transportation system could have easily been adapted for proper use but fortunately for us, as the invention was out too early, the inventor painted the box blue, put a light on the top and used it for TV and not for real. By the time the programmes were finished, the original purpose was forgotten and the Transporter's codes were lost. But the public did realise that transport by this device might be possible even though it was clearly for the distant future."

Peter pointed to the screen as a short film explained how the Transporter was used. A man aged about thirty and dressed in colourful ski gear stood in front of the box. He had his skis and poles in one hand and a piece of paper with some numbers listed on it. With his right hand he tapped the numbers into the pad on the door. He then pulled the silver knob, stepped in and closed the door behind him. The scene changed to a similar box positioned at the top of a mountain next to the top of a gondola lift system. The weather looked perfect and the ski conditions were superb. The knob turned, the front door opened and the man emerged, dropped his skis onto the snow and clicked his boots into the bindings. He then used his poles to move forward and skied happily down the slope and away.

"There are various sizes," the inventor said. "This is the single occupant, economy version. Many people will have one of these at home and use it whenever they fancy a break. They can go skiing, motor racing, scuba diving, boating, deep sea fishing, whatever they desire."

Steve thought that this was marvellous. "So when will it be available and how much will it cost?" His business mind was active.

"It will be invented properly as the world's supply of oil runs out and it will cost about the same as a small car did when you passed through. Of course the motor car will eventually be obsolete, the only time later generations of motoring enthusiasts will get the opportunity to drive a decent car is when they visit Heaven, or depending on the road conditions, Hell. Peter added that larger versions of the Transporter would be available at various locations so that couples and groups could transport together. He then paused and smiled. "But what interests many of us is the potential to tease and to see how far we can go before someone loses their temper." Steve didn't understand and said so.

"When someone enters the location co-ordinates there is a chance of error."

He tapped his nose. "Not necessarily by the user, but possibly by a mischievous spirit." He grinned.

The film showed the same chap in the ski wear press the buttons and enter the Transporter. This time it opened, not on a mountain but by a beautiful Caribbean beach. The man emerged, skis and poles in hand to be faced with miles of sand, a warm sea and glorious sunshine where lovely topless girls and handsome men relaxed on sun beds. Some of them saw him and called out.

"Hey the snow's over there," and, "sorry it's all melted," before dissolving into laughter. The skier stepped forward, his boots sinking into the sand. He threw his skis and poles down, stamped about and then collapsed onto the beach undoing his gloves and throwing his hat to one side.

"He's booked a day's skiing and he'll now spend the time sunbathing." Peter smiled, "and he'll be writing his letter of complaint to the suppliers of his machine and demanding compensation no doubt."

"You are not a nice spirit are you?" Steve said. "Have you any more nasty tricks up your sleeve?"

"Do you mind? I'm not nasty." Peter was offended. "You should recall that nothing you ever had on Earth worked perfectly. The designs and manufacture were good enough of course but how could we test the resolve of individuals if nothing ever went wrong?" He paused as Steve thought this through.

"Individuals handle irritations in different ways and these ways are judged."

He looked at the screen again and a series of cameo performances were shown. A golfer sliced a ball into some trees, clearly it wasn't his first bad shot of the day as he stamped his foot and hurled his club to the ground. He kicked his golf bag, it fell over and he stood there fuming.

A driver was looking for a space to park and drove slowly along the road. Suddenly he saw a space on the other side. He pulled past the gap and was about to reverse in when another motorist sneaked in behind. The unlucky driver watched the other man get out of the car and walk away. He raged against the rudeness of the other driver and punched the steering wheel with all his might before accelerating away and nearly colliding with another car.

The film changed to show a man at his computer screen, he was obviously very frustrated. He continued to type but his left hand was clenching, then the screen crashed yet again and the words came up. 'Closing Down' At this, the man punched the screen hard, the monitor flew off the table and landed on the floor. Everyone in his office looked at him.

Then another set of short films appeared. A lady struggled with heavy shopping bags in the rain. Suddenly one of them gave way and the groceries tumbled to the pavement. She looked in dismay at the mess but instead of getting upset she shrugged. As she bent to try and gather up the tins, a man appeared and offered to help. He pulled a carrier bag from his pocket and smiled as he put the fallen items into the bag for her.

Another short film showed a man getting out of his car at the side of the road. He looked at the flat tyre and then opened the boot. He lifted out the spare but when he put it on the ground; he could see that this tyre was also flat. Instead of kicking the car, the chap shrugged, got back into the car and called for help on his mobile.

Peter said, "We see how someone will react as soon as they realise that things have gone wrong. Clenched fists and gritted teeth indicate a mini storm brewing. What we see is the start of a totally wasted effort in ranting and raving. But when we see someone shrug their shoulders, maybe even grin or laugh, then we know that the person is at peace with themselves and is nearer to God than the others."

Steve could appreciate the logic of this. "So when things go wrong, it's like a mini test of character. And it's always done deliberately to wind people up to see how they'll react?"

"Not exactly," Peter said. "in some cases the problem is induced by a spirit as a test but sometimes equipment does malfunction because of a mistake in design or manufacture and then it's not our fault. Here's a problem on one of the group Quadrantal Transporters."

The screen showed a family group off to a wedding. The dad was in top hat and tails, his wife in a flowery pink dress with an enormous hat. The children were dressed as pageboy and bridesmaid and granny had a smart blue outfit and a pretty white hat. Grandad looked splendid in his morning suit. They had spent ages getting ready and they were nervous. Tempers had already been tested a few times that morning but they were relatively calm as they stood waiting to enter the Transporter. Dad was very careful to press the correct numbers onto the pad and the family trooped inside. The scene switched to the wedding where a portable Transporter had been placed to receive guests. When the family emerged, the effect was hilarious. Dad was still dressed as he had been on his top half but his wife's rose covered pink dress and shapely legs supported him. Mum was no longer Mum but half Grandad and the two children had come through with their heads transposed. Steve found this funny and laughed as the group started grabbing each other. The children tried to pull at their heads as if they could remove them. Then one of the ushers arrived. He was apologetic and took Dad by the arm. He showed him the other guests. All were wrong. Half women, half men, all in different non-matching outfits, they looked ridiculous.

The usher said, "My apologies Sir, the system has a small error but as you can see, you are not the only ones to discover this. Please join the wedding party, you will all be returned to normal after the ceremony, we hope to have the machine ready to correct you all before you go to reception."

The family joined the other guests and everybody seemed to be examining each other's new form. One joker in the top half of his morning suit was showing off his shapely legs and pulling up his skirt to reveal his suspenders. His wife who had a low cut blouse leaving little to the imagination strutted forward on her short, fat legs in striped trousers, punched her husband and said, "Pack that in you pig!"

CHAPTER 18

If you are looking for sympathy,

you will find it in the dictionary between sex and syphilis.

(The angry wife of a man who discovered that he had been unfaithful)

Peter and Steve left the inventor's room and Steve was still giggling.

"Do you think I would look nice in a dress with her legs?"

Peter didn't think so. "Come on, we have to continue with your court hearing now and I will offer you some advice. Don't try and bullshit. If it appears that you did bad things when you were alive, accept it, don't deny it or make excuses. Accept what you did with good grace."

Steve was worried. "What will they drag up, just my bad things, my sins?"

"Goodness knows, you may see things that you have done or said that you will be proud of. Well at least I hope you will." Peter looked at Steve. Steve looked even more worried.

They re-entered the courtroom. Rosie was settling at her desk, others had filed in at the back and there were people ready to take notes. Again there was no one where the judge would normally sit. The egg was there, sitting on its box and the colour was clear. The opposing side was there too. Helen Crompton seemed in a happy mood and she was laughing at something her assistant was saying. Then she turned and looked at Steve, she smiled but Steve thought that it seemed to be a smile of triumph. He wondered what was in store.

Rosie stood and spoke. "Your childhood was without serious blemish except when you teased your neighbour's cat and tormented insects." She stopped speaking as the court film started. The screen showed a small boy of about ten as he sat in the garden playing with a spider. He trapped the spider and grabbed it, he opened his hand and plucked one of the legs from the spider. He then plucked another leg off and another and the spider was eventually separated from all of its legs. The boy looked up from his handiwork and called out to his friend and another child came into view. Steve recognised his school friend Patrick.

"Hey Pat, where do you find a spider with no legs?" He paused but the other boy didn't reply. "Where you left it." The boy Steve laughed at his own joke.

The adult Steve sitting in the courtroom didn't laugh, neither did anyone else.

Rosie asked, "Why did you do that Steve?"

Steve stammered. "I don't know, I didn't suppose that spiders were important. It was only a spider. I feel ashamed now but ..." he paused, "come on, I was only ten or eleven. Lots of small boys do that sort of thing."

Helen Crompton interrupted. "What do you think it feels like to have your legs pulled off?" Steve didn't reply. Suddenly he felt a vibration and he and everyone else looked at the egg. It had turned black. Immediately Steve felt the most horrendous pain in his left leg and he squirmed in agony. The pain suddenly stopped. Then he felt it again in his right leg, this time it felt as if his leg muscles were being slowly torn from the rest of him. He clenched his teeth, his hands became tight fists and he thought that he would pass out from the pain.

The agony lasted a few seconds and it left Steve with tears pouring down his face. He looked down, half expecting to see his legs missing but they were still there, he could feel them, but they did ache.

The film moved on. Steve and another boy had a lad of about nine years old in their grasp. Steve and his friend were dressed in red school blazers. Their victim had a blue school blazer. He looked terrified. He tried to wriggle free but he was held too tight. He lashed out with his leg but missed his target.

"Caught you!" Steve sneered. He held the boy with one hand and punched him with the other. The lad doubled up in pain, his face contorted in agony and fear. Steve shook him.

"You County High school boys aren't allowed to use our bus stop, you will pay a fine, how much you got?" The boy cringed, all he had was his bus fare. Steve and his friend took it from him and punched him again. The boy burst into tears, picked up his school bag and ran off, he would have to walk home.

Steve and his friend went into the sweet shop. Steve held out his hand to show that he had money and asked for some sweets in a jar behind the shopkeeper. She turned to get the jar and Steve's hand flashed, grabbed a bar of chocolate and gave it to his friend. The woman saw the movement.

"What did you take? Come on, what did you take? I saw you take something."

Steve showed her his hands, one was empty, and the other held the money he was buying sweets with.

"Nothing lady, I didn't take nothing." He smiled sweetly.

The shopkeeper didn't believe him but she had no proof. She threw the sweets on to the scale, bagged them up and demanded her money. Steve paid her, took his sweets and the two boys left the shop grinning.

Rosie asked for the film to rewind to the point where Steve stole the chocolate.

The film froze and Steve's spirit could be seen standing to one side. He didn't look happy. Another spirit, dark and grey was whispering the word 'Now!' into Steve's ear. The film started and Steve's hand grabbed the chocolate and passed it to his friend.

Helen Crompton spoke. "When you were a baby you didn't know any better and when you were tempted to throw the rattle at the cyclist you were forgiven because you were too young to know the difference between right and wrong. But at eleven years old you did know the difference so please explain now, why did you bully that boy, why did you think that you should take his money and why did you think that it was okay to steal from that shop?"

Steve wasn't sure what to say and he tried an excuse. "It wasn't my idea, Derek Brown suggested that we grabbed the boy from the County High." Immediately the egg vibrated and turned black, but Steve felt no pain and he watched as it turned clear again. He realised that this was more serious, a black mark had gone against his record and Rosie looked at him and frowned. Too late he remembered Peter's advice. 'No bullshit!'

Helen Crompton spoke again. "We'll press on."

Steve appeared aged about seventeen. He was lying on a sofa with a pretty girl of about fifteen and as he kissed her he slid his hand up her thigh and under her dress. She resisted and tried to push him back.

"No Steve I'm not ready for this, stop it."

Steve tried harder and said, "You said you loved me, I love you so if you really love me, prove it." His hand struggled with hers and he moved his hand from her leg and fumbled at the buttons on her blouse. The girl didn't know what to do, she thought she loved Steve, he had said that he loved her, yet she wasn't ready for what Steve wanted. She felt that they should wait and she made a firm decision.

"No! Stop! I don't want to." She pushed Steve away, he fell off the sofa onto the floor, it was comical. The girl sat up and straightened her clothing. Steve was angry.

"You said that you loved me. If you loved me you'd prove it." Steve stood up and picked up his coat. He adjusted his trousers, he was obviously in an excited state and very frustrated.

"I do love you. Look Steve, I will make love with you, I promise but my sister is due home any minute. Meet me tomorrow after school, we'll go to my dad's shed, no one will see us."

Steve insisted. "Come on, what's wrong with now? You said you wanted to do it. Let's go to the shed now."

The girl hesitated and Steve took her in his arms.

"Look if you don't want to, if you don't feel ready for true love yet, I understand." He paused and looked at her. She looked at him.

"You do love me don't you Steve?"

"Course I do, come on."

The teenagers left by the back door and went into the shed closing the wooden door behind them. The film moved forwards and the scene changed. The girl was with her friend in the shopping precinct.

She saw Steve and called out to him. Steve heard her voice and looked around. He blushed and whispered to his friend,

"There she is, quick let's go." Steve and his friends laughed as they ran to the escalator and ran down the steps, dodging in between the shoppers.

Helen turned to Steve as the film ended.

"You know what happened don't you Steve?" Steve didn't reply, he did know what happened but Helen continued.

"That girl had an abortion Steve. You thought you were cool and you didn't give a damn!" She emphasised the word damn and Steve looked at her coldly.

"How did I know it was mine? She could have been going with every boy she met." Steve tailed off. He remembered Peter's advice and changed tack. "Yes, you are right. I was too young for a relationship, my friends would have laughed at me and yes, well maybe she was sleeping around. She might have been."

The egg changed to black and vibrated. Steve felt a severe pain in his heart. He clutched his chest and shut his eyes tight.

"You hurt that girl Steve and you didn't care if she became pregnant. If you had been, you would have used a condom. You also knew that she was a virgin, she told you, she trusted you. You hurt that girl and now you have a taste of the pain you caused her."

The film moved forward, it showed the girl and her sister with her mother and father. She had confided in her sister that her period was late and her sister had told her mother, she in turn had told her father. There was a family row, her father called her a slut, her mother defended her and the girl refused to say who the father was. The scene moved on. The mother and daughter were going into a clinic. She was about to have an abortion. The film ended and the court was in silence. The egg looked decidedly grey. Steve wasn't confident and wondered what else would be brought up.

Rosie spoke. "We move on five years to when you were twenty-two years old. By that time you had several girlfriends and you had finished your studies and started work. Nothing of note occurred until you went to that party where you drove home afterwards. Do you remember that party Steve? Do you remember what happened afterwards?"

Steve nodded and looked down at the ground. The film showed

Steve enjoying himself at a party. He was standing in the hall, the music was loud, people were having a good time and Steve was swigging from a bottle of lager. He was smartly dressed and proud of his new suede jacket. He looked as if he'd had a few beers and he flirted with a girl. Steve liked girls in tight jumpers and short skirts and was doing his best to make her feel special. Sue Grainger had only recently left university and all her friends were as broke as she was. She liked Steve, found him sexy and was impressed with his stories of how much he earned and of his fancy West-End flat. She kissed him and suggested that they look for a taxi. Steve felt for his car keys.

"It's raining hard, I have my car outside. We won't get a taxi easily, come on, I'll drive."

"But you are a little bit drunk, come on let's get a taxi, I'll phone for one from the pub." Steve grinned.

"This is my third, I'm not drunk. Look." He stood on one leg and tottered. "Honest, I'm okay, come on."

Steve and Sue got into his car, it was raining hard and Steve turned on the engine, pulled his seatbelt on and clipped it into place as he drove off. The scene showed the car on the main road and Steve moved his left hand to squeeze Sue's knee. She smiled; they both knew what would happen when they got to his flat. Steve only smiled at her for a split second before his expression changed. He wouldn't have seen the cyclist in time anyway. He had no lights, his black jacket and dark trousers weren't of any help either. Steve tried to brake but it was too late. The bicycle clattered under the car's wheels, the man hit the bonnet, the windscreen cracked and the man's body fell behind the car. Steve was shocked and just sat there. The rain came down harder.

Then after a moment, the girl opened her door and got out. She looked at the cyclist. He was dead.

"Shit! Shit! Shit!, Bloody Shit! Steve shouted. "Get in the car. Now! The girl looked again at the body, there was no doubt, the man was dead. She looked at his face, it was matted with blood and his eyes stared wide open.

"No, we can't go. We must get help." She looked around but the road was deserted. She called to Steve. "I'll call the police, I'll get an ambulance."

Steve's mind raced. He'd killed the cyclist. The stupid woman was phoning the police, he would be arrested and he'd end up in prison. He got out of the car. Part of him wanted to help, part of him wanted to run. He looked at the body, he too could see that the man was clearly dead. He looked at the girl, she dialled 999 on her mobile phone and was about to speak.

"I'll park over there." Sue nodded as she started to speak to the operator. Steve started the engine. He moved off slowly and took the first turning on the left. He knew that he should stop and park by the kerb but something in him told him to keep going. A hundred yards later he knew that he'd made the decision. He would go home. The girl didn't know where he lived, she didn't even know his surname. He relaxed. He had gone to the party on the recommendation of a friend from work who hadn't turned up. He didn't know anyone there and no one knew him. She wouldn't have taken his registration, she thought that he was simply moving the car to park.

CHAPTER 19

The film stopped and Steve looked down at his feet.

Rosie spoke. "Well?"

Steve sighed. "I should have stopped but there was nothing I could do. The man was dead. All that would happen would be that I would probably go to prison.

What was the point? I reasoned that if I had a chance to get away with it I should take it. As it was I did get away with it. I didn't get caught, the police never came."

Steve could feel everyone looking at him and the feeling wasn't pleasant. He was ashamed.

Rosie spoke again. "In your defence, it was evident that the cyclist was to blame. Watch the film."

The film started. The cyclist had come out of a town centre pub and he was clearly drunk, he unlocked his bike with difficulty and moved off from the kerb. A couple walked by on the pavement and the man shouted at the cyclist. 'Where are your lights?' The cyclist half turned and raised one finger in defiance and shouted back 'Bollocks!' He put his head down and raced on as fast as he could go. He was difficult to see in the poorly lit road and the heavy rain. When he got to the road, the cyclist was going much too fast, he leaned forward to brake but the rims were wet. The cyclist entered the main road at almost full speed, straight into the path of Steve's car. The cycle clattered to the ground as it hit the car and the cyclist struck the windscreen, rolled over the roof and fell to the ground, breaking his neck instantly. Steve winced at the horror of it but he felt marginally better. Everyone could see that he accident wasn't his fault.

Rosie and everyone else heard his thoughts, 'It wasn't my fault.'

"You were still to blame because you were over the drink driving limit. If you had been sober you may have spotted him a split second earlier, you may have swerved, he may have been injured instead of killed. In any event, the police would have blamed you and you would have deserved your punishment. But I want you to tell the court now what you did afterwards. Talk us through it Steve."

Steve looked up. "I read about the accident in the newspaper and found out that the dead man had a wife and two children. He was twenty-nine and he was a tyre fitter. The police were looking for witnesses, they didn't mention the girl I was with and maybe she ran off too. I never saw her again. I don't know what happened to her."

"I looked up his name in the telephone directory and found the address." Steve paused and looked around the court. "I knew that I couldn't do anything to bring him back but I knew that I could help in some way. I had the car fixed and I sold it, cashed the cheque and took the money to the house in an envelope. I rang the bell and a child answered the door. I gave his son the envelope and said that I was sorry to hear about his dad and that I hoped that this would help."

"Did you think that giving the family that money excused you?" Helen looked at Steve.

"No, of course not, but as you saw in the film, the accident wasn't totally my fault. I shouldn't have left him, but then he shouldn't have rode into a main road at full speed, with no lights and in dark clothing."

Steve looked at the egg. It remained clear.

Rosie continued. "We move on. We now see you on your twenty-fifth birthday. You have been promoted at work and you are now a sales manager. You and your friends have had a drink in the pub and you have decided to go to a nightclub. As you approach the club you see someone being beaten up in the alley. Roll the film please."

The film showed Steve and his friends walking down a side street to the nightclub. There was a queue at the door but it wasn't too long. As the group walked past the entrance to an alleyway, Steve looked down it as he heard a noise. A woman and a man were struggling and the woman was crying out, "Stop! Leave me alone." The man grabbed her by the lapels of her leather jacket and he threatened her.

"I've paid you, now do it!" The woman pushed the man away but he came straight back and hit her to the side of her head. She fell and Steve heard himself cry out.

"Hey you, pack it in." The man left the woman who was trying to get up and he stepped out from the shadows to face Steve. He was furious and Steve saw a knife in the man's hand. He looked rough in his dirty anorak. The fake fur around the collar made him look cheap.

"Come on then. You got a problem? I'll sort your problem." The man brandished the blade and challenged Steve. He froze. This was nothing to do with him, he was now in danger and all over a tart and some yob. Steve didn't move, he sensed that his friends had stopped and were watching. They would surely back him up. Suddenly he felt very alone. No one moved to help him but he knew he couldn't retreat. He opened his hands to show that he wasn't armed and decided to try and reason with the man.

"Come on now, no need to get upset. No one has a problem. Leave it. Leave it.

The man stood his ground. "She took thirty quid from me and then tries to run. I want my money back, I want it back now!" He shouted the last words and waved the knife at Steve and then pointed it at the woman who was sitting on the ground.

"Put the knife away. I'll give you thirty quid, just put the knife away."

The man was suspicious. "Why would you give me thirty quid? Is she a friend of yours?" He became aggressive. "Are you in this together?" He moved forward.

Steve spoke quickly. "I'm with my friends, look. I don't have anything to do with this but I'd rather give you thirty quid than get stabbed and it's not worth getting stabbed for thirty quid is it?" Steve attempted a weak smile.

The man held out his hand. Steve felt for the notes in his back pocket. He found two twenties and held them out. The man moved closer but he was careful. He held the knife in one hand and snatched the money with the other. He put it in his pocket and moved to pass between Steve and the wall. Steve took a step back and let him pass. The man turned the corner and disappeared into the shadows. Steve went to the woman. He helped her up. Her mouth was bleeding, her make-up had run and she was crying.

"Come on," Steve said, "go into the Club and clean yourself up in the ladies loo."

Steve took the girl by the arm and approached the doorman. He said a few words to him and pointed at the girl. The doorman could see that she had been attacked and he stood by to let her and Steve pass.

Rosie spoke. "You risked your life for that woman. You could have run away when you saw the knife in that man's hand and you knew that he was stupid enough to use it. Why did you give him the money?"

Steve shrugged. "I was frightened, I don't fight very well but I can sometimes talk my way out of situations. I didn't have much money but I guessed that if the man got his money back, he would be satisfied and have no more reason to hit her or stab me."

"So you agree that what you did was pretty stupid?" Steve looked up at her and saw that she was smiling.

"I suppose so, but I'm glad I did it. If I hadn't intervened, he might have killed her."

"And what happened then?"

"The woman cleaned herself up, I bought her a drink and she offered me the thirty pounds that she'd taken from the man."

"But you didn't take it did you?"

"No. I could see that she needed it and told her to forget it. She then left the club, she spoke to the doorman and later he thanked me, he told me that anytime he was on the door, I could come in free."

"So what did you learn from that Steve?"

"Sorry, I'm not with you."

"You did a stranger a favour and you risked your life for someone you didn't know. You wanted nothing from her in return and yet you made a friend of the doorman and every time you and your friends went back to that club, you were treated as a member and got in without paying."

"Yes I suppose so."

"Exactly. What you discovered is that when you help someone else, the favour is always returned. Not necessarily by the person that you helped but it comes back to you in another way."

Steve thought about this. He could see the logic.

"There were lots of other instances in your life that we could look at but the ones that we have seen give a good indication of the sort of person that you were when you were alive." She picked up her notes. "I see that you have been shown parts of Heaven and parts of Hell. Do you have any questions before you pass judgement on yourself?"

"I pass judgement on myself?" Steve was surprised at the statement. "Do I pass judgement on myself?"

"Why are you so surprised Steve? Who do you think passes judgement on you?"

"Well God of course."

"And do you see God here in this courtroom?"

Silence followed, Steve didn't know what to say. He looked around and he looked at the egg, it remained clear. He looked at Rosie, then at Helen Crompton, then at the others in the seats.

"But God is in this courtroom." He paused, unsure and then added, "Isn't he?"

"Of course he is, where do you think he is exactly?"

Steve was stumped, was this a riddle set to trick him? He thought back to his experiences with Michael, with Peter and with the others that he had met. The truth suddenly dawned. "God is here, he's everywhere. He is inside us."

"Precisely!" Rosie smiled. "He's in you, he's in me, he's in all of us and everywhere. He is a part of everything and he is everything. Now that you have understood that you can decide on your own judgement."

Steve chose his words carefully. "What exactly are my options?"

CHAPTER 20

Helen Crompton stood up from her seat and interrupted Rosie.

"I'm sorry for mentioning this now but before we progress any further with this judgement I think that Steve Rogers should be present when his wife is informed about his death."

Rosie objected immediately. She seemed worried. "I disagree. Whilst it is normal for someone who dies to be present in spirit form when their loved ones are notified about their deaths, no worthwhile purpose would be served by Steve being present." Helen stood firm.

"On the contrary, as it is normal for the spirit to be present I do not see why Steve should not attend. Can we have a decision please?" She looked at the egg and it remained clear.

"I respectfully request a decision with regard to my suggestion. Can Steve be present when my daughter, ahem, his wife, is told that Steve is dead?" Helen and everyone else looked at the egg. For a moment nothing happened and then it vibrated and remained clear.

Rosie then put her views. "I suggest that Steve is not present when his wife is told that he is dead." She didn't have long to wait. The egg turned black and vibrated.

"That's settled then, Steve must attend." Helen was triumphant.

Rosie turned to Steve and mouthed the word 'sorry'.

Michael left his seat and walked to where Steve was sitting. He didn't seem happy at having to take Steve home and he half apologised.

"Sorry about this Steve but you and I have to be present when your wife is visited by the police to be told that you were killed in your accident."

Steve shrugged. "Look that's fine with me. I feel as if my accident happened ages ago but I remember that you said that there is no time here and only a tiny fraction of Earth's time has elapsed." Steve followed Michael out of the courtroom, others were leaving too. Helen put her papers together and as Michael pushed open the door leading to the main hall, Helen walked through. Michael realised that she wished to go with them.

"Do you think that's a good idea?" He looked at Helen, he wasn't pleased.

"Normally no but if you don't mind I would like to be there when Steve arrives and you know you can't stop me anyway. Like you, I can go where I like and when I like."

Michael shrugged. "Okay, I will take Steve and we will see you there, I need to have a chat with him first."

Helen stood her ground. "Oh no you don't. You can chat to him afterwards. I want him to see what he should see."

Michael gave up arguing. He pressed the lift button and as the doors opened Helen entered. Steve followed and Michael came in last and pressed a button. The lift didn't seem to move and the doors opened again, they were no longer in the court building but on the pavement outside Steve's home. The house was well lit, it was raining slightly and the street lamps illuminated the front garden of the tidy semi-detached house. Steve noticed a police car coming slowly up the street. The driver was looking at the numbers and he stopped outside Steve's house.

Michael spoke to Helen. "Is this really necessary?"

Her eyes shone. "Indeed it is, indeed it is. Come and stand by the front door." The three spirits stood by the door as the policewoman rang the bell. Her colleague stood slightly behind her and straightened his tie. George Saunders hated telling people that their loved ones had been killed or injured. It was the worst part of the job. He was glad that Anna Witherwood had volunteered to do the talking. She was an excellent WPC and George liked working with her. She was always professional and had a human touch and could often defuse difficult situations by talking quietly and gaining people's trust. But this job didn't involve gaining anyone's trust, they were bringing news that would be bound to have a tragic effect on the victim's widow. Just a minute! Did the victim have any children? He was about to ask Anna when the door opened. A young woman aged about thirty wrapped her dressing gown around her body and pulled it tight. She frowned when she saw the police but she relaxed and listened as Anna spoke.

"Excuse me, I am WPC Anna Witherwood and this is my colleague PC George Saunders. Are you Jane Rogers?"

The woman looked at them and said, "Hold on a second please." She turned and called up the stairs. "Jane it's for you, it's the police." They could hear a voice from the top of the stairs. "Hold on a minute." A woman appeared. She was pulling on a T shirt over her head and doing up her jeans. She had obviously been changing her clothes.

"I am Jane Rogers, can I help you?" She looked at the policewoman and said, "Is anything the matter?"

Anna asked politely if they could come in. Jane's friend moved back and the police walked into the hall. Anna politely asked Jane's friend her name.

"I'm Vicky, Vicky Thompson."

"Well Vicky, I need to speak to Jane," she turned to Jane, "would you prefer Vicky to be present or should we speak alone?" Jane looked worried.

"No it's okay, Vicky's my friend. What is the matter please? You are worrying me."

Anna sighed, she would never get used to breaking bad news. "I'm afraid that we have some bad news. Your husband Steve Rogers was involved in a very serious traffic accident this evening. I'm very sorry Jane ..." Her words tailed off. Jane stood there, she didn't move. Her mouth opened, she tried to speak but she couldn't.

Vicky said, "Oh my God!" Anna put her arm out and touched Jane gently on the shoulder.

"Perhaps you should sit down, is there anyone that you'd like us to call?"

Jane stood there, she hesitated and then sat down heavily on the sofa. She tried to regain her composure but her hand covered her mouth. Anna and George never knew what to expect when breaking this kind of news. Sometimes people would just sit there without speaking; sometimes they would burst into tears and sob their hearts out. Once a man punched George hard in the stomach when George gently told him that his son had been killed in a motorcycle accident. The father said that he didn't believe it and shouted at George for playing such a terrible trick on him. That was George's worst ever experience. But as George watched Jane he realised that she was not taking the news well at all. She put her head in her lap and started to shake. She then lifted her head, there were no tears and she said,

"Are you absolutely sure it was Steve and do I understand that he's actually dead?"

Anna tried to be diplomatic and said that they were sure as they could be, they had found Steve's wallet containing his credit cards and diary and someone had told their colleagues who attended the accident that the victim was Steve Rogers. Jane's eyes flashed.

"This someone who told you it was Steve Rogers, would that someone be a woman by any chance, smartly dressed, blondish hair, dyed?"

Anna was embarrassed. "We wouldn't know, another crew took the details, we were asked to come and see you to tell you what happened and to ask you to identify ... " She didn't finish her sentence. Anna looked astonished as Jane clenched her fist and said,

"Yes, Oh Yes. Yes, Oh Yes!" George had been watching Jane carefully. There was almost a look of triumph in her face. Certainly there were no tears.

"Identify him? Certainly, I can identify him." She looked at Vicky who still looked shocked. "Do you want us to go now or shall we do this tomorrow?" Anna paused, she hadn't expected the victim's widow to act like this. She knew that shock might be delayed and she suggested that Jane attend the hospital in the morning.

"No, that's fine. We'll do it now if you please. I would like to know for sure, for absolutely sure, tonight." She turned to Vicky. "Get dressed Vicky; we need to do this tonight."

Steve, Michael and Helen watched the whole episode unfold. Steve had been surprised to see Vicky undressed except for a dressing gown. She was often spending time at their house, Vicky was Jane's best friend.

Jane ran upstairs and called out, "I won't be a minute, I'll just get a coat. Get dressed too Vicky, I really want you to come with me." Vicky followed her up the stairs. Helen nudged Steve and winked at him.

"Well big boy how do you feel about this then?" Steve gave her a puzzled look. Jane came down first and fastened the zip of her ski jacket. Vicky was dressed now and came downstairs and stood by the front door. Anna and George put their hats on as they walked to their patrol car and Steve watched as the two women got into the back of the car and George made sure that Anna and the two women put their seatbelts on before starting the engine. Steve watched through the car window. He could see Jane holding Vicky's hand very tightly. Then she leaned forward and whispered in her ear.

"I love you."

Steve flinched

"Satisfied now?" Michael whispered.

Helen smiled at him. "I think so. See you later Michael." She left and her spirit vanished.

"Do you want to go to the mortuary?" Michael could see Steve was stunned by what he had discovered.

"No thank you." Steve thought for a moment. "Do spirits of recently dead people normally go to the mortuary?"

"No, but they can if they want. Most spirits are there when their relatives are told of their death, that's of course if they aren't there when they die. Spirits can and do try to comfort their relatives and close friends and as you saw when that boy died in hospital, his spirit put his hands on his mother and father. They impart a tremendous amount of healing and warmth when they do that."

"I don't think Jane needed much healing then," Steve said.

"No I don't suppose that she did," Michael replied. Michael asked Steve a question, "Would you like to continue with the judgement hearing now or would you like to go to your funeral? It's just about to start."

*

Steve was surprised. Did he want to be there? Who would turn up? Would people cry? He wanted to see his dad again. His mother was dead but he would like to see his dad. "Yes, I would like to go please."

Michael and Steve walked along a leafy lane through the park. They had a few moments and Steve could see the first black hearse entering the cemetery gate. He wanted to ask Michael a question.

"Michael, when the egg turned clear and vibrated for Mrs Crompton and when it turned black for Rosie, was that God sitting in judgement and making a decision?"

Michael was patient with Steve.

"No it wasn't God. It was a decision made by everyone present. The egg reflects the feeling of those involved and it understands all the criteria needed to make the right decision. It rejects any bias that anyone may have and it reaches a decision that really, we all know is the right one. It effectively mirrors the feelings and judgement of everyone involved.

The two spirits walked to the grave as the mourners, all dressed in black, stood respectfully to one side. Steve could see his dad. Next to him was his mother, but that's impossible, he thought, his mother was dead and supposed to be in Hell. He then realised that his mother was there as a spirit. His father's eyes were moist. Next to him stood some relatives of his dad that Steve recognised. His Uncle Barry was there with his second wife. His Auntie Barbara wasn't there, a shame as he liked her. He noticed a group of the salesmen from his office. Sharon was dressed in black with a hat and a black veil. Her skirt was too short and next to her stood Mike Steadman and he was standing closer than Steve would have liked. He then saw Sharon's hand reach out for Mike's hand and he watched as Mike clasped Sharon's hand. Steve noticed Sharon nod to Mike and tilt her head. They watched as Jane arrived at the grave with Vicky. Maybe Sharon was pretending to be with Mike so that Jane wouldn't be upset. Sharon wouldn't know if Jane had guessed about her and Steve. Michael and Steve watched as the coffin was lowered into the grave. The priest said some nice words about Steve being a decent man and a good husband and he looked at Jane. He saw that Jane had her head covered by a veil and he was glad that he couldn't read her thoughts even if he wanted to. He preferred not to try.

The ceremony finished and Jane spoke quietly to the mourners and asked if they wanted to come back to the house for a drink, but something in the way she asked the question indicated that she wouldn't be too upset if they refused. People shuffled their feet and wanted to get away. His sales colleagues said that they needed to get back to work but instead they were going to the pub. Steve watched Sharon and Mike get into Mike's car and heard them say that they would meet the others at The Fox. Michael asked Steve if he wanted to go to the pub. Steve felt quite sad and heard himself making a weak joke.

"Do they serve spirits?"

Michael looked at him. "It's best that we don't go to the pub Steve. I have a better idea, come with me."

Michael saw that another funeral had just finished at the other end of the cemetery. They walked over and Steve noticed that the mourners were older. The spirit of a recently dead woman stood to one side with several other spirits of men and women in their seventies. As the ceremony ended, one of the mourners was passing out news to the others. "We are off to the house for a drink. Come along, everyone is most welcome."

CHAPTER 21

Michael and Steve slipped into the huge black Daimler just as the mourners got in and the spirit of the dead woman got in too and winked at Michael and Steve. Her husband sat down and the spirit of his wife sat on his lap. He couldn't see or feel her but he felt okay and was coping with this awful day far better than he thought he would. His brother, sister-in-law and his best friends took up the rest of the places. Even though there were six adults on the six seats, there seemed to be plenty of room for the spirits too.

"Well that went well as far as funerals go," said Jack Reilly.

"Sure, Patsy would have loved it," her sister joked. "Patsy loved funerals."

"More like the wake afterwards you mean."

Sean had been married to Patsy for forty-four years. He was a handsome man and as he watched his lovely Patsy being lowered into the grave he wished with all his heart that he was with her in heaven. How would he cope without his Patsy?

Jack noticed his brother trying to be brave. He knew his tears would flow again before the day was over. He put his arm around him and squeezed him.

"Come on Sean, we'll have a drink or two with the others. You are doing well, it will be okay, you are doing fine."

His sister-in law was Patsy's closest sister and now she was the last one of the Steed girls left alive. At seventy-two she was in good health and she and Patsy loved to sit for hours talking about their lives and looking at the family photographs. They had laughed a lot over the years, now it was over. Patsy was dead and Sheila was on her own. The spirit of Patsy looked at her sister and Steve watched as her hand reached out for Sheila's hand, she held it and squeezed it. Patsy smiled at Sheila who suddenly said,

"Come on, let's make this wake a true Irish send off for a great Irish girl."

The car stopped outside a pleasant family house with lots of flowers all over the garden and in baskets on the walls. The lights were on, the front door was wide open and within a few minutes everyone had arrived and people were clinking glasses and toasting Patsy and each other. As they drank, they exchanged stories about Patsy and everyone found time to spend a few moments with Sean to agree with him what a wonderful girl Patsy was. Steve and Michael spoke to Patsy in the hall.

"Sure I have a lovely family. Sean is a wonderful man and look there are my wonderful children and beautiful grandchildren." She turned to introduce another spirit. "This is my sister Phyllis. She passed on a few years ago but she was there to welcome me through after my operation. It was lovely to see you then Phyllis and lovely to be with you now. The surgeon was so upset that the operation failed, he just couldn't stop the bleeding."

"He did a good job and no mistake. After you died I remember thinking, I've never seen you looking so well."

"Excuse my daft sister gentlemen. You stay as long as you like. I'm going to suggest that they put some Irish music on now and have some dancing."

Patsy and Phyllis left Steve and Michael and went to whisper in Sheila's ear that it would be a great idea to put some music on. Steve asked how her husband would cope. Michael said that he would struggle but that he would be all right even though later on in the evening when Sean Reilly went to bed he would feel terribly alone. An image formed in Steve's mind.

*

Sean Reilly washed his hands as he finished in the bathroom. His starched pyjamas hung awkwardly and when he took his false teeth out, he suddenly looked old. He pulled back the covers of the bed that he'd shared for so long with Patsy and he lay there quietly. He thought about Patsy, that she had died and that he wouldn't see her again on this Earth and as he started to cry, his sobs shook the bed.

Steve saw a shimmering light approach Sean's bed. It was the spirit of Patsy. She sat on the end of the bed and Sean was startled. He definitely felt the pressure of someone or something sitting on the bed. Patsy stretched out her hand and stroked Sean's hair.

"There now, it will be alright Sean my love, you'll be just fine." She sat there on the bed as Sean stopped sobbing. He wiped the tears from his eyes with the edge of the bed sheet. Within a few moments he was asleep and the image in Steve's mind faded away.

"Come now," Michael suggested and he and Steve left the house to the sound of Irish music as several people got up to dance. "Everyone does it differently but by and large the best funerals are the Irish ones. They don't mourn their dead so much as celebrate their lives. They have a good attitude to life and death do the Irish."

"You sound almost Irish yourself Michael."

"Sure, haven't we all got a tiny bit of the Irish in us somewhere?" He did a little Irish jig and laughed. Steve was more thoughtful.

"And do most people who die come back to visit their loved ones?"

"Indeed they do, sometimes spiritual people who are alive on earth can feel their presence and some actually see them. You'll often see birds close to people after someone has died. Often a spirit will be around as a robin or as another bird that they liked though it's not really the done thing to soar overhead a street in suburbia as an eagle. Robins and sparrows and thrushes, are more suitable, or sometimes butterflies if it's the right time of year."

"So spiritual mediums who claim they can see spirits and help loved ones in grief, they are all genuine?"

"Woooah! Just hang on. No they are not all genuine but some of them are. Some mediums are genuine and can help grieving relatives and friends to come to terms with someone's death but not all mediums are genuine."

"So how can someone tell?"

"It's difficult but there is one rule of thumb that is right in ninety per cent of cases."

"And what's that?"

"If the person claiming to be a medium and able to contact spirits offers to do so for money or valuables then the chances are that the person is a fraud. They might have some abilities but the more they use their gift to earn money, the more they have to rely on guesswork and trickery. But if a medium refuses money or helps someone through a church or does it purely out of love then that's the best indication that the medium is genuine."

"So the spiritualist churches have the right idea?"

"Yes, but so do most of all the other religions. Basically any religion that isn't concerned with money, power or control will have good people who are able to communicate with spirits. Their priests, pastors, vicars, rabbis, preachers, healers whatever they may be called, their spiritual leaders are also in tune with spirits. Every religion in the whole world that believes in God has many people who can help grieving relatives to come to terms with their loss and whilst they might not always fully realise it, they are in touch with spirits who have died. Their gift is as natural as breathing."

"And who has this gift, is it a calling, is it really a vocation?"

"For some yes, but in reality, every single person has some ability to feel or see spirits besides their own spirit. Indeed children are often very psychic. Some children continue to feel and see other spirits as they get older, many lose the ability. But when they die, their own spirit is free and is then easily able to see other spirits just as you saw me and your grandad and now other spirits. It's natural isn't it?"

"You said that some spirits come back as birds. Is it just birds or other animals?"

"All animals, all birds, all living things have a spirit. From your own experience you have seen cats snuggle up and purr against some people but spit and hiss at others. You've seen dogs go to some people and wag their tails and then bark at others. Every animal has a spirit and spirits communicate with other spirits. Some happen to be nicer than others, just as some humans are nicer than others. Not every spirit gets on with every other spirit. Between you and me, I'm not over keen on Helen Crompton, your ex mother-in-law." He smiled.

"You and me both," Steve said and laughed. "So if every animal, bird and insect has a spirit, people shouldn't kill or eat them."

"They shouldn't be killed for pleasure or for sport, though sometimes Mother Nature will need humans to balance her world with culling. If a particular species is taking control, then yes, it needs to be reduced and Mother Nature may influence men to do her work if disease or accidents or freaks of nature aren't effective. Food too is obviously important as many animals are part of the food chain for the planet. The best indication is this. If an animal eats meat then it's not normally supposed to be part of the food chain but if it doesn't eat meat, then it may be. It's not one hundred per cent correct as we don't obviously see human vegetarians being eaten but it's a good guide. Some people eat dogs, though I wouldn't recommend it for everyone and some people eat horses, though I personally wouldn't as some of my best friends in spirit are horses. The spirits of those animals that we eat know that they are part of the human food chain, they don't mind, it's all part of their learning and understanding of how all spirits progress. But I tell you what does upset animal spirits." He looked at Steve to see if he was still listening. He was. Steve was fascinated.

"They hate it when they are part of the food chain and they are killed and then discarded. It's right to kill an animal for food, that's okay. But to kill it for sport or because killing it is enjoyable, well that's wrong."

"So people who go big game hunting for lions etc, people who kill animals for trophies …" Steve stopped talking. Michael urged him to be quiet. They had been walking through the streets and into a park. The scene changed. Steve and Michael were now in a National Park in a place that Steve guessed was somewhere in Africa.

Michael got down behind a bush. He pointed to a lion and whispered to Steve, "We are not in any danger from the lion of course but I don't want its spirit to see us just yet. Watch what happens."

The lion paced slowly through the long grass. It had smelt something. Away in a copse of trees there was a dead tree, by the dead tree sat a lioness, her cubs were resting quietly against her body. The lion picked up the scent of a recently slaughtered animal and as he came into a clearing it saw the remains of a shot zebra, its stomach cut open, the blood oozing onto the grass. The lion stopped and looked around, it saw no danger. Slowly it crept towards the zebra. A shot rang out and the lion rolled over and jerked for a few moments. A man dressed in khaki ran towards the lion and pointed the rifle at the beast ready to shoot again as it was clearly still breathing. A few hundred yards away, the lioness flinched again as she heard the second shot. Within moments other men had joined the hunter and they tied ropes to the dead lion. The carcass was pulled onto a trailer and hitched to a Land Rover. The hunter celebrated his skill and the others joined in.

"We are going back to finish your judgement now," said Michael, "but we'll just look in on something first."

Steve had been disgusted to see such a fine animal gunned down. He wasn't sure that he wished to see what Michael wanted to show him next.

CHAPTER 22

Michael walked to a tree and climbed it. He invited Steve to follow and they sat on a branch looking down. The tundra stretched for miles, there was no sign of the dead lion, the lioness or the cubs and the Land Rover and trailer had disappeared and the sun was setting. A beautiful red glow covered the horizon, the wind blew softly and there was no sign of the killing that had been done earlier. The world seemed at peace.

Steve heard a movement below. A man dressed in khaki shirt and shorts stumbled through a patch of thorn bushes, his hat fell off as he tripped and he cried out in pain as he grazed his knees badly. Steve recognised the man as the hunter that had shot the lion.

He had seemed joyful at his kill then, now he was scared, very scared. The man tried to get up and stumbled again. He lay very still. He listened. He crawled forwards to the base of a tree and pressed his back against the trunk. He was obviously exhausted and Steve watched him as he held his head in his hands. A rustle in the bushes startled Steve and he looked to his right. The hunter heard it too and his eyes flashed as he searched for the cause of the sound. Then he saw it. A magnificent lion moved through the brush and into the clearing. It stopped as it saw the man sitting there and it didn't move when the man raised his rifle to his shoulder. He pulled the trigger but all Steve could hear was a click. The gun was empty. The lion walked slowly towards the man, it stopped again and growled. The lion lifted his head and roared. The earth shuddered. Steve and Michael felt scared too even though the lion couldn't touch them. The hunter held his useless rifle by the barrel, he lifted it over his head as if he intended to defend himself with it but it made a useless club against an angry lion. The lion leaped at the man and he immediately fell over. The enormous jaws clamped over the man's head and the lion's teeth found their target as blood spurted from his neck. The lion stepped back from its kill and sat down. He twitched his head as a fly bothered him and relaxed. The lion seemed to have no further interest in his prey. Steve watched as a man and a woman walked calmly into the clearing. They were wearing casual clothes and they seemed to ignore the lion that was watching them. The man bent over the dead hunter and shook him. He moved a bit, then managed to stand but he was obviously in great pain. His head was badly bitten and there was a wide open bloody wound where his neck had been. The hunter was obviously very distressed but the man put his arm around him and asked if he was okay. The hunter nodded.

The man asked, "Which was worse, being hunted or being ripped apart?" The hunter tried to answer and managed to gasp.

"When I realised that I couldn't escape I felt the most fear. It was awful. When the lion pounced I thought that my head would explode but suddenly the pain stopped and I just drifted away." The woman looked up and saw Michael and Steve watching from their branch.

"Hi Michael, come down, it's over now." Michael slipped from the branch and landed neatly on the ground. He turned to Steve and suggested that he jumped too. Michael introduced Steve to Jerry and Margaret. The hunter was still rubbing his neck and Steve could see that the wound was healing fast.

"David is going through his Life Appraisal," Jerry smiled at Steve.

"Have you had your head ripped off by a lion yet?" Steve wasn't sure if he was joking, then he remembered.

"No I haven't but I did have my legs pulled off." He rubbed his thigh as he recalled watching himself as a small boy pulling the legs off a spider.

"That hurt but maybe having your head chewed off by a lion hurts even more?"

"I wouldn't recommend it." David tried to force a smile but his wounds were still aching. Margaret smiled at Steve.

"If people on Earth knew that they would have to suffer whatever pain they caused to others during their Life Appraisal then perhaps they would think twice. It's all very well being a big game hunter or a sports fisherman but if you decide to inflict injury or death on another living being then you have to appreciate that whatever pain you caused will all be returned to you. And if you hurt someone, who is already weak, or a child or an old person, when you get to taste your pain, it's multiplied by seven. And that can hurt believe me!" Steve shuddered. He thought about people who abducted and killed children. Margaret read his thoughts.

"Those monsters not only inflicted harm on their victims, the pain and anguish was also experienced by their victims' families, friends and neighbours. When they come to their Life Appraisal we have special teams waiting for them and can you guess who is in those special teams?" She looked at Steve and wondered if he knew.

"Sorry I've no idea. Devils?" Margaret laughed.

"Not bad! Not devils exactly but close. They meet spirits who have also tortured and killed. They meet spirits similar to themselves who took pleasure in their cruelty and didn't care how much they hurt others."

Steve shuddered. "So that's why he's here today. He hunted and killed a lion for sport and he's had to experience the feeling of being violently killed too."

"Do you think that's fair?" Steve paused and recalled the pain of his legs being pulled off.

"Yes it probably is. It's a shame that people on Earth don't know about this. They might behave differently."

"Funny you should say that but people who deliberately hurt or kill do know deep down that they shouldn't be doing it. After a while they manage to suppress their feelings but they do know. Believe me. They just don't listen to what their own spirit is telling them." Michael had been stroking the lion. He stood and said to Steve,

"Say goodbye Steve, we are going back now to finish your Life Appraisal David is halfway through his but yours is nearly over." Steve shook hands with Jerry and Margaret and the lion came up to him and rubbed its giant head against Steve's leg. It purred and Steve put his hands to the lion's ear and rubbed. The lion enjoyed that and Steve bent down and looked at the superb animal's face.

"Lovely to meet you Mr Lion. You take care of yourself." Steve jumped when he realised that the lion could speak.

"Nice to meet you too. My day turned out quite nicely after all."

CHAPTER 23

A haze covered the tundra and Steve noticed that the visibility was fading fast. He felt Michael close beside him and as the mist lifted Steve found himself back in the courtroom. The egg sat there on its box and Rosie and Helen Crompton were dressed in their gowns and wigs and sitting patiently at their places. Rosie turned in her seat and looked at Steve, she nodded to him and he smiled. He felt a little more comfortable. He had learned a lot and he knew that his judgement was nearly over. Rosie stood, cleared her throat and spoke. She carried on from where she left off when Helen insisted on Steve being present when his wife was informed of his death.

"You asked about the options available to you. Your options are these. You can ask to go straight into Heaven…" as Rosie spoke, the film showed Steve and Michael in the corridor looking into the room with the golfers. Steve was dressed ready to play and Michael was telling him that he could play later. The film then showed Steve skiing with Michael. Steve looked across at him and saw Michael sitting in his seat, he was blushing and looking down.

"Ahem! Apparently Michael can resist anything except temptation." Steve looked again at Michael following Rosie's gentle criticism. He blushed even redder and was clearly very embarrassed.

The film continued. Michael was briefing Steve not to say anything in the bowels of Hell and Steve was nodding, then the scene changed to the part when Steve's mother fell at his feet and Michael pulled him away. Steve felt that it would be all right to interrupt.

"Michael told me that my mother's presence in Hell would be

explained to me? Is that possible?" Rosie didn't say anything, she sat down and folded her arms.

Michael left his seat in the courtroom and came to the place where Rosie sat. He picked up a hand-held remote control and pressed a button. The film changed and showed Steve's father and mother in their younger days. Steve's father wore a pinstriped suit and his mother looked smart but tough in her business suit.

"Your parents bought properties in the town. They were cheap because they had tenants who were paying low rents and who could not be evicted. Your parents were supposed to treat those tenants with respect and not to hassle them." The film showed the couple talking to an elderly woman in one of the houses. His father was speaking.

"Don't worry Mrs Ridley, we will send the workman in this afternoon. The window frame is rotten, we are replacing it for you and it will stop the draught." The old lady wasn't sure but she thanked them and Steve's mother added, "they'll take out the old window and put in a new one. It will be much warmer."

The next scene showed two workmen removing the window frame and leaving a gaping hole in the wall. They put the frame into the back of their van and left. The old woman looked at the hole in dismay. Michael continued, "Your parents knew that the new frame hadn't been ordered. When Mrs Ridley phoned them later that afternoon, your mother said that the new window would be installed either late that afternoon or first thing Monday."

The film showed Mrs Ridley speaking.

"But I can't wait until Monday, it's freezing and I have to sleep in that room." His mother said, "I'm sorry Mrs Ridley but we are making improvements and you need a new window. You'll be much warmer when it's fitted." Michael pressed the pause button.

"Your parents had no intention of fitting that window in the foreseeable future. Mrs Ridley tried to keep warm that night but she couldn't. Her daughter collected her the following morning to take her to her own home but Mrs Ridley didn't recover. She caught pneumonia and died a few days later."

Steve was shocked.

Michael added, "Your parents bought houses with sitting tenants, they then pretended to make improvements but there were always problems with the replacement fittings. They took a bath out of one flat and left two elderly sisters with no water for over a week. They complained but your parents just made excuses. In the end, Social Services arranged for them to go into a home. Your parents doubled their money on that house within two months."

Steve felt ashamed. "That's terrible," he whispered.

"Your parents were known for their tricks but they didn't care. Laws existed to prevent abuse of tenants but your parents always claimed that they weren't abusing their tenants, they were improving their homes. They claimed that it wasn't their fault that builders and plumbers were unreliable. They might have got away with it when your mother was alive, indeed they made a lot of money and were only fined twice, and even then only paltry amounts." Michael continued, "After your mother was killed in an accident on holiday, she watched her life on this film and she was deeply ashamed of herself. She decided that she wasn't fit for Heaven and should be sent to Hell. She's there now and doing a totally useless job carrying fuel in buckets to furnaces that create heat for no-one. We don't need heat in Heaven, she does her work even though she knows it's futile. Your father is still on Earth, his judgement day is yet to come."

Rosie spoke. "So Steve, you've been shown quite a lot and you have a much better understanding of Heaven and Hell than when you first came here. What happens to you now is your decision. Are you worthy of Heaven or do you think you should go to Hell? It's your choice.

Steve tried to think. If he chose Heaven he would have a wonderful time, playing golf, skiing, doing all the things he would have loved to do on Earth. If he chose Hell, he would be able to help his mother, she hadn't lived a blameless life but she did appear to be suffering now. It was tempting to choose Heaven at once but Steve hesitated.

"Thank you for everything you have done and shown me." He nodded at Michael who smiled back at him and he nodded to Peter. "Of course Heaven looks wonderful and Hell looks awful, I expected that but I can't really accept Heaven and enjoy it knowing that my mother is in Hell and having a really bad time. Can I go to Hell and help her and maybe go to Heaven later?"

The egg suddenly turned black and vibrated.

"Oh, I see, it's not allowed." Steve thought hard, he remembered what Michael had said when they discussed Heaven and Hell and in between. "Contrary to popular belief, there is no purgatory where souls can go to be punished and then forgiven and sent to Heaven. It's a nice idea and some religions used it to persuade people that they could be forgiven for their crimes against others and then sent to Heaven."

Michael spoke clearly and added, "What did you learn from our journey through parts of Heaven and parts of Hell?"

Steve thought back to that time in the black car when they listened to the radio and talked. He remembered the radio being on and Michael tuning to another station because a preacher was asking for donations and promising salvation to those who gave. Michael had said, "We don't listen to that station."

"I feel, and I may be wrong," he paused, "Heaven and Hell are one and the same. It's not a separate place or two separate places but is something that is within us. It's how we relate to God and others and how we relate to ourselves." As he spoke he felt more confident. "Heaven is here, it's all around us, so is Hell," he paused again. "And so is God, God is within us and is not a separate being."

The courtroom burst into applause.

Helen Crompton smiled nicely at him and spoke. "So where do you choose Steve?"

Steve was firm in his reply. "I am in Heaven and Heaven is within me, I now realise that Hell is within me too and that it's my choice which state I live in."

The door of the courtroom opened and his mother came in, she was smiling.

His grandfather came in too and to Steve's surprise and delight, the lion followed. It swished its tail, walked slowly to the front of the courtroom and sat down. Steve saw that everyone he had met was in the courtroom and the egg was bright white and vibrating happily.

Helen spoke kindly, "You have achieved what was expected of you Steve. You are now ready for further training for more experiences. You will be part of the team that meets spirits as they depart from their mortal lives and come to be judged. You will help those spirits to judge themselves just as you have judged yourself."

Helen smiled and sat down.

Rosie took Steve by the hand, she beamed at him and he stroked her fingers.

"I feel that I have known you forever Rosie," She looked into his eyes.

"You will Steve, you will."

BOOK TWO

CHAPTER 24

Eternity really is for ever and ever and ever and ever and ever and ever and ever...

Deal with it!

(Shaman)

"Eternity isn't really forever – is it?"

The transition for a spirit from life as a human to the next life isn't normally too traumatic, after all, the spirit is within the human form and whilst it doesn't have total control over the mind, body and actions of the human, it is responsible for the human's behaviour and is often very happy to be released.'

Steve Rogers put the heavy book face down on the table and thought about what he was reading. His judgement was over, he was told that he was successful and his spirit guides Michael and Peter warmly congratulated him.

"The hard work starts now, but don't worry, you have the whole of eternity in which to do it." It seemed simple when Michael explained about eternity but Steve was worried. He tried to get used to the concept that he would live forever, not for a million or a billion years, not even for twenty trillion years. But forever. Wow!

And he was lucky! His judgement had ended well but it could have been a lot worse. Michael told him what happens to some spirits who fail to grasp the meaning of life. One woman that Michael had guided had seemed to understand what she was being shown but when she was asked at her judgement what she wanted to do, she replied that she loved shopping and asked if she could be sent back to Earth with a credit card with no limit and no demands for payment. As the others in the courtroom gasped, the egg vibrated and turned grey and she made things worse by asking if there was anywhere where she could have her hair done first.

Her defence had tried to save her by pretending to laugh at what must be her joke at the court's expense and asked her to say what she really wanted to do. Unfortunately she missed her cue and continued to file her nails. She was then asked to leave the court whilst a decision was made and it was decided that she would be sent back to Earth as a human for another twenty years but she would have to work in the cosmetic department of a huge store and learn to say, "Can I help you Madam?" and "Would you like to try this new perfume currently on special offer?" Apparently she was delighted and she was allocated a special guide who was able to stand for long periods under bright artificial light and talk about nothing in particular for hours on end to other spirits.

Steve was told to read his study books. Michael would come and see him to talk about any points that Steve wished to raise but Steve was bored. He didn't read much and preferred to learn by listening and discussing topics. He forced himself to concentrate and picked the book up again.

'Every living creature is affected by his or her spirit. In addition to the spirit allocated to each creature being born, other spirits would intervene from time to time and whilst some would be welcomed by the guide spirit, others would not. It is part of the spirit's duty to protect his creature from spiritual harm and to guide it successfully to a full and complete understanding of the meaning of love and life.'

Steve didn't regret the decision he made at his judgement. He chose to be trained to welcome spirits as they died and bring them through to be shown Heaven and Hell just as Michael and Peter had showed him around. But first he had to study and understand the role of the spirit within the living being. Steve had not been surprised to learn that all living creatures had spirits but he was shocked to discover that all insects, fish and even macrobiotic creatures all had an individual spirit too. He was told that he would meet some of these later and that he would talk to them about their lives and struggles. Steve had never had a conversation with an ant or a wasp before although he had killed a few in his time on Earth. He wondered if he would meet any that he had dispatched to an early arrival in the spirit world.

Steve looked up as the door to his room opened. Michael peered around the door and smiled at Steve. He was delighted to see him sitting on the edge of his bed and reading the books that Michael had given him. Steve was pleased at the distraction and welcomed Michael. He got up from the bed and pulled a chair across the room for Michael to sit down. Steve had chosen his furniture and furnishings himself and he had his room just the way he liked it. The large bed with a soft blue quilt dominated half of the room and Steve had chosen a smart desk and comfortable chair for his computer. At first he had selected a computer similar to the one he'd used as a human but he soon changed it when he learned about the latest models available containing 'Girl Friends Reunited', 'Select a date" and 'Celebrity Choice.' Steve would switch on his computer and play for a while after Michael had gone. In the meantime, he would have a chance to ask Michael if he could pass on from the theory lessons to the more enjoyable practical experiences. Michael pointed to Steve's computer and asked him if he was enjoying it. Steve was happy to put away his book and explain what he had been doing.

Last night Steve had sat with his computer and played happily for hours. Girl Friends Reunited intrigued him. He entered the name of an ex-girlfriend, her location when he last knew her and within seconds her image and details appeared on the screen. The image showed her as she was then, a click would move her on five years and another series of clicks would age her by five years at a time until she was two hundred years old. Once he had chosen the age at which he thought her to be most attractive, he could put on a headset and a pair of sensual vision glasses. He could either stay sitting at his chair or lie down on his bed. A handset enabled him to choose a place and a date and Steve punched in the most expensive hotel he knew of in the Caribbean. He selected the penthouse suite and planned a weekend with an ex-girlfriend doing all the things he liked doing, and more important, all the things he wanted to do to her. Last night he clicked on Cars, selected a red 1965 Ford Mustang convertible, chose the most sensational evening wear for a girl he remembered from school as Georgina Mackie, advanced her age from fifteen to twenty-five and dressed himself in a suit to shame James Bond. They then drove out along the coast road on a perfect balmy evening and discovered a wonderful seafood restaurant. At first he mistakenly selected Indifferent as her attitude for the evening and he couldn't understand why she wasn't so pleased to be going out with him. Then he realised his error and clicked Adoring and smiled as she snuggled up to him in the car and gently blew in his ear. He thought about experimenting by clicking Obsessive and Possessive to see what might happen but he decided to take things one step at a time on their first computer date.

Michael then noticed Steve's black eye. Steve blushed. At first he didn't want to tell Michael what had happened but Michael wasn't going to leave until he found out.

"I tell you Michael, Georgina Mackie is gorgeous. Just look at her picture on the screen save." Michael leaned forward, he was impressed. "We took the Ford Mustang, found this superb restaurant and had the most romantic meal. Afterwards, we drove slowly back along the coast road to the Hotel Terrifico and I invited Georgina back to my room. Of course she couldn't wait to get there…" He paused as Michael repeated, "Of course …" and he wondered for a moment if Michael was laughing at him. "I poured us some champagne and chose just the right music for a slow and very sensual dance." He paused and gently stroked the bruise on his left eye. "I was sure that she wanted me to kiss her and so I put my hands gently on her cheeks, pulled her slowly towards me and just as I was about to kiss her in the most wonderful way I know how, she took a step backwards and clouted me with all her strength." Michael covered his mouth with his hand so that Steve wouldn't see his smile.

"And why do you think she did that?" Michael couldn't help but grin.

"At first I had no idea. I was so shocked that I pressed Exit. I just wanted to get away. Then after a few minutes I switched the computer on again and entered her details. This time I read the instructions and could see that I had made a fundamental error. I had failed to discover what became of Georgina Mackie after she left school. I didn't believe it at first. She had only become a bloody nun!"

Michael roared with laughter. "You made another mistake too. You can select your ex-girlfriend, choose a location and a date to take her out but if you try kissing her or anything else you first have to ask her to put you in her own computer favourites. Just because you might like her, she has to like you too if any relationship is to occur, even if it's only on computer."

"But why did she agree to go out with me if she'd become a nun?"

"She didn't agree, you didn't ask her, you just assumed that she would come and so you pressed all the buttons to plan a date. Georgina Mackie remembered you when she was fifteen and you were seventeen. You apparently asked her out and she was delighted. Then after you had spent an evening smothering her in slobbery kisses and manhandling her, you had the nerve to tell her that you really liked her friend Katie Chapman and would she mind if you asked Katie out as well? As you can imagine, Georgina wasn't impressed with you and one of the reasons she agreed to accept your computer date was to give you a good smack." Michael leaned his head slightly to the right and peered at Steve's eye. "She did hit you rather hard, didn't she?"

"Umm, yes she did." Steve brightened. "I was going to study for a bit longer and then try Celebrity Choice this evening. But I think I'll read the instructions first."

"Who will you choose?"

"I thought I might take Kylie Minogue out, or maybe Sharon Stone or maybe Marilyn Monroe." He paused, "Or maybe all three!"

"Good choices but do get some experience first before taking classy women to classy places. If you choose a busy restaurant or nightclub idiots will pester you. I suggest somewhere quiet at first where you can talk and then if you like them and they like you, you can ask the girl to put you into her Favourites and then it's up to both of you where you go from there." Michael offered more advice. "And don't go taking out more than one at a time until you are very experienced and have lots to talk about."

"Lots to talk about, like what?"

"Exactly, you can't just ramble on all evening how you once had a Porsche and that you caught a taxi just after someone famous got out of it. That will bore them stiff. You need to get some experience and star in a few films or be a Prime Minister or something."

"How do I do that?"

"Easy, you log on to Be a Star Tonight, scan in your image and c.v. and the computer will appoint you an agent and he'll get you some part offers in new and old films. If you fancy playing say James Bond in *The Man with the Golden Gun*, you will be cast, trained and then given your lines to learn. You will be taken to beautiful locations, treated like royalty and have the most wonderful time. Then when you take Kylie Minogue or anyone else out for dinner, you will have something to talk about."

"This is marvellous, I'm really going to enjoy it here in Heaven."

"Oh this isn't Heaven, playing computer games and pretending you are a film star isn't Heaven Steve. You won't be in Heaven until you know that you are in Heaven."

"And how will I know?"

"Well for a start, it's not being in or going to exotic places and having wonderful material things that will bring you Heaven but proper relationships. And not just relationships with pretty pop stars or sexy actresses but one to one relationships with people that really matter to you. You'll find that happiness in the simplest of places. That's Heaven. Don't confuse what you are doing now with that. The games you can play here are just for fun and for you to experiment and learn from."

"So how come you knew all about Georgina Mackie being a nun? You were watching me on some closed circuit television system weren't you?"

"Of course not, I don't need to. Just one look into your mind tells me everything that you have been doing, what you have been thinking and what you intend to do next."

"My goodness, you would make a typical wife on Earth. I would have hated to be married to you."

"Why Steve, most men are married to wives that know everything. Tell me, is a man at his cleverest before he makes love to a woman, during their love making or afterwards?"

"I have no idea, before I expect?"

"No, it's during their love making, that's when he's connected into Miss Know It All." Michael smiled and Steve roared with laughter. Neither Steve nor Michael heard the door opening behind them and they didn't see Rosie come into the room.

"Ahem!" Steve and Michael turned and faced her.

"Oh hi Rosie, Michael and I were just…"

"I know what you were just..." Rosie grinned at Michael. "I see Steve is playing games instead of studying. Yes he does have all the time in the world but if he's going to help us with the new arrivals, he'd better get a move on. We are expecting a full complement of passengers from an air crash and any help Steve can give would be appreciated."

Steve blushed. "Yes I'm sorry, I'll put the computer away for now and I'll read up on my lessons. Sorry, I really would like to help."

Michael stood up and went to the door. "Read the chapter titled 'Sudden Transformation,' if you can help with the aircraft passengers that would be appreciated. In the meantime, read as much as you can and someone will come for you when we need you."

CHAPTER 25

'When a spirit leaves its body it is for one of two reasons. The human body is either too frail to support life or it has been damaged too badly by disease or injury to continue living. Every creature dies from one single cause. A lack of oxygen to the brain. If the head of a creature is removed from its body, the brain will continue to function as long as oxygen is fed in the correct dosage to the brain. The spirit can only leave the body once the supply of oxygen has ceased and the brain ceases to function.'

Steve read this and sat deep in thought. He recalled reading about executions that took place during the French Revolution. As the masked operators of the guillotine despatched the French aristocracy to a messy death, they sometimes held the head of the despised victim high in the air so that the public could jeer. Historians noted that although the heads were totally separated from their bodies, the expressions of the dead would change and several members of the aristocracy were seen to scowl at the mobs that cheered their demise. One report described an executioner who lifted a head from the basket by its hair and showed it to the crowd. Their gasps of horror caused him to look at the face full on and he was astonished to be presented with an evil look that had obviously been created after the blade had severed the head. He dropped the head in shock and it bounced into the terrified crowd that broke and ran away in panic thinking that the ghost of the dead man was after them. Steve thought that this was funny and he chuckled.

'When the spirit leaves the body it doesn't immediately leave the area of death unless it specifically wants to. Usually the spirit will wait a while especially if relatives and friends of the deceased person are present. The spirit will meet with other spirits and may try and help the bereaved to be calm and to come to terms

with their loss. The same will happen with animals and other creatures. When a bonding occurs with any other living creature and sadness and pain is present, spirits will do what they can to make the transition easier for all those involved whether they are present at the death or not.'

Steve made a mental note to ask Michael some questions. Was the spirit in the brain of a person? The book stated that the brain would die once there was no supply of oxygen and that the spirit would leave when this happened. Did the brain therefore contain the spirit?

Steve put the book down and lay back on his bed. He stared up at the ceiling and thought about where he was. He knew that the ceiling, the walls, the furniture and the room didn't really exist as they had done when he was alive and he accepted that everything was an illusion designed to help him to adapt the transition of his spirit being in a human body to a non-bodied spirit in a totally different world, yet in a world intertwined with the world he had just left. When he thought about it, everything seemed to be simple and uncomplicated. It was a person's spirit that was permanent, not their body or their looks, or their possessions. Michael had once suggested that he should regard the living body as one would a vehicle. When a vehicle is being operated properly and is in good condition, it will transport its occupant wherever it chooses to go. The vehicle needs regular attention and sustenance and if it's well looked after it will be more efficient than if it isn't. But when it can no longer function, the vehicle will return to its basic components and will no longer be serviceable. That's when the occupant needs to move on, either by itself or in another vehicle.

A buzzer sounded somewhere inside Steve's room. Then someone knocked on Steve's door and a voice called him to come to Reception because some new intakes would soon be arriving from an aeroplane crash. Steve knew what he had to do but he felt nervous. Michael showed him that when spirits arrive from their earth bodies they are met at the point of death by other spirits, some are relatives, some are friends and some are there, as Michael was for him, to welcome them through and ease their panic. Sometimes when someone died, no spirits would be present and as the body started to deteriorate, its spirit would be left near the body or the place of death awaiting help, guidance and instructions. If they weren't helped they would wander around until another spirit met them. Sometimes a spirit would be confused and would not go with other spirits. They might want to stay with their earthly body or the place where the body had died and they would flatly refuse any help offered. These spirits became frustrated and angry and would try and manifest themselves or cause commotion. Steve had read about ghosts and poltergeists and he knew that the only way to exorcise a troubled spirit was by persuading other spirits to help it to move on. He had once read a story about two children who were living in a large and draughty old house. They were playing hide and seek with their cousins and discovered a marvellous hiding place under a windowsill. When they lifted a wooden lid, they found that they could push past a flap and hide in a tiny alcove but they were trapped when the flap closed and they couldn't escape. The other children failed to find them, they called for help and scores of people searched the house from top to bottom but they couldn't find them either. Years later, the house was abandoned because no one could live in it. There were many sightings of the children as ghosts and poltergeist activity wrecked the living areas. Eventually priests trained in exorcism were called and one of them acted as a medium to contact the children's spirits and those of their long since dead relatives. The medium was told about the hiding place and when it was opened, the children's bodies were found. They were removed and buried and the ghosts and poltergeist activity ceased. The spirits of the children had refused to pass through to the spirit world until the mystery of their death had been discovered.

The buzzer sounded again. Steve guessed that the arrivals from the aeroplane crash had arrived and that he would be required to help. Michael told him that he would be trained to welcome spirits and to help them pass through and then eventually show them around Heaven and Hell and help prepare them for their Life Appraisal, just as he had been. Steve was nervous about his first contact.

The reception area was very busy. Around two hundred people were moving in lines and Julie had been joined by other spirits to help process arrivals and to issue nametags. Most of the people seemed very confused and tired. Some however were acting aggressively and one man was pounding on Julie's desk in anger. She continued to smile at him and as she handed him his nametag he snatched it from her and stuffed it in his pocket. He demanded to know the reasons for the delay to his flight and as he became angrier, he stamped his foot. Steve saw Michael moving smoothly through the queues of people waiting in line behind the angry man. Michael politely and gently made room for himself behind the man's back and he raised his right hand and placed the palm of his hand gently against the back of the man's head. Instantly the man became quiet, his aggression left him and he stood silently. Then he wiped his mouth with the back of his left hand and apologised to Julie.

"I'm sorry if I was rude. It's just that we have been badly messed about. The flight was delayed, we had endless security questions and once we actually took off ..." he paused, Steve could see he was confused. "Once we took off... er. Look just how did I get here, we were in the air not five minutes ago? We didn't land anywhere. I'm sorry young lady but could you please tell me how I got here?"

Julie looked around and saw Steve, she called him over.

"Excuse me Steve, could you please help Mr Owen, he's a new arrival and seems to be quite confused?" She turned to Mr Owen. "If you would kindly go with Mr Rogers, he will explain everything, thank you Steve."

Steve was flustered. Julie had passed him a difficult passenger who had just been killed and she had accepted Steve's ability to handle the situation without question. Steve needed to think quickly.

"Hello Mr Owen. If you'd like to come with me, I'll see what I can do to help you." He looked at Michael who was still standing at the head of the queue. Michael smiled at him and made a suggestion.

"Why not take Mr Owen into that room. All you need is in there. You know how to operate the screen."

Steve looked to see where Michael was pointing. He suggested that Mr Owen should follow him and he left the main reception area and pushed open the door of the small room.

Steve invited Mr Owen to be seated on a comfortable brown leather sofa. He then sat on the edge of a table and tried to appear relaxed. He knew that he had to be calm yet remain in control. It was important for him to be in charge of the situation and he didn't want Mr Owen to become upset again and start shouting.

"Can you please tell me what's going on? Are you an employee of World Airlines and what is your position here?"

Steve remembered how Michael had introduced himself at Reception and how he had shown a film of Steve crashing his car. He picked up the remote control device from the table and pressed the play button. As he did so, a screen came down against a wall and the lights dimmed.

He said, "Let's see what happened to you Mr Owen." The scene opened to show a queue of passengers waiting to check in their luggage and receive their boarding cards. Mr Owen was an impatient man. He clicked his teeth and tapped his right foot. He didn't have a suitcase, just an overnight bag and a laptop computer in his briefcase. He was only going for one night and he needed to be back on time ready for a director's meeting. He wasn't looking forward to the meeting with his client either. Mr Owen had been entrusted with getting local authority planning permission for the client's new building and it had transpired that the local authority had complained because the application hadn't been completed properly. Not only did Jack Owen have to placate the client, he also had to ask the planning official to accept a new application form and backdate it.

The queue for ticket allocation moved forward very slowly. The red-haired check-in clerk asked everyone if they had any electrical items and if they had packed their own bags. No Mr Owen had not been asked to carry any items for anyone else. He picked up his ticket and boarding card and sighed as he saw yet another, even longer queue. He would need to join that queue now if he wanted to catch his flight and he realised that he had no time to buy a newspaper or a coffee. The film continued to roll and the camera left Mr Owen and zoomed in on two men and a woman who were also passing through the security control. One of the men seemed very nervous and he almost dropped his bag. The woman hissed at him from the corner of her mouth and he apologised. Sweat broke out on his forehead. The nervous man put his bag on the conveyor belt and the X-ray machine displayed its contents to a bored security officer. Her eyes scanned the interior of the bag and it looked fine. His companion's bag was also scanned and the woman put a small briefcase on the belt but held onto her handbag. A security man asked her politely if she could place it on the belt but she refused. She said that she had important film in her bag and that the X-ray might destroy it. The security man explained that the film would not be damaged but the woman insisted. She had once had a whole film ruined and she was unwilling to put the film through the X-ray but she was happy to empty her bag of the film and put it through without the film. The security man could see the line of passengers getting restless. He took the bag from the woman, removed three rolls of film and put the empty bag through. His colleague scanned it, it was fine. He then took the bag from the belt and dropped the film into it and smiled. The woman thanked him and put the bag on her shoulder.

Jack Owen watched himself going up the steps of the aircraft. The plane would be late taking off and his client would be irritated at its late arrival. He slumped down in his seat and snapped his seat belt into the lock position. He could work on his laptop later and he reached for the in-flight magazine in annoyance because he didn't have a newspaper. The two men and the woman sat in the row immediately in front. Jack Owen didn't take any notice of them, he was hoping that no one would sit next to him and he deliberately left his laptop on the adjacent seat. As the passengers boarded, the seats filled up and he sighed as he tugged the laptop out of the way to make room for a plump woman and her overweight husband.

As the final passengers boarded, the stewardess shut the heavy cabin door and the safety announcements began. Jack had seen these hundreds of times before and he casually looked away as if watching the safety demonstration gave him away as a nervous flyer. Jack Owen wasn't a nervous passenger but as he travelled by air so often he did feel that one day he would be on an aeroplane that would be involved in an emergency. He looked casually at the passenger on his right. He was squashed up against the window seat and the lady's arm was on his side of the seat divide. He decided against asking her to move it as his attention was caught by something unusual. The man in the middle seat of the row in front was showing signs of discomfort and kept mopping his brow and beads of sweat ran down his face and neck. He looked a strange colour and the man was clearly terrified of flying.

The film showed the aeroplane taxi to the holding position. The pilot completed his checks and lined the nose wheel on the yellow line. They were cleared for take-off and as the nose wheel straightened, the pilot applied full power and the engines roared into life. The nose wheel lifted as the pilot pulled back on the controls and the aircraft and two hundred and three passengers and crew climbed through a thin scattered cloud base and towards an altitude of thirty thousand feet. As the pilot reached four thousand feet, he banked the wings to the left and headed out towards the centre of the city with the coast dead ahead.

The woman in front of Jack Owen was busy. She took the film containers from her bag and placed them on her knee. The man in the aisle seat reached into his bag and pulled out what looked like a pencil. He handed it to the woman who looked at the sweating man in the middle seat. She nudged him hard and he put his hand in his inside pocket and pulled out his wallet. He opened it and took out a small thin bag containing a white powder. He seemed even more scared as he handed it to her. The woman screwed what looked like the pencil into the film canister. She took another canister and prised off the lid. She tore the paper of the bag holding the powder and poured it in. She then pushed the plastic cap back on. She placed the two film containers together and she pressed the point of the pencil rod against the film case. She then nudged the man in the middle seat. Jack Owen hadn't seen any of this during his flight but he was carefully watching the screen now. The man in the middle seat didn't move at first, the woman nudged him again, harder. He leaned forward and took off his shoe. It wasn't really a shoe, more a heavy working man's boot with a thick sole. The man in the outside row lifted his newspaper in front of him. He didn't want the stewardess or the passengers in the next aisle to see what they were doing. The stewardesses wouldn't have seen anyway, they were firmly buckled into their own seats for the take-off.

The Boeing completed its turn at six thousand feet and Jack could see that they were right over the centre of the city. The woman in front of him held the film canisters and the pencil rod firmly in both her hands. The sweating man in the middle seat brought up his arm with his heavy shoe held firmly in his right hand. A passenger on the other side of the aisle looked up, he'd seen the movement despite the carefully positioned newspaper. The boot came down, the reinforced heel struck the pencil rod and it pierced the top of the first film canister, went straight through the middle of it and into the second canister. The explosion blew a gaping hole in the side of the aircraft and the plane tilted to one side. The passengers in the rows in front and behind the bomb were killed instantly by the blast and others started to scream as the dust and papers flew around the aircraft. The terrorists had chosen their window seat carefully and the woman knew that her seat was right over the bolts securing the port wing. As the pilot fought to control the stricken aircraft, the port wing almost held but as the floor took most of the force of the explosion, the strut buckled and as the wing slowly curved upwards, it tilted ninety degrees into the airflow and its mountings tore off. The pilots wrestled with the controls but the control column waggled uselessly. Like a giant sycamore leaf, the aircraft tumbled out of the sky and exploded as it fell into a park. If the explosion had occurred just five seconds earlier or later, the stricken plane would have landed on a school or a factory.

Steve looked at Jack Owen's face. It was white and Jack didn't speak at first, then he muttered under his breath. Steve caught the word 'bitch'.

Steve watched Jack's face with interest. He remembered his own feelings of confusion when Michael told him that he had been killed in his crash in the Porsche. Steve thought that someone was playing a practical joke and setting him up. When he watched the film of his own death, he felt very much alive but odd. He asked Jack to describe his feelings on watching the film of his death in the bombed aircraft.

Jack sat quietly, he then put his head down, raised his hands and held his face covering his eyes. Steve waited for Jack to speak. Jack lifted his head and looked at Steve.

"I feel weird, I know that I am dead but I don't feel dead. Indeed for the first time in months the pain in my back has gone. I trapped a nerve in the bottom part of my back last year. Everyday I've had to take pain killers but they never got rid of the pain totally." Jack stood and stretched. "The pain has gone, I feel bloody fantastic!" He laughed and Steve smiled at him.

"What happens now, and how come you are here?"

"I died in a car crash. A lorry pulled out of a side road and I tried to avoid it. My car was a beautiful silver Porsche 911. It rolled and I was killed instantly. Like you I arrived in Reception and my Guide showed me a film of my death so that I could understand what happened to me. He then showed me around Heaven and Hell and I was able to meet other spirits and find out the answers to any questions that I wanted to ask. I expect that the same will happen to you. Then I was taken into a courtroom where my life was shown. Not all of it, but there were important parts and I had to explain my reasons for the bad things I did. At the end a decision was made on what would happen to me and this is where I've ended up, helping you to come to terms with your death."

"Why have you come to help me specifically?"

"I don't know really, I expect it was because you were making a fuss and being a nuisance. Everyone else seemed to be waiting in line and they were being patient. I was asked to help generally and then I was asked to help you specifically. Sorry but I can't be any more help than that."

"You said that you were shown Heaven and Hell, will I be shown Heaven and Hell?"

"I expect so but I can't show it to you."

"Why not?"

Steve hesitated. "Because I don't know where the rooms are that Michael showed me. I don't know the way to Hell. I'm really new to this and I am trying to take it all in." Steve looked up as the door opened and Michael entered the room.

"I'm sorry I had to leave you Steve, it's chaotic out there and we are trying to get everyone sorted out." He looked at Jack. "Have you seen the film of your death?"

"Yes I have, I didn't feel a thing when I died, one minute I was sitting in the aircraft, the next I was here." He glanced at Steve. "Steve's been telling me that I'll get to see Heaven and Hell and that I will be judged but that he doesn't know where Heaven is yet."

Michael raised his eyebrows and looked at Steve.

"Steve doesn't know where Heaven is?"

"He means the rooms. You remember. You showed me the rooms, we went skiing…" Michael interrupted.

"But that's not Heaven Steve, I thought that you understood, Heaven isn't going to exotic places or doing nice things, Heaven is when you are truly happy in yourself and that's most often experienced in a relationship. All those hobbies, pursuits, tangible things, they are all pleasant enough but they aren't the real Heaven. You haven't been there yet but you will and maybe you will experience Heaven very soon." Michael opened the door. "Jack, Steve, come with me please, we have to get started."

The reception area was chaotic. Julie and her colleagues did their best and other spirits were helping. Passengers were taken into a large room with lots of round tables and hundreds of chairs. Spirits sat at some of the tables and were scanning the faces of the passengers as they entered the large room. Some called out to the passengers.

"Hey Donald, Donald Price, over here Donald."

Another spirit shouted, "Mary Purrell, can you hear me Mary, come and sit here?"

Some spirits had already found their passengers and they were chatting happily at the tables. The passengers looked relaxed and happy to be with their old friends and relatives and some had cups of tea. A few of the tables had children and one old lady bounced a baby on her knee. She was happy to be there and the baby gurgled with pleasure.

A woman called out, Steve thought that she was talking to him but then she said Jack's name.

"Jack Owen, it is you, how the devil are you?" Steve and Michael winced at the term devil but Jack stood transfixed. The broad smile on his face was of pure pleasure. He threw his arms around her and clasped her tightly. He then dropped his arms and stood back.

"My God! Valerie Pemberton. It's wonderful to see you, is it really you? You look wonderful." He paused and turned to Steve. "Valerie meet Steve, Steve's been helping me, I haven't had a good journey." He frowned but Valerie burst out laughing.

CHAPTER 26

Valerie was still laughing when she sat down. She pulled a chair close to hers and she squeezed Jack's hand tightly. He sat next to her and looked up at Steve.

"Valerie and I were good friends once."

Valerie interrupted. "We were more than good friends Jack." She blushed slightly and smiled at Steve.

"We were lovers and we were going to get married. Unfortunately I was a victim of a serial killer and I arrived here thirty-five years too early. I felt so sorry for you Jack."

She still held Jack's hand as if she couldn't let go. She had a happy face and a slightly plump figure. Her hair had been dyed red so many times it was starting to look thin but overall she was pleasantly attractive and she looked younger than her thirty-eight years. Steve suggested that Michael and he left Valerie and Jack to talk about past times but Michael said that they would stay awhile if that was okay with Valerie and Jack. Steve saw a movement and a pot of tea, four cups and a jug of milk appeared on the table. Steve looked at Michael, he didn't have to say anything as a plate of éclairs arrived as well. Steve sat down and reached for an éclair and Michael moved behind Valerie and pulled up another chair. Valerie smiled.

"I can't do that yet, I can't make pots of tea and chocolate éclairs arrive just like that. I can do glasses of water though." She squinted her eyes and held her breath. Nothing happened at first but then a goldfish bowl arrived full of water and with two fish swimming around. Michael grinned at her. Steve and Jack were astonished and Valerie burst out laughing again. She certainly seemed to be a very happy person.

"Oh would you look at that? It's Romeo and Juliet, they were my fish when I was a little girl. They are with me now but I left them in my room. I wanted water, I got my fish." She giggled again.

Steve was starting to get uncomfortable with her constant laughing and giggling. 'She's starting to drive me mad,' he thought but stopped as he sensed Michael frowning at him.

"You'll get the hang of it. Don't just concentrate only on the water, concentrate on the glasses as well. If you just think about water, anything could arrive from a thimble full to a swimming pool, concentrate on the glasses as well and they'll come too."

"Moving liquids and matter by thought transference is great fun but I'm always getting it wrong. I'll take your advice though Michael. Thanks."

She turned to Jack. "I've asked if I can be your Guide around Heaven and Hell and to help you with your Life Appraisal, would you like that Jack?"

Michael spoke. "Valerie you are not yet ready for this level yet but I can advise you that you can be part of the training process. Indeed, Steve needs to learn much more too and I have been authorised to allow you both to watch Jack's induction and his Life Appraisal." He turned to Jack. "Will it be alright with you if we have two trainees along for the ride?" He expected Jack to agree and he wasn't disappointed.

"No, that's fine. I'm so happy to see Valerie again. I did love you so very much Valerie …" He stopped as a commotion was heard in Reception.

The two men and the woman that Steve and Jack had seen blowing up the aircraft were involved in a scuffle in Reception. Michael turned to watch through the large glass partition separating the room from the Reception area.

The woman was shouting something and Julie was standing up at her desk and trying to calm the woman down. As she spoke, three men in white uniforms arrived and grabbed the arms of the woman and her two male colleagues. They were invited to go with a men in white uniforms and there was no fuss. Steve watched too, he was fascinated, he hadn't seen any signs of officialdom at all on his tour through Heaven and Hell or at his Life Appraisal. Clearly there was a force of some kind to maintain law and order.

Michael spoke. "The woman and those two men, they were responsible for blowing up the aircraft and they won't go through Reception in the normal way. They will be taken to a different part and they will have a specialist team working with them. Before they can see Heaven or Hell they will need to spend some time reflecting on their actions and thoughts and they will need a lot of anger management training before they can even start to understand what they have done."

"But won't they go straight to Hell?" Jack asked Michael.

"You will find out about Heaven and Hell just as Steve did and is still doing. If you wish we can look in on their induction course as we go through your Life Appraisal. The teams that work with terrorists, political murderers and those who have been brainwashed have to help their subjects come to terms with how they are thinking before they can be even close to being judged. It's a fascinating experience for the guides involved and you may find it very interesting too." He smiled at Valerie.

"How do you feel that you are progressing?"

"Oh I'm doing ever so well." She giggled again and Steve stiffened and muttered under his breath.

"If she giggles once more, I'll…"

Michael interrupted. "It's just nervousness," he said to Steve. "We all handle stress in different ways and whilst most of the stress you had as a human is almost gone, you will feel some stress for a while longer. When something or someone seems to irritate you, instead of thinking about what is annoying you, think instead of something that you like about that person, you'll then be able to cope much better."

Steve was embarrassed and he looked at Valerie sure that she would be annoyed with him. But Valerie and Jack hadn't sensed Steve's annoyance at her constant giggling and they hadn't heard Michael's advice. They were busy talking to each other and whispering. Steve could see that they were both delighted to be in each other's company.

"I had to confront my murderer." Jack was surprised.

"He stole your life and he killed others too. What on earth did you say to him?"

"Before I met him face to face I watched a film of his life and I learned a lot about him."

Michael stood up. He smiled at the others and said, "It would be lovely to sit and chat all day but we really do have a lot to do. Steve, you and I have to look in on some of the initial interviews with passengers that have just arrived."

"Valerie," he turned to face her, "why don't you take a walk through the gardens and tell Jack about your progress here." He smiled as he patted her on the shoulder. "Valerie's main job lately is to help children who have just arrived, it's a challenging job but you do it so well," he looked at her and she beamed at him.

"I love my job Michael," she gripped Jack's hand, "come on Jack, we'll walk through the Garden of Eden, mind you don't tread on any snakes." Jack looked worried but Valerie shrieked with laughter.

"Only joking, darling." Valerie and Jack walked to the windows leading onto a terrace, the doors opened as they approached and Steve and Michael heard her giggles as she teased Jack about snakes and apples.

"I can see I have a long way to go," Steve said as he and Michael left the seating area and walked through into Reception.

"Really?" Michael frowned slightly.

"I know that I have to be tolerant but her giggles and silliness are irritating, you have to admit that just even a tiny bit." Steve was ashamed to feel like this especially after Michael had told him to look for her good points and to concentrate on them but Steve was finding that difficult and he was relieved that Jack and Valerie had gone. He hoped that Michael would agree and he looked at Michael's face to see if his minor blasphemy was accepted.

Michael paused before he spoke. "Everyone handles their stresses differently Steve. Valerie is basically shy and thinks that everyone else is good at their jobs, good with others and that she is failing in her tasks by a long margin. She lacks self-confidence and when she was in her human life she really did struggle. But now she is beginning to realise that everyone is different and that she can be as good as she perceives others to be. Actually she is even better in many respects than the others in her team who welcome children here after their passing. The children take to her really quickly and their spirits adore her. She's currently the best in her team and as she realises that, she becomes more assured and even better at her job. It wasn't an easy induction for her though but what made it happier was when one of the team told her that she was finding her own job easier once she had studied and copied Valerie's easy going way in which she helped children understand what was happening to them. Being told that she influenced others in a positive manner greatly improved her performance and her happiness. She really feels now that she is making a worthwhile contribution and this makes her feel really good about herself.

"So why does she still giggle so much?"

"Oh that's because she's daft!" Michael grinned at Steve who realised that he was joking and he burst out laughing.

"Yes daft as a brush."

Michael put his arm around Steve's shoulder as he lowered his voice. "She may be a little daft but the next person you will meet will come across as being evil. You might even prefer Valerie's giggling."

CHAPTER 27

Most people are very nice until you upset them.

(Shaman)

Michael put his finger to his lips as he grasped the door handle. Steve waited patiently as Michael listened. He opened the door and Steve saw that the light was off but there was a glow of blue light in the corner of the room. Michael pushed the door open and went in, Steve followed. A small lamp with a dim blue bulb sat on a plain wooden table. Its beam made a small circle of light and the rest of the room was almost in darkness. A man sat with his back to the wall, his elbows rested on the table in front of him and another man sat opposite. The man with his elbows on the table looked up at Michael but he didn't smile or scowl. He seemed as if he didn't care who came in or maybe he was used to people coming and going. The man sitting opposite turned and smiled at Michael. Steve was surprised to see that this man wore a suit of gold. It seemed almost ridiculous. His hair was swept back and was jet black with hair oil. His thin face broke into a smile and he said to Michael,

"Hi Michael, maybe you and Brian can have a chat, I seem to be getting nowhere and Brian is not interested in talking to me about his life in any way, shape or form." He looked up at Steve.

"Or maybe you Steve, maybe you can talk to Brian and find out what he thinks of it all?"

Steve was surprised that this man knew his name, he had certainly never met him, he would have remembered that face and as for the gold suit, well the suit was almost comical.

The man stood and stepped away from his chair. At once Steve saw that his shoes were gold lamé! His socks, they were gold too. Steve looked at the suit, even in the blue light he could see the wrinkles, what on earth was this chap doing, why did he wear such awful clothes?

Michael walked over to the wall and picked up a chair. He placed it alongside the other one and he sat down whilst motioning Steve to sit next to him. Steve did as he was bid and as he sat he looked at Brian. He was a man in his middle fifties and his build betrayed a life on junk foods and no exercise. His belly bulged at his shirt and the belt around his trousers was loose. There was a dull, dark stain on his chest and it covered the front of the shirt. His open collar was clearly dirty, he hadn't shaved for a week at least and his eyes were tired. His manner was that of one who was tired, fed up and totally disinterested in anything. He scowled at Michael and then at Steve and said nothing.

Michael seemed to ignore him. He turned to Steve and spoke as if he was making a report to a superior. He spoke about the man as if he wasn't there.

"Brian Nichols arrived a short time ago; he met his death at the hands of his wife who stabbed him in his heart as he slept in his chair. He had been watching television but he dozed off after drinking nearly half a bottle of whiskey. He has no interest in where he is now, he has no questions and rejects any attempts on our behalf to explain what has happened to him and what may happen to him. It's as if he didn't care." Michael turned his attention to Brian.

"Aren't you the slightest bit interested in what will happen to you Brian?"

Although Michael had asked the question in a mild manner, Brian just stared at him and looked away. Then he rubbed his nose, scratched his ear and said just one word.

"No."

Steve looked at Brian, then he turned to Michael and spoke. "Any chance of a game of pool Michael? I used to play a lot of pool and since I have been here, no one has let me have even one game."

Michael was astonished.

"Pool?" he said, "Pool? You want to play pool?"

"Yes," said Steve firmly. "I have asked if I can play pool on many occasions but you have always said that we have other things to do. Well I am fed up with all these discussions, your questions and the interrogations. Just let me have some time to myself, I want to play some pool."

Michael looked at Steve, his mouth opened but he didn't speak. Steve had never mentioned pool before; indeed he knew Steve's interests very well and Steve's sudden obsession with playing pool was a mystery. Still he would go along with what Steve wanted.

"Okay, you can play pool if you like but I'm not playing pool, I have other things to do." Michael pointed to a door. "There's a games room in there, maybe there's a pool table." He stood and pushed his chair back and Steve scraped his chair as he moved away from the table and over to the door. He opened it and both he and the two men could see a pool table in the other room as well as a darts board. The table was set ready for a game, they could see the white ball on its spot and the red and yellow balls in a triangle. There was even a bar with beer and lager taps and the optics on the wall offered various spirits. The room was well lit and a welcome change from the dull blue light in their room.

"That's more like it," Steve said and he went into the games room, took a cue from the rack on the wall and took up his stance against the white ball. He played the shot and the red and yellow balls clattered as they rolled against the cushions. One red ball hesitated against the middle pocket and then dropped in. Steve smiled.

"Come on Brian, have a game, I bet you a pint of lager you won't pot anything before I finish. He looked at Brian who didn't move, he just sat in his chair staring at Steve in the games room. A clear five seconds passed and no one moved or said anything. Brian then stood up and pushed his chair back. He left the blue room and entered the games room. Steve turned his back on him and prepared to hit the white ball against a red ball. Brian picked a cue from the rack and examined the tip. He looked for the cube of chalk, found it hanging on a string and he wiped the end of his cue with it. He seemed satisfied and as Steve finished his go by cleverly leaving a red ball over the end pocket, Brian took his position and swiftly pocketed one yellow ball, then another, then another. He didn't notice as Michael went quietly to the door and let himself out.

Steve did his best but Brian beat him easily in the first frame.

Then Steve lost the second frame after fouling and knocking the black ball down. He and Brian hardly spoke as they played the third game and this time Steve played very well and he grinned at Brian as he cleared the last three yellow balls and pocketed the black preventing Brian from sinking his last red.

"Nice one!" said Brian.

"Shall we help ourselves? There doesn't seem to be anyone here." Steve didn't wait for Brian to answer, he went behind the bar and took a pint glass from the rack, he placed it under the lager tap and pulled the lever. The lager flowed out and Steve placed the full glass on the bar as he pulled a second pint. He put his glass to his lips as he motioned to Brian.

"Cheers Brian, Happy days."

Brian picked up his beer and didn't need a second invitation.

"Cheers," he grunted as he took a long swig.

Steve sat down at the table. Brian looked around him and Steve followed his gaze to see what he wanted. Brian's gaze was on the back of the bar, he looked for something, Steve asked him what he wanted.

"Fags, got any fags?" Steve didn't know if there were any but he offered to look. Brian joined him behind the bar and together they searched through cupboards and drawers. Finally Brian found a packet of cigarettes and this cheered him greatly.

"Brilliant," Steve said as he found a lighter on the bottom shelf. As Brian took a long draw on his cigarette he watched Steve as Steve lit one up too. He seemed happier and he relaxed.

Two hours passed and Brian and Steve sat back in their chairs. The ashtray overflowed with dog ends and their lager glasses had been supplemented by whiskey glasses after Steve pulled a bottle from the optic to save getting up, well that's the excuse he made as he unclipped it and plonked it down on the table.

Steve looked up through a haze of smoke as Michael entered the room. Michael was clearly very displeased and he spoke sharply to Steve.

"If we have had enough …" he stressed the *we*, "if we have had enough" he repeated, "then it would be nice if we could get back to work. You have duties, so have I, you can play pool later if you like but for now, I would be grateful if you would come with me."

Steve hesitated. He had never been spoken to like this before by Michael or anyone else. He felt like a naughty schoolboy and he was flustered. The man in the gold clothes then came in too and ordered Brian to stand. Brian ignored him as he held his whiskey glass in front of him. Clearly Brian wasn't leaving until he finished his drink. The man in gold snapped his fingers, Brian paused, put his glass to his lips and downed the lot in one go. He wobbled slightly as he stood and spoke to Steve.

"Thanks for the game and the drink, see you around." He burped as he brushed past the table and he followed the man in gold out of the door.

Michael sat down next to Steve, he smiled.

"Well done."

"Well done bollocks!" Steve was angry. He was also quite a bit drunk. "Well done bollocks!" He repeated. And with that, Steve struggled to stand, "I need a piss."

*

"Hangovers in Heaven … Excuse me but no way did I expect to suffer a hangover in Heaven." Steve groaned as he lay on his bed. He looked up to see Rosie sitting on the edge of the duvet, she had a wet towel in her hand and she leaned forward to wipe his forehead.

"We don't get hangovers in Heaven." Rosie smiled. "We only get hangovers in Hell."

"So am I in Hell then?" Steve didn't expect an answer.

"Well actually yes, you are," Rosie smiled as she placed the wet towel on his head and left it there. Steve closed his eyes to block out the light.

"I didn't deserve this." He paused. "This has to be the worst hangover I have ever had and believe me I have had a few. Have you any tablets or whatever?" Rosie shook her head.

"Surely there's something I could take?" Rosie felt sorry for him but there was nothing he could take.

"You'll be alright in a few hundred years."

"What?" Steve tried to sit upright as he heard what Rosie said.

"Only teasing Steve," and as she smiled, she moved her hand across his forehead and at once the pain disappeared.

"Umm that will make it better," she said and Steve blinked at her.

"Wow, I feel fine now, thanks."

"Michael and Inspector Gold are very happy with you Steve. Thanks to you Brian Nichols is talking freely to Inspector Gold and his team and they are helping him come to terms with his crimes. You obviously said something to get him to co-operate, they are very happy with you indeed."

"His crimes?" Steve was puzzled. "I thought he was murdered by his wife."

"He was, he was stabbed to death, she couldn't take any more and when she found out that he had been touching her daughter she finally snapped and killed him whilst he was drunk."

"So he was a bad man, I thought that he was okay actually, he relaxed after a drink and a game of pool and we got on fine."

"There were two reasons for that Steve. First you had no idea what he had done in his human life and secondly you treated him like a normal person and with respect and friendship. He hadn't been spoken to kindly for many years and your acceptance of him as a normal person encouraged him to open up."

"But I had no idea, what had he done anyway."

"You don't want to know Steve but basically he was a danger to children, he tempted them, he got their trust, he abused them, he terrified them and he got away with it for many years. Then he was caught by accident on a chance police stop and they found things in his car that connected him with unsolved crimes from years ago. His DNA convicted him and when he was finally released from prison he met a woman with a young daughter and within a few weeks he was abusing her. The mother discovered by accident that he was a registered sex offender and when she told her daughter what she had discovered, her daughter burst into tears and the truth came out. That's why he was murdered but he wasn't the victim, he was the criminal, he had abused children for years."

"That's awful, I had no idea." Steve was shocked. "What will happen to him, surely he will be in Hell forever?"

"Maybe, but as we know, Hell isn't a place but a state of mind where we suffer and he too will have to understand what he did and why he did it before he has any chance of being free from torment. If Michael agrees, you will be able to watch his reviews and his Life Appraisal and see how it progresses and how things end for him. I think that it should be part of your next training programme. But it's up to Michael, whilst you are under his guidance, he makes those decisions."

Steve heard a knock at the door. Michael came in.

"Hi Steve, how's your head?" He smiled at Rosie, "Ah I see that you have used your healing hands, couldn't you have let him suffer a little longer?"

"He suffered enough, besides you and Inspector Gold have had a breakthrough with our chap Nichols and that's down to Steve as you well know."

"Maybe. Steve you did well getting him to accept his situation, how did you know that he played pool?"

"I noticed the chalk marks on his ear, they didn't show up that well under the blue light but when he rubbed his nose and scratched his ear I saw what it was. How did you arrange for the pool table, games room and bar to be already there anyway? That was a bit of a coincidence."

"Nonsense, no coincidence at all. You remember those blank empty rooms you saw when you first arrived. You wanted to see a pool table and that's what you got when you opened the door. The dartboard and the bar were there to help you both to relax in comfortable surroundings."

"So it was all a set up to get me to make friends with him, that scumbag who touches children?"

"Well yes actually, you had no idea of his background, you were ideal and what's more you learned something as well?"

"Did I?" Steve wasn't so sure. "What did I learn?"

"You learned that if you treat someone with respect, with good manners and as an equal, they will usually respond positively, even if they are really evil. But now that you know about him, you will probably treat him differently and he will realise that. What you have to do Steve is to be able to treat him in the same way as you did before you knew about him and you will really find this difficult. But you have to do it if you are to truly understand what made him do the things he did. And you will have to accept it before you can represent him at his Life Appraisal." Steve was aghast.

"I have to represent him? You are joking."

"Not at all. You had Rosie to represent you, now you will be trained to represent him. Oh and before I forget, Inspector Gold will be on the opposing side. He can be quite ruthless you know."

Steve felt sick. He wasn't ready for this, not by a long way. Meeting people who had just come from one side to the other seemed challenging enough but to represent someone at their appraisal, well that was a tough challenge and whilst he thought that perhaps it wouldn't matter if he failed and Nichols spent eternity in a state of hell, then perhaps it wouldn't matter, he would deserve it. Yes it must be that Michael, Inspector Gold and Rosie wanted this chap really punished, that's why they gave his case to him, a complete amateur. They knew that he would mess it up. But then Michael dashed those thoughts.

"Of course if you do a poor job and Brian Nichols has to experience plenty of fear and terror then you will have to share some of those experiences with him. It's in your best interests to find the good side to him and hope that you can convince everyone that he's not a bad sort after all. I did think that you would respond well to a challenge Steve. We will soon see what you can do."

CHAPTER 28

"Was I the first person that you represented?" Steve looked up from his book as Rosie sat on the chair opposite. She too was reading about past case studies.

"Yes you were, we met at that pub where you sang like Elvis." Steve blushed.

"I didn't sing like Elvis and yes of course I remember meeting you." He thought back to that evening and his astonishment at seeing Elvis sitting near the stage and clapping when Steve had finished.

"Actually you did sound like him but that was down to the equipment." Steve was indignant, he was happy to be coy about his success that night but certainly didn't want anyone thinking that he was an average singer that only sounded good because the sound system faked it.

"The karaoke machine at that pub can be adapted to make the singer sound just like the original artist. When you sang Elvis's song, you sounded just like him. It's all down to technology."

Steve was disappointed. He had been proud of that performance and when Rosie had joined in the clapping he felt good, now that he knew that the machine changed his voice, he was upset, but he tried not to show it.

"I didn't hear you sing Rosie. Do you sing?"

"No I don't sing but if we go there again, you can sing your song without the machine helping you and it will be your voice that we hear, okay?"

Steve made a mental note to ensure that the equipment would be set to change his voice to mimic the artist perfectly.

"So when you represented me, were you asked to or did you volunteer?"

"Volunteer? Goodness no. I didn't want your case at all, you were a complete cheat as a husband and you had the morals of an alley cat. You certainly wouldn't have been my choice of a man when I was a human, I would have avoided you at all costs. I only took your case because I was promised that I could choose my next one if I made a half decent job of yours."

Steve considered this carefully and he was quite wounded. He really fancied Rosie, mind you he really liked that Julie too. In fact there were some really gorgeous women here. He could see that he could be quite happy. Unfortunately he had forgotten that Rosie could read his thoughts if she chose to. She snapped at him.

"You are a typical man."

"Whoops!" Steve smiled to himself. Then a thought struck him.

"But you were really nice and sweet to me when we met. And as everything progressed you gave me the impression that you liked me, I actually enjoyed that."

"Yes well you would. What you need to realise that I needed to get the best from you, to get you to be less defensive, to admit your failings and to understand why you did the bad things that you did. If you and I were working together rather than against each other, then your chances of a successful outcome were much better and I would have a good result."

Steve thought about this for a few moments, then another thought occurred to him. "So this child abuser that I have to represent, have I got to pretend to be his friend too, have I got to get him to think that I like and admire him." Steve was hurt, he had honestly believed that he and Rosie were good friends and that she had been genuine in her friendship. Was it all a scam and would he have to do the same to this Nichols chap, someone who should have had his balls cut off?

Rosie smiled at him.

"When I first looked at your case file Steve I must admit that at first I thought that you were a flashy, arrogant, woman-abusing bastard. As I got to know you better, I realised that my first impressions were totally correct. But I must admit that when I read more about you, when I met you a few times and got to know you I still thought of you as all those things but I could see the good side in you. Yes I do like you, yes you are basically a decent person, that frankly is why you are here and doing what you are doing. Yes I am happy that you are my friend and that I am your friend and I am glad that we are on the same team."

Steve didn't know whether to feel insulted or flattered. Then he realised something with a shock.

"So whilst I got on okay with Brian Nichols and played pool, got drunk and talked to him I now discover that he's the lowest of the low as far as human beings are concerned and not only do I have to pretend to like him, I have to look for something that I admire in him so that I can represent him to my best ability."

"Well done Sherlock. You are learning fast."

CHAPTER 29

Rosie, Michael and Steve paused as the lift doors opened. Michael stood back to let Rosie out first and she nodded as she stepped onto the floor. She knew where to go and as she turned right, the others followed along the corridor. Rosie stopped by a closed door, a red light above was on and she hesitated before knocking. There was no reply but Rosie didn't wait, she opened the door and went in. Michael followed and he whispered to Steve that he should be quiet.

The room was small and the walls had the sort of material used in recording sound studios. The thick square panels were painted white and lots of wires hung from the low black ceiling. A long desk faced a panel of clear, thick glass and Steve could see into the room beyond. A small table with green baize was positioned between three upright chairs, one on one side, two on the other. Steve was reminded of the interview rooms that he had seen on television in police dramas. There were three black vinyl-covered office style chairs in front of the table in their room. It was obviously an observation room where interviews could be watched and heard without the interviewee being aware.

Rosie and Michael sat down and Steve didn't wait to be asked. As he leant against the back of his chair the others picked up the headphones in front of them and Steve picked up the set that were there for him, he put them on and glanced at Michael. He felt good. He imagined for a moment that he was a high-ranking police officer ready to hear a suspect's interview and possibly his confession as well. He smiled at Michael but Michael wasn't paying attention to him, his eyes were on the room next door and as they watched through the secret window the door opened and the man in the gold suit came in followed by Brian Nichols. Inspector Gold sat down and motioned that the other man sat down too. He leant forward, pressed a button on the wall and started to dictate.

"Interview between Inspector Gold and Brian Nichols, reference G1-993555."

Steve noticed that Inspector Gold didn't give a time and date and he was suddenly interested in knowing what day and what time it was. He realised that he hadn't given the date and time a single thought until this moment, he would have to ask Michael or Rosie later.

Inspector Gold leaned back in his chair and spoke clearly and evenly, there was no trace of anger or urgency in his voice. In fact he seemed slightly bored as if this interview were one of many in a long day and as soon as it could be finished, he could pack up for the day and go home.

"We've covered your childhood until your seventh birthday, what happened when your Uncle Trevor came to stay at your house?"

Brian Nichols looked down at his hands, they were shaking slightly. Steve and the others could see that the man was very nervous. He paused before replying and then spoke in clear short sentences.

"At first nothing. He was okay. He was fine to me. I liked him. He took me out to the park. We went shopping. He was nice to me. He liked me and I thought he liked me."

He stopped. Steve was puzzled at the last sentence. "He liked me and I thought he liked me."

"What do you mean?" said Inspector Gold. "He liked you or you thought he liked you?"

Brian Nichols hesitated. "I thought that he liked me because he was my uncle and that I was fun to be with or maybe because he liked me because … maybe he liked me in the way that normal people like normal boys of seven years old. I don't know. All I know is that one night he came into my bedroom when I was nearly asleep and he sat on the edge of my bed. He started talking to me and he was whispering a lot. I couldn't hear all of what he was saying but he kept saying that he liked me. Then he stroked my hair and I started to fall asleep. The next thing I know, he was pulling back the bedcovers and getting into bed with me. He said that he wanted to sleep in my bed with me because I made him feel nice. He asked me if I minded, he asked me if I liked to feel nice, then he touched me and he asked me if that felt nice. I was too surprised to say anything."

"How long did this touching go on?" Inspector Gold's question was vague. Did he mean in minutes for that one time or in years for all the time that the boy was abused?

Brian Nichols sighed and then he spoke. "He left me alone when I was thirteen. It was after I stabbed him in the hand with a compass, you know, those things we used at school. By then I was scared, very scared and I knew that I had to do something."

Inspector Gold spoke quietly, "Did you ever think of telling anyone? Did you ever tell your mother about what your uncle was doing to you?"

"No," he softly replied.

"Why not?"

"Because he told me that if I ever told anyone about feeling nice then everyone would be very angry, I would be beaten and sent away to a horrible school and never come home again. In fact I would probably be killed. He told me that 'feeling nice' was a sin and it was one that couldn't be forgiven, you know, a mortal sin."

He hesitated for a few seconds.

"He told me that it was his sin too and that if he ever told anyone about our 'feeling nice' both of us would get into trouble and he would keep our secret and I would have to keep it as well."

"And did you?"

"Yes, I kept our secret."

"And it all stopped when you stabbed him with your compass?"

"Yes, I was given a math's set to use and it had the usual things in it, a ruler, a protractor, a compass, you know ..." Gold nodded. "I had done my homework and I was fascinated at the sharpness of the point. I had a strong urge to stick it in myself, you know. I hated myself, I hated everyone and I wanted the touching to stop. I didn't feel nice anymore, I felt dirty. I realised that I didn't care if I got into trouble. No one or nothing could be worse than what was happening to me." He paused. "The night I did it, I put my books and stuff back in my bag but I put the compass under the pillow. Uncle Trevor would come in to say goodnight to me when everyone was asleep and ..." he hesitated, "and then he would pull the covers back and he would get into bed with me. This time he screamed, I don't remember actually doing it but I must have taken the compass from under the pillow and the next thing I knew he was screaming. My father came into the room and he saw his brother holding his hand and my compass was in deep, right up to the end of the point, right in the back of his hand. My father shouted at me and I was terrified but I didn't care anymore. I suddenly felt brave and I shouted at my father, 'Tell him to leave me alone.' I never forgot the look on my father's face, I think that I disgusted him. He grabbed my uncle by the shoulder and pulled him out. I lay there trembling and after a while my father came into my room. I thought he was going to shout at me and tell me that I would be sent away. But he didn't. He asked if I was alright but I was too scared to say anything at first. Then I asked if I would be sent away. He looked puzzled and he said that no I wouldn't be sent away, that I was a good boy and that I must get some sleep. I must have fallen asleep for only a moment as I awoke when I heard shouting downstairs and I heard the front door slam. Then my mum came to my room and she gave me a glass of hot milk. She stayed until I went to sleep again. In the morning my uncle had gone. He'd taken all his things and I never saw him again until I was in my twenties when he came to my gran's funeral.

"What happened after your uncle went away?"

"At first nothing. I expected my dad to say something but he didn't. I then asked my mum if Uncle Trevor was coming back. She looked at me and said, 'He is never coming back. You will never see him again, he's very upset with you because you stabbed him after he offered to help you with your homework and he said that we were lucky that he didn't call the police.' I started to tell her that it wasn't like that, that he wasn't helping me with my homework and that … but I stopped because she told me to shush and that it was all over now. Later my dad came back from work and I asked him if my uncle was ever coming back. He said that he wasn't and that there had been a lot of confusion and that the matter would be dropped and never mentioned again."

"And was it?" said Inspector Gold, "was it ever mentioned again?"

"Yes." Brian Nichols looked down at his hands, they were still shaking slightly. "At my court case, my defence lawyer asked me if I had ever been touched like I had touched that Simpson boy. At first I was ready to deny it but I realised that I had to break free of my demons, that I had to tell someone and that something inside me was saying that the right moment had come. Yes I told them about my Uncle Trevor and what he had done and you know what, I wasn't believed. My case was adjourned and someone did some checking. They found Uncle Trevor, he told them about me stabbing him with a compass and said that he had heard me screaming in the night and that he had discovered that I was having a nightmare and when he tried to calm me, I stabbed him. As it was an accident and as there was no really serious injury done, he didn't make an official complaint. He denied ever touching me and there was no evidence and nothing was proved. My parents were interviewed but they were old and said that my uncle's story was correct."

"And then you went to prison," Inspector Gold prompted Brian Nichols to carry on his story.

"Yes I got five years and I was put in a special prison, we had group discussions and it turned out that most of the others had been touched when they were children, they too felt the need to touch other kids when they were older. When I came out I was released on probation and put on the Sex Offender's Register. You know the rest. I met Julie Travers, she and I lived together for a few months, we were very happy and then one day she got it into her head that I had touched her daughter up and she stabbed me. I hadn't touched her daughter at all. My thing was for young boys."

Steve jumped. He was shocked and he looked quickly at Michael and Rosie, they didn't seem to have been struck by the comment. Inspector Gold was winding up the interview and switching off the tape and Steve was sweating. He had believed Nichols' story, he had even had sympathy for him and could fully understand that someone could be abused and then go on to abuse others, that didn't exonerate them of course but in listening to the interview he had started to build up a defence case to mitigate the crimes. But then Nichols had said it. "My thing was for young boys."

In the corridor Steve turned to Michael and said, "Thank you for the honour of asking me to represent someone at their Life Appraisal. I am honestly touched at the faith you have in me but there's no way I can defend Brian Nichols. His story might have been true, I don't know, all I do know is that the man is evil and I cannot and will not try and excuse him at all, not in any way, shape or form." He looked at Michael and then at Rosie, no one spoke for a moment.

Then Michael said, "Yes I know, Brian Nichols is a liar, he's perverted and he disgusts me, you and anyone who knows anything about him. But he has to be represented at his Life Appraisal and you Steve, you don't have a choice in the matter. His case is part of your training programme and you have to succeed before you can move on."

Steve was upset. "So I have to lie or find some technicality that gets him off before I can be promoted?" He was incredulous. Michael gripped his arm and looked straight at him.

"Remember where we are Steven." His voice was firm. "This isn't an enactment from a TV court drama on Earth where tricks are applied and people are misled. There's no chance of anyone being conned and the wrong judgement being reached here. We know what Brian Nichols has done and why, we know his life story better than he knows it himself. We know absolutely everything that can be known about this person and why he did what he did, we are not here to judge him just as no one judged you at your Life Appraisal."

Steve was taken aback at Michael's firmness. "Then why are we going through this?" He hesitated, almost scared to say it, "Why are we going through this charade?" Michael sighed and then he spoke very gently and softly to Steve as Rosie looked at him.

"Because whilst we know what Brian Nichols did and why he did it and that he's a weak-minded evil person, it's Brian Nichols himself that has to understand what he is, what he did and why he did it before he can understand and find any peace at all in his wretched soul. Your job my friend is not to defend him or get him excused or to have him 'released' on a technicality but to help him come to terms with what he did when he was on Earth, to understand and feel the suffering he caused and to help him to accept and understand. Your job Steve is not to defend him but to help him."

Michael heard the commotion first, they looked up and something hard slammed against one of the doors in the corridor. It splintered under the onslaught. Brian Nichols lurched into the corridor and saw Steve. Inspector Gold followed him out of the room and was powerless to stop him. Brian Nichols lunged at Steve and grabbed him around his throat. His grip paralysed Steve, his knees bent and he collapsed to the floor with Nichols' fingers tightening. Michael stepped forward and placed the palm of his hand on the back of Nichols' head. Nothing happened at first then his grip on Steve's throat started to relax as Nichols stopped squeezing. Brian Nichols collapsed on the floor but Inspector Gold leaned over him and grabbed his arm pulling him to his feet. Steve sat on the floor, his back was against the wall and his neck felt as if it had been crushed. He fought to breathe. Rosie soothed him with gentle words and she stroked his neck with her hands and the pain ceased. Inspector Gold looked at Steve, then he spoke to Michael.

"Some you win, some you lose. Maybe we will have him next time."

Steve, Michael and Rosie left Inspector Gold gripping Brian Nichols' arm. He had clearly lost the desire to fight anymore. They got back into the lift and Rosie and Steve looked at Michael. He shrugged and said,

"Well Steve, it looks like Brian Nichols didn't want you to represent him. In fact he doesn't want anyone's help at all, he's not interested in progressing any further or in coming to terms with his future. As far as he is concerned he doesn't have a future worth having and he has unfortunately elected to remove himself from our care. It's his decision, frankly I'm not surprised, I have expected it. But," he paused, "he had to have his chance, which he got, and now his fate is sealed until maybe he asks to be reconsidered again. But that won't happen for a very very long time."

Steve's neck had stopped hurting. He opened the door to his room and his bed looked extremely inviting. He lay on it as Rosie came in and shut the door behind her. She said goodbye to Michael who left them to rest and to talk about what had happened.

"Where will Brian Nichols go? What will he do? Will he experience what you have told me about being in a state of Hell? What will happen to him now?"

Rosie looked at Steve. "You are about to find out what happens to the souls of those who don't make it through their Life Appraisal or who reject the concept of Heaven and eternity. I hope that you are not too squeamish." She smiled but Steve sensed that his next adventure wasn't going to be very pleasant.

CHAPTER 30

"Most people are very nice until you upset them. Then some of them can get very nasty indeed." Steve recalled Rosie's parting words as he met the prison officer.

"Hello! What is this that you have brought me?" The small, thin man in a dark green overall didn't smile as Steve was shown through the heavy metal door. Steve and Brian Nichols had already passed through seven similar doors, all were very high and stretched from the floor to the ceiling. They comprised of thick iron bars spaced wide enough to get a hand through and they were rusty at the bottom but not rusty enough to be weak. These doors were the strongest prison style doors that Steve had ever seen. The man looked up from his board. There was a list of names and a coding alongside each name. He looked at Nichols, his small, black eyes showed no light and Steve thought that this man was probably the coldest and nastiest man that he had ever met. A shudder passed through Steve as he looked at him.

"Name!" he demanded.

Brian Nichols didn't reply. He ached all over; he had been beaten steadily and without a break for twelve hours. Two men with rubber truncheons and with the skills to know how to inflict the maximum pain without causing their victim to pass out had taken turns to whack Brian Nichols until they had been told to stop. As they finished, one had said to him, "nothing personal mate, have a nice day."

All Brian Nichols wanted to do was to sleep; every part of him was bruised except for his face though he did have the beginnings of a fine black eye. He had been told to keep his head still as he knelt on the floor to take a beating to his shoulders but he had disobeyed and moved his head and the baton caught him across the face. His torturer had apologised, "sorry mate, nothing personal."

The small man wasn't happy to be ignored and he didn't ask again. Instead he moved towards Brian Nichols and swiftly brought his knee up hard into the man's groin. His head flew forward as he doubled up in pain and dropped to his knees. The warder quietly spoke.

"My name is Mr Ball, I am called that because I have the lucky ability to be able to knee or kick a man in just the right place at any time I want and wherever I want. I have just introduced myself to you, the least you can do is to introduce yourself to me."

He waited. Brian Nichols coughed and his hands clutched his groin, tears streamed down his face and he wanted to throw up. He opened his mouth and tried to speak but all Steve could hear was a muffled groan.

"Excuse me!" said Ball.

"Nichols."

"Nichols," shouted the man, "Nichols what?"

Brian Nichols hesitated, then he realised what he had missed.

"Nichols Sir!"

Mr Ball was pleased.

"Excellent, you will find us very friendly here. We are all on first name terms, I will call you Pervert so that you are reminded of your previous existence and you will never forget who and what you were. You will call me by my first name at all times, do you understand?" He looked at Nichols in contempt.

"My first name is Sir. Do you get that? Everyone you meet here has the first name Sir, if you forget to be nice and to call us by our first name then you will be gently reminded." To emphasise the point he pushed his knee to within an inch of the man's face as he continued to kneel before him.

"We have really been looking forward to your arrival Pervert, at one time it was thought that you might escape us and opt for a Life Appraisal. That would have been extremely disappointing as we have so much planned for you. We have a very special course designed for people who get their pleasures from touching children and it's geared just right to suit you right down to the ground. Indeed Pervert, you are one of the lucky ones. You never actually killed a child, that's a real bonus for you but what you don't realise is that you caused some children to live a life of torment and pain and as you are so qualified for our extra care course, we can't wait to get you started."

Steve was shocked to hear this. His experiences in his new life had so far been pleasant and he could cope with his courses well enough to enjoy them. He was surprised to see that there was a hidden, deeper side, a very nasty side where people were beaten and tortured. Mr Ball must have read his mind, he turned to him.

"You were asked to bring Pervert to us, you will accompany him through his early experiences and you might even share some of them." He paused as Steve shuddered, his hands went involuntarily to his groin. Mr Ball smiled but without humour.

"No you won't get kicked or punched but you will taste some of the things that our friend here has to taste, he deserves it, you, on the other hand, will share the experience for your own benefit."

Steve was not at all pleased and didn't think that whatever this horrible man could dish up would be of any benefit to him at all.

*

"Good morning boys, my name is Mr Fly and my job is to help you to survive. I am not very good at my job as some of you will quickly find out and I consider myself to be a bit of a failure. Still, never mind, there's always plenty more of you lot to take up the places on my course so if you do find yourself not able to survive, then don't worry, you won't be missed."

Steve looked at the teacher. He sat next to Brian Nichols in a wonderful reproduction of a classroom at an English school in the 1950s. His wooden desk was covered in scratches and ink blots and some of the names and initials were still decipherable. But he wasn't looking at the desk now. He sat in a class of around thirty men and they ranged in race, size and age. Most seemed to be in their fifties, two were around twenty-five and one chap was clearly nearly eighty. All looked worn out and dejected and most of them looked as if they had been fighting. Black eyes, swollen lips, one had a plaster covering a badly cut ear. They all listened as their new teacher tapped the huge blackboard with his stick and he pointed to the title. 'The Life Cycle of a Fly.' Around the wall Steve could see tatty photographs of various angles showing a fly, some were sitting, some were in flight and there was one that was eating something. Steve's attention was on the teacher, he seemed to have a problem with his jacket. In common with many teachers of the nineteen-fifties he wore scruffy black shoes, brown corduroy trousers, and a silver grey worsted jacket with a leather patch on each elbow. Ink stained the left breast pocket, leaky pens were obviously still a problem. The man's hair was thin and the strands were combed across his bald head and the many lines in his face revealed years of smoking strong cigarettes. But the jacket fascinated Steve, the collar at the back seemed to be moving up and down by itself with no input from the wearer. Others had noticed it too. The teacher continued.

"You have heard of reincarnation. Yes reincarnation is an important part of your existence; you will be delighted to know that as you are on a special care course you will experience reincarnation. You are all very lucky." He emphasised the word all and he repeated the phrase as he looked at Steve. "You are all very lucky to be able to enjoy reincarnation and I hope that you will find the process interesting." Steve wondered why he had been included, he wasn't supposed to be on the course, he was just there to observe Brian Nichols. He wondered if any of the others were in the same position or were they all molesters of children who had been selected for a special punishment. He looked around him but whilst all the men there seemed creepy, they all looked totally normal as well. Steve realised that he assumed that they were all like Brian Nichols but really he had no idea, he decided to wait until after class to speak to the teacher. Suddenly his attention was brought swiftly back to the movement in the teacher's jacket and he watched as the teacher sighed and then took his jacket off. Steve and the others were riveted. There on the man's back were two enormous fly wings. They looked in astonishment at the man's face as the eyes grew bigger, his face became pointed and two black cheeks pushed out from around his mouth. The teacher was turning into a fly right before them. Steve suddenly felt a stab of pain, his face was changing too, he looked at Brian Nichols. His face had become pointed too, his eyes were turning black and red and Steve looked around, they were all becoming flies.

"Follow me." The teacher moved up and away from his desk and towards the open window. Steve realised that the room had suddenly become very large, the ceiling stretched way overhead and the desks and chairs were a thousand times their normal size. Mr Fly led the way and darted towards the window. Steve realised that if he beat one wing faster than the other he could control his direction as he nearly bumped into another fly. Steve realised that he no longer had any human form at all, neither did the others. Mr Fly passed through the open window, the others followed and Steve was in the middle of the small swarm. They flew towards a tree; Steve felt a huge rush of air as a giant fluttering creature passed him at about three times his speed. It was huge and it had a sharp beak. The creature feinted to the right and grabbed the fly next to Steve, it disappeared into the beak and was crushed in an instant. Steve was too shocked to be scared.

"Over here." Steve looked for the source of the command. A fly was calling to him from beneath a huge leaf on the ground at the bottom of a tree. Steve dived and found that if he brought his wings up to the stall position he could slow down and stop. He landed next to the fly who had called him and as he did so, the others arrived.

"We lost two then." Steve realised that the teacher was the one giving the commands and talking now.

"Keep your eyes out for birds, they are fast, and if you fly at dusk you can get clobbered by bats, they are blind as you know but they have fantastic radar. If you move, they can get you; if you keep still, you will be marginally safer. Oh and look out for spiders. You don't need me to tell you that spiders are much cleverer than us, once you get caught in a web you will be stuck fast, you may be eaten straight away, this actually hurts by the way, more likely you will be wrapped in a silk rope and kept for later. When the spider wants you he will come at you slowly and he will suck all the blood from you as you are still alive. That's a nicer way to go than being eaten as it doesn't hurt as much and you will feel yourself falling asleep and that will be that. There are lots of different spiders and they use many different methods of catching us but you will only ever get to meet one kind." The irony wasn't lost on Steve, his first encounter with a spider would be his last.

"Now, listen carefully, try and keep alive for a little while. As a fly you can travel to most places but do keep away from water, you might find its smoothness attractive but once you land on it you will not get off again. And don't fly too close to water either. If a fish grabs you, you are history. Fly carefully, keep to surroundings that you know and when you are hungry, go and eat shit!"

"Pardon?" said Steve. "We have to eat shit?"

"Of course you do, we flies are the lowest of the low in the animal and insect world, we are all here because we have acted in a disgusting manner when we were humans."

If Steve had a hand he would have raised it. "Excuse me, I don't know if you are aware but I am not actually supposed to be on your course, I am supposed to accompany Brian Nichols who I believe is being punished and taught harsh lessons. I am not actually in his class."

"Oh dear," said Mr Fly. "No one told me that. I assumed that because you were there you were on my course, I am dreadfully sorry. Look there's nothing I can do about it now, you will have to continue. I don't suppose that you will survive as sadly no one does but instead of flying with us and eating shit, you can go off by yourself and see some of your old haunts, oh and you don't have to eat shit either, I can spare you that, you can eat dead carcasses, jam or cake."

"Dead carcasses, jam or cake?" Steve wasn't impressed with the choices.

Mr Fly continued. "Dead carcasses are safer and they are quite delicious to a fly compared with shit but they do taste pretty disgusting as well. Now jam or cake, they are gorgeous but far more dangerous. You are likely to get fat and slow after eating sweet things and the chances of getting flattened with a newspaper or a fly swatter are very high indeed. If you make it back from your adventures meet me here in three days, if you get eaten, squashed or blood sucked then I am afraid that you will have to start again. If this happens too many times then you may forget who you were originally and you'll have to go through all of the 423 trillion stages of life. That will take a while, fortunately you have the whole of eternity to do it in."

The other flies waited patiently as Mr Fly told Steve how to get to the area where he used to live. Some of them asked if they could go off on their own too. The teacher told them to wait until Steve was off.

"Your Mr Nichols will stay with me Steve, don't worry about him and if you do see Michael or Rosie give them my love, it's a pity that they didn't fill in your forms correctly."

Steve made a mental note to have a firm word with Michael and Rosie. He wasn't supposed to be here, he was not supposed to be a fly. He was in great danger of being killed or worse still, forgetting his origins and going through, how many was it? Ah yes, the 423 trillion stages of life.

Steve followed the directions that he had memorised. He flew between the trees and close to the trunks, which made it more difficult for the birds to pick him off in flight as they would risk colliding with the bark. He mustn't fly too low either as the spiders had their webs near to the ground. Avoiding two trees close together was also advisable and he could see water droplets hanging on web strands giving away their position. As he came out of the woods he saw a path leading from a school to a main road. The path was busy as mums and children walked to their cars, others to the bus stop. The birds and spiders weren't comfortable around people so Steve flew close to a mum with a pushchair. A six-year-old boy skipped alongside. Steve was tired and he landed on the pushchair where the baby was asleep and didn't notice. Steve was attracted by the smell of the baby's skin and he moved a few inches to land on the child's cheek. The mother saw him and waved her hand. Steve saw it coming easily and took off, he flew around the mum and noticed that her shopping bag was open. He dived for the safety of the top of a box of cornflakes and sat there. He could see and hear the noises around them.

Steve was rested after his journey on the cornflake box and he took off to see where he was. He recognised the High Street where he lived as a child and he remembered that his uncle lived in a flat over the betting shop. He flew across the road neatly avoiding a bus but then he cartwheeled through the air as the bus whooshed past. He tumbled down towards a dustbin almost out of control. He steadied himself and was about to land on the edge when he heard an angry voice.

"Clear off or I'll squash you flat." He looked into the bin. A huge bluebottle sat in the lid of a polystyrene box, the remains of a burger looked wonderful and Steve realised that he was very hungry but the bluebottle was in no mood to share.

Steve moved backwards and up. He left the bin and decided to wait until later, that burger was far too big for even several bluebottles, he would return.

The window was open and Steve flew in. He recognised his uncle's modest furnishings and his threadbare carpet, at least he could rest here and be safe from birds and spiders. He found a place in the sun and looked down at the bluebottle chomping away at the remains of the burger. After a while the bluebottle moved away in search of a drink and he found it in an empty bottle of orange, there was just enough to quench the thirst of a well-fed bluebottle gorged on the best that McDonald's could offer. Steve lost no time, he hit the burger box at full speed and skidded to a stop. There was plenty of burger left and he sighed with pleasure as he stuffed himself. Life as a fly wasn't too bad he thought, so far he had managed not to have to eat shit.

The sun was going down as Steve flew back up to his uncle's flat. He paused on the windowsill and saw that his uncle was home. He glided through the window and parked himself on the vertical cupboard door right in front of his uncle's face.

"Hi Uncle George, don't be alarmed, it's me your nephew Steven."

His uncle looked away from the kettle that he was filling and spoke directly to Steve.

"Clear off you pesky fly," he picked up a tea towel and Steve moved swiftly away as the cloth hit the cupboard door hard.

"It's me Uncle, It's me Steve!" Steve dodged and ducked as his Uncle swore at him and waved the tea towel. Steve was much faster than his Uncle's wrist and had no problem keeping clear of the flaying towel. His heart sank as he realised that his uncle couldn't hear him and he flew up to the curtains where he watched his uncle throw down the tea towel in disgust.

Uncle George then made a cup of tea and took a biscuit from the cupboard.

"Oooh Jammy Dodgers, my favourite." Steve gazed at the biscuits. He was tempted to swoop straight down and land on one, maybe if he did his uncle would see him and hear his voice calling out to him. But Steve wasn't stupid and he realised that his uncle would never be able to hear him.

Uncle George leant forward and switched on the TV. He sat back in his chair and flicked through the channels. Steve realised that he had missed TV and he settled down in his vantage point on the curtains and watched the film. Uncle George was tired, his eyes closed as the TV blared out and Steve watched him fall asleep. In a second he was down. The cup and saucer loomed closer as he banked to the right and his wings flicked up as an airbrake as his feet touched down on the plate. The remains of the Jammy Dodger looked wonderful. Steve settled on a large crumb and as he looked up he noticed the film on TV and he recognised it. The film was about an epic journey from America to Europe. It was the story of Charles Lindbergh who flew alone across the sea in a plane called 'The Spirit of St Louis.' The plane was so full of fuel it could hardly take off and there was no forward screen, the pilot could only see outside through the side window. Steve remembered this film and with a start he recalled that a fly saved Lindbergh's life. The story unfolded, the helpers wished Lindbergh luck as he attempted to take off and they gasped as his overweight aircraft just cleared the trees at the end of the long grass field and no one saw the fly dart into the cabin where it hid behind the seat. As the plane flew towards Europe Lindbergh ate his sandwiches and he noticed the fly as it buzzed around the cockpit. He even spoke to it, "Hullo little fella, I guess I thought I was alone on this trip but you are here too." After many hours in the sky and with nothing to look at but the waves the pilot started to nod off. The fly noticed that the engine pitch had changed and that the plane was starting a shallow dive towards the waves. The fly screamed at the pilot. Steve could clearly hear it. "Wake up, wake up, we will hit the sea." Of course the pilot couldn't hear the fly and the fly started to panic. A crash would doom both the pilot and the fly and the fly had to do something. He did. He settled on the pilot's nose, sleepily the pilot brushed it away. So he hit the nose harder this time, landing at maximum speed, then he flicked over to the cheek and brushed that with wings at full tilt, finally it flew at full speed right at the pilot's nose and didn't even attempt to slow for a soft landing. Lindbergh woke with a start and was just about to swat at the fly when he noticed the waves a few feet below, immediately he pulled back on the control column and applied full power. He breathed a sigh of relief as the plane climbed back to its cruising level. "You saved my life little fella." The fly was so proud and Steve was proud too. Clearly that fly was a hero and it helped other flies too because Lindbergh completed his epic voyage and he never forgot that fly and he never killed another fly as long as he lived. Steve had finished all he could eat of the Jammy Dodger by now and he was entranced by the Lindbergh story. He didn't notice that his uncle had woken and he didn't notice him leaning forward to pick up a slipper. He did however feel the rush of air that precluded the arrival of anything threatening and if he hadn't eaten the burger and the biscuit he might have made the safety of the curtains. As it was, Steve felt the pressure of the slipper hard on his back. His tiny body was crushed and his lungs collapsed. He landed upside down by the wall and he felt his life slipping away from him as his uncle leaned over him and swept him unceremoniously into the dustbin. The lid clattered again as the last crumbs of the Jammy Dodger biscuit tumbled around his body. They lay together until Monday when Uncle George put the bag out for the bin men.

CHAPTER 31

Steve landed with a thud on the floor, he opened his eyes and looked up. Michael and Rosie stood over him and looked very relieved to see him. Rosie asked if he was alright.

"Oh yes just perfectly fine, you try being flattened by a slipper two hundred times bigger than you and see if you like it." Steve struggled to his feet and Michael took his arm.

"We are terribly sorry, you weren't supposed to go as far as Brian Nichols into his course, you were only supposed to make sure that he got there and meet him afterwards, as it is, he has progressed past the fly stage, through several hundred other stages and you'll meet him later on. He's a cockroach in prison at the moment and about to be eaten by a starving drug dealer, he then goes on to be a rat for a while."

Steve groaned, he didn't want to see Nichols ever again but he did want to ask some questions and Michael and Rosie seemed genuinely sorry.

"We can go to one of the rooms," Michael said. "You can play golf, go skiing, ride motorcycles, whatever you want. I owe you one Steve, it couldn't have been nice being told that you had to eat shit." Michael stifled a grin.

Steve thought. Yes he would like to go to one of the rooms and yes it would be a change to do something enjoyable for a change but Steve sensed an opportunity.

"Look Michael, a game of golf would be great but could we first find somewhere nice to sit and could I ask a few straight questions?" He paused. "And you answer them without showing me or getting me to experience anything? Just some straight answers to some straight questions?" Michael agreed and he opened a door to one of the rooms. Ahead stretched a beautiful beach with white sand, palm trees blew gently in the breeze and the surf rolled over their feet as they walked along the water's edge. They were dressed in shorts and they both carried a towel. A smiling Thai bar owner welcomed them to his bar and pointed to two sun loungers. As they sat down he arranged the beach umbrellas to give them shade. Steve settled onto his lounger, Michael smiled at the bar owner.

"Sawadee Krap. Two Singha beers please oh and glasses please, not bottles."

The man brought the beers and a woman approached.

"You want massage?" she said.

"Maybe later," Michael smiled, he turned to Steve. "Have you ever had a Thai beach massage?" Steve hadn't.

"This place is the nearest that anyone can get to Heaven on Earth. It's just wonderful, a lovely country with lovely people, but don't upset anyone here. You'll find a touch of Heaven in Thailand but do something wrong or hurt someone and you'll find no tougher place to be on the planet. Some of the ideas for Heaven and Hell are taken from Thailand and some people experience both. There are many other countries in Asia which are the same." He relaxed into his sun lounger. "Okay let's have your questions."

Steve found it hard to look back on his experiences with Nichols when he met the warder and was kicked by Mr Ball. He saw the bruises on his back after the torture and he knew that Nichols had made his own decision to refuse a Life Appraisal. It was his own fault but Steve was concerned.

"It's not the actions of a civilised society to beat up its prisoners after they have been convicted. Hitting them for hours on end or kicking them in the balls is not something that was condoned in Britain when I died. Convicted criminals, even nasty ones like Nichols and perverts like him were at least treated with some decency. I would have thought that here everyone would be more enlightened and people would be treated with some respect."

"To begin with, we are not treating people, we treat spirits, the people that bore those spirits ceased to exist when the person died. What you are, what I am, what Nichols is, is a spirit. That spirit begins a new journey when he passes out of human form and it's my job, and Rosie's job, and your job, to help those spirits come to terms with how they acted as a person and they need to understand that before they can move on." He sipped his beer before carrying on.

"Yes it can appear brutal but if you remember when you had your own Life Appraisal you were shown what pain you caused, what suffering you caused and you experienced some of that pain for yourself." Steve remembered feeling the pain of having his legs pulled off and he remembered that man who killed lions for sport and the pain he experienced when the lion caught him.

"If people like Nichols knew that they would experience the pain of child abuse and that they couldn't escape when they then died and felt the fear and suffering that they had imparted to others, do you think that they would have chosen to enjoy themselves hurting children if they knew what would happen later? No they would not."

"But they don't know," Steve argued. "They do what they want, they hurt others and then when they do discover the truth it's too late. The damage is done."

Michael was patient with Steve. "If that were true there would be no need for me, for Rosie, for you, for thousands of other spirits like us. It's our task to get the message through to others who are still alive and who can influence and affect others."

"But we aren't on Earth anymore." The beer made Steve forget his caution and he wanted to argue freely. "We might be able to punish those who caused pain and suffering but unless we can get the message through to people who are actually living their lives, the whole thing is a waste of time."

"Precisely," said Michael. "But we are winning. I told you about bad spirits and good spirits and you saw the effect of bad spirits on people such as yourself when you did bad things as a person. But you also saw and met others in your life who were different too. You met selfish people, you met bullies, you met those who had to control others, you even met those who got their pleasure from actually hurting others. Those people exist as humans as well as spirits. But remember some of the more pleasant people that you met. Those who had feelings and time for others, those who gave up contended lives to help those less fortunate, people who put the wellbeing of others before themselves. You remember knowing about those?"

Steve nodded.

"Well that's the difference, that's how we know that we are making headway, those people are enlightened spiritually and they are aware of what really matters. They are not driven by having bigger and better homes, by faster and flashier cars, they don't even bring true pleasure to those who have them. No Steve, the ones who experience the real pleasure, the real Heaven, they are the ones who understand what I am saying and they find their happiness through relationships with themselves and others."

"Through relationships with themselves? How can you have a relationship with yourself?"

"Do you remember what you said at the end of your Life Appraisal when you asked where God is and then you gave the answer?"

Steve thought back.

"Yes, God is everywhere and he is within us." He stopped as he remembered those last four words.

"Exactly! Steve you are ready to move on now, you are ready to work in the same team as Rosie and me. The times are changing on Earth. People are discovering that there is more to life than fine material things, they are discovering that they can work hard and enjoy material successes but the real happiness, the real joy in their hearts comes not from what they have built or bought, it comes from relationships with others, our family, our friends but from most important of all, our relationships with ourselves. If we can get everyone to understand that then we can relax and go and play." Michael stood and shook the sand from two snorkels and masks and he waved to the bar owner who brought him two pairs of bright yellow fins. "Come," he said. "Let's go and say hi to some Angel Fish."

CHAPTER 32

The three little words 'I Love You' can, if you are not careful, lead to the longest

sentence known to mankind. Only say them if you really mean it.

(Shaman)

Steve enjoyed the peace of being on his own and he lay on his bed and thought about all the things that had happened to him. He didn't dwell on the word eternity anymore even though the thought of being somewhere forever really rattled him at first as the concept is almost impossible to imagine.

His eyes looked up at the ceiling, he still felt that he had his old body and when he met with others, they had bodies too. He had been told often enough that the illusion was there for the benefit of those who had recently arrived and he sometimes felt himself to be not in human form but in a vague, dreamy spirit, a bit like he would imagine a ghost to be, slightly shimmering, moving effortlessly through space and in a state of total serenity. Steve enjoyed the sensation but he found that when he was needed to stay mentally alert or to face a challenge, he needed to feel the presence of his human form; just to make it seem easier to deal with. He sat up and swung his legs over the edge of the bed and then he moved his legs one at a time so that they were tucked into the top of his thighs. He had seen the yoga position but had never tried it before. As a human he would have struggled to achieve the proper position but here it came effortlessly. Steve put his hands on his knees and straightened his back, he allowed his head to bend forward and he closed his eyes and took a deep breath. His lungs filled with air and he held it for a few moments. He sat like this for a long time gently breathing in and out. He then felt a strange sensation, his spirit seemed to be leaving his body and moving upwards. Steve opened his eyes and looked down to see his body, still in the yoga position as it sat on the edge of the bed but he was now clearly out of his body and he could see the detail of the room as he looked down from the ceiling. Then the detail started to fade until the room seemed shrouded in mist. He allowed himself to drift in a cloud of consciousness and he felt wonderful, his mind became clear and he could almost feel the silence. His heart seemed to swell and it felt like it wanted to burst. Steve had never felt like this before, it was amazing. He moved to the left, then he moved to the right, he found that he could drift forwards, then backwards. As he glided serenely though a mystical space he felt that he could understand everything. He felt totally at peace. Then in the distance he heard a bell, it seemed to be sounding for him. Not the shrill of an electric alarm but the steady chimes of a church bell far away. Steve moved towards the sound, he seemed to pick up speed and as the wisps of light cloud around him moved past he felt that he was moving incredibly quickly, he wasn't frightened.

The bell stopped ringing and Steve felt himself descending very quickly, he looked down and saw his body still in its position on the bed. His spirit entered it and Steve felt the presence of his arms and legs, he lifted his head but otherwise kept perfectly still, he opened his eyes, he was back. Another bell sounded outside his room, an electric bell with a shrill sound. Steve had heard it before when he was called to help with the plane crash victims, should he stay or should he go? The door to his room opened and Rosie shouted at him. Her face was flushed with pleasure.

"The eagles are here, and the dolphins, come and see them, they are fantastic!"

Steve was puzzled, he couldn't understand why the arrival of some eagles and dolphins would create so much excitement. He stood and followed Rosie out of the door, the corridor was filled with hundreds of people, they were all going in the same direction towards the lifts but when they arrived where the lifts were they filed through two huge doors into a giant arena. Steve gasped, there were hundreds of thousands of people here seated patiently and all looking at the centre where there was a circular track and the centre was covered in lush grass. Steve had never been here before, the size of the arena impressed him and as he followed Rosie down some steps he saw her turn and move along a row of seats. She checked to see that he was following and she stopped at three empty seats and they sat down. Someone touched his arm and he noticed that Michael had arrived and was sitting on his left. Steve smiled at Michael and looked around at the crowd. The arena reminded him of a huge sports stadium and he tried to guess how many seats it held, he spoke to Michael above the gentle murmur of voices all around him and said,

"How many seats does this place have?"

Michael looked at him and was puzzled. "As many as it needs. Shush it's starting."

Steve saw six dolphins appear from the side of the stage, there was no water, they moved effortlessly through the air and they were joined by six more from the opposite side. The twelve creatures moved in harmony and Steve was reminded of the water shows that he had seen on Earth where dolphins had swum and done tricks for an admiring public. Then six more arrived and the movements got higher, Steve watched the dolphins rise, turn and twist and dive down again. Then more arrived, and then more. There must have been a thousand dolphins streaking through the air, one came up to where Steve and the others were sitting. It came so close that Steve could see its face clearly as it twisted and turned and then rolled over as it twirled through the air. Somewhere on the far side of the stadium another dolphin did exactly the same manoeuvre. The air filled with even more dolphins, all turning and swooping, the crowd started to clap and cheer. This made the creatures go even faster still. Suddenly each dolphin stopped and hovered in the air at the very top of the arena. Each nose pointed down, each creature held the exact same poise. Steve couldn't count them but guessed that there must be twenty, no, thirty thousand of them. Suddenly and as one they dived down together, Steve felt the rush of air as two dolphins passed just over his head and they all reached the centre of the arena together. They stopped and formed a circle around the edge, there was no space between them, each dolphin pressed up against its neighbour. Their noses pointed to the centre of the grass and there was silence, nobody moved, no one even whispered. In the distance Steve thought that he could hear wings beating, he looked up but saw nothing. The beating grew louder and then he saw them. As they came over the top of the dome Steve gazed at the eagles, they were huge and magnificent. They soared over the heads of the crowd, they swooped, checked and climbed, some turned in the air and others glided effortlessly. Whereas the dolphins had synchronised their display, the eagles did their own thing. One by one they glided down to the centre and Steve noticed that someone had put out hundreds of podiums, each eagle chose one and as they settled down, they gripped the poles with their talons and folded their wings.

"What happens now?" Steve nudged Rosie who pointed at the centre.

A tall man in a white shimmering gown appeared from the centre of the arena, he stood on a tiny platform that seemed to rise from the grass. He held his hands high over his head as if in greeting and as he rose, the platform turned all the way round and it kept turning so that he could see everyone and everyone could see him. He spoke, there were no microphones, no loudspeakers, no amplification at all but Steve could hear each word clearly.

"Adopt your positions please. Do it on the count of three. One … two … three."

There was a huge commotion and a fluttering of wings, squeaks and shrills filled the air and Steve could see glorious rainbows of colour, the noise was incredible. Steve attempted to put his hands over his ears but he had no hands. He was shocked, he looked down at his hands but saw two white paws instead, he was amazed. He twitched his nose and sat bolt upright. Rosie had been next to him, now her place was taken by a fawn. The last time Steve had seen a fawn was when he watched the film *Bambi* as a child. His nose twitched again and he looked to where Michael sat, he had gone too but there was the most magnificent stag, its antlers took up the space of three seats but luckily Steve was small.

"Wow!" said Steve. He looked around him and everyone had transformed into animals, birds and insects. There was a cockroach on the seat in front of him and over to the left a huge spider sat perfectly still, he looked behind him and was transfixed by the sight of an enormous black bear. Down on the seats stretching in rows to the grass circle were countless creatures, the air was filled with the noise of squeaking, clucking, squawking and grunting. He looked down at his paws again, they seemed vaguely familiar. Then he remembered; he was a white rabbit identical to the one he'd once had as a child. He loved that rabbit, he wondered, was he a new, quite different rabbit or had he turned into his pet Bumpy? He was about to speak to the fawn, he felt just a bit intimidated by the stag and he wanted to ask what was going on. Before he had chance to answer the voice came again from the centre of the circle.

"Now on the count of three transform yourself into the creature you want most to resemble. One … two … three."

At once every animal, bird, insect and fish vanished from their seats and in their places sat hundreds of thousands of eagles, there were a few dolphins too but most of the creatures were eagles, they sat proudly on their seats, their talons gripping the edges.

The man spoke again. "And back please. One … two … three."

Steve hadn't changed into either an eagle or a dolphin, he seemed to be a lone white rabbit surrounded by probably the most two intelligent and wonderful creatures on the planet. As the voice gave the command, everyone changed back into human or animal form but this time, each had a wispy cloud over their heads. Steve was pleased to see Rosie as he knew her, it was difficult for a rabbit to speak to a fawn and absolutely impossible for one to address a stag so he was delighted to see Michael as he knew him before.

The man at the centre spoke again. "I see that everyone is back to normal and yet again the vast majority of you aspire to be eagles. As I am sure that you are all well aware, you have much to do before you can achieve eagle status and as for those who wish to be dolphins, may I politely remind you all that achieving dolphin is only for the most dedicated spirits. I am not saying that it is impossible but to reach the best, you must be totally pure in spirit and in thought. Now I see from the question marks above your heads that most of you have a query." Steve looked around and saw that the wispy clouds had formed themselves into question marks.

The man continued. "You, over there, yes the man in the bright red, yellow and blue jumper, what is your question?"

The man in the colourful jumper spoke, there was no need for a microphone, he spoke clearly and at a normal voice level that seemed odd for a man, maybe the speaker was a woman? Everyone could hear the question.

"Does the panel think that eternity is long enough for most of us to become eagles and maybe even dolphins? I for one am fed up with being a parrot and being spoken to by humans who keep asking me who is a pretty boy then? For a start I am a lady parrot, I do have some intelligence and I resent being treated like this." The audience roared with laughter and many of them clapped. Steve looked down at the circle, he could now see that a panel of eagles and dolphins were sitting around a circular table and in one of the chairs sat the man in the shimmering gown that had addressed them a few moments ago. He turned to one of the dolphins and addressed her.

"This is one for you Miss Universe, what do you think?" Miss Universe was well known for her attacks on anyone who was even the slightest bit aniphobic. To her all animals were equal and she didn't think that any should be treated differently. As far as she was concerned an ant was on the same level terms as an eagle or a dolphin and should be treated as such. This caused her to be admired by ants and other small-sized life forms but she was mocked by lions and tigers and others from the jungle. It was all right for her to have her views, she after all was a dolphin and she could look down on everyone else, and she frequently did. But Miss Universe hesitated in her reply, the last time she had expressed her views plainly she was laughed at by everyone. Some bright spark had politely enquired how she could have been elected Miss Universe when all the other contestants had also been originally from Earth. She stumbled and had no reply and felt the pain of ridicule as even the tortoises laughed at her. She had been standing up for the American sport of baseball and supporting their claim to call their championship a 'World Series' when clearly only American teams took part. She didn't want to make the same mistake twice.

"I think that Ms Parrot has a point." At this, all the spirits who were female parrots clapped enthusiastically. She continued. "Clearly Ms Parrot needs to demonstrate that she is not a pretty boy but a pretty girl, sorry I meant an intelligent girl. What Ms Parrot needs to do is simple, she needs to lay an egg." She stopped, flushed with excitement at her clever and witty response. The chairman turned to one of the eagles.

Major Hawk beamed at him because he wanted to speak. He knew what it was like to be laughed at. Being an eagle was wonderful, he had worked hard and played the political game and sure enough he had reached the position of eagle long before others from his military school had even got to stag or tiger shark. But being stuck with the name Hawk meant that he was the regular butt of jokes especially when he was in his less heavenly moods and this upset him. He decided to support Miss Universe, indeed he always admired her from those days that she had been a pin-up in 'Playboy.' It was a shame that she had campaigned hard to shut that magazine down along with all the others of its type and it was a particularly sad day for him when 'Big and Bouncy' ceased publication too. Still all that was behind him and no one would know that he had enjoyed a personal subscription as he'd been clever enough to buy it in his son's name. He decided to assist Miss Universe by supporting her suggestion.

"Laying an egg is a wonderful idea Miss Parrot," he couldn't bring himself to use the title Ms. "It seems simple enough, lay your egg and they will realise that you are a lady parrot." The chairman looked at Ms Parrot for her response.

"That's easy for you to say as I understand that you have laid a few eggs in your time Major, unfortunately I can't produce an egg as I have no mate, I live in my cage alone and quite frankly if I had to have a companion I would far rather that it would be a female companion, I have no time for men at all."

The audience fell about, uncontrolled laughter filled the stadium, Miss Universe and Major Hawk blushed. Miss Universe was furious, she had hoped that Major Hawk would have his own suggestion, now everyone was laughing at her again. Steve enjoyed this, it was very funny.

The chairman then pointed to others to ask the panel questions and some were frivolous and a few were serious. The panel showed that some were brighter than others and it was obvious that if you had a problem that needed solving at a high level you wouldn't bother with Miss Universe or Major Hawk, you would ask someone sensible like Eagle Mayor, the most famous leader London ever had or his successor, Eagle Lord Bungle, who in his day was a well-known novelist and political motivator. Both were clever and interesting characters. The former had succeeded in turning one of the best- known capital cities into a green and beautiful park and everyone who didn't work for a local authority or for public transport had to move out. Businesses failed by the hundred and whilst some recovered at the new capital city of Greater Milton Keynes most gave up and moved to other parts of Europe. Eagle Mayor finally died at the age of 128 when the staff at the Livingstone Hospital in Whitechapel had to turn off his life support machine after three power cuts in two days. His body had to be carried through the streets as he had left strict instructions for no vehicles to be used in the centre of London unless they were for wardens to patrol searching for untidily parked cycles. He had wanted to be buried at Westminster Abbey but that had been leased out to Disney as a theme park. Eagle Mayor's whizzing idea to turn Britain into the United Magic Kingdom and thus encourage Americans to visit failed after the dollar fell to 100 dollars to the British pound. President Hedge's successor had proudly announced that following an assault on him by a disgruntled Arab working as a waiter in a pizza restaurant from then on America would look after America and everyone else could go hang. The Israelis were not happy to lose their protection and hit America where it hurt, right in the wallet and the dollar plummeted to its lowest ever level.

Eagle Mayor's human body was eventually laid to rest at the site of the old Millennium Dome because that was the only place big enough to house his headstone and the engraved list of his achievements.

His successor Eagle Lord Bungle had also reached number two status and was campaigning hard to be a dolphin but apparently his application was being delayed by dolphins unknown. He had become Lord Mayor of London amidst much protest but it was really a stunning coup for him. He wrote a thrilling novel where the villain planned to exterminate Britain in a cloud of deadly gas. No one took any notice at first because read copies tended to be hidden under the seats on airplanes or stuffed into rubbish bins outside Starbucks coffee shops. Having read the book, no one dared to lend it or pass it on because the revelations and implications were too horrible. Apparently the hero of the book was a formerly disgraced author and political figure. He had been wrongly accused and sentenced by 'Enemies of Britain' and had been sent to prison where he had met a clever mastermind and the hero had tricked him into revealing his plan to mix two simple ingredients and to create a gas that would kill every man, woman and child apart from anyone who had the word Lord in their name or title. First, however, the hero had to get his title back which took him fourteen chapters but the finale saw the hero save the country on the last page. Cleverly the author kept the secret of the ingredients safe but subtly mentioned that if he was reunited with his former title and voted in as Mayor he would dispose of the clever mastermind and would keep the secret safe for ever, or until he was ever unlucky enough to be voted out of office. The British people fell for it and welcomed him as a hero, he was elected unopposed, even by his rival who had cleverly ensured that he was out of the country. He had bought a package deal from Saga Holidays but found that he was too old and infirm at 106, so he changed the booking to their sister company Gaga Holidays and he was being safely pushed from one karaoke bar to another along the streets of the British area in Benidorm when the election took place.

Steve realised that men of action such as these were clever enough to run Heaven until the chairman ended the programme with this announcement.

"This brings this round of Question Time to an end. In the chair tonight we welcomed Miss Universe who graced us with her beauty," she glared at him, "Major Hawk representing Old America, His Royal Highness Eagle Mayor and of course, The Master of the Universe, Eagle Lord Bungle," (he couldn't bring himself to drop the title when he promoted himself to Master of the Universe and changing his first name to Lord was a brilliant idea suggested by his wife Maria from her separate bed in Cambridge) "and of course our other two guests, our sporting heroes. In the red corner we had Eagle Emmu ex-chairman of Manchester United FC who sadly did nothing but chew gum all the way through the event and in the blue corner, Eagle Cumon da Bluz who blocked his chances of being invited again when he accused the chairman of spoiling the occasion by not acting impartially." The audience had booed him and he sulked for the whole time.

A member of the audience who looked human even though he apparently existed on a diet of just chips and gravy asked the leading question, "Can the panel er like confirm er like that Manchester United er like is the world's greatest er like football team?"

The chairman had ignored Cumon da Bluz's laughter and turned to Eagle Emmu who continued to chew gum, he uttered just one word.

"Yep."

Cumon da Bluz had expected the chairman to ask him next but he had turned to Major Hawk instead who had changed the subject and had waffled on about a team of red socks or blue socks or whatever. Everyone got bored and the chairman moved on to the next question.

"What were the thoughts and intentions of the first person who accidentally discovered that if you tweak a cow's udders it will provide milk? And should whoever it was be allowed to work with animals in the future?"

The event ended and everyone clapped, Michael and Rosie had enjoyed it immensely and Steve was still chuckling when they finally left the arena. Michael explained that whilst he might recognise some of the characters from his own time as a human, others from different countries would be seeing their version. The Cubans for example had Eagle Castrato who apparently had lived up to his name well when dealing with his enemies and the Americans had so many to choose from, they had to be given notes, except of course when listening to Papa and Baby Hedge. Baby Hedge as usual had answered every question asked of him with the pledge to fight all known terrorists to the death or until they were exterminated whether they be from Iraq or Iran, he wasn't sure, he was going through the alphabet in his pledge to protect the civilised world that was the 'World Series of America.'

"I noticed that you see yourself as a stag then Michael?" Steve teased him but he thought that Rosie as a fawn was simply fantastic; she was so beautiful, gentle and feminine.

"Yes, well I do actually. Stags are fine, brave creatures, they live in the wild with Mother Nature and everybody loves and respects them." He lowered his voice, "Unfortunately it gets into the head of some who should know better, to shoot at us and put our heads on their walls. I shouldn't tell you this but a certain prince is going to be very put out indeed when I put his head on the wall over a fireplace in my Scottish castle."

"But you haven't got a Scottish castle," said Rosie.

"I'll get one." He paused and then laughed. "I'll call it Immoral Balmoral, that will annoy him even more."

CHAPTER 33

Rosie sat back in the comfortable armchair as Steve settled down in the one next to her and they gazed out onto a beautiful mountain scene. In the foreground was Lake Como and they could see tiny Italian villages nestling in the hills. A waiter brought them a chilled bottle of white wine and poured two glasses, he then returned with a plate of small pieces of cheese and some bread, not enough for a meal but something to nibble with the wine. Steve was at peace and with his favourite person and Rosie grinned at him as she picked up her glass and took a sip.

"Heaven's not a bad place is it Steve?"

Steve couldn't disagree but something troubled him. "I'm getting mixed messages about it all." He put down his glass and placed his index finger into his palm. "I am told that Heaven is not about enjoying ourselves in a materialistic way but here we are in one of the most beautiful places on Earth, drinking the most delicious wine and here am I with the woman I'd rather be with than anyone else I have ever known. Michael said that being in Heaven is about relationships and not having expensive toys or doing great things but here we are …" his voice tailed off.

"And where would you rather be Steve?"

Rosie's question caught him unawares, especially as she seemed very disappointed. He didn't mean to offend her.

"Nowhere, nowhere at all, this is wonderful."

"Do you see the other people at those tables also enjoying their pre-dinner drinks?" Steve nodded. "Do you think that they are in human form on Earth or here as a spirit in Heaven?"

Steve looked around. The couple in the corner looked at each other dreamily, they were obviously in love. The man wore a white jacket with a traditional cravat around his neck, he looked about sixty and his black trousers were immaculately pressed. The woman facing him was in her late forties but looked ten years younger. She didn't smoke and waved her hand at the cigarette offered to her. Steve had just been about to decide that these were fellow spirits in Heaven but the cigarette refusal made him unsure. He looked at another couple sitting by the balcony, they were much older and the man must have been at least eighty, his jacket was old, very well made but no longer fashionable. The woman with him seemed about the same age and she was plump with a cheery face. She pointed at a boat on the lake and her companion looked up from the paper he was reading.

"It's difficult to tell," said Steve.

"What about them?" Steve looked to where Rosie was pointing. A couple in their early twenties stood by a silver car in the car park. Steve recognised it as a Maserati. The man was leaning against the rear wing and the woman held him in her arms, he held her tightly and caressed her hair, she looked up at him and kissed him passionately.

Steve had no idea but he was expected to guess so he did. "The couple there are in spirit form, the older pair are still on Earth as they are out for an anniversary meal and the two in the car park are on Earth because we don't need cars in Heaven, they would have arrived as we did," he paused, "however that was!"

Rosie laughed. "Absolutely wrong! The first couple is in Hell. They have been having an affair for four years and the woman's husband has discovered it and thrown her out, he wants a divorce. She has just told her lover and he's so flustered he's offered her a cigarette even though he knows that she hates smoking. Indeed her lover is in deep trouble, he has a wife and four children all in the family business. He has just discovered that his mistress has told her husband everything. That will mean that his wife will find out, his children will refuse to speak to him, he stands to lose his wife, his family and his business and he will be kicked out of his home too no doubt and no one will help him. The mistress is saying that it's okay, they will be together and find a way to survive but they both know that it's impossible as they live in a society based on family values. In fact he has already decided in the last ten seconds to get home as quickly as possible, he will tell his wife that his secretary forced herself on him and being a weak, stupid man, he couldn't avoid the temptation, he will tell his wife that his affair is over and she will forgive him and not tell the others. She won't be happy about it at all but she will agree because the alternative is too awful to contemplate. Well that's what he hopes will happen as he prises his hand from his mistress's hand and stands ready to walk out. She will have to be fired of course but he can give her some money to placate her."

"Oh dear," said Steve. He had played around and knew of the dangers of getting caught, he could see the anguish on both their faces.

"The second couple, those two in the corner, they actually passed to our side just after the Second World War. They used to own this hotel and were very happy here, they come here as often as they can, they were married for sixty-three years before the husband died. Mama died not long after. They say that they like to keep an eye on the place especially now that their grandson is the owner. He is doing a great job and everyone says that it has a fantastic atmosphere, indeed the old couple's happiness greatly adds to that."

Rosie looked down into the car park, the man and woman by the car were still kissing.

"He's in Heaven." Steve could see that, the man was obviously besotted by his Italian beauty, he kissed her again and stroked her hair, the girl adored him.

"But look closer," said Rosie, "it's not just the car that comes with extras."

Steve was puzzled and looked at the girl, she was truly stunning. But hey, wait a minute, she couldn't be, no that's impossible, he looked at Rosie.

"Sorry but I don't understand."

Rosie was patient. "Antonio is in Heaven, he's alive on Earth and not due to pass through until he's an old and very tired great grandfather. But he won't be marrying his Roberta for the simple reason is that his beloved Roberta is still Roberto and he doesn't know. Now are they in Hell or in Heaven, what do you think?"

"I'm not sure," said Steven, "but if they are in Heaven I think that it might be temporary."

The waiter arrived and said that dinner is served, they left the terrace and went into the restaurant which was very busy. They were shown to their table and several pairs of eyes watched as Steve held the chair for Rosie and then sat down, the perfect gentleman. Steve had no idea as to how he could tell who was who and said so. Rosie helped him to understand.

"Heaven and Hell are both present on Earth, you know that because Michael showed you. We are spirits who can travel freely between Earth and Heaven and Hell and we chose to spend this evening on Earth and in Heaven, like you I can't think of anywhere I would like to be tonight or who I would rather be with. Some of the people here with us tonight are still alive as humans, others are like us. We are all experiencing Heaven or Hell, it depends on our state of mind. Unfortunately some of us thought that we were in Heaven but as we know others, like that couple having the affair know too well what Hell feels like this evening. Antonio may have the fastest transition known to man as he goes from Heaven to Hell at some time after midnight tonight and poor Roberto, well he's never really been in Heaven because he didn't know how to tell his lover that he's not a girl that Antonio can introduce to Mama. He secretly hopes that Antonio will forgive him and love him anyway but deep down he doesn't hold out a lot of hope."

"Well as long as he doesn't hold out anything else." Steve burst out laughing at his joke and others looked at him.

"That's a bit unkind," said Rosie. "Transvestites need love too you know," and she squeezed Steve's hand and dropped her voice an octave and said, "Darling!" She saw the look of shock on Steve's face and added in a husky voice, "I hope that this won't change anything between us. I am not joking."

Poor Steve didn't know what to think or what to say, he had known for a long time that he was in love with Rosie but now he was stunned. He put the glass of wine to his lips but it didn't taste so good anymore. He forced himself to look into Rosie's eyes, he stared at her and she gazed at him lovingly. Then he saw it, she winked at him. Oh for goodness sake, she had played a joke on him, he grinned and sat back in his chair. Rosie smiled at him.

"Let's try and understand our feelings Steve. You had strong feelings for me because you were attracted to me at first and then you found yourself liking my personality a lot more. As we got to know each other and as we went on courses together and worked together you found yourself even more attracted to me, is that right?"

Steve nodded, yes he did feel that way about her.

"But now, just for a moment, your illusions were shattered because you thought for one second that I might have been born a man and had a sex change at some time. Tell me Steve, if you loved me when you believed I was a woman, why wouldn't you love me after you thought that I might not be as you thought? Did you love me for my looks or for my spirit? Which was it Steve?"

Steve looked into Rosie's eyes. He knew what he had to say, he had to tell the truth.

"When I first saw you in that pub where I sang I was knocked out by you, your smile, your body, your personality ... I thought you were gorgeous. As I got to know you and discovered what you were like I found myself falling for you. I didn't dare tell you although I guess that you are probably aware of what I am thinking all of the time, after all you have been a spirit helping others for a lot longer than me and as you were and still are one of my mentors, I guess that you know what I am going through and what I will do next."

Rosie stopped him. "I have no idea what you are thinking unless you tell me and certainly I don't know what you will do next. I am only aware of what you are thinking when your thoughts are so apparent to everyone by your words and actions."

Steve held Rosie's hand in his. He clasped her fingers and decided to let her know what he was thinking, it was the only fair thing to do.

"Shall we order? I'm hungry."

CHAPTER 34

Steve put his spoon down by the empty plate. "That was delicious."

Rosie nodded. The food had been superb and they both felt that they had eaten well but were not uncomfortably full. The dessert served was zabaglione and it was exquisite, few Italian chefs bothered to make the delicate whipped egg yolk with Marsala wine but the chef at this hotel knew that his customers adored it especially when a night of love was planned.

Steve had put his scare about Rosie out of his mind. Well he had tried to but the thought haunted him. 'What if she was a man and had a sex change, no for goodness sake, pull yourself together Steve, she's one hundred per cent girl, get on with it.'

"I'm sleepy," said Rosie thinking of the huge double bed in their room. She had wanted to dive on that golden quilt and bury her face in those giant feather pillows as soon as she saw the suite but now she couldn't wait to do it.

Steve tensed, so this was it. Rosie had not just invited him out to the Italian beauty spot for a nice meal and a lesson, she really did have feelings for him and now they were about to sleep together. He felt a tingle of excitement that reminded him of his terror on his first proper date with a girl he really fancied.

"Why did you tease me?" Steve lay with his arm around Rosie, her head rested on his chest and he stroked her lovely long hair as he spoke.

"I didn't tease you," she said, "I just didn't want to rush things, you seemed so impatient."

"I didn't mean that," Steve replied. "I meant about you being a man."

Rosie sat up and looked at him. "I didn't say that I was a man you idiot, do I look like a man, do I feel like a man, do I smell like a man?"

"Of course not."

"So why say that I am a man then?"

"I didn't say that you were a man."

"Yes you did."

"No I didn't."

Rosie was silent, Steve wished that he hadn't said anything but then he realised, there was no way any man would have logic like that. He was now totally convinced that Rosie had been teasing him, he decided to lighten the conversation.

"Our first argument and we've only been lovers for such a short time."

"Yes it was a short time, four minutes I think, could I use you as an egg timer?"

"Ha ! Very funny," Steve was pleased to change the conversation away from sex changes and he was happy to be teased by Rosie. They had made love for considerably longer than four minutes and as Steve touched and caressed her he knew in his heart one hundred per cent that he really loved Rosie and that he wanted to be with her forever. Rosie felt the same, he knew that and she knew that he was aware of that too. Steve had had sex with scores of women and he easily justified the nickname that one girl had given him.

"I will call you Butterfly," she said, "you flit from flower to flower and you'll never know what true love is until you stop seeing sex as some kind of conquest." At the time he had laughed off the jibe but now he understood. Rosie said, "When you are totally in love with someone and you honestly believe that they are totally in love with you, that's when you know that you are in Heaven and that doesn't matter if you are a human on Earth, or if you have passed through to the spirit world. Of course people think that they are in love but most of the time it isn't love, it's lust and the feelings die when one partner no longer fancies the other because the initial spark has gone."

"So how does someone know that they are truly in love and indeed how do people fall in love, what is the mystery?"

"There is no mystery, it's very simple. When someone falls in lust rather than love they desire the other person and they want them for themselves, they want to possess them, they want to make them theirs. At first if the feelings are mutual, the passion is immense, it's stunning, and it's frightening. But after a while one or the other, sometimes both, look at themselves, they look at their relationship and see that it's not really going anywhere. That can happen in a short time or a medium length of time but rarely after a long time though it can happen. The problem is of course that if one or both partners realise that they are not really in love after children have been born and there are financial burdens then whilst the love or lust has failed, the couple find themselves trapped into staying together, hence the rows, the adultery and the break-ups. Many couples are together making the best of a bad situation because the problems and expense of splitting up are worse than staying together."

"I can understand that but how do you know when it's real love that you feel for someone and not a lusting love?"

Steve's question didn't faze Rosie, she had experienced lust and real love when she was a human and she had studied the textbook *Heart of the Soul* that Michael had given her on her Human Performance course.

"When two humans on Earth fall in love properly or when two spirits fall in love in Heaven, the love is spiritual and not just physical. You are going to ask me how love can be spiritual and I'll make it easy for you. You know that every human has a spirit, or soul, call it what you will. When that spirit meets another spirit and there's a bonding, then and only then can the physical part of the human fall deeply in love, deeply into a proper, long-lasting love. Of course in Heaven we don't have a physical side, yes you could see and feel your body in the early stages of your learning and indeed to a certain extent now, but you won't be lusting or feeling the need for carnal pleasures with strangers or people you hardly know when you meet them here. You would have done that on Earth and indeed you did on many occasions but here you are in a different spiritual environment and if and when you fall in love it's because you and your spirit have fallen in love." She paused. "But this presents us with a problem."

Steve was surprised, he didn't expect spirits to have problems in Heaven, he started to interrupt but Rosie cautioned him to wait.

"The problem occurs in Heaven as well as on Earth, it occurs when the spirit falls in love more than once." This time Steve couldn't keep quiet.

"More than once? And have two or more ongoing relationships?"

"No, not like that. It's just that you could feel deep love for me now and I could feel the same for you and yes, although we are destined to be very happy, there could come a time when one or both of us fall out of love. That happens to spirits just as it does to humans."

"Well I know that I love you Rosie and I feel deep down that you love me, I have never felt so strong a love, so strong a power inside me that I feel for you. You are the girl that I always searched for when I was on Earth and now that I have found you, I will never let you go."

"What a load of twaddle!" Steve was amazed at the rebuke. "When you first saw Julie in Reception you felt exactly the same about her." Steve had to admit it.

"Yes she is lovely and yes I must admit that I really fancied her, but Rosie she couldn't hold a candle to you. I have got to know you in the time that we have been together so far and I honestly believe that you and I are right for each other."

"And if I was a man?" Rosie looked at Steve straight in the eye. At once Steve knew what she meant and why she brought up the farce earlier of her having been a man and having a sex change.

"Yes." And he understood. He didn't love Rosie in a shallow way because she was pretty or because she had the figure that he desired, he found that he loved Rosie because he knew that his spirit loved Rosie's spirit and that his spirit and he were not two separate beings but one whole being.

"Now maybe you understand why people fall in love with non-sexy, unattractive people, why couples stay in love with each other when the beauty and passions of youth are long gone, why they stay together after rows, break-ups and traumas. Those are the lucky people who are really in love, they are in a spiritual love relationship and that never dies as long as one thing remains."

"And what's that?"

"The ability to love unconditionally."

"What does that mean?"

"If there is unconditional love then there is an excellent chance of the love developing into a spiritual love. I'll give you an example. A couple might think that they are in love because they are always saying 'I love you' and indeed they both mean it. But have one partner not return the statement and the other is wondering, 'do they still love me?' Or let's go a step further, one partner wants to spend all their free time with the other whereas the other wants to do different things alone or with other people, if there is unconditional love, both partners will acknowledge that there needs to be space and freedom on both sides and no attempts at control or possession. If you think about couples that you knew who were very happy together you will realise that their love for each other was unconditional, in other words, they loved the other whatever happened.

"I'll give you an example, let's say a couple loved each other but then one of them decided that they had to go alone around the world and explore and find new adventures. You might think that the would-be explorer must have fallen out of love with their partner if they could entertain the idea. We take it further, the partner to be left at home really does love the would-be explorer and whilst they are sad and upset at the personal loss of the partner for a few years they know that they really want to do this and they encourage them and help them to prepare and leave. That love is an unconditional love and it transcends time and space."

"But suppose that explorer went to the other side of the world and met someone else and fell in love with them, would that abandoned partner still love them?"

"If they had a spiritual, unconditional love then yes they would still love them, and even more surprising, they would be pleased that their ex-partner had found happiness, if indeed that's what they had found."

"That's far too much to accept," said Steve. "If my wife ..." he paused and looked at Rosie, "if my wife cleared off on some find-myself type trek and fell in love with another man, then I would hardly be pleased, I would feel betrayed and abandoned and I would want a divorce and that would be it."

"Yes," said Rosie, "you and millions like you, but think for one moment that we are not talking about an ordinary love but a deep, spiritual, unconditional love, it's hard for you to accept this now so soon after your arrival here but believe me, unconditional love is the sweetest love of all."

Rosie took his hand and held it.

"We are going to be apart for some time, then we will be together on one of the courses and then we will be apart again. Of course I don't hope that you will meet someone else but if you do and you are happier with them than with me then I will love you enough to be able to let you go and truly I will be happy if I know that you are happy."

Steve was sad to discover that they were soon to part and he wanted to reassure her that he would never want to be with anyone else other than Rosie. She knew that and there was no point in saying it again, instead he wanted to know more about the different types of love and said so.

"There are many different types of love and believe me that they are really different. The deepest of those are unconditional too, do you want some examples?" Steve nodded. "Okay, a mother's love for her child is totally unconditional and it's totally natural of course. The child doesn't know or reason that it is loved but it feels and senses that love and responds to it. As the child gets older it may rebel against its parents who may be thoroughly upset at the child's behaviour especially if the child abuses their trust or creates trouble, commits crimes etc. But the parents, especially the mother in the vast majority of cases, will still love their child. They may not like them, they may indeed be extremely upset with them, but they will still love them. Now you could say that this unconditional love is something that we have naturally for our children and you'd be right, but it will also happen when we have that feeling of unconditional love for a good friend. They may please us, annoy us and sometimes may act or speak in a way which we find shocking. We might even have huge rows with them. But if we love them unconditionally then we will forgive them and our love will become stronger."

"And if the mother doesn't love her children or if someone doesn't love their friend or partner?"

"Yes that's sad and it does happen, but we can't choose who we love and who we don't love, not when we are talking about spiritual love. We can choose who we are attracted to and often when we get to know them we discover that our feelings for them turn into love. It's a complex state but luckily when it happens we are fully aware of it especially if there's a chance that we might lose that person."

Steve said, "You said earlier that we will be separated for a while, will that be for long?"

"We have no time here, you know that, but yes it may feel like a long time to you, it will feel like an eternity for me because I have a good idea where you are going."

Steve immediately wanted to know but something told him that Rosie wasn't too keen to tell him. He would have to wait until he saw Michael. Rosie leant back against the pillow, she had a look in her eye that Steve recognised and he moved towards her and kissed her.

"Come here lover," she whispered. "Your next assignment starts in the morning and you won't have time to think of me for a while so come and make love to me again."

Steve felt a mild panic, the word 'again' was the one that men feared most when with their lover. Would he have to rise to the occasion for many more 'agains' before she would let him sleep?

CHAPTER 35

"I love you Michael."

Michael looked up in astonishment at Steve who was reading one of the books that Michael had given him. He felt wonderful, truly wonderful, he had slept the sleep of contented lovers after Rosie had finally closed her eyes and he held her in his arms all through the night. When he awoke he found that she was looking at him intensely and he met her gaze. She stroked his cheek with her fingers and told him that he was a wonderful lover. He wasn't sure whether to be pleased with the compliment or not. How many lovers had she had? Having decided that it was none of his business he read the chapter on Communication and the need to tell people that you loved that you loved them. His statement right out of the blue shocked Michael.

"Yes, well, er right, er exactly!" Steve grinned, he hadn't seen Michael flustered for ages, Steve sensed Michael's discomfort and decided to amuse himself.

"Don't you love me Michael?" Steve was determined to look serious and not let on that he was teasing him.

"Well, er, yes, I mean, yes I do love you Steve but ..." His voice tailed off as he searched for the right words to maintain his teacher/pupil relationship. "But I love you as a ... er, as a friend, as a pupil, I love you because you are who you are Steve."

Steve smiled, Got him! "Well that's all right because I love you unconditionally so that even if you didn't love me I would still love you Michael."

Michael thought. Then he understood. "No way Steve!"

"No way what?"

"No way am I letting you dodge out of your next project. You are doing it and that's final, indeed you have to do it otherwise you can't

247

go to the next stage." Michael assumed that Rosie must have let slip to Steve what his next course assignment was but Steve hadn't got a clue.

"I have no idea what you are talking about," said Steve. "I just want you to know that my heart and soul are full of love and some of that is for you."

"I think that we need to have a nice chat about that sometime Steve but in the meantime do you think that you can put yourself in the right frame of mind for what I have to tell you, whether you like it or not, you have to go through this state, everyone does, there's no alternative, you might even find it fun."

The word 'fun' chilled Steve. That meant that it wouldn't be, he wanted to know more.

"You remember when you were a fly?" Steve did, indeed how can anyone forget living the life of a fly, he was just happy to eat jam and not … and that whack with a slipper that had killed him had been totally painless. But he didn't want to be a fly again.

"Well the good news is, you are not going to be a fly again."

"Oh great, so maybe a cockroach or a spider, no thanks."

"Actually you don't get to choose, I do and as I do like you," he decided to tease Steve in retaliation for his outburst, "as I do love you, I have decided to let you do the Fish route."

"The Fish route?"

"Yes. You have been a fly and I could have put you through the Insect route or through the Animal or the Bird route but I have decided that you are doing the Fish route. It's my decision, you can argue but it will make no difference unless I get annoyed and if I do, you'll have to be a fly again."

"I'm not arguing," said Steve quickly who had no desire to be a fly again. "The Fish route will be fine. I like fish."

"You are not going to eat fish you twit," Michael immediately saw his mistake. "Well actually you probably will eat fish but if you do, it will be as a fish."

"Oh, you are going to make me a fish, and I am going to eat myself am I? Will I be filleted and grilled or served up raw like in sushi?"

"Right!" Michael was slightly annoyed. "That does it. You will start as an anchovy and see how you get on, if you do well, I might move you up to being a mackerel. Do well at that and we'll look at other species but screw up on being an anchovy and you'll be right out of Fish and into Insects, do I make myself clear?"

Steve remembered his dislike of anchovies, he would never have one on a pizza, they tasted disgusting. He sighed, now he was to become one.

Michael and Steve left Steve's room and they walked down the corridor, Michael put his hand on the door handle and paused before he opened it.

"Good luck Steve, do a great job of being an anchovy and you'll progress, mess it up and, well I don't need to tell you do I?" Michael pushed the door open and stood back to let Steve enter. He saw a doctor's waiting room, the floor and the walls were white and in the centre of the room was a doctor's couch with a light shining down onto the pillow from a large angle lamp. Steve saw no one but heard a voice.

"Come in, remove your shoes, your trousers and your shirt and lay down on the bed, I'll be with you in a moment."

Steve went in and he was alone in the room, he did as he was told and looked for somewhere to put his clothes. He felt silly in just his underpants as he lay on the couch and placed his head on the pillow. The voice spoke again.

"Look up into the light and don't look away as it gets brighter, don't worry you'll be a fly in a moment or two, it won't take a moment, you won't feel a thing."

Steve felt panic rising in his throat. "Excuse me, I understand that I am not to be a fly, I'm supposed to be an anchovy."

"An anchovy?" The doctor spoke loudly, he was surprised and irritated.

"Yes, an anchovy, definitely not a fly please."

"No one tells me anything, oh well, just a second and I'll change the setting. Good luck as an anchovy young man, I am sure that you would have made a wonderful fly. Now count ten seconds and you will go to sleep, just like having an anaesthetic."

But Steve didn't want to count to ten, he was so relieved not to have to be a fly again he decided to spend the ten seconds telling the doctor a joke.

"Did you know what Disraeli said just before he died?" The doctor had no idea and said so.

"I think I'm feeling better." He could hear the doctor chuckling as he suddenly started to feel very drowsy, the bright light above him shone straight into his eyes and even as he closed them he could still see the light as it faded. Then it grew again in intensity and Steve opened his eyes, it wasn't the light of the bulb that he could see but the light of the sun as it flickered through twenty metres of warm blue water. The silver rays of light darted above him with a trillion tiny bubbles, sunlight reflecting off every single one of them. He looked to his left and right and saw that he was swimming with countless other anchovies, he felt warm and secure and he felt that he was particularly close to the anchovy swimming closest to him.

"Welcome my son," she said. "Enjoy your life, stay safe, I …" and with her sentence unfinished, she turned left and disappeared into the shoal and he never heard her last words. Steve could feel the shoal moving up and down and as it swirled left and then right he heard the voices.

"Big fish coming, pass it on. Big fish coming, pass it on." The murmur grew louder until it was coming from the anchovies nearest the centre of the swarm.

"Big fish coming, pass it on. Big fish coming, pass it on."

There was a pause and a silence. Then the anchovies next to him said it again, even louder.

"Big fish coming, pass it on. Big fish coming, pass it on." He felt compelled to repeat the warning and he did.

"Big fish coming, pass it on." The anchovies to the right of him, swirled and dived up and down, the tiny bodies darting through the water.

"Hold on!" said one older one next to him. "How do you know there's big fish coming?"

Steve didn't know, and said, "I don't, I just passed on the message I heard."

"Please do not do that, you will cause panic in the shoal and you know what that will do to us all?" Steve didn't and he continued to swim as if his life depended on it. He liked the closeness of the other fish, he enjoyed the warm water and being part of a huge crowd, he felt powerful, almost invincible, the shoal moved down deep into the ocean, then it suddenly rose extremely quickly.

"Big fish coming, pass it on." This time the words were coming from the fish on the edge of the shoal, the anchovy that had rebuked him earlier, turned to Steve and Steve saw the panic in the older one's eyes.

"Big fish coming, pass it on." But it was too late for Steve to speak; at once he heard a new, louder command.

"Form a ball. Form a ball." The anchovies huddled tightly together and Steve felt himself almost crushed in the grip of the anchovies as they pulled tighter. Their speed increased and the shoal moved in circles, ever tighter and the ball got smaller and smaller. Their speed picked up and Steve was dizzy, the shoal twisted, turned, fell and rose, ever tighter. Anchovies in the middle of it were suffocated and died but Steve didn't know that, his attention was on a flurry of movement and lots of bubbles ahead of him. He could hear cries of pain. Suddenly he was out of the shoal's defensive ball and darting to keep clear of huge teeth and eyes that flashed in anger. He swerved and just missed being eaten and as he spun over pointing down into the ocean he saw the ball of fish attacked by hundreds of terror fish, he had no idea what they were but he knew that his comrades were being slaughtered.

To one side he saw a group of anchovies being urged to form another ball by several older fish and he realised that he could reach this ball safely. As he dodged and ducked the carnage around him he saw countless anchovies disappear whole into the mouths of their attackers. He tried to reach the new ball and as he was hit by the wash of a predator taking the anchovy next to him he tumbled out of control, he straightened up and there was the ball ahead of him. Next to him was a baby anchovy, it had just been born in the melee around him, the poor mite had no idea what to do and Steve could see that if it remained where it was it would be swallowed in a second. He grabbed the baby and pulled it close, it weighed nothing at all and Steve reached the edge of the ball and accelerated to pick up speed. He had to match the velocity of the outside of the ball before he could duck inside for protection, it was no good being on the outside as he didn't have the stamina. With the baby tucked close, Steve pushed others aside. He could see that they were terrified but he knew that he had to reach the middle. In time the attackers would finish their meal and would swim off somewhere else, he and the baby would be safe if he could survive just a little bit longer. Then he heard the all clear.

"Slow down, not our turn this time. Slow down, not our turn this time."

Steve felt the pressure of the ball easing and he knew that it was slowing down. He looked around and there were tiny particles of dead anchovy everywhere. He could sense the relief in the shoal and also a terrible sense of loss as anchovies moved around searching for their loved ones, trying to find relatives and friends who they had been sharing their lives with before the attack.

"Two hundred and twenty thousand dead." That was the news spoken by those that knew within the shoal.

"I suppose it could have been worse," said an old veteran anchovy who swam up beside Steve. "I remember that attack we had just off the Azores. It was a terrible day, we lost fourteen million that time, by far the worst one ever."

"Nonsense," said another. "I was in the Pacific one time when we lost twenty-seven million, you don't know anything about disasters, you are just a minnow."

The anchovy was embarrassed and changed the subject.

"You did well to save that baby, your bravery was noticed. It will be good for you in your next life." Steve was surprised and then he noticed something odd about the anchovy that had spoken. It was his eyes, they reminded him of someone that he knew. Yes, that's it, he had the same eyes as Michael. He was about to ask him when suddenly he felt a tremendous blow and the sea erupted from under him. He and a million others were pressed together and Steve thought that his lungs would burst, he felt himself being pulled upwards though he wasn't swimming, he was totally under someone or something else's control. He gasped as he left the water, he heard the screams of horror from those around him and for a second it all went black. Then he felt the sun hot on his back and he looked around, water dripped from everyone. They moved up and away from the surface, they stopped and for a second Steve hung in space, it was surreal. Then he was falling, it seemed like miles, others were falling too, he tried to swim but swimming doesn't work out of water and his flying abilities were poor. They hit hard. An anchovy cried out as Steve landed on his stomach, then another one smacked into

Steve as he wriggled clear of the one he had just collided with. Steve rolled over, he wasn't hurt but he thought he was winded. No it was worse than that, he wasn't winded at all, he simply couldn't breathe. He closed his eyes as he felt the warm sun on his face, others lay still around him, a few twitched, Steve tried to move a bit but it was useless. Then everything went black and suddenly Steve was very cold, very cold indeed, in fact it became colder than hell and Steve tried to get warm by pressing against the anchovy next to him, but he was freezing too and the last thing Steve felt was being cold and suddenly very sleepy as he passed from being an anchovy and he landed on his bottom beside the chair in Michael's office. His feet and hands were still cold and he was soaking wet. He looked up at Michael who smiled at him.

"And how was it?"

Steve held the cup with both hands as he sipped the hot tea that Michael produced and handed to him. He was shaking, he was still very cold but getting slightly warmer. Going through the fish experience wasn't too bad, it could have been worse. Indeed swimming around in a warm blue sea was much more preferable to being a fly but he did wonder what had happened and he asked Michael who pressed a button on a remote and a screen lit up showing Steve his life in the Ocean. It showed the shoal of anchovies moving in time and space, it looked beautiful and Steve remembered having watched the Blue Planet series of films.

"There's you," said Michael and his stick pointed to a single anchovy amongst millions. "And there's me ... And there are those old timers who told you about previous survival battles." The scene changed to show a trawler. The crew clapped as their net collected a bumper catch of anchovies, the tiny fish hit the deck as the net was released and as the trap doors opened they tumbled into the ice cold freezer. That's where Steve died along with thousands of his kind.

"So that's what happened to me in the end." Steve was intrigued but Michael had more to show him. The scene changed to a happy gathering of four young men in their late teens sitting in a restaurant, they were laughing and teasing each other as their meals were presented and one of the men looked at his pizza in mock disgust.

"Ooh I can't stand anchovies." And his fork dabbed and picked up Steve's lifeless body and dropped it into the ashtray.

"Hey I would have had it," said his friend. "Too late now though," as he looked to see the tiny fish covered in ash next to a dog end. The waiter picked up the ashtray, poured the contents into the kitchen's rubbish bin and chucked the ashtray into the washing up bowl.

"Well that's VERY nice," said Steve. "I've survived a giant fish attack, been caught, died and been frozen and for what? To be dished up on some moron's pizza who didn't even want me anyway." Michael laughed.

"That's the second time you've been thrown in the dustbin Steve, you must be getting used to it and didn't you once prise an anchovy off your pizza too?"

Michael had enjoyed being in Steve's adventure. The swim had refreshed him and he asked Steve if he had recognised him when he congratulated him on saving the baby.

"Yes I think I did. It's those eyes Michael, you can't disguise your eyes."

"So true," said Michael. "You did well in that life, you have a few hundred more to go before you get an idea of what's going on, but you can enjoy a rare privilege, you can choose your next species of fish."

"Oooh aren't I lucky?" Steve wanted to be sarcastic but if Michael noticed, he didn't comment.

"What are my options?

"Before we discuss those, can you please, and for the record, just tell me what you learned as an anchovy?" He picked up a pad and pencil as if to make notes.

"Pardon?" said Steve, "I don't think I learned too much in the short life I had."

"A lesson was taught to you and either you picked up on it or you didn't, if you did, you will tell me and we can progress, if you didn't, then back you go for another swim in that shoal."

Steve was stuck, he thought back to the feeling of being in that shoal, it had been quite pleasant but then the rumour started. 'Big fish coming, pass it on.' He had repeated the words and had been told off. Then the warning had come again, but this time from the edge of the shoal not the middle. He thought about this long and hard.

"There was a rumour, it was about an imminent attack but the information was coming from the wrong direction, I would have ignored it but the pressure on me to be part of the group and do what they did was overwhelming. I felt that it was wrong at the time but I still found myself being swept along with the crowd. They were saying it so I did too."

Michael was pleased. "And then you heard the news of a genuine attack from those who would have had more information, those who were in a position to see and hear for themselves."

"Yes," said Steve. "I was too heavily involved with those around me to realise that I was doing what I was bid to do, I wasn't making my own judgement I just went along with everyone else."

"And is that a good thing?"

Steve didn't need to think before answering. "No it's foolish and dangerous. Next time I won't be rallied by a crowd of others, I will search out the facts for myself and make my own decisions." Steve thought back to his previous life and the TV reports showing crowds protesting and chanting slogans, he could see how easy it was to get carried along with others and to act without rational thought.

"Right Steve, your lucky prize is to be able to choose your next species. What will you be next?"

CHAPTER 36

Steve flicked through the book of the world's fish. Michael meant what he said and Steve could choose his next species. Gosh some were ugly, others were beautiful, some had bright colours, others were transparent and some could change colour to suit their surroundings. What did he fancy? He couldn't be a dolphin, that had been ruled out but he could be a shark. Did he fancy being a shark? He wasn't sure. Steve was experienced enough to realise that death would be inevitable and this was at the back of his mind as he looked in detail at each page. A shark might have a horrible death as the victim of other sharks and being torn to pieces wasn't really what he had in mind. So what then? A tiny fish ready to be swallowed whole and painlessly? No that would be after a boring life of hiding and dodging everyone else. Then he saw the clown fish, what a beautiful creature and it lived in lovely warm seas, it had good defences too and was likely to survive. He wasn't sure about predators and then he laughed as he remembered an old joke from a Christmas cracker. 'Why don't clown fish get eaten by other fish? Because they taste funny! Boom boom!'

Michael looked up from his book to see what Steve was laughing at and he told Steve that he had a few seconds to decide, otherwise he would choose for him. Steve wanted to ask for advice and Michael suggested that he become a trigger fish and he pointed to the page. It looked interesting and Steve liked the small mouth with the very sharp teeth, it wasn't colourful either so he wouldn't attract too much attention. He decided to be a trigger fish.

Steve didn't need to be told to undress and the voice had his chosen species right this time. He gazed up at the bright light on the doctor's couch and as it faded it was replaced by a much murkier, dull glow from a rain-covered surface thirty or forty metres above. The visibility wasn't as good as before and as Steve looked around he glimpsed another trigger fish looking at him in wonder.

"Hi I am your brother, it was fascinating watching you being born, Mama's got to rest now. I am so pleased to see you, I have had to patrol on my own for ages and it's not so much fun alone. We'll have great sport now that you are here. Come, we are on duty in five minutes, get those teeth sharpened and gleaming, I feel lucky today."

Steve hadn't a clue what was expected of him but he was pleased to be able to follow someone who seemed as if he knew what he was doing and was friendly. No shoals for him then, it looked like he would be swimming with his new brother.

"Oh and my name is Sebastian but my nickname is Cop because I'm a good one. You have great teeth for biting so I will call you Jaws."

"My name is Steve actually but yes I like the sound of Jaws, you can call me Jaws."

Cop led the way to the surface and Steve swam close to hear what he was saying.

"It's dead easy, our territory starts from that point down there next to the sunken boat, look you can see its funnel. Be careful if you go in there, a family of lobsters lives in it and if one of them catches you with its claw you will have a nice scar as a reminder.

Our patch starts at the bottom and forms a cone from there to three metres below the surface. Now if anything or anyone passes through our cone we attack first and ask questions later. At night it's fairly quiet but during the day when the sun is overhead we have great sport with humans." Steve, or rather Jaws, was puzzled.

"We meet humans here? Wow!"

"They come every day, usually about twenty of them, they swim around a bit, make loads of bubbles and they are harmless. If they keep clear of our cone then we ignore them but if they enter it then we attack."

"But why do we attack if they are harmless?"

"Oh my goodness, what a question. We attack because that's what we trigger fish do, that's our job and it's expected of us. If we didn't attack anyone and just floated around trying to make people laugh like an idiot clown fish we would have no real fun at all."

Steve was pleased that he hadn't chosen to be a clown fish. "Do we allow anyone through our cone Cop?" Steve was getting into the mood.

"Well yes, we allow sharks, or rather we don't actually allow them, we stand back and they come through, best to keep away if you see a shark. Oh and moray eels too, they can be insolent and they think that they can go anywhere."

"And can they?"

"Well, yes."

"Anything else?"

"Look, the list of who can come through and who can't is too long to go through now, basically if some soft stupid jerk tries to get through our cone we hit him hard, rough him up a bit and then fine him."

"Fine him, what do we fine him?"

"Anything he has, if he hasn't got anything, then we give him a nasty bite and tell him not to come back." Cop looked up, he heard the sound of a boat approaching and then the engine stopped, a few minutes later they heard the splashes as divers jumped from the boat into the water, they formed a group at the back of the boat and then started their descent. At first Cop was disappointed, the divers were heading away from their cone. Steve saw a clown fish approach and bared his teeth.

"Oh you won't frighten me," said the clown fish rudely. "You go for me with your teeth and I'll tickle you to death." Steve backed off. The clown fish continued.

"You won't see any divers today boys; they have gone to Anemone Reef. Apparently the coral there is alive with colour and the fronds will be attracting your humans with all the fish that swim around them. Anemone Reef is stunning."

Cop wasn't impressed. "There are some super fronds growing beside our cone, we have been looking after them to attract our own divers." Cop turned and swam to the funnel, the fronds, long and green waved in the current, they were lovely and thousands of tiny colourful fish swam around and through them.

"You are right," said the clown fish. "I'll spread the word for you, we'll have the divers over here in no time at all." He paused. "After all, wait for it, wait for it - with fronds like these, who needs Anemones?" The clown fish roared with laughter and Cop went for him but the colourful joker was too fast. Steve grinned at the awful pun and Cop saw the bubbles coming from his mouth.

"Don't encourage that idiot. We haven't got time to stand around joking with fools, come, we need to get into position, we'll have visitors soon."

"Stay out of sight, be careful." Cop hid behind the old funnel. He looked inside, the lobsters were asleep. Jaws waited next to him.

"If they see us they will turn away. They know what's good for them. Get down, I can see the Divemaster."

Bruce Allen couldn't give a four x about trigger fish; he had seen plenty in his time not only here but at scores of other dive sites too. But he wasn't stupid either, he wore a full wet suit made of very good quality material, he'd been bitten once by a trigger fish and it bloody well hurt. The bastard had bit him hard on the head and it felt as if someone had cracked a beer bottle over him, the blood poured from the wound and when Bruce climbed back on to the boat the captain took one look and ran for the first aid box, a hole the size of a coin had been clearly bitten. Bruce was in agony and swore never to swim without a full suit, booties, gloves and a proper hat even if the water was really warm.

Cop and Jaws watched Bruce lead his divers right through their cone. Cop whispered that he would give the command, he paused and then ordered, "Now, go now, stick by me."

The fish accelerated from their hiding place and with less than a few centimetres apart they weaved left and right, away from the base of the cone and as they looked up they could see the Divemaster coming to the far boundary. They dived deeper and hugged the bottom, darting around the coral and as seven divers passed them Cop picked his target. A lone Englishman separated from his buddy trailed the group, he was nervous, he used his air up quickly and as he took in large gulps, his bubbles could be seen for fifty metres. Cop covered the ground quickly and Steve swam beside him, Henry Whittaker looked down and saw them.

"Hmm they look like two motorcycle police riders." Cop would have been ecstatic if he knew what Henry thought. Henry Whittaker didn't recognise them as trigger fish, indeed he saw a lionfish and recognised that and the clown fish was an easy one to spot too, he'd been told of the dangers of trigger fish and to keep away from them but how do you keep away from something that's hunting you? His instructor had told him to swim away from a cone and not to go up but which way was away? He had to stay with his buddy too. Henry was intrigued by the arrival of the brown fish with the small mouths but he pressed on and tried to catch the others.

Cop looked up. He couldn't believe the cheek of the divers, they had passed right through the centre of his cone and the last one, the fat one with lots of bubbles was taking a liberty. He wore a dive shop T-shirt with a picture of a lionfish and his buoyancy jacket was buckled tightly around him. He wore cheap, blue swimming shorts and a belt with more weights on than most to get his fatter body to sink. The buckle on the weight belt was loose and two of the weights hung down in front of him instead of being around his back and fortunately they protected Henry's manhood. Cop wanted to catch Henry and sink his teeth into the warm flesh of Henry's privates but the loose flapping weight belt made him cautious, he'd bitten a weight once and the lead taste was awful. Henry would never know how lucky he was that day. Henry Junior who came along a year later would never know that he owed his life to a loose weight belt.

Cop saw the huge yellow fins.

"We'll go for his big yellow feet; a good swift bite is bound to hurt him." Cop and Jaws released their brakes and shot after Henry. Cop got there first and sank his teeth into the tough plastic.

"Yuck this tastes awful," thought Cop as he gripped harder and pulled. Henry felt the tug and turned round, he had thought at first that another diver was trying to catch his attention but all his team were ahead. He looked in astonishment at his fin, a large brown fish was tugging at it.

"Get Blob," Henry shouted, forgetting for a moment that you can't shout under water with a respirator in your mouth.

"Piss Ob," Henry tried again and this time he waggled a stern finger at Cop. Cop was astonished and tugged harder, then he let go in disgust.

"Bloody cheek, he comes straight through our cone as if he owned it, I then bite him hard enough to draw blood and he just laughs at me and tells me to clear off. You have a go."

Steve aka Jaws sped after Henry, he was leaving the cone but Henry didn't know that. Steve decided to go in for one good bite of the diver's knee but as he aimed for his spot he felt the temperature of the water change ever so slightly and he realised that Henry had cleared the cone. He heard Cop calling him and he swam back. The divers disappeared into the distance. Henry didn't know how close he had been to disaster.

"You did well stopping," said Cop. "Were you tempted to bite him after he left the cone?" Steve thought about it.

"No not really, you told me where the boundary was and that I can only attack within it. You stated the rules clearly, I obeyed them."

"But weren't you even tempted to hit him just outside the cone? It was only a few metres outside?

Steve was about to respond when he noticed Cop's eyes. "It's you, it's you, it's Michael."

Cop turned away, he was disappointed, he had been recognised again and now Steve would expect him to appear as his fellow creature every time he went on a lesson. It was a shame, Michael enjoyed swimming around and he'd always fancied being a trigger fish and patrolling the deep, playing cops and robbers. He wanted to test Steve too, catching divers and biting them was great fun, they were the talk of the diving world and rarely would a post-dive bar chat go by without the famous trigger fish being mentioned at least once. But he had to know, would Steve cheat, would he deliberately agree to honour rules and then break them to suit himself, others had done it and people had suffered. If you make rules then you keep them yourself, otherwise you lose all credibility and no one will believe you or trust you ever again – not even your friends. Steve had obviously passed this lesson too. It was time to go back. Cop led the way with Steve close behind. Cop knew where the Barracuda would be waiting, poor Jaws wouldn't even see it coming. Michael could come and go as he wished, Steve still had to pass through life properly and birth and death were essential to his growth and progress as a spirit. Michael hoped that it would be painless.

Steve wiped the blood from his legs and stood up straight, his hair was still wet and he knew he was back in Michael's room. Michael looked up from his reports and put his pencil down and Steve asked,

"Er what was that by the way?"

"What was what?"

"That giant creature that snapped me in two?"

"Oh that was a Barracuda."

"But how did you know? You were swimming ahead of me, that thing grabbed me from behind, if I didn't see it coming then either you did and you didn't warn me or you knew it was there."

Michael didn't know what to say, he had been rumbled, he muttered a few words that sounded like an apology and then straightened. "It may have been a Barracuda, it took you and then sped off in another direction, I only got a glimpse of it. Anyway, it's all water under the ... er, Barracuda now. So tell me Steve what lesson did you learn this time?"

Steve picked up a towel and dried his hair, he went to Michael's door and opened it ready to leave. As he went out he paused and turned and looked Michael in the eye.

"What did I learn this time?" He took a big breath for maximum effect. "If you ever go diving, choose a buddy that you can trust!" He shut the door after him, Michael smiled and sat back in his chair and ticked the pass box, Steve had learned about setting rules and keeping them. By not breaking the limits of the cone in order to hurt his enemy Steve had shown that he was a valiant warrior in battle. He had nothing to be ashamed of and wouldn't have to make hundreds of personal apologies to innocent victims later as a certain iron lady would have to do before she could progress as a spirit. He was looking forward to meeting her.

CHAPTER 37

Rosie and Michael faced Steve, he sat in a comfortable chair and his two teachers smiled at him. Steve had done well so far and they were pleased with his progress and said so, but they still had to make sure that Steve was learning properly and that he understood what they were trying to teach him. Michael had prepared some questions and they covered more than Steve had been taught. It would be interesting to discover if his line of thought would be correct.

"An easy one to start with. Why do arrivals into Heaven have to become animals, fish, birds or insects if they go on a course similar to yours?"

"Because …" Steve stumbled. "Because before a spirit can progress and understand more, it has to live other lives in order to understand the meaning of life and how it affects everyone and every creature on Earth." He stopped, was that enough?

"Go on," said Rosie. Steve was stuck for a moment.

"Oh and so that the spirit can learn something valuable from each stage of life experienced." Rosie beamed at him and Michael ticked a box.

"And what if that creature learns nothing from being a particular life form, what happens then?" asked Michael.

"I expect that they have to go back and do it again."

"Not exactly, if you were born as a tiny fish and got gobbled up as soon as you arrived you would not come back as that fish but you would move straight to the next stage and consider that quick entry and departure as a pass."

"What's the point of that?" Steve was puzzled.

"It's bad luck that's all, remember that Mother Nature is working hard doing her bit and we can't control her, if you don't make it through the early stages of life and you die before you have had a chance to understand and appreciate anything then you aren't at fault, you just move on."

Steve's wife Jane had a baby brother who died not long after birth and he remembered her telling him that whilst she was too young to know too much at the time, her parents were inconsolable. He asked if babies were born again as babies if they died young or did they go on to be other creatures?

"Ah that's an interesting question," Rosie said. "Mother Nature doesn't always get things right as you know although she does do her best and sometimes creatures and humans are ready to be born and they discover that because of the way they are made they will not survive very long. They do know this in advance and because everyone knows that they will not live long enough to learn or understand anything they are given a unique advantage, they are allowed to choose their parents." Steve was shocked and said so.

"They can choose their parents?"

"Yes, they get to see many sets of parents awaiting the birth of their babies. They are able to learn about their personalities and more important, their spirits. Then, when they have got down to the final selection, the baby's spirit gets to meet the spirits of the chosen parents and they all agree on how best to handle things. Yes it's a very tough time for the parents when a baby cannot survive or when it dies naturally or is tragically killed but whilst Mother Nature reserves her right to be tough and allow these things to happen, she does not interfere when the spirits concerned need help from each other in assisting the parents to overcome their grief."

"And does the baby suffer?"

"Good heavens, not at all. The spirit of the baby lives for eternity and is reunited with the parents and others close when they move through eternity too."

"But what happens when a foetus is aborted? Does that baby come back again?"

"The spirit of a baby doesn't enter the body until the time of birth and it will only do so if the baby's body is alive. It's quite simple, a spirit enters the body at birth and leaves it at death. If a baby is born alive and then dies shortly afterwards, then the spirit of that baby lives on forever."

"I remember a man on television once saying that ill or disabled people suffer in their human lives because they did bad things in their previous lives. I thought it was rubbish. Was there any truth in it?"

Michael interjected. "Actually, we are supposed to be asking you questions but as you ask, the answer is a definite no. You've seen what happened to Brian Nichols, he did shameful things to children and he has been sent to live many lives in the insect world. He hated life as a fly and suffered the most gruesome death when a spider bound him up nice and tight and then bit into his neck and slowly sucked the blood from him. After that he was born as a cockroach in a smelly, disgusting prison somewhere in Asia and he was eaten by a starving drug dealer in a squalid cell. After that I think he moved on to become a praying mantis, quite apt really because after he was seduced by a female he was just about to relax in her arms when he found to his horror that she was holding him down by his head and steadily munching her way through his body, he would have hated that. The last I heard, he was flying around light bulbs trying desperately to get back to see Rosie and me. You see that as each creature passes through from life back to here it recalls that when it first arrived it came through a very strong white light just as you did. Those insects you saw trying to get into a light bulb are mad and deluded and they are experiencing even more of their Hell programme."

"And will he get back to Rosie and you?"

"What through a light bulb? I think not. No, he will be chomped up by another creature in a painful and horrible death and he'll stay at the bottom end of the insect world for a long time yet. He and others may have thought that they got away with their crimes when human and even if they were caught and put in prison, they would have had a relatively nice time. But here they are punished for their crimes against the spirit and they have a lot of suffering and unpleasantness to catch up on before they are ready to get to where you are now. Can we go to my questions if you please?"

Steve settled back in his chair, this wasn't too difficult and he wanted to pass whatever test they had for him so that he could move on and learn more.

"Right Steve. What two creatures are considered to be the most revered. Not spirits, you are not ready for that, just give me the name of the bird and the fish.

Steve smiled. This was easy. "Eagle for the bird, dolphin for the fish."

"Nope try again, and by the way, dolphins are mammals not fish."

Steve was flustered. He had seen the eagles and the dolphins and when everyone was invited to be what they wanted to be most chose eagles and a few aspired to be dolphins. He racked his brain.

"I'll give you a clue," smiled Michael. "What superb creature was absent on that day when you saw the eagles and dolphins?"

Steve thought back, he hadn't got an idea, he looked at Rosie for inspiration and he hoped for a clue from her. She obliged him by sitting back in her chair, she then extended her arms to their fullest stretch and she gently, oh so gently, moved them up and down. Steve still didn't get it.

"Goes for long trips without stopping," said Michael. No light dawned.

"Huge wingspan," said Rosie and stretched her arms out even wider. Steve scratched his head.

"Travels the oceans alone."

"A whale?" said Steve, the others sighed.

"With wings?" Rosie was exasperated.

"Don't worry, only teasing. You mean the good old, now extinct, dodo."

"No we do not!" Michael almost shouted.

"Ever heard of the albatross?"

Steve had and he said so and muttered an apology.

"The albatross travels the oceans in search of knowledge which it passes on to us, the eagle might oblige us by showing off and gliding about a lot and looking severe and the dolphins adore being clapped and getting free fish but the Lord and Master of them all would never deign to bother himself with trivialities. He has dedicated, serious work to do and he never allows himself to be deflected from it."

Michael put his hand over his mouth and whispered, "Bit of a boring character though, he might be graceful and thoughtful and able to transmit lots of interesting facts like whale migrations etc but have him in a bar with you and ready for a couple of beers, well I'd almost prefer to chat with … well with anyone!"

It was time for some harder questions and Michael told Steve not to say the first thing that came into his head but to think things through. Steve would need to draw on his personal experiences and think of what others had told him. He would also have to apply logic, not just the logic of Steve as a human but Steve as a spirit.

"Okay, here's one to think about. Tell me Steve do you think that every spirit starts as human, lives a life and after passing through it then starts the journey that you are on now? Or …" and he paused, "or do some spirits start as insects, fish, birds, animals etc and progress until they reach the human level at the top?"

Steve thought about this and dismissed lots of possible answers simply because they didn't feel right. After a while he spoke carefully.

"Mother Nature's job is to maintain a balanced planet. She needs to populate it with all creatures from the tiniest microbe to …" Steve thought how big and then chose a whale over an elephant …. "a whale! Spirits enter the planet at every level and some come straight in as say wasps and bees and others come straight in as tigers, monkeys and yes, as humans. They all are expected to live as best they can following their basic instincts but when they die their spirit moves on to learn tougher lessons."

"And to answer the last part of my question, do they progress until they reach the human level at the top?"

Steve answered that they did. Michael made some notes.

"You got the first part right, spirits can sometimes choose what level they want to come in at and yes they do start as all sorts of animals, birds etc, but you got the last part wrong. Humans are not at the top of the cycle of life. They might think they are, indeed, some are very intuitive and some are brilliantly intelligent but some are not very spiritual at all and have no concept of their own spirits, let alone the spirits of others. I have met ants who are more spiritual than some humans and I have met humans who are so near to understanding themselves and their spirits that I take lessons from them."

Michael turned to Rosie and asked if she would like to ask Steve a question regarding relationships. At once Rosie appeared business-like and she picked up a writing pad and a pencil but she didn't write anything, she just held it firmly in her lap. Steve knew that she was going to ask a question about love and she didn't disappoint him.

"A short but tough one Steve, define love."

Steve sighed, 'how do you define love? Are we talking about the love a mother has for her baby, or the love a man has for his brother or his close friend? Or are we talking about the love we feel for our parents or the love we feel for our hobbies and passions? Or are we talking about the love we had as teenagers for a pop star or for a hero? Or are we talking about the love we feel for our partner when we know that we want to spend the rest of our lives with them and we want the world to know about it so we celebrate in a wedding ceremony? Are we talking about one type of love or a description of a love that covers all these things?' Steve struggled with his thoughts, he looked to Rosie for a clue but she just smiled at him. 'Did he love Rosie?' Yes he was sure of that and the thought of her not being there felt awful, it felt like someone had a hand up inside his stomach and was trying to pull his heart out and down from the inside. He wondered if he loved Michael too. Yes he did, he felt warm, safe and comfortable when he was with Michael. Michael looked after him, made sure that he was okay and that he was learning and progressing through spirit. Michael would set him hard tasks but he wouldn't abandon him. Yes he loved Michael and he loved Rosie too. Then he thought, 'do I love other people?' He reflected on others that he had met both as a human and later as a spirit. He could see that he now had a love for others that he hadn't experienced before, he knew that when he watched people struggling in disasters and caught in wars that they were suffering and when he watched those TV scenes with Michael he felt a love from inside himself for those people too. Steve struggled with the definition. What could he possibly say that defined all of the love he felt for everyone he loved or had ever loved? He sat there and said nothing. Rosie noticed that he wasn't able to reply and instead of prompting him, they all three just sat there and said nothing.

Finally Rosie spoke. "Don't worry about it Steve. It's not an easy question to answer and although you will one day know the answer it's one that you have to discover for yourself. It's not one that I or anyone else can rattle off in a few words because love means different things to everyone and an individual's appreciation of love is as different as their character and spirit. But I do know that you are very close to it and that's why I recommend to Michael that you progress further with your training, it will be tougher now and you will have to battle with the hardest and toughest enemy that you have ever come across. Do you think you are ready for that Steve?" Rosie looked at Michael who was nodding when Rosie said that she would recommend Steve for a pass. Now he looked at Steve and quietly asked him,

"Who do you think held you back when you were a human? Who tried hard to stop you from doing the right things sometimes? Who did you think set out to destroy you Steve? In a nutshell, who was your hardest and toughest enemy?"

Steve had absolutely no idea. He thought of all the people he knew, he dismissed all of them, even that kid at school who used to pick on him. No, Steve was sure, if and when he was to meet his hardest and toughest enemy then he would be ready to be enlightened as to his or her identity and yes was he ready to fight if necessary.

"Come and meet him," said Rosie and she stood. Michael got up from his chair too and picked up his note pad.

"Good luck Steve. Don't let him hit you when you are not looking." Michael held the door open and Rosie and Steve went out into the corridor. Michael said goodbye and Rosie led the way to Steve's room.

"There's a picture of him in your room." she said. Steve was intrigued. Was there? It must have been put there recently.

Rosie opened Steve's door for him and stood back. Steve went in and immediately looked at the walls, nothing new or out of place there, he then glanced around but saw nothing out of the ordinary. He was puzzled. He went into his bathroom, nothing in there either. Then he turned and was about to go back into the bedroom when he caught a sight of his reflection in the mirror. He looked worried, he could often feel his human form when it was necessary and whilst he was more and more in just spirit form he needed to feel his human form and the physical surroundings of everything for a bit longer, he wasn't ready yet for a full-time spirit existence. Steve looked at his reflection, he was still as good looking as he was as a human and to be honest his tummy looked flatter than it was just before he died. Too much beer and good food with not enough exercise had been taking its toll, but here in the mirror Steve saw himself as perfect as he'd ever be. Youthful, fit, strong, handsome even? Yes, he was pleased. Rosie came into the bathroom.

"Ah! I see that you have found him."

CHAPTER 38

Make your worst enemy your friend and you'll live happily ever after.

(Shaman)

Steve looked at himself in the mirror for a full minute. He was aware that Rosie stood close by, he could feel her but although her reflection should have appeared next to his in the large glass he could only see himself. She moved away from his side and went back into the bedroom. Again Steve noticed that although she had definitely passed opposite, her reflection should have shown up but it didn't. He stared at himself some more and then he moved his right hand. Amazing! His reflection remained perfectly still. Steve then moved his hand on his left side but the Steve in the mirror stayed perfectly still.

Steve moved his right arm up high, the Steve in the mirror remained unmoved. He deliberately and slowly walked away from the mirror into the bedroom. He turned and put his head around the opening. Steve's reflection had gone. He went back into the bathroom and stared at the mirror, there was no reflection, just the normal mirror image of the bathroom, the toilet and the bath. As Steve stared he saw that these reflections were fading, he watched mesmerised as the bathroom's image totally disappeared. He looked behind expecting to see everything in its proper place but everything had gone. He moved into the bedroom. Where was the bed, where was the cupboard, where was the shelf with his books? His whole set of Human Performance textbooks had vanished as well. He could still see Rosie but she wasn't in human form anymore, she was … it was difficult to tell, yes he could see her outline, he could easily see her face and her expression as she looked at him smiling but she had no clothes, neither was she naked. Her form took up a shimmering, light silver mist, it was beautiful and whilst the main colour was a silvery white, other colours were present too. The area where her human heart would be was red and there were strands of blue and gold running from the outline of her head to her feet. Steve saw for the first time that Rosie was the most beautiful spirit that he had ever met. His heart ached with love for her.

"You cannot say goodbye to the old Steve until you have confronted him," she continued. "Now that you know who your enemy is, how will you face him, how will you overcome his demons so that he cannot hurt you anymore?"

Steve hadn't a clue, for a start he didn't expect to find that his worst enemy was himself and he certainly didn't know how to go about destroying himself. Surely if he fought and beat an enemy it would die or run away. Could he fight himself like that?

Rosie quietly spoke. "I am going to go with you now as spirits to a rather sad and unpleasant place. You will see and feel things that will greatly upset you and you won't understand. You will see young humans battling with their real enemies and a few will win yet sadly some will lose. All we can do is watch, we cannot interfere too deeply, these battles have to take place and the outcome is not always affected by us even though we do our best. Come."

Steve felt strange, he looked down at his hands and feet, he could still see them but they were blurred and silvery white, he moved towards the door to follow Rosie but he was no longer walking, he was silently and swiftly gliding, he felt fantastic. His body had been replaced by a ghostly shimmering form and it moved so beautifully. He could see Rosie's spirit ahead and he knew that he should follow.

He drew close and she took his hand and said, "Breathe." Steve was surprised but he took a deep, deep breath and he found that he was moving at an unbelievably high speed, the surroundings became cliff walls, open fields, then lakes and mountains, the air was warm and there was no wind except from the swooshing sound they made as they accelerated to above the speed of light towards a massive build-up of clouds ahead. Steve could see white fluffy cumulus clouds, towering storm clouds were there too and as they got closer, Steve and Rosie steered comfortably to the left to avoid sheet lightning far off in the distance. Steve wanted to ask where they were going, he was enjoying the sensation of flying very much but as they got closer to the storm he was worried. The huge clouds were all around them now and there was a crack of lightning to their left, Rosie turned a few degrees to the right and started to descend. Steve followed her and he could see more dark black clouds ahead. They passed the few wisps of cloud on the edges of the storm. Steve looked up, he could see the top of the anvil-shaped cloud way above. They were at least thirty thousand feet from the ground and the visibility was awful. Steve didn't have any flight instruments of course but he had been this high in a commercial jet and he had once been close to a storm and the pilot had avoided it but Rosie was taking him down into the centre of it. Was she mad?

A golf ball just missed him! A golf ball? Was he seeing things? Then one hit him but it didn't hurt, it just passed right through his hand. Well it was his hand and Steve could see its shimmering outline and if it had been his human hand that ball of ice would have smashed it to pieces. Rosie continued downwards. Now the hail was hitting them both but as it passed straight through them there was no pain and no injury. Steve couldn't see anything now, just fierce blackness all around with regular flashes of the brightest blue and white light he had ever seen. Suddenly they were no longer flying but falling. Steve could sense that Rosie was close but he couldn't see her. Ah, there she was for a split second, she was just ahead. Steve wasn't frightened but he didn't like this storm much and wanted to be clear of it. Then they were in free air. Steve could see the towns below and the rain fell steadily from the cloud layer above his head onto the cold uninviting Earth. He could see the lights of cars on the motorway but the traffic was hardly moving, the cars moved slowly in the longest jam Steve had ever seen. It was in both directions and in the distance Steve could see flashing blue lights dazzling through the light rain.

He felt that they were slowing down and he tucked in close to Rosie as she appeared to stop and hover above a housing estate. Steve had no idea where they were and he saw Rosie looking for a landmark, she found it and as she descended Steve noticed a long shimmering tape of light coming from Rosie and into Steve's spirit. He knew that he wouldn't get lost and as they came lower Steve could see the houses closely, a typical English housing estate on the outskirts of a city.

They stopped outside a house, the road was wet from the rain and a few cars were parked outside the houses. Most of the homes looked clean and tidy but the garden of the one Rosie stopped at was overgrown with weeds. The door was a dirty brown colour and the front of the house needed new paint. The window in the front had a great crack running from top to bottom and someone had stuck some brown parcel tape over it to hold the glass together. Lights in the other houses were on but there was no light coming from this one. Rosie was close, the tape between them had gone. Rosie silently passed from the pavement across what used to be the front lawn and into the front room and she didn't disturb the cracked window or the heavy curtains that were drawn. Steve followed and was surprised to find that he could pass through the front of the house too. They looked around the room. There were two dirty single mattresses on the floor and piles of discarded smelly clothes, old tin cans and pages of newspaper littered the room and the door to the hall was open. Steve recognised a picture on the wall over the fireplace, it was of a purple coloured woman, typical of the cheap prints sold in Britain in the nineteen- seventies. The fireplace had the remains of a fire in it, old screwed up charred newspaper and half burnt sticks, the last attempt to make a fire hadn't been a success.

Rosie shimmered out of the room and upstairs, Steve followed and as he passed the kitchen he looked in. It was a mess and there was rubbish everywhere, a torn black plastic bag spewed household waste onto the floor, the sink was dirty and full of unwashed plates. There were full ashtrays made from torn up cartons and tins, the smell was of dirt and decay. Steve was disgusted.

Rosie was at the top of the stairs, she stopped outside a bedroom and she motioned to Steve to join her. They passed through the wall and stood by the window of the single room. A girl lay on the unmade bed. The sheets were filthy and the blanket was half on the floor, half on the bed. The girl didn't move. She was slim with very white skin and long black hair that lay over her shoulder. Her head was to one side of a dirty striped pillow and she was asleep. On the floor beside her bed was a syringe and an empty cigarette packet, it had two dog ends inside the lid.

Rosie left the girl's room and pointed to another larger room at the front of the house, the door was closed but Rosie passed straight through it. A man lay comatose on a double divan bed, he had no pillow and his body was curled up against the edge of the bed, a grey sheet covered most of him and a blanket lay across his legs. Steve could only see the back of his head and the pale white skin of his shoulders. There was a cot in the corner and Steve looked into it, there was no child, just the base of a thin cot mattress. A discarded baby's bottle lay where the child would have been and a tiny pink teddy bear was tied by a ribbon to the rail of the cot. .Steve looked at the clock on the sideboard. It was a cheap, plastic alarm clock typical of a Sunday market stall. The time on it was a quarter to twelve, it was nearly midday.

"Where are we Rosie?" She was surprised.

"Where do you think, don't you recognise this place?"

Steve looked out of the window at the drab housing estate. "No idea, London, Birmingham, Manchester? These estates all look the same." He looked into the distance but low grey clouds covered what hills there might have been. "No I have no idea where we are."

Rosie looked at him sadly. "I'm surprised that you don't recognise it. We are in Hell Steve, look around you, does this look like Heaven to you?" Steve realised his mistake, he had been looking for a geographical fix when that mattered not a bit. It was the state that they were in now, their spirits moved through the carcasses of two ruined lives and an empty cot. Rosie spoke quietly.

"We can help this couple to leave Hell and to find Heaven," she looked inside the cot, "and we can help them get their baby back if it's not too late. Let them sleep now, they won't be waking until this evening so we can go and get things moving for them."

Rosie and Steve shimmered out of the house. Steve was getting used to having no human body and he liked moving as a spirit, they accelerated away from the squalid house and arrived at a town hall. Rosie seemed to know exactly where to go and she entered a large room with a very high ceiling and a huge table and around the table sat fourteen or fifteen people. A man in a corduroy jacket at one end was going through an agenda and a thin woman at his right was making notes. The people at the meeting seemed bored, they had been here since ten and the woman nearest to Rosie was fidgeting. Steve could see that each person at the meeting had a spirit behind them but to his amazement he could see that each spirit seemed to be asleep! Rosie moved to a position behind the woman's spirit and woke it up.

"Oh hi there. I wasn't asleep honest. I concentrate better with my eyes closed." The woman's spirit looked at Rosie and smiled. Rosie asked her the name of her human.

"Her name is Dawn Atkinson," she lowered her voice in case she was overheard but of course she wouldn't be. "She's Assistant Head of Human Resources for the borough, she's extremely important, she earns twice as much as a head teacher but between you and me she is a twit, she couldn't organise an office party in a pub."

"Could she arrange for a house to be inspected and the occupants put in rehab?"

"She could but she wouldn't, she would be worried that someone might criticise her or ask her to spend some of her budget surplus that she needs to keep if she is to receive her bonus."

Rosie spoke firmly. "Get her out of here, we will go to her office and I need you to help me, that's if you are not too busy." Dawn's spirit knew not to argue with Rosie, she had seen Steve and had no idea who he was or where he was from, he might be part of her assessment team and she wasn't looking forward to her next appraisal. Watching over Dawn Atkinson might be boring but Dawn's spirit had settled into her role and taking the easy way was something she liked. It also allowed her to spend time with the spirit of Ken Harrison, Head of Human Resources. Dawn and Ken were having an affair and whilst she was well aware that Ken was married to Patricia Harrison, the marriage was a cold, loveless arrangement. Pat Harrison had her lover, Ken had his mistress, in a way they were happy, neither wanted to change things.

Dawn's spirit leaned forward and spoke to Dawn's inner consciousness. She suggested that Dawn had grown bored with this meeting and that she needed to go back to her office to check on the state of the Cunninghams. Their baby Karen had recently been taken into care because Wayne and Sue Cunningham obviously couldn't care for her and Dawn had made a mental note to arrange for someone to visit the parents to see how they were getting on. Dawn Atkinson found herself apologising to an astonished Ken Harrison and asking to be excused because she had a meeting to go to. Ken had never been so surprised, he had just got to the bit about fighting the government's budget cuts and he felt sure that everyone, especially Dawn, would be anxious to see how they would be affected. He blinked as Dawn gathered her papers and left the room.

The three spirits followed Dawn down the corridor and Dawn unlocked her office door with her personal key. She never left her door unlocked; someone might come in when she was absent and see that the files on her desk contained cases that had faded away long ago. But now for some strange reason she had a purpose, she needed to find the Cunningham file. She looked under C but it wasn't there. She looked under R for rehab in case it was in that file. It wasn't. She then looked under K for Karen Cunningham and there it was. She pulled it out and opened it. Rosie read it over her shoulder. Baby Karen had been taken into care authorised by Dawn Atkinson and countersigned by Ken Harrison because her parents were heroin addicts. There was a copy of a letter to Social Services team member, Simon Blake asking for his report on the parents but no reply had been received and there were several sheets of paper concerning the moving of baby Karen to a Mrs Dryden. Mrs Dryden had four small children in her care and Karen would be treated well and with love. Best of all, Mrs Dryden was cheap, some of the other adoptive carers wanted more than Dawn was prepared to pay but Mrs Dryden wasn't motivated by money, God bless her. Dawn's budget surplus would be safe if everyone was like Mrs Dryden. Dawn was concerned as she thumbed through the papers. It wasn't like Simon Blake to be behind with his paperwork and she picked up the telephone, he answered straight away and that was odd, shouldn't he be out on house calls? Simon stiffened when he heard Dawn's voice, he had been meaning to write a report to her about the Marlon family but he hadn't got around to it, he relaxed when she asked about the Cunninghams.

"Yes I went there as you asked. Mr. Cunningham told me to eff off and the delightful Mrs Cunningham threw a bottle at me, it's in my report."

"Well I haven't had your report yet but I need you to visit again." Simon Blake was surprised but he couldn't see Rosie whispering into the ear of Dawn's spirit and Dawn's spirit whispering into Dawn's ear.

"I need you to visit again, tell them that even though their council rent is long overdue we need to make general repairs to the house and we will house them in a guest house whilst the work is being done. Don't go to their house before noon, preferably visit at around five before they are out of their minds. Take Bruce and Wendy with you in case they object and take them to 53 Victoria Road. Geoffrey Barford will sort them out."

Simon Blake was astonished. "53 Victoria Road, that rehab place? Who is going to pay, it's not coming out of my budget is it?" Dawn Atkinson hadn't even thought about the budget but she gasped, the court made her send a heroin addict to rehab only last month and the bill was for over ten thousand pounds. Dawn thought it cheaper to give the addict two hundred pounds and let him go and overdose, there was no way that they could solve the town's huge drug problem by sending everyone to rehab. Dawn heard herself saying that she would worry about the budget, Simon had his instructions.

Simon Blake and his two assistants let themselves into the Cunningham house. Simon couldn't find the council's keys when he looked but the master key worked. He found Wayne in the lounge watching television. Wayne stood up when he saw him and his companions.

"What the fuck do you scumbags want coming into my house uninvited?" Sue Cunningham was in the kitchen and when she heard Wayne's raised voice, she came in with a bottle in her hand.

Simon wasn't frightened, he could break Wayne's arm if he tried to fight him. Sue's bottle though was something else. He tried to placate them.

"I did knock but the door was open and I thought I heard you say come in." He showed his identity pass and pointed at the other two. "These are my colleagues, we have some good news for you both." Sue relaxed her grip on the bottle and Wayne blinked at Simon.

Sue spoke. "Does that mean that Karen is coming back home, you had no right to take her?" She shouted the last few words and then stopped, she knew enough to sound reasonable and responsible if these bastards were ever going to return her baby.

Simon was used to lying. "Yes we have come to arrange for Karen to come home." He looked around the squalid house. "But first we have to send in someone to clean up the house and decorate it and get it ready for her, there's no way she can come home to this filth."

Sue protested. "We can clear it up can't we Wayne?" Her husband didn't respond and she carried on. "We can get this place lovely again," and she picked up the overflowing dustbin bag but it split even further and old tins clattered to the floor.

"We have professional cleaners who will do that, don't worry." Simon told the Cunninghams to sit down and he patiently explained that once their house was clean they would have Karen back. He added that new health and safety regulations meant that Wayne and Sue would have to move out for a few days until it was done and immediately they protested, they had nowhere to go and their income support just about paid for their daily fix, there's no way they could get credit from their dealer. Simon patiently explained that they would be living in a guest house not far away, they would have their own room, a satellite TV and breakfast and evening meal. They could come and go as they pleased and when the house was finished they could come back with Karen. Wayne was suspicious but Sue was ecstatic.

"When do we go?" she asked Simon who said that he had a car and they could get some things together and go now. Wayne hesitated and whispered something to Sue. She told him not to worry, she had it safe in her wash bag. Sue went upstairs and rooted through her clothes trying to find the least dirty ones, Wayne would go as he stood.

They got in the back of Simon's car and Bruce sat with them. Wendy got in the front. They were both heavyset people in their mid-twenties, Bruce used to play rugby but his sporting achievements never went further now than watching rugby on the TV. Wendy was a big girl too, she would have made a fine prop forward but she had no interest in sport or men. She lived with Louise in a Victorian flat conversion. Louise was about the size and build of Sue Cunningham, Wendy loved Louise and wanted her and Louise to get married in a civil ceremony. She had no pity for the Cunninghams, they had their life on a plate if they wanted it, they scrounged off the state and treated their council house like a rubbish dump. Wendy had no sympathy for drug addicts at all, they were fools as far as she was concerned. Fortunately she was able to keep her personal opinions to herself otherwise she would have never got her job.

Geoffrey Barford was expecting them as the car stopped outside his clinic. He liked to call it a clinic although it wasn't really. A large twelve bed-roomed Victorian house on the edge of town, it had seen many uses in its time. A rest home for retired transport workers, a period as a school for girls in the forties and it was scheduled as a midway house for refused asylum seekers before someone realised that refused asylum seekers were now being deported immediately and not left to appeal and disappear.

He greeted Wayne and Sue Cunningham as they walked up the drive. The red marble tiles gave the floor a regal look and the huge front door opened wide to let them in. Wayne and Sue looked up at the high ceiling and the wooden staircase. Sue clutched the dustbin bag that she was holding as if frightened to let go of her personal belongings and Geoffrey smiled at them and said that he would show them to their rooms. It didn't occur to Wayne and Sue that he used the word in the plural as they followed him up the stairs.

CHAPTER 39

Steve and Rosie watched from the ground floor as Wayne and Sue Cunningham climbed the stairs. For some reason Steve knew only too well what would happen to them and he felt an affinity with Wayne in particular. He had no idea that Rosie knew exactly what Sue felt like as she followed her husband. As they walked along the landing to their rooms, two spirits appeared and came to stand by Steve and Rosie.

"Thank you so much," said one. "We tried but we couldn't cope with them anymore. We did everything we could but we were hopeless."

"Don't worry," said Rosie, "we will take over here, you'll get them back when it's all done." The two spirits thanked Rosie and Steve again and then faded away. Rosie motioned for Steve to follow, they needed to catch up with Wayne and Sue.

Wayne was protesting. "We don't need separate rooms, we can share." Sue however had entered the room designated for her; she sat on the bed and noticed that there was no other furniture in the room apart from a small cupboard. Wayne had inspected his room too and asked where the TV was.

"It's in the communal lounge." Geoffrey Barford suggested that Wayne tried the bed for comfort but as soon as Wayne sat down, he closed the door and locked it. He spoke through the closed door and told Wayne that he would find some sandwiches and bottled water in the cupboard.

Sue couldn't hear Wayne shout and Wayne couldn't hear Sue wailing. The initial shock at being locked in two separate rooms had turned first to anger and then to frustration. Then it started. Wayne began to sweat and shiver. He was coming down from his last heroin fix. He raved, he screamed but no one came. A few doors away Sue was going through her personal hell too. To her side lay Rosie, Rosie felt every pain that Sue felt, she would have cried out too but no one would hear her screams either. In Wayne's room Steve writhed on the floor, every shudder of pain that racked Wayne's body was felt by Steve too, he had never known such agony. For three days and three nights Wayne and Sue confronted the demons from hell as their bodies finally accepted that it would be getting no more heroin. The humans were watched over, fed and given vitamins but of course Steve and Rosie got nothing.

On the fourth day Geoffrey Barford opened Wayne's door to find him fast asleep on the bed, the sheets were pulled over him and Geoffrey could see that they were soaked with sweat. The room smelt and Geoffrey opened the window with a special key, fresh air flooded into the room.

Geoffrey spoke quietly and clearly. "There's a bathroom next door, go and shower and then we can have a little chat. Come on Wayne, there's a good lad."

Wayne turned on his back and looked up at Geoffrey. His mouth was dry, he was very hungry and he felt strange. His head seemed clearer than before and he knew that whatever happened he had to get out of his bed. His body ached but he managed it, he stood up shakily and moved towards the door. Geoffrey Barford introduced his assistant.

"This is Jonathan, Jonathan is an ex-heroin addict, he's clean now and he's helping you to get clean and stay clean but only on one condition."

"What's that?" mumbled Wayne.

"Quite simple really, you have to want to get clean. If you want to get off heroin you will have to say it and mean it. If you don't, it's back to your previous life and probably an early death. If you don't do it for yourself, do it for Sue and for your baby Karen." Geoffrey left Wayne in the capable hands of Jonathan who took Wayne to the bathroom, he turned the shower on for him and made sure the temperature was right. He placed a towel on the chair; Jonathan asked if Wayne was hungry.

"I'm fuckin' starvin'."

"Get washed, get dressed, there's a new T-shirt and pants for you and see if those trousers will fit you, they are mine, you look about the same size. Then when you are ready you can come down and eat. How's bacon, two fried eggs, sausage and beans sound?" Jonathan didn't wait for the answer. Wayne was in the shower washing his hair with proper shampoo, something he hadn't done for ages. Steve was next to him. He didn't feel hungry or dirty but he did feel as if he'd had his complete insides torn out and put back in the wrong place. Wayne was a bit shaky on the stairs but Jonathan was there to help if needed. He entered the communal dining area and saw Sue sitting with another girl. She looked up at him and smiled.

"Hi darling, how are you feeling?" Wayne wasn't sure but he knew that he was ravenous and he picked up a knife and fork as Jonathan put a plate in front of him. The rest of the day was spent with Wayne talking to Jonathan and Sue talking to a woman called Katie. Both counsellors had been previous addicts and both were trained to assist others. Wayne and Sue were interviewed and examined by the doctor and Wayne had to have his hair properly cleaned. Sue was so disgusted to hear that she had nits that she wanted to shave her head, Katie persuaded her not to, she would be fine and had to use a special shampoo for a while.

At five everyone gathered for their evening meal and others came in to meet Wayne and Sue. They were introduced to heroin addicts, alcoholics, people who were on speed and other tablets and everyone seemed really nice. Rosie and Steve were able to sit and talk with the spirits of the other patients and they all found that they had so much in common.

After their evening meal Geoffrey invited Wayne and Sue to have a talk with him together. They sat away from the others in a large conservatory and Geoffrey asked them both if they would like to take part in a rehab programme. Wayne wanted to ask if they were still allowed some heroin or would they have methadone to help them get off heroin but Sue was more interested in asking if they would get Karen back if they finished the programme. Geoffrey said that he would make them no promises, certainly there would be no heroin or methadone and he added that this wasn't a prison, they could both walk out at any time and never come back. If they stayed they had to be willing to stay and they had to want to break their drug habit. He then went on to explain that the treatment would start with a month in a hot sauna with five to six hours spent in it each day. The sauna would cleanse them of their drugs and purify their skin. He added that they would not just get them clear of heroin, they would talk to them in great detail about their past lives and see what had happened. If they had demons they would expose and deal with them. They were warned that it would be tough but the reward was that they would be clean for as long as they wanted to be clean. He repeated that they could leave at any time but if they did stay they could qualify for a certificate confirming their success on the course. Whilst he couldn't personally promise anything, that certificate would help ensure that Karen's return would be a possibility.

As their treatment continued Wayne and Sue got to talk with the other patients, they were reminded that they weren't to be addressed as patients but as students and if they passed their courses then they would 'graduate.' That meant little to Wayne or Sue but it helped the patients who had been sent there from good homes and felt better about being regarded as students rather than patients or inmates.

As their course progressed Wayne and Sue were permitted to have days out in the local town, they were near the sea and whilst the wind blew cold in the winter, there were some lovely sunny days too. Jonathan and Wayne and Sue and Katie enjoyed their long walks but one day Wayne stopped dead as he held Sue's hand. Jonathan had been talking about life after rehab when he noticed Wayne stop suddenly. Jonathan looked to see what Wayne was looking at and he saw a black BMW saloon with tinted windows and very shiny wheels. The driver was parked on double yellow lines and was coming across the road to greet them.

"Hello my man," he called and he lifted his hand in a five high greeting. Wayne looked away, he felt ashamed but didn't know why.

"Yo fella, how's it goin'?" Maybe the small white man in a tight black suit and shiny pointed shoes felt a need to talk like a black rapper and he looked first at Wayne and then at the other three, clearly he felt no threat from any of them and he put his hand down after the rejected greeting and he stuck his thumbs into his belt as he stood blocking their path. Steve and Rosie had been walking behind and enjoying the salty sea air, now they were watching this man and Steve was looking straight at his spirit. This wasn't a nice spirit at all, he was grey in colour and small and furtive. The spirit noticed Steve's stare and whispered in his man's ear.

The man stepped to one side. "Well Wayne you know where I is if you wanna come callin'. Got some mighty good gear for ya, no sweat man, no sweat at all."

Wayne didn't reply and the four of them walked on. As Sue passed the man she stuck two fingers at him, he was amazed.

"Hey man what did I do wrong?"

Jonathan and Katie said nothing, it was obvious that the man had sold heroin to Wayne in the past and it was interesting to see Wayne's reaction. Sue had pleased them with her two-fingered salute but was Wayne so resilient? Would he go back to heroin when he was clear of rehab? Only Wayne could answer that.

Steve ignored Rosie's warning and moved after the drug dealer's spirit. He caught up with him and warned him to stay away from Wayne and Sue.

"Or what?"

"Pardon?"

"Or what? What exactly will you do if I don't?"

Steve was stuck for an answer. He explained that Wayne and Sue were getting clear of heroin and that they would leave rehab with a chance at a new life and their baby back. They would have a chance to find Heaven and to be happy. The grey spirit laughed in his face.

"I'll make a bet with you. Within one month of leaving your so-called rehab place Wayne will be back on the Smack, Crackle and Pot. If he is, I will come to Heaven as your guest to look around at your dreamy wonderland but if he isn't then you will come to my place in Hell and see life for what it really is."

"Just a second," said Steve, "I hope that Wayne and Sue will win their fight against heroin and if they do I come to visit you, if they don't then you come to visit me. Shouldn't it be the other way around?"

"No it's like I said. If you are right, you visit me, if I am right, I visit you."

Steve agreed and the grey spirit laughed again. Steve didn't like him at all.

Rosie was annoyed with Steve. "Michael will be angry. You are in a no-win situation, if Wayne and Sue succeed in their battle and give up heroin then you have to visit that slime ball in Hell. If one of them goes back on the drugs then you have to invite him into our place. Michael won't be happy with this at all, he tricked you. And by the way what is Smack, Crackle and Pot?"

"It will be okay. We have to make sure that Wayne and Sue stay clean and to answer your question, smack is heroin, crackle is crack cocaine and pot is marijuana. If I have to visit him I will ask you or Michael to come."

Rosie was aghast. "There's no way that I am going there and Michael won't either. He was tricked once by a clever, sneaky spirit like that one and he was nearly …" She stopped. Steve pressed her to continue but Rosie refused. "It looks like you will confront your demons sooner than you thought."

CHAPTER 40

Steve hadn't properly understood what they meant when Rosie and Michael said that he'd meet his worst enemy and then after that he would have to confront his own demons. He could appreciate that a person might be their own worst enemy but wasn't that to do with good spirits and bad spirits battling it out to control the human? And weren't our demons those bad spirits? It was all so confusing. He had been to Hell and back in that room with Wayne Cunningham and he did not enjoy feeling all that Wayne had gone through for himself, he wondered why he'd had to do that. It's not as if he had been a drug addict in his human life, he was quite well conditioned by his parents and by what he had read in the newspapers and seen on TV to know that drugs usually led to tragedy, so why did he have to experience the cold turkey? And Rosie had to do it with Sue, she had been very quiet afterwards and she listened intently when the counsellors were talking and listening to Wayne and Sue's life stories.

The spirits of the counsellors had talked with Steve and Rosie too and whilst the discussions were chatty and informal Steve couldn't help feeling that there was a structure to the questions and topics. The worst part of the cold turkey was the nightmare, waking in darkness and in pain, having to struggle to overcome harsh tests run by horrible people and being drowned over and over again before surviving that last long fall into ice-cold water after finally getting that trapdoor open. Why did Steve have to endure this Hell, he didn't deserve it at all, not like Wayne. But then if he thought about it, did Wayne deserve that Hell either? He was so confused, so scared and so alone but he could sense that there would be an ending, a positive ending that was worth waiting for.

"Strive to improve," said one of the counsellor's spirits. "There's no point otherwise." Steve thought about his words. He heard them again when Wayne and Sue finished their rehab course and Steve was very proud when Wayne collected his diploma confirming that he, Wayne Cunningham, had completed a successful rehab course at Barford's Clinic. Sue was delighted with hers too and she intended to frame it and put on the wall at home. Her counsellor suggested that she showed it to the care worker who was responsible for Sue's baby and then she should put it in a safe place and make both the addiction and the rehab a part of her past. She would need to show Wayne's certificate as well to prove that Wayne was clean.

Wayne lasted more than a month without heroin. On the Thursday morning just thirty-three days after Wayne's departure from rehab, his dealer followed him and offered him some drugs for nothing, for old time's sake, to show that he was a pal. If Wayne had been tempted before then the offer of free heroin was just the last straw. He put his hand out and accepted the small wrap, the dealer grinned at him, then before he could blink, Wayne had the dealer in a grip as his right hand seized the dealer's neck. He pulled him forward and brought his knee up hard into the man's groin. His mouth opened wide and he screamed. That's what Wayne wanted. He held the dealer's throat and pushed the heroin hard into the man's mouth. He squirmed and twisted but Wayne was too strong for him. He forced the wrap down between the man's teeth, his grip on the man's neck was tight, all the fury that had been pent up inside him was now coming out in his anger. When it was down as far as it could go, Wayne kicked him again and threw him to the ground. The dealer tried to get up and rolled over, he made it to his feet and produced a knife. Spitting hatred he lifted his arm to stab Wayne but Wayne was ready, he grabbed the arm and twisted it hard, the dealer screamed again in pain. He yanked the arm back and heard the bone snap. The knife fell to the floor.

"You come near me and Sue again and I will kill you, do you understand?"

The man spluttered and swore, tears of fury ran down his cheeks. "I will get you for this, you wait."

Wayne realised that the drug dealer would come after him, the dealer was in great pain but he didn't stop threatening.

"I know where you live, if I don't get you I'll get your wife and child." Wayne was angry, he leant forward and picked up the dealer's knife, it was an Italian switchblade, the sort of knife a gangster would carry. It had a long pointed blade set into a black handle and was beautifully made. But Wayne didn't stop and admire it, the dealer was still on his knees, he had pulled the wrap of heroin from his throat and thrown it to the ground. The man was holding his arm and staring at Wayne, his small, thin face full of hatred. Wayne grabbed his hair and stepped behind him at the same time yanking his victim's head in a sharp backward movement. The dealer's eyes opened wide in astonishment as Wayne brought the knife down in one smooth slashing swipe across his throat. The wound in the neck immediately widened as Wayne yanked his head back further and drove the knife hard into the side of his throat. He pushed his head forward and let go and as the dealer tumbled forward onto his face, blood gushed from the wound.

"I'll see you in Hell." Wayne spat at the dying man and he stepped away and was gone.

Steve and Rosie watched the murder and they witnessed the last few moments of the drug dealer's life as his blood mixed with the dirty rainwater in the gutter. They saw the grey spirit of the dead man leave his body and stand to one side on the pavement, he looked down at the corpse and kicked it but it didn't flinch. The grey spirit glanced up and saw Steve and Rosie, he shimmered towards them and immediately Steve felt a cold, black presence.

"So we meet again and so soon."

Rosie didn't want to stay in this spirit's presence and wanted Steve to leave too but Steve didn't move, the grey spirit faced him and smiled.

"We have a deal, your man will not be tempted anymore by me or any other and as long as you keep your side of our bargain, then he will not be caught. But if you break our bargain, I will see to it that Wayne Cunningham is caught and tried for murder and he will get the heroin he needs in prison to die from an overdose. He will never live that life of happiness that you wanted him to have with that woman and their baby. I will personally see to that and if you break our bargain, then that is what will happen."

Steve knew that this wasn't an idle threat and he moved towards

Rosie who was really upset.

"He's tricked you. He doesn't care about Wayne Cunningham or his wife or their baby. He was quite happy to sacrifice his human to get a chance with you, now you have to go and I have to tell you Steve, I am worried." She moved closer to him so that they were almost one.

"I have no idea what will happen to you. Michael lost a pupil once when he too had to honour a promise and we never saw him again. I am really concerned for your safety but you have to go, you do know that."

Steve was unsure, he had to honour his promise but he didn't want to leave Rosie. Rosie didn't want him to go either but she knew that he had been tricked and that he would have to go with this grey spirit to Hell. She would tell Michael and Michael would be very upset and they would have to accept that Steve's destiny lay in his own hands. She didn't worry about Wayne Cunningham and his family, she could see into his future and she knew that he would be alright. He wouldn't be caught for the murder, indeed the detectives wouldn't be too upset to see one of their nastier, known dealers killed and they would only make a token attempt to find the culprit. Wayne wouldn't have to suffer or to account for the death at his Life Appraisal either, drug dealers, paedophiles, petty thieves and other criminals who lived their lives benefiting from the suffering of others were held to be at the same level as mosquitoes, dung beetles, wasps and hornets, it was okay to kill them as their spirits were grey or black. They would have a chance to review their human lives and a very small percentage would progress immediately through a Life Appraisal and be accepted as Steve had been. Most however would choose not to be assessed and would go the same route as Brian Nichols and only after much pain and suffering would they flit as demented insects towards any bright light and beg for forgiveness and a release from their torment. They would all do this in the end and then their Life Appraisals would begin.

The grey spirit smiled at Steve but it wasn't a smile of friendship, it was one of victory.

"Come," he said, "come meet your destiny."

CHAPTER 41

Steve followed the grey spirit, they moved away from the murdered drug dealer and Steve stayed close as ordered as they glided through the streets. They didn't feel the rain and the blustery wind didn't affect them either. Steve didn't recognise the town or the river as the grey spirit slowed, he looked once to see if Steve was following but he knew that his charge was obedient and Steve knew that if he didn't keep a watch on his guide he would lose him and that would mean desertion. They travelled down a street where terraced houses lined both sides and there were few cars. They moved neither over the pavement nor in the road but a few inches over the gutter where the rainwater found the drain. At the end of the road, Steve saw the rusty hull of a merchant ship and as they got closer he saw cranes towering over the grey roofs and lots of steel containers, all had numbers and they were stacked in rows. Men walked amongst them and the cranes moved lazily lifting containers of all colours onto the deck.

The grey spirit stopped moving and Steve looked to see where they were. A warehouse door was next to them but it was locked and it looked as if it hadn't been opened for years. Beside it was the grid of a drain and Steve watched the grey spirit pass through the iron bars that protected the opening. Steve followed and as he entered the shaft he felt a cold that he remembered from the cold turkey and the tests that he had to either pass or drown in his nightmares. He shuddered, he didn't normally feel temperatures as a spirit but this was unmistakable, he looked down but he couldn't see anything, there was no light, just a black, wet and cold void. As they descended further and further into the darkness, Steve felt even colder and he looked again hoping to see some light ahead. Then he knew that they had arrived, the pressure seemed different and although Steve still couldn't see anything he felt that they were in a large cavern. He could hear noises too, the dripping of water and in the distance an eerie wailing. He shuddered. Was his nightmare dream going to come true?

Then the lights came on, just two low wattage bulbs hanging from long flexes that hung from the top of the cavern. Steve looked up but he couldn't make out the roof, it was too dark and too high to see. Steve looked around him, there were thousands of faces looking straight at him, they didn't seem to have proper heads or bodies just sad, tired faces. None smiled. There was no greeting, no sense of curiosity, a sea of round faces, all looking straight at him, not one mouth moved, not one eye blinked. The grey spirit spoke.

"I said that I would show you around." Steve was surprised. Would the grey spirit act like a tour guide?

"You passed along a metal staircase once, it was not far from here yet you would never have seen or felt the presence of this cavern." Steve remembered his trip with Michael after he first arrived. He saw his mother for the first time and he saw the shapes of people he recognised, but it was all a trick wasn't it? He had met his mother again at the end of his Life Appraisal, was she back here, was she in Hell? Steve thought back to his early lessons too, Hell wasn't a different place but a state of mind or a state of being, there was no actual place called Hell just as there was no place called Heaven. The grey spirit guessed what he was thinking and wanted to change the subject.

"Would you like to go back?" Steve was surprised. An invitation to return to Rosie and Michael was the last thing he expected right now.

"No I don't mean back there. Would you like to be born again and go back as a human? You can even have your old life back, you can be Steve Rogers again and we'll take you back to the night when you were killed. But we won't let you be killed this time Steve, you will see the lorry much earlier and you will brake in time and stop. You can go right back, let me think, ah yes weren't you due to meet Sharon in a hotel? You could go back Steve, you could go back." Steve thought about it.

"What was Sharon wearing? Do you remember? She really is a sexy girl Steve and boy did she have the hots for you."

Steve wasn't going to be tempted, he decided to change the subject and looked at the sea of sullen faces looking at him, there must have been a hundred thousand that he could see and he felt that there would be many more, further back in the huge cavern. "Who are they?" he asked the grey spirit. But he just dismissed them.

"Oh don't worry about them, they are no one, they are nothing. Now stop delaying, this offer to go back ends today, indeed it's a once in a lifetime special offer, just for you Steve. Do you want to go back to Sharon, Yes or no? Decide now!" Steve was startled to hear the grey spirit raise his voice; he didn't need to be asked again.

"No, I do not want to go back and see Sharon, No, I don't want to be Steve Rogers again. Thanks for the offer but I have a feeling that you would be my spirit guide and nothing personal ..." he stopped, "I don't even know your name, what is your name?"

"Boo!," he replied, "B and then double O and don't forget the exclamation mark."

He continued, "So what's wrong with me being your spirit guide? I am very experienced, I would make sure that you didn't get into any trouble, indeed you would make lots of money and have a wonderful life with all the things money can buy. You will travel the world, you'll have boats and planes and the latest cars. With me as your guide you will make a fortune. Come on, it must sound tempting Steve? And you can marry Sharon or you can have a whole string of beautiful women. You will meet them in Monte Carlo, in Hawaii, the Bahamas, everywhere that you want to go. There's nothing that we cannot do if you agree to go back." Steve thought of Rosie.

Boo! read his mind. "You like Rosie? You can have Rosie instead of Sharon, or you can have her as well, she can be introduced to you tomorrow, what do you say Steve, your old life back, your affair with Sharon, an affair with Rosie, wouldn't you like that?"

Steve realised something with a shock. 'He doesn't know. Boo! doesn't know. I'm already in a relationship with Rosie and he doesn't know. Now why doesn't he know? He knows everything else.'

Boo! looked at Steve oddly, normally he could read Steve's thoughts but these ones seemed jumbled and scrambled, he knew that he had Steve tempted and the thought of riches and Sharon should be enough to get him back. He really wanted Steve, that drug dealer, what's his name? Ah yes, Simon Speed, well named that man for a drug dealer, but he was weak, he wouldn't always do what Boo! wanted him to do. Steve would be a tough nut to crack but once he had him, he could deal in death, misery and really get some pleasure from the chaos he caused. Boo! needed Steve. He needed someone with good in their soul; he needed someone that he could corrupt properly. Picking a person with a poor or bad spirit wasn't good enough, he wanted someone who had a good spirit, he wanted someone who could lead him to trap Michael!

Yes he wanted Michael. Michael was his enemy, his opposition, he yearned to get Michael, to corrupt him, to bring him under his control. He could have gone after Rosie but Michael wouldn't have come to save Rosie. He would have missed her and would have been devastated at her corruption but Boo! knew that Michael had special plans for Steve because Steve was a chosen spirit, Steve would eventually be working on an equal basis with Michael and might even rise higher. Steve and Michael together were quite capable of destroying Boo!, he knew this and had to either corrupt Steve or get Michael to come after him now to rescue him before Steve was as skilled as Michael. Either way Boo! would win. Yes either way Boo! would win!

"I'll do a deal, if you don't want to go back to Sharon and to your life as a wealthy traveller and playboy permanently, why not go back for just a little look? You can move around with me and see the life you could lead and then if you want it you can say yes and I will make all the arrangements, but if you still don't want it, then that's fine too."

Steve was tempted but before he could decide there was a commotion somewhere in the sea of faces. Boo! was concerned and looked around to see what the matter was. A low hum came from the faces, it gradually became a wail and got louder. Boo! tried to move away from them but Steve could see that they were totally surrounded. The sad faces stared at them, each one emitting a wail that slowly started to get louder and louder until it became a scream. The noise was deafening. Boo! looked for an escape, there wasn't one. He didn't want Steve to witness what was obviously a revolt. Steve looked hard at the face nearest to him. It was the eyes, the eyes, he knew those eyes. As the scream turned into a continuous high-pitched shriek. Boo! shouted over the noise to Steve and urged him to follow. Boo! rose up above the sea of faces and they climbed towards the roof of the cavern. The faces followed them up and the face with the eyes that he thought he recognised rose with them until they reached the top. The rock was hard and cold and Boo! and Steve had nowhere else to go. The noise stopped, the faces resumed their low hum and they descended to the floor of the cavern. Just one sad face remained with them and this time Steve was sure. It was Michael. Boo! recognised him too and mocked him with a scowl. The face that was Michael didn't flinch and he spoke.

"Steve, you are coming back with me. Well done Boo!, I'll settle my debt with you later. Nice one!"

Boo! smiled at Steve. "You did well Steve, a lesser spirit might have been tempted by my offer." He turned to Michael. "You were right Michael, Steve is worth training. Good luck with him. Thankfully that Simon Speed isn't a human anymore and I don't have to train his spirit. I suppose he will be coming to you soon for his Life Appraisal, can I sit in?"

"He's already been and he refused it, just as Brian Nichols did. But he'll be back begging for another go soon. We've started him off as a wasp and he wasn't happy, he wanted to know what his purpose was other than annoying people at picnics and barbeques but no one knew and no one could tell him. When he's been a wasp for a while we'll let him drown in an overdose of strawberry jam and then he can spend some quality time as a sea urchin trying not to get pricked by his really boring family. Cheers Boo!, Steve and I will bump into you sooner or later."

Rosie was glad to see Steve back.

"Well! Don't keep me waiting, did he pass or fail?"

"He passed sure enough. Well done Steve, are you ready for your next assignment or would you prefer a weekend away with Rosie, in Italy, perhaps?"

If Rosie and Steve were still in human form they would have blushed, indeed spirits blush too and both Rosie and Steve reddened.

Rosie was sure that Michael was unaware of their affair and Michael would never have known if Steve hadn't realised that Boo! didn't know either. When Boo! tempted Steve with a night of passion with the sexy Sharon he added that he could have an affair with Rosie. Michael hadn't told Boo! because Michael hadn't known either, but when Steve's thoughts were read by Michael who was tuned into him all through the conversation, he then realised that

Rosie and Steve were closer than he thought.

Steve looked at Rosie.

"What do you think? Italy again or shall we go somewhere else this time?"

Before Rosie could answer Michael stopped her.

"I need to chat with you Steve, sorry Rosie but do you mind leaving us for a while? Steve and I need a debrief." Rosie blushed again. She wasn't normally excluded from Michael's chats with Steve but this time she clearly wasn't wanted. She left them to it, there were other things she could be doing. Michael and Steve relaxed as only happy spirits can, their shimmering forms lay on two sunbeds on a beautiful beach, the warmth of the sun rested them and Michael lay back.

CHAPTER 42

"I'll come straight to the point," said Michael. "I don't trust Boo!. What did you think of him?"

Steve didn't like him and said so, he added that when he first met Boo! he felt revulsion when close to him. But Steve was puzzled, why would Michael trust Boo! to test Steve with the offer to go back to being a human if he didn't trust Boo! himself?

"Boo! is not typical of the spirits we normally deal with, he's not a black spirit but a grey one and he says that he wants to defect and join us. He took a keen interest in you for some reason and he offered to show you around Hell, it was his idea to tempt you with a return to human life and all those riches. I told him that he was wasting his time but he felt sure that you would agree. He made a bet with me and he lost, now he has to accept my invitation to visit me."

"And what will you do with him, what will you show him?"

"He wants to see what's happened to other grey spirits that defected. If he is impressed then that may make his defection all the more likely."

"He may be tricking you. He may be pretending to defect in order to find out what happened to the others and to find out where they went in so that he can find them and exact revenge. He may want a lot more than he appears to want."

"I have thought of that Steve. I don't trust him at all and his interest in you concerned me, but I had no choice in the matter. You made a bargain with him over Wayne Cunningham and he lost, therefore you had to visit him. When Rosie told me I went straight to him and asked him to test you as part of your programme, he could hardly refuse if he wanted to be seen to be keen to defect."

"Umm, that's clever, so you turned his trick on him so that I would not be in any danger."

"Yes I suppose I did but he's a very tempting spirit and his offer for you just to have a look with no commitment was very hard to turn down."

Steve didn't speak for a minute, he had very nearly accepted Boo!'s offer to have a temporary visit, he was about to decide one way or the other when Michael started the commotion. He asked Michael who were those faces.

"They are spirits who behaved very badly towards others when they were human so they are awaiting their chance to be flies, mosquitoes, dung beetles, wasps, hornets, grubs, maggots and other such creatures. There's plenty of opportunities and each one could start their programme now but Boo! and the other grey spirits like to keep them waiting until they are really fed up. Then they will let a few go at a time and they won't pick them in sequence, they'll let them go when they feel like it, this really annoys the ones that have been there a long time."

"How did you get them going on their wailing and screeching, that shrieking at the end was deafening?"

"I became one of them and told those nearest me that I was going out soon as a butterfly and that got them wailing and moaning."

"Would Boo! have honoured his promise, would he have arranged for me to go back as a human and to arrive in time to avoid my car crash?"

"Oh yes, he wouldn't break his promise but you would have to join the faces for a while and he didn't mention that did he?"

Steve was silent. No he didn't mention that at all. "Why wouldn't you let Rosie come to our chat?"

Michael needed to know something before replying, he wanted to know how Steve felt about her and Steve was doubtful, not about how he felt for Rosie but because Michael needed to ask, surely he already knew what Steve was thinking.

"I often know what you are thinking but I don't always know how you feel. How do you feel about Rosie?" Steve was pleased to learn that his feelings weren't an open book to Michael, at least he had some privacy. He asked Michael why he wanted to know.

Michael said that Steve's next project would involve Boo! and it would involve Steve going back as a human for a short period, there was a good chance that Boo! would trick Steve again and that Michael might not be able to protect him. If Steve survived he would be tasked with bringing Boo! back as a genuine defector. If he failed, Steve may spend an eternity with the other faces.

"So you see Steve, if you succeed then Boo! will come and join us, if Boo! is faking his intentions to defect then you will find that out and you might not make it back here. If that happens Rosie will be upset."

"I won't be too happy either," said Steve.

Steve and Michael set out a plan to test Boo!. If the grey spirit was serious about defecting then they would give him an opportunity. Steve wondered why Michael couldn't just read his thoughts but Michael told him that he couldn't read grey spirits' thoughts and they and the black spirits couldn't read their thoughts. Instead of comprehension, there's a jumble of words as if the thoughts were deliberately scrambled. They are not of course, it's as if they and we are on different wavelengths. Steve asked why Boo! couldn't simply defect. What was stopping him from just arriving and staying?

Michael explained that because Boo! couldn't be trusted yet, he had to prove himself and the best way to prove himself would be to arrange for a good many faces to be released into Michael's care for Life Appraisals. If Boo! was serious in his intentions then he would arrange for the releases from within but he mustn't arouse suspicion in the other grey spirits. Boo! in turn would need to trust Michael. If Michael cheated, he could gain thousands of faces and then not let Boo! defect. Steve asked what his role would be and Michael and Steve hatched a plan. They didn't tell Rosie.

*

Michael wasn't allowed in Hell unless invited and Boo! couldn't come to Heaven unless he was invited. This truce had been made long ago and it wasn't clear who suggested it. Neither broke the arrangement as it suited both not to have the other coming and going whenever they wanted and messing up each other's programmes. The other strict rule concerned promises. If either party made a promise then that promise would be kept, even a black spirit would keep a promise made to a white spirit. If they didn't then there would be no further possibility of liaison or mutually beneficial arrangements. Sometimes Michael and his team would be forced to give up on someone such as Brian Nichols who rejected all forms of help and who refused point blank to co-operate. In contrast there would be spirits in a state of Hell who genuinely wanted to change and have the privilege of a Life Appraisal, it was necessary therefore to keep a dialogue open between the two sides in order to make transfers. Steve understood the ground rules concerning Michael and Boo!. Did they apply to him and Rosie too?

Michael explained that the arrangement would be strictly between Boo! and himself. Steve and Rosie were progressing through their programmes and if and when they ever reached Michael's level then they would be expected to honour the pact as well. For the meantime however they would be expected not to arrive in Hell without an invitation and not to make promises that they didn't intend to keep.

Steve hadn't seen Boo! since Michael had appeared as one of the faces. Boo! wasn't happy with Michael's arrival as a face and he said that Michael must be careful. Whilst he was happy to see his future mentor appear as a face and be in Hell without an invitation, the other grey spirits would not be so obliging. Boo! cleverly walked the fine line between being seen as a keen defector and upholding the rules of his masters. Michael was very relieved to arrive before Steve made a decision to have a temporary visit to see what Boo!'s suggested life would be like, he felt sure that Steve was about to agree, it had been a close thing.

Steve had his plan worked out and it involved Rosie but he wouldn't tell her just yet. He told Michael that he was ready and Michael arranged for Steve to accidentally meet Boo!. He knew that two Englishmen and an Australian couple had been sentenced to death in Thailand for trying to smuggle heroin and he sent Steve to attend their execution to see if he could bring their spirits for Life Appraisals. Michael guessed that Boo! would be there too to try to take the spirits back with him.

They both arrived at the Bangkok prison at the same time and Steve whispered to Boo! and told him that he'd appreciate a few quiet words. Boo! nodded and they waited for the prisoners to arrive but there was a delay. Upstairs in the governor's office a row had broken out. The drug smugglers had been caught and properly tried and claims that they made at their trial had been rejected, now however there was new evidence to be considered. The two Englishmen were on holiday in Bangkok when they were approached by the Australian couple. In brief, they had made an arrangement to finance a parcel of heroin to be sent inside a bronze statue. The statue would be lined with lead and it would be classed as freight. If the statue got through they would be clear and rich for life. If it was stopped they would claim that someone at the freight company must have hidden the drugs and as the statue wasn't actually in their possession, there would be no case to answer. Unfortunately none of the four knew that the supplier of the heroin was also the owner of the freight company and that he had an arrangement with the assistant head of customs to betray and catch the smugglers. Both he and the customs officer would keep the money paid for the drugs, they would get a good reward and they would also be able to keep the heroin to sell again. When the freight company owner appeared in court to testify that his diligent staff had found the drugs, the accused pointed to him as the organiser. He laughed off the claim and the court chose to believe the Thai national rather than the foreigners, but justice had a strange way of being done especially when Michael got involved. On the day before the execution, the freight company boss had a furious row with his wife. She had long suspected him of having an affair with her younger cousin and now she had the evidence of her own eyes. She had come home early from a shopping trip because she wasn't well, her husband and her cousin were in bed together and they could no longer deny the truth. The wife, in true example of a woman betrayed went to the head of customs along with her lawyer and told him that her husband made millions of baht smuggling drugs with the help of a corrupt customs officer. The arrests took place as the execution was being planned and the authorities had no option but to cancel the killings. Michael congratulated himself on getting the export man's wife to eat that contaminated ice cream to make her unwell enough to go home and the trap was set. Boo! and Steve were able to have their chat and now it was up to Steve.

Boo! listened intently, he smiled as Steve explained that he would be very interested in taking up Boo!'s offer for a look at what his life might be like if he went back just before his untimely death.

"The way I see it is that I could enjoy the life that I was denied. I would have Sharon, maybe Rosie too and with you as my spirit I would have a great life."

"And when you died, what would happen then? Michael is hardly going to welcome you back with open arms and let you do another Life Appraisal."

"Why not? With your defection safely completed you won't be making any protests and Michael loves a repented sinner – not that I am going to sin much anyway."

"Why do you think I would defect?"

"Michael told me, he said that you wanted to defect to join him and Rosie so the way I see it is I can't lose. I get my old life back but with the riches you promised and when I eventually die of old age, preferably being shot by a jealous husband when I am 102, I will come back to Michael and Rosie and carry on where I left off."

"So Michael told you I wanted to defect, that's interesting."

"Maybe but not surprising, Michael doesn't keep secrets from those he trusts."

"Does Rosie know?"

"I think so but she's involved on scores of other projects and she hasn't been involved in this at all."

"Does Michael know that you have approached me to run your life again?"

"Oh yes, he said that I must do what I think is right and that at the end I will be older and wiser and no harm will be done."

Boo! thought for a while, this new twist excited him. Steve would come under his guidance and seemingly with Michael's blessing, he could turn Steve easily and then he could have Steve go back to Michael but not as Michael's rising star but as Boo!'s.

"Alright. You are on, come with me back now and I will make the arrangements. There may be a short delay before you go back, you don't mind that do you?"

"No delays, no time spent as a face, thanks but no thanks. Unless you can promise to send me back straightaway then the deal is off."

Boo! was surprised but didn't say anything. Michael had obviously told Steve about the faces and their long periods of waiting. Something else struck him.

"You are agreeing to go back now? No look-around, straight back to being Steve Rogers just before your accident?"

"Yes, take me back there now, no delays, no being a face."

Boo! agreed and Steve made him promise. He did and the pact was made.

*

The road was wet and Steve was driving carefully, he saw the lorry start to pull out of the T-junction on the right, he braked and slowed down, the lorry kept coming and didn't stop. Steve swore under his breath and reduced his speed and almost stopped. He sighed as the lorry blocked his path completely and Steve checked his mirror. Sharon hadn't slowed, he could see her headlights getting closer, the light blinded him, he heard the swishing of her tyres as Sharon saw the danger far too late and she slammed on her brakes. Her VW Golf hit the back of Steve's Porsche at around fifty miles an hour. The Porsche buckled under the impact and the car spun around. Steve was unconscious and Sharon was out cold too. The lorry driver was oblivious to the crash that he had caused and the Volvo driver arrived a few moments later.

The doctor stood at the foot of Steve's bed and looked at him, Steve was covered in bandages and a wire frame held the blankets from Steve's legs, he didn't feel any pain but then he realised that he didn't feel very much anyway. He looked at the doctor and tried to take in what he was saying. It was something about technology and the words quality of life were mentioned. Steve was confused but when he tried to feel his toes he found that he could move them, this reassured him, at least he wasn't paralysed but he couldn't understand why the doctor was still talking so much and he rudely interrupted him.

"Get to the point will you, when will I get out of here?"

The doctor took a deep breath, he had explained the damage as best he could but this patient refused to accept it, he tried again.

"I am sorry to tell you that you broke your neck and back in that accident and we had to amputate both of your legs below the knee, you may regain some movement in your arms but you will not be able to stand or walk naturally ever again. You are lucky to be alive, none of us thought that you would make it."

Steve didn't believe him. "I can feel my toes."

"Yes that is quite likely, the nerve endings still have some sensation; that might stay, it might go. Look, we have been trying to

305

find out who we can contact, your jacket containing your wallet and papers were destroyed in the fire and we have not been able to trace anyone for you. The police got your name and address from your car registration but there was no one at home when they called." Steve couldn't take all this in and changed the subject.

"What happened to Sharon?"

"Who is Sharon?"

"She was in her car behind me, I think that she must have hit me when I stopped for that lorry."

"Oh yes, a lady was brought in from the same accident, she's in intensive care still, she's had skin grafts. Is she a relative or a friend of yours?"

Steve lay back in the bed and stared at the ceiling. He was very angry. "Of course she is a bloody friend of mine,"

"Her father and mother are by her bedside, would you like them to come and see you?"

Steve closed his eyes and lay on his back, he could feel the pillow against his head and he wanted to put his hand to his face but he couldn't. He tried to sit up but that wouldn't work either. The doctor backed away from him and closed the door quietly as he left the room. Steve couldn't sleep and he called out for a nurse, he had to shout loudly three times before the door opened.

"Now then, what's the matter love?" Steve looked in disgust at the nurse. He didn't want to be called love and he didn't take to this nurse at all. At five feet two inches and weighing nearly ninety kilos, Nurse Mary Day wasn't a vision of loveliness though she could look quite nice with her make-up on and her hair brushed back. But Nurse Mary Day didn't bother with make-up or hair brushes anymore and she had long given up on looking nice. Dr Browne would never take an interest in her, she knew that and for the last four months she had embarked on an affair with someone who never said no, someone who was always there for her whenever she came home or got up in the morning. Nurse Mary Day was having an affair with her fridge. She patted Steve's arm and checked his drip, everything was in order. She spoke to him in a cheery way and this annoyed him even more.

"Just give me something to help me sleep."

"Are you in pain?"

306

"Of course I am, I am in agony." It wasn't true but Steve wanted something strong to knock him out. Nurse Day had the authority to dispense what was needed and she prepared a high dose. She felt sorry for this young, handsome man, he would have a tough time ahead. She watched as the drug took effect and Steve closed his eyes and slept the sleep of the dead.

CHAPTER 43

Steve's spirit left his sleeping body and rose to the ceiling. He looked down and saw Nurse Mary Day fussing around the bed. She gave him enough to send him into a really deep sleep and as he looked down in disgust at his broken body, he felt the presence of Boo! and he moved towards him.

"That wasn't our deal. Look at me, I will be in a wheelchair for as long as I live and you told me that I would have riches, Sharon, and Rosie too if I wanted her, look at me, I am a wreck."

Boo! didn't apologise.

"I didn't make the arrangement. Michael did."

"Michael?" Steve was aghast, "why would Michael want me like this, what can I achieve with half a body? I am not happy Boo! this isn't what you promised me, you've cheated me."

"On the contrary, I haven't cheated you at all. Sharon's car hit you because she didn't see the lorry pull out and you stopping. That was an accident. If you don't like it, complain to Mother Nature. As for your injuries, that's not my fault either. You chose to have a rear-engine Porsche. When Sharon's car hit yours, the engine came right through your seat, it broke your back and your neck. Your feet were crushed under the pedals and the Volvo driver managed to pull you out just before your car burst into flames, Sharon nearly died but her air bag saved her. She will never be as pretty or as sexy as she was but I haven't gone back on my deal, you can have her close to you for as long as you want. But don't worry if you want Rosie, she will be there too, she has been scheduled to meet you when you go for therapy, she will teach you to swim in a special pool designed to keep you active."

"But you said that Michael arranged it?"

"Yes, he told me that he wanted you badly injured to see how you would cope with it. He said that he told you that everyone has to know suffering before they know joy and you didn't really suffer much when you were a human. This is your chance, he says, to understand what others have to go through."

"And what about the riches, what am I supposed to have, a gold plated wheelchair?"

"If you want? You will receive a very large payment from the insurance company that insured Sharon's car. It will be enough for you to live a very comfortable life and you can travel all over the world, you will never have to work again and you can practically go anywhere and do anything you want. You are only hampered by your own limitations."

"Oh yes, and having no legs is a limitation, and not being able to fully move my arms, isn't that just a tiny limitation too?"

"Yes if you see not having them as limitations. But they are only limitations if you want them to be. You can still get around, sure you will need some help but you can afford it and you will still have your mind, your spirit and of course me to help you through it. You can have a good time for the rest of your life, it's entirely up to you."

"And then what? When I die will I go back for a Life Appraisal or will I join you as a face and queue up to be a fly?"

"Michael said that's entirely up to you, your Life Appraisal will be based on how you love your life, how you love yourself and what decisions you make."

Boo! started to move away. "That drug that the nurse gave you will wear off soon Steve, you will wake up and then you have to make your own decisions on how you spend the rest of your life. Do you wake up frowning and feeling miserable? You can if you choose, it's up to you. Or do you wake up smiling and feeling positive about yourself and your future? Again that's entirely up to you; no one can make that choice for you. Go ahead, you choose." Boo! drifted away and Steve felt himself descending from the ceiling back into his broken body, he could hear Nurse Day near the bed and he woke, she looked at him and smiled.

"Good morning love, fancy some breakfast?"

Steve's rehabilitation went remarkably well considering his

injuries. He learned to swim using his arms only and whilst his left one was weak, his right was stronger and that meant he swam in circles a lot. Rosie was his therapist and she enjoyed her work and they liked each other. Steve was a challenge in that he was sometimes moody but most of the time he was bright and funny and he had her and Nurse Day in fits of laughter. When Steve wasn't swimming he had other things to do, he started to write a book about his life in therapy and he learned to play the organ. He made tapes of soft music for companies that supplied music to department stores and they discovered that having one kind of music encouraged customers to spend more than another kind. He read too and spent many happy hours with Nurse Day and two other patients playing bridge. He liked poker and enjoyed low-stake tournaments, he developed an interest in the spirit world and read about Healers and Mystics and he bought a book that showed him how to read The Tarot. He practised with the book and the cards and did readings for anybody who wanted one, he found them to be uncannily accurate and this mystified him but he would never do a reading for himself; something inside told him that his future as a human would not be a long one.

The walks in the park were Steve's favourite and Nurse Day said that she enjoyed being with him, he found her funny and said so, she blushed. He then suggested that they went to the cinema together and she agreed. Afterwards they went to a pub and Steve got a bit drunk and told her that he loved her, Nurse Day giggled and told him not to be silly.

Steve never saw Sharon again after the accident. Nurse Day told him that she had mainly recovered from her injuries but the fire had left her face badly scarred. Steve wrote to her and she replied with a small get well card which Steve thought was odd, he invited her to visit him but she didn't reply.

It may have been the walk in the park or maybe Steve picked up a bug somewhere. The doctor told Nurse Day that Steve had a bronchial disease and that he didn't have long to live. Steve had an idea that he was ill but he was surprised when Nurse Day brought him his Tarot book and the deck of cards. She asked him not to do his own cards but to do hers again, she wanted to know what her future held in store.

"What after I'm gone?" said Steve.

Nurse Day blushed.

"No, not at all. I just want to know what will happen to me in the next few months."

Nurse Day shuffled the cards and lay them out in the spreads as instructed in the book, Steve checked each card against its prediction and smiled as he announced that Nurse Day would be glum for a while as she had to handle sadness but that she'd be happier not long afterwards. She'd be rich too, maybe an aunt would leave her some money in a will?

Her Tarot reading confirmed that she would stay in a caring profession and that she would marry and have a baby boy. Her husband would be a good father and parent and they would be a happy family. Steve closed the book and put the cards back in their box. 'Tarot For Your Future' might be accurate for Nurse Day but what would they hold for him? He had never read his own Tarot but now he was alone. Nurse Day went to make some tea and he hesitated. Then he dealt his cards.

Steve sat and looked at the spreads but it didn't seem to refer to him at all. The cards said that he was going on a journey and that he would experience many new adventures. The death card didn't faze him because he knew that this card meant a new dawn, a new period of life. He was surprised to see that The Tarot advised him that he was in a loving relationship with someone that he really cared for and who cared for him and he looked up as Nurse Day set a cup of tea in front of him. Then he saw it, she brought out a box of Jammy Dodgers.

"I've been hiding these, they are just for us."

"Nurse Day, can I ask you a question?"

"Sure," and she unwrapped the packet.

"Nurse Day, will you marry me!"

"Good Lord no," she placed a biscuit by his saucer, "and ruin a perfectly good relationship?"

Steve Rogers and Nurse Mary Day were married in a chapel not far from where they lived. The insurance money provided a lovely bungalow and Steve had a specially adapted car, he could park it wherever he wanted and that pleased him. They had three happy years together and Rosie came to visit a lot. She was there when Steve collapsed whilst writing his book and she helped Mary to put him to bed. The cause of death was pneumonia and everyone said that it was a release, but it wasn't. Steve didn't want to die and he struggled to stay alive. Mary Rogers and Rosie held hands at the funeral and behind them Steve and Michael watched as Steve's body was lowered into his grave.

Michael spoke, "Before we go for your new Life Appraisal we have to visit someone." He and Steve glided away from Steve's second funeral and travelled noiselessly through the town until they reached the rows of terraced houses near the docks. Michael stopped by the drain, the strong bars made a menacing barrier.

Michael and Steve passed through the ironwork; didn't they need to be invited? Steve wondered if Michael knew that he was breaking his agreement with Boo!. They sped down through the drains and tunnels and the blackness seemed to mock them, they arrived in the cavern and the two low wattage lights glowed softly, a million faces looked at them, none blinked or changed expression.

Boo! spoke quietly, "And to what do we owe this unexpected pleasure?"

"We have come for you Boo!."

Boo! was surprised. "But I am not going anywhere."

"I'm afraid that you are." Michael spoke softly but something was wrong and he realised that they were surrounded by around two hundred black and grey spirits. They wore hoods to match the colour of their souls and they positioned themselves menacingly in front and behind Michael and Steve. Behind them the faces waited, motionless, what would be happening?

Michael said, "I've come to invite you to leave this place and to come and work with Rosie, Steve and me. You might not realise it Boo! but you were set a test and you passed. Well you passed in one way and you failed miserably in another." Steve heard the murmurs starting up; the faces were going to wail.

"I didn't take any tests," said Boo!.

"Oh but you did. When Steve's spirit left his body in that hospital bed and spoke with you, you gave him some very valuable advice." The murmur grew louder and Steve realised that it was the grey and black spirits making the noise, not the faces.

"You showed compassion, sympathy and love in that moment Boo!. You showed that you should not be here with these spirits but that you have a chance with us. Where you failed was as a grey spirit, you are supposed to be totally evil. Unfortunately as a grey spirit you are a disgrace to your brothers. Come now, come with us, defect!"

Boo! looked terrified, the grey and black spirits were making a horrible moaning noise that was getting louder and louder. They advanced on Boo! who could feel their hatred and their pure evil. He decided to accept Michael's offer but the grey and black spirits barred his way. Steve realised that he'd have to do something, he called out to the faces.

"Hey faces, if you want to stay here in your miserable tomb and hope one day to be a fly and eat shit then say and do nothing, you will stay here. But if you'd like to come with us and swim in the oceans and start off as an anchovy or as a prawn then make your noise, come on, start wailing, start screaming, start shrieking."

At first there was a stunned silence, even the grey and black spirits were quiet. Then they heard it, a low murmur, it grew louder, it became a growl, then a scream. After a moment, the scream became a shriek and as one, the faces rose shrieking towards the ceiling. Michael, Steve and Boo! rose too and when the grey and black spirits tried to rise, the faces cut in front of them and the mass of faces held the grey and black spirits to the floor of the cavern. As one, they rose to the same level of the dim light bulbs and up still further. Michael reached the opening to the tunnels before Boo! and he turned and said, "What is your decision, are you coming or staying here, it's your choice."

Boo! looked down at the sea of faces staring up at him. He wanted to go, he hated being a grey spirit and deep down there was some compassion. No he hadn't felt it when his drug dealer Simon Speed was killed but he did feel it when he saw Steve in the hospital and he thought that Michael had shown a streak of cruelty when insisting on the broken body. His desire to break Michael and have him share his life in Hell suddenly seemed to have no value. But Michael hadn't been cruel at all. It was his purpose, his test of Steve, his test of Boo!. Boo! knew that his decision was right.

Boo! pushed his way forward to face Michael and cried, "I'm coming with you, I'll follow you anywhere."

Michael laughed, "Well follow from the front then."

The three spirits shot up the drain tunnels till they reached the top. Behind them a million round faces left a deserted cavern floor and they followed, their speed increasing all the time. But the grid was barred; there was no exit for Boo! and he stopped suddenly when he realised that he couldn't pass through the iron prison.

"What's the matter?" said Steve as he felt Michael judder to a stop and he nearly disappeared into Michael's spirit. The pressure of a million faces was incredible and they all pressed tightly against each other as they waited a few more moments for what must be freedom.

"I can't pass through," said Boo!.

"Why not?" said Michael who wanted to be away before the grey and black spirits arrived.

"Because I haven't been invited," said Boo!.

"Oh for heaven's sake!" said Michael.

"Excuse me," said Steve, "it would give me great pleasure if you would accept my invitation to join us in Heaven."

Michael was astonished, he was supposed to say that, who did Steve think he was?

Boo! smiled, "I'd be delighted." And with that he passed through the iron bars followed by Michael, a grinning Steve and just on a million faces all hoping for a better life as an anchovy or a prawn.

They arrived in Reception and an astonished Julie Waters pressed her bell, she would need a lot of help dealing with this lot. Jack Owen came out of one of the rooms followed by Valerie who giggled when she saw all the faces. Now they were all smiling. Other spirits stopped whatever they were doing and came to help with the processing of the new arrivals, they had never seen a million faces at one time and everyone seemed to be so happy.

Rosie came out too and Inspector Gold in his wonderful suit. They saw Michael and Steve and waved. Rosie approached Steve and took his hand in hers, she was surprised to see Boo! but today seemed to be a day of surprises.

She leant towards Steve and kissed him, "Hi Steve, been anywhere nice?"

Printed in Great Britain
by Amazon

14365441R00190